W9-BXA-136

Praise for

BEST EUROPEAN FICTION 2015

"An appealingly diverse look at the Continent's fiction scene."
— *The New York Times*

"The work is vibrant, varied, sometimes downright odd. As [Zadie] Smith says [...]: 'I was educated in a largely Anglo-American library, and it is sometimes dull to stare at the same four walls all day.' Here's the antidote."
— *Financial Times*

"With the new anthology *Best European Fiction* ... our literary world just got wider."
— *Time Magazine*

"The collection's diverse range of styles includes more experimental works than a typical American anthology might."
— *Wall Street Journal*

"This is a precious opportunity to understand more deeply the obsessions, hopes and fears of each nation's literary psyche — a sort of international show-and-tell of the soul."
— *The Guardian*

"Readers for whom the expression 'foreign literature' means the work of Canada's Alice Munro stand to have their eyes opened wide and their reading exposure exploded as they encounter works from places such as Croatia, Bulgaria, and Macedonia (and, yes, from more familiar terrain, such as Spain, the UK, and Russia)."
— *Booklist Starred Review*

"We can be thankful to have so many talented new voices to discover." — *Library Journal*

"There is sex, and there is history, and there is the uncanny." — *Gorse*

"[A] widely varied collection of stories by both emerging and established writers has been assembled." — *Irish Examiner*

"Has something for everyone." — *Irish Independent*

"A kaleidoscopic view of what is being written on the European continent today in a single anthology." — *The Millions*

"What the reader takes from them are not only the usual pleasures of fiction — the twists and turns of plot, chance to inhabit other lives, other ways of being — but new ways of thinking about how to tell a story."
— Christopher Merrill, *PRI's "The World" Holiday Pick*

"The book tilts toward unconventional storytelling techniques. And while we've heard complaints about this before — why only translate the most difficult work coming out of Europe? — it makes sense here. The book isn't testing the boundaries, it's opening them up." — *Time Out Chicago*

"The English-language reading world, 'wherever it may be,' is grateful." — *The Believer*

"Does European literature exist? Of course it does, and this collection . . . proves it." — *The Independent*

BEST
EUROPEAN
FICTION
2016

Copyright © 2015 by Dalkey Archive Press
Preface copyright ©2015 by Jon Fosse
Preface translation copyright ©2015 May-Brit Akerholt
First edition, 2015
All rights reserved

Please see rights and permissions on page 295 for individual credits

Partially funded by the Illinois Arts Council, a state agency

Please see Acknowledgments on pages 291 for additional information
on the support received for this volume.

www.dalkeyarchive.com
Victoria, TX / London / Dublin

Dalkey Archive Press publications are, in part, made possible through the support of the University of Houston-Victoria and its program in creative writing, publishing, and translation.

Cover design by Gail Doobinin, composition by Mikhail Iliatov
Printed on permanent/durable acid-free paper

BEST
EUROPEAN
FICTION
2016

PREFACE BY JON FOSSE

 DALKEY ARCHIVE PRESS

Contents

PREFACE

The Majority Is Always Wrong

WHAT IS LITERATURE? At the very least it is a distinctive category, something you can set limits on, and therefore what we call literature must also have certain characteristics that it should be possible to say something about. But any effort to do so soon leads to disagreements about what these are. And thus to disagreement about which works belong to literature, and which works don't.

Throughout the centuries, what we call a western literary canon has developed, beginning with Homer—and I would say with the Bible as well—and continuing to the Greek tragedies and making its way up to our own times; Franz Kafka's works, for instance, belong without any doubt to the western literary canon.

What are the unifying traits of this canon of fictional works? Obviously, the fact that it is fiction, that it is literature in which form and content is one and the same, and that what is written is fictional in the sense that it is something represented, something imagined, imagination, instead of something referred to: that is, something other than the kind of text in which the words pretend to point directly towards a reality beyond language.

When you read these canonical works, you're struck by how coherent, how unified, how harmonic each of them is. And by how each work is totally original, unique, each its own cosmos. And each work's cosmos is born by the fact that it is written in a different way—yes, world literature, to use this concept which Goethe is said to have been the first to coin, is in a way a collection of distinct writing styles; quite a lot is written on verse, whether we are talking of lyrical, dramatic, or epic writing, and when verse is not used and we are talking about prose, it is still always a form of prose in which the rhythm of the sentence and the weaving of the sentence, the sentence texture—and the etymological meaning of the word "text" is "to weave"—is conclusively important, whether it refers to the already mentioned Franz Kafka, or Joyce, or Flaubert, or Proust. Or Beckett, or Faulkner. Or Knut Hamsun. Virginia Woolf, herself a part of the western canon, of world literature, says that the act of writing is "putting words on the backs of rhythm." We may say that all the works of world literature, all the cosmoses there, are held up by rhythm, each by its own rhythm.

But it is the unique, the wholly idiosyncratic, that characterizes each of the works. It becomes obvious if you look at the verse forms, the extent to which a work is metrically bound—and then always freely bound; in Homer it is hexameter, in Dante terza rima, in Shakespeare blank verse, in Racine alexandrines. As far as prose is concerned, Kafka's rhythm doesn't have a name of its own, nor do the rhythms in the works of any of the other great prose writers. Still, that doesn't mean the rhythm isn't there, nor that it is not as distinctive in the works of each prose writer as the alexandrine is in Racine or blank verse in Shakespeare.

What do these different cosmoses, held up by such unique rhythms, say anything about?

There is always something unknown, something foreign that meets you, and that, through taking possession of the work, you finally no longer experience as foreign, but as something almost self-evident. Often it is as if you are left in the end with the feeling that, yes, I've always known this, I just haven't been aware of it. And thus you see reality in a different way after your meeting with strong literature, yes, what you experience as real looks different after a meeting with a canonical work, but the same is true after reading works of strong literature written by totally unknown contemporary authors. By authors whose work is their own, who manage to create their own voice, who manage to write in their own voice, authors who have what I call their own writing voice.

And there are many strong and good authors, they come from all countries, they write in all the world's languages. Most of them are unknown; unfortunately, that is how it is and how it must be. But you can meet some of these authors in, for instance, this year's edition of *Best European Fiction*.

In most places where people allege you can find literature, it is not literature you find, but the opposite, you find something that alleges to be literature, but is not. That is how it is with almost all literature that becomes popular—yes, it may almost be said to be a rule: a bestseller is not literature. You see it most clearly in suspense literature, which is often the kind of literature that sells best, together with literature that deals with sexual fantasies, usually dressed up as romance.

For what is literature, true literature, really about? Literature that tells its story through a union of form and content, and in a way unique to each single strong author, not to mention to each single strong literary work?

It is always about the eternally human, about love, death, and the sea. Yet always seen in new ways, and as such, good literature is always fundamentally new.

But what happens in best-selling literature?

The unique, the foreign, what makes literature literature, is exchanged for the conventional, the traditional, for the most sentimental, maudlin consensus. Literature dressed up as romance is merely pornography, and thus hardly anyone cares to regard such novels as literature, unless they have a very broad concept of what we call literature.

On the other hand, many people genuinely regard suspense literature, or crime fiction, as literature, and there are countries, Norway among them, that believe that production and sales of such literature ought to be supported on the same level as real literature, what we usually call serious literature.

But crime fiction is not literature; it is the opposite of it.

For what literature is truly about, deep down, is death, what it means to die. You learn to die from strong literature, not to live, says Harold Bloom. And nothing can be truer than that.

The enigma of death is in a way the enigma of life itself. Life, existence, is a border station at the edge of death, as Martin Heidegger says. To live is freedom from death, as he says, because the human being is always standing face-to-face with death and can choose to make the step from life into death at any time. And when a child is born, isn't that also a dead person being born? Isn't love, including sexuality, exactly what we use to defend ourselves against death, and what at the same time creates death? It cannot be understood.

And literature, strong literature, doesn't give an answer, but each work makes it easier to live with these yawning paradoxes.

But what does crime fiction do? It reduces the greatest of life's ugly questions and paradoxes to a riddle, to a murder riddle, which can be solved by clever old women or tough men, and when the riddle is solved, peace and calm may descend and we can live happily ever after. Crime fiction is a lie that represents an untruth—that is, it is fake—while real literature is a lie that represents the truth.

You learn from crime fiction that it is conformity that provides salvation, whereas from literature you learn that it is—yes, what is it? Harold Bloom says that in the dark days of his youth, he learned from "strong literature" that there is something in the human being that can never die because it was never born. There is something totally unique in every human being, the way there is something totally unique in every good literary text, canonical or contemporary. And what is totally unique in the human being is similar to what is totally unique in literature. You could even say that what a strong author does is to transfer something of his or her innermost idiosyncratic uniqueness to a universally understandable and accessible literary unity of form and content. That something at the very core of the human being becomes, as it were, linguistically accessible through the literary work of art.

To me, as a Christian, strong literature bears witness of "that of God in everyone," as the Quakers say, while crime fiction, and trivial fiction on the whole, just tells us how it is possible to get away from one's inner self, away from God in everyone; tells us how a simple piece of advice can disappear in the rush and roar of the world and just be like everything else, as far as this is possible. The majority is always wrong.

In *Best European Fiction* 2016 there are many examples of strong literature. Perhaps even written by an author who will belong to the canon of world literature in a few decennia, and who, at least in some instances, may have a safe place among the literary canon of his or her own language and national literature already. And as such, works to make life endurable for others in their home country, in their own language, in their national literature, and now, in translation to English, also works to make life endurable for the many who cannot read anything but their mother tongue or the world language, English.

JON FOSSE

TRANSLATED FROM NORWEGIAN BY MAY-BRIT AKERHOLT

BEST
EUROPEAN
FICTION
2016

JOSEF WINKLER

The Word Flew Away

THE WEATHERED FENCE in my mother's vegetable garden always looked desolate, gray-flecked, worm-eaten, and rotting, the nails crooked and rusty. This vegetable garden, lying at the foot of the village built in the shape of a cross, in front of the cemetery wall in the so-called church field, was a small section of a larger parcel my father leased from the church, where he cultivated grain. If my father was feuding again with the pastor and the unspoken threat of the lease's revocation were in the air, I would walk around fearing the loss of the vegetable garden by the cemetery wall; we wouldn't pull up any more radishes, parsley, or lovage in the garden where, as a child, the idea had sprung from my morbid and overheated imagination that poison from the corpses had seeped under the cemetery walls and contaminated our vegetables, and that, especially in dreams, we would be able to carry on conversations with the dead. When, on summer days, with a deeply flushed face and a hand-woven beige straw hat on her head, my mother was pulling up weeds, I would keep close to the cemetery wall, taking the tin watering can from grave to grave and freshening the pink and white cardamines with cool water—"The cardamines are grateful flowers, they even hold out in the summer heat," she used to say—halfway up the graveyard, not neglecting the three or four unkempt graves of nameless children with their meager adornment of wild dog violets, daisies, and dandelions, capped with crumbling plaster angels. No one dared to clear away the broken-off angels' wings.

Often, after some difference of opinion, my paternal grandmother and my mother would stop speaking to each other. My fat grandmother would exit the kitchen indignantly and shut herself up in her room on the second floor. "It's been five years now since your mama dropped off," my grandmother is alleged to have said to my mother, referring to my deceased maternal grandmother, who had lost three sons in the full flower of youth in the Second World War and had died of a broken heart. "You talk about an animal that way, not about a person!" my mother said to me many times later. "Repeatedly in Giotto's mourners: the upper lip swollen from grief." For weeks my paternal grandmother would not set foot out of her room on the family farm, and day after day, she had my mother bring lunch and dinner up to her. At that time, there was still no running water on the second floor of the farmhouse, and in the mornings my mother used to go with a full washbasin, slowly and carefully up the sixteen steps of the staircase, and leave it on a footstool in my grandmother's room. She combed the old woman, smeared violet oil in her thin, grayish-white hair, and wove two braids which she would then twist together in a bun-like shape on the back of her head. With a rag my mother would soak up the water drops around the footstool in front of the dark-gray divan that our uncle Hans, the confectioner from the Rabitsch pastry shop and chauffeur to Josef Köstner, the Bishop of Gurk, had brought to us from Klagenfurt. One spot on the divan, where the old woman sat day after day twiddling her thumbs—speculating, as she called it—was bowed in from holding her, she weighed more than a hundred kilograms. After a few weeks my grandmother would thaw out, as they said, and walk downstairs deliberately in her boot-shaped felt slippers, which made a clapping sound against the floor of the house's narrow corridor, then sit down wordless in the kitchen, glaring into space before her lips began to move and she would utter a word of halfhearted reconciliation. "The danger of all these abstractions and formulations is of course that they tend to become independent. When that happens, the individual that gave rise to them is forgotten—like images in a dream, phrases and sentences enter into a chain reaction, and the result is a literary ritual in which an individual life ceases to be anything more than a pretext." Thus writes Peter Handke, in *A Sorrow Beyond Dreams*.

When visiting my now lonely grandmother in her room, I would often open the bottle of violet oil, sniff at it, smear a few drops of it into my hair, sit down with my back to the window, beyond which the death bird lurked on some spruce branch—"Seppl! Did you hear the jaybird? It's cried out again! I'll surely die soon!"—and open a drawer, taking out a thick photo album with a padded turquoise cover and staring at the photo of a child lying in repose, so beautifully arranged that I would gladly have lain down next to her, if only there were enough space. The dead child lay in an old-fashioned hand-woven carriage with a retractable shade. The head of the perished farmhouse princess rested on an embroidered white pillow. It was adorned with a bouquet of cloth flowers and white wax blossoms in the form of lilies, so that only her brow was visible. The dead girl's mouth hung ajar from beneath the cleft in her upper lip. The closed eyes looked like horizontal slits, the nose with the large nostrils was blunt, the cheeks were chubby, the hands, wound in a wreath of roses, were folded in prayer, the fingernails, which had gone on growing faintly, were sharp. I would lay the photo album quietly back in the drawer, because I did not want my bedbound grandmother to discover the purpose of my numerous daily visits was simply to look at the dead child's picture.

For a year, my mother carried on with this song and dance, as it was called, up and down the sixteen steps of the staircase: in the mornings she went with the washbasin and spread a tea towel on the lap of the old woman lying in bed, to set her hot soup down on top of it. In the afternoon she brought her coffee substitute—a blend of Linde malt coffee and Melanda coffee, made from figs—with a thick donut, and sometimes two baker's rolls and the cubes of soft cheese with the blue Gentian printed on the label, which I would buy for her in packs of six from the German general store, getting a piece to eat as a reward. For a long time she could still eat the soup on her own, later she had to be fed by my mother. "Mouth open! Mama! You hear me?" "I'm not hungry anymore!" "These two dangers—the danger of merely telling what happened and the danger of a human individual becoming painlessly submerged in poetic sentences—have slowed down my writing, because in every sentence I am afraid of losing my balance," writes Peter Handke in *A Sorrow Beyond Dreams*.

Somewhat later, my toothless grandmother cried "Jogl! Jogl!" for nights on end, so loud that we could hear her clamoring from our childhood bedrooms. "Jogl! Help me!" Jogl, her son, my father, stood up under the large sacred image of the *Madonna della Seggiola* in its black frame, walked past the vanity table with its broad framed mirror, carved out of walnut by his father-in-law, atop of which stood a bust portrait of his deceased mother-in-law, Grandma Aichhotzer, who had lost three sons in the full flower of youth in the Second World War. On a nail over the vanity hung a green glow-in-the-dark Jesus. He went into the bedroom and lay next to his old mother in the bed where, two years before, her husband had died. To calm her down, Jogl slept through the night at his mother's side, until five in the morning, when he got up to work in the stables.

"I don't want to die! I don't want to die!" she screamed the next night, once again waking up her grandchildren. The following morning she began to gasp heavily in her bed. My father ran down the left-hand beam of the village built in the shape of a cross, to the inn, which had the only telephone in the village, and called Doctor Plank. Shortly afterward the white Volkswagen of Doctor Plank appeared—he had broken an early appointment, leaving the patient in the waiting room of his office. He rushed with his doctor's bag down the corridor, up the sixteen steps, and into the death chamber. After a half-hour he left the house, with tears streaming down his face, and drove back to his patient, on the far bank of the Drava River. My father pressed his balled-up handkerchief, stiff with snot, into his red eyes, and said softly: "It's over." He leaned against the warm stove in the kitchen and I sat down on the divan. We nodded to each other. Two newborn death-birds, soundless and furtive, must have slipped from her left and right nostrils. My mother exhaled. The tyrant was dead.

Tresl, the dear soul, as she was known, my grandmother's eldest daughter, was so shocked by the sight of her mother's corpse that, according to my father, she refused to believe it was real and knelt wailing beside her deathbed. She climbed the sixteen steps holding the white enamel wash basin with the thin blue border full of warm water, and under her arm, a freshly washed linen hand towel with Enz, my family's common name, embroidered on it in red. She spared my mother the washing of the corpse. Some time later, I no longer know why, I followed after her, climbing the stairs and stepping over the threshold without knocking. Sobbing, with the damp towel in her hand, Tresl lifted her head, stared at me sternly and gestured for me to go away. I ran frightened down the stairs and kept what I had seen a secret. I was ten years old. I never spoke of it in the decades afterward, not with my mother or father or even my siblings. As a child, I would wake up and go to sleep with this nightmare image in my mind; it was not seldom that it slipped into my dreams. "Every man dreams for himself," writes Peter Handke in the diary *Traveling Yesterday*. My mother stood at the kitchen counter, peeling the onions one after the other and wiping tears with her forearms from the corners of her irritated eyes. She didn't mourn a single second for her mother-in-law. She was glad it was over, over forever, forever and ever it was done with.

It was also the aforementioned Tresl who seven years before, when I was three years old, walked up the wide staircase of the home of my maternal grandparents into the mourning chamber of my grandmother and lifted me up over the catafalque arrayed in periwinkle. With one hand she clasped me tight, with the other she lifted up the pall and said: "Look, Seppl, look!" I stared long at the ash-gray face of my grandmother, who had lost three sons in the full flower of youth in the Second World War. It may be I have Tresl to thank for my macabre imagination. Never, not even decades later, did I dare to speak of this to my father, whom I knew for fifty-five years. How many thousands of times must this scene be repeated, before this coffin will be pulled from me and taken to its grave, be it in Heaven or Hell? Only once, when I was well over forty, did I tell this story to my mother. "She shouldn't have done that!" was her response. She never spoke of it again. "Strip me of my tongue, that I may finally speak."

After the corpse had been washed and my grandmother laid out in bed, dressed in the folk costume she wore on Sundays, with her hands folded in prayer, and after the Priest Franz Reinthaler had performed the last rites, my father hurried back to the inn and phoned the undertaker Stimniker in Feistriz-on-the-Drava, and within a half-hour the black Mercedes with the mysteriously tinted windows behind the driver's seat pulled up to the mourning house. With a wool blanket, my father and the undertaker carried the cumbersome deceased through the corridor of the second floor of the house and down the steps. I stayed in the kitchen, I heard the slow, tentative footfalls over the smooth-worn steps, the creaking, the panting of the corpse-bearers in their struggle, wary not to slip with the body and make a jumble of the living and the dead. They laid my grandmother on the floor, lifted her from the drab dark-green wool blanket, grabbing the corpse by the hands and feet and setting it in the coffin. The undertaker righted her head, which had fallen to one side, and refolded her hands, which slipped apart while they were carrying her. Tresl stood over the coffin, laid her own hands over those of her mother, folded now in prayer, shook her, so that the coffin began to rock, and cried: "Mama! Mama!" It never occurred to anyone to wash the blanket in which my grandmother was carried down the stairs from her death chamber. In wintertime, on the divan, we bundled up with the musty scent of the dead. "What is writing for me? The deciphered evocation of childhood," writes Peter Handke in his book of observations, *Mornings at the Rock-Window.*

Unlike my grandfather, who died two years earlier, my grandmother did not lie exposed in the old farmhouse. Instead, the servant's quarters, stinking of Austria 3 brand cigarettes and a damp straw mattress, were cleared out to make room for coffin and corpse. "Seppl! Run up to the inn and bring me back a pack of 3's!" the servant used to say to me. After the old woman had been interred in the village cemetery and we were once again back in the family home, my cousin and I drained the half-empty wine glasses scattered about until I was stumbling through the house, and had to lie down for two hours in the pungent hay and sleep off my drunkenness.

In my mother's family's farmhouse, where there hung on one wall a black-and-white photo of her three brothers who had fallen in the full flower of life in the Second World War, I took a sheet of stamps from my uncle's desk, went into the empty kitchen, moistened the stamps with my spit and laid them on the large hot plate of the stove, which served both for cooking and heating the kitchen. In the center of the plate, through a small, round hole, a yellowish orange flame would sometimes come tonguing up; lying over it, the head of Austrian president Adolf Schärf, which was printed on a jagged-edged stamp, went up in flames. The stamps bordering it smoldered and burned on the metal plate. I ran up the unpaved village street to my parent's house and hid the stamps I had spared. "What a treasure, in retrospect, the emptiness, the uneventfulness of childhood becomes—or was it already so even then?" A few days later, while my mother was working in the kitchen, preparing lunch, I must have made a remark to the effect that I had found some stamps, and she said, without reproach, "I see!" and took hold of the bundle of rods they used to punish us, which was dangling from a coat hook near the kitchen door, where my father used to hang his greasy hat. It was made of twigs from the birches that stood at the forest's edge. Firm and loud she said to me, "Pants down!" Shuddering, I unbuttoned the elastic suspenders—trouser-straps, we used to call them—and while my mother tugged at my black underwear, reeking of urine, I began to moan and cry. She shouted, "Lie down on the chair!" and beat the supple birch rods against my rear end until I could smell the sweat from her exertions. With my eyes swollen, my teeth clenched, my face deep red, I stared at the kitchen floor and gripped the legs of the chair tight in my trembling hands. After the long punishment—it was the longest of my life—I was in so much pain that I could only manage to walk slowly, with my legs spread far apart. The bundle of birch rods had shrunken in the course of this punishment, splintered fragments of it lay to the left and right of the chair.

At seven in the evening, after the call to prayers, when it was time to go to bed, I was afraid to take off my clothes, and pulled down my pants in shame, and one of my siblings jumped at the chance to pull up my nightshirt smudged of feces and call out: "He's got rainbows on his ass!" The next morning I pulled on my black underwear beneath the bedcover—we only changed them once a week, on Saturdays, after a bath in the smoke kitchen. At my school desk I wriggled back and forth. "Can you not sit still for once!" the teacher screamed. I swallowed my pain and pressed my pencil harder into my notebook, until the tip broke off and I had to use the pencil sharpener. The red marks from the lashes stayed on my skin for a long time, I looked at them daily in the mirror, when I knew I was alone in the kitchen, while my mother was working in the vegetable garden by the church wall near the unkempt children's graves and my brother and sister were still at vocational school in Feistritz.

My uncle was pleased as well, a week later, when I was hunting for peacock feathers and our eyes met as I walked across his yard. My mother had settled the debt with her brother, she had paid for the stamps, I kept what was left of the sheet hidden for a long time and later burned it in the oven and watched with great zeal as the churches, mountains, and castles portrayed on the stamps quickly vanished, along with the heads of Austrian President Adolf Schärf, of Viktor

Kaplan, the inventor of the water turbine, of the poetess Paula Preradović, composer of Austria's national anthem.

"Watch your step, I'll tan your backside!" my mother often used to say, or she would remark derisively, reminding me of the event: "You'll get a switching till there's rainbows on your ass!" "You've got a good one coming," she would threaten, meaning a box on the ears, not with the flat of her hand, but with its bony outer side. Now and then she would mock my small fingers: "He's got tiny little fingerlets!" Ashamed, I would look down at my hands. Once again I would be left speechless for days. And when I was a child and used to ask her something she would often say tenderly: "Boy, I have no idea!" "Grief: in the end, I have no opinion," writes Peter Handke in the diary *Traveling Yesterday*.

In a garden in the Indian city of Pune, where I saw a peacock crying slowly and majestically, because its feet had gotten tangled in plastic as it pranced across a waste heap, and which would have to be caught so that its feet could be freed, it occurred to me that I used to often go to my maternal grandparents' farmhouse and look for peacock feathers, in the stable, in the shed, and on the hay ramp. If I didn't find any, I would sneak up on the peacock pecking at grains in front of the door to the house, grab it by the tail and tear a few feathers, bloody at the roots, from the screaming bird. Together my mother and I would place the feathers behind the framed bust portrait of her mother, who had died early after losing her three sons in the full flower of youth in the Second World War, just under the green glow-in-the-dark crucifix.

Years before I began to steal money from my father to buy books and go to the cinema, I would rob my mother and buy sweets in the German general store, especially chocolate-covered marshmallows. Her wallet was in a drawer in the pantry. Once I said to my younger brother that I had found some money in the village, and I showed him my cache. He didn't believe me and tattled to my mother. Without asking me or even confronting me, she believed my brother. She didn't hide her wallet, but now she counted out her five- and ten-schilling coins. After a while she forgot about it, and I started up again.

Mother and father were standing at my crib while the diminutive, white-haired Doctor Plank was readying a penicillin injection. Before he had touched me with the needle, I said to him: "Shove off!" This anecdote was repeated in the house for decades, accompanied by my parents' laughter. Whenever my father would retell it, it was with pride at my rebellious attitude, but he did not like it at all when I contradicted or disobeyed him. Once he hit me so hard my nose bled, the blood streamed down over my chin, dripping onto my shirt and the floor, and my mother got between the two of us and cried: "Do you want to beat the boy to death?" With his filthy, snot-stiffened kerchief, he wiped the blood from my nose and mouth. But seeing the fear in my father's face, I would happily have embraced him, I wanted to grab onto his feet as he turned around and walked out, to be dragged across the floor and outside, down to the cesspit.

In the evenings, when I could hear my mother rummaging in her bedroom, I would kneel on the bed before the image of the guardian angel and pray, "Angel of God, my guardian dear, to whom God's love commits me here, ever this day be at my side, to light and guard, to rule and guide." It was so loud, she must have heard it in her room.

Aunt Nane, my mother's youngest sister, who came to visit us from Klagenfurt several times a year, told me she had often seen me holding a pencil in the first year of my life. I was left-handed by nature, but when my mother saw me scribbling or drawing, or later writing, she would take the pencil from my left hand and place it between the thumb and forefinger of my right, until at last I gave up the struggle and began to write with my right hand. "Won't you hold the pencil in the nice hand!" she would shout, turning to face me from the sideboard, where she was preparing the meal. Or she would just say, "Will you not . . . ?" and then I knew what I would have to do. "Writing, to allow a sculpture to build itself inside you, a breath sculpture whose contours the hand need only trace."

Especially in winter, I would leave my bedroom at four or five in the morning while my four siblings were still asleep—for years I had to share a bed with my younger brother—and lie down between my mother and father in their room under the holy image of the *Madonna della Seggiola* and slide over, usually toward my father. When my parents got up to go work in the stables, I would lie in my mother's bed and contemplate the bloodstains that I often found on the large flannel bed sheet in the middle of the bed. My mother bled, my father didn't! I thought. And I asked myself when she would bleed to death. Sooner, or later?

"Nerves," she often used to say, and groan softly, "Nerves!" For decades she was given psychotropic medicines by the "nerve doctor" in Spittal-on-the-Drava. Once, when they needed to change her medication, the doctor told her: "We'll clear you back up!" "You're white as a sheet!" my mother used to tell me often. As a cure for my blood deficiency, as it was called, I was prescribed speckled, foul-smelling iron pills. This may have formed a special bond between my mother and me, as only she and I were allowed to swallow tablets, no one else.

Because I had deep rings under my eyes, I was once sent to convalesce in a children's camp in Ledenitzen, not far from Villach. My father had found an ad for it in the weekly *Carinthian Farm Journal*. With a travel bag, my mother and I went to the bus stop in Kamering and rode to Villach. Across from the station, where parents and children were gathered, I stepped into a bus that was already idling, ready to take us to the resort. Looking out, I saw my mother press a kerchief against her eyes and nose and look for me behind the gleaming bus window. As we set off, I waved to her, she bashfully raised her hand, her lips quivered. "The most stirring sign of life: shyness," writes Peter Handke in the diary *Traveling Yesterday*.

In the village, my mother lived in utter isolation. After the death of her father, whose wife, also called Maria Winkler, survived him by half a decade, she would occasionally visit her brother and her mother-in-law at her parents' house. She hardly ever set foot in any other house in the village. She went to church and back, and she went to the vegetable garden by the cemetery wall and back. "There should be pencils and fountain pens and so forth that only write with a specific slowness."

Once she told me she had really wanted to run away, to leave her husband, but that she had stayed on account of the children, had swallowed everything back up and held on. She is supposed to have gone to her father numerous times, to have complained to him, but he always calmed her down with the words, "It'll get better! It'll all get better!" When she was pregnant with her sixth and last child and Aunt Tresl came to visit, my father grinned and declared there might yet be another child after the sixth, and I heard my mother say clearly, in a strident tone: "No!" Nothing else, not another word.

Once my mother and I took a boat, the so-called ferry, to the far bank of the Drava, to Ferndorf, where Doctor Plank had his office on the premises of the Heraklith factory. A thick iron cable was attached to the boat to harness it to the pyramid-shaped concrete bollards on either shore. On the Kamering side we banged a clapper several times against a rusted, jagged circular saw blade until a woman emerged from a tiny house on the other bank, rowed to Kamering to fetch us and then back to Ferndorf on the Drava's other shore. Doctor Plank gave me general anesthetic before pulling two teeth from my lower jaw. When we were back in the boat and seated, the hope struck me—with the taste of blood in my mouth, and my tongue burrowing relentlessly into my wound—that the boat would sink and mother and I would drown together, and all the others, my siblings and my father, would be left behind alone.

TRANSLATED FROM GERMAN BY ADRIAN NATHAN WEST

NIJAT MAMEDOV

Streaming

1.

Predominance of consonants/samit sets the direction/səmt to "the Semites, whose name means 'name.'" (J.D.) What did Jesus do for 21 years, beginning from the age of 12? The answer is beyond any doubt: he looked at himself in the mirror. Getting involved in the contest of the Creator, who opens lovers' wounds. *Meraj*[1] or mirage? What does it matter? As long as we have tongues and index fingers, we are who we should be. Women cannot avoid pleasure, men cannot avoid obedience, edification, lessons. Obviously, any speech is *vird*[2], since any word is word. *Simit* in Turkish means 1) bagel; 2) life buoy. Spinning of *seme*—"not indifferent difference" (G.B.), spinning of the Mevlevi—*sema*. From accentuating to accenting. Deep gloss levels out differences between speaking/λᾰλέω and muteness/lallıq. But what about writing, as long as they write that Christ and Buddha never wrote anything?

2.

Diary was my catharsis, Sh. was a mana personality that helped clear up the shadow (*The Parting with Narcissus*) and thereby come to L.—to anima, psychopomp (*Aspects of a Spiritual Marriage*).

My dream before waking proved the above-mentioned: in a basement-level used bookstore, with streams of light struggling their way in from the street, I buy some books, consulting with a noble and prim fair-haired woman, keeper of that temple. I want to buy new editions but she gently advises old ones. Authors whose names begin with the 26th letter of the Russian alphabet and the 32nd of the old Cyrillic Azerbaijani one (the 33rd and last was the apostrophe. Əski means 1) old junk, 2) rag. Aren't we like Sufis, brother? We get our clothes from second-hand stores ... Must thank Ayaz for the tip.) Shekhinah? Upon waking, I recalled how people in old patriarchal villages of Baku had shown great respect for Velimir Khlebnikov, regarding him as a dervish.

I met a stunningly magnetic girl in the metro the other night. Slim, slightly taller than my shoulder, brown hair ("Dein Haar ist nicht braun." You're not mine.), graceful head, like that of my Tutankhamun ashtray, eyes of a houri but without that typical oriental tristesse, finely moulded nose; I can tell the flower between her legs is fragrant and beautiful; sensual mouth, lips like a shell. There is a salt sea hissing inside her.

... eating of the rose in Jodorowsky's film ...

3.

Lévy-Bruhl's approach and the Sapir-Whorf hypothesis can work in liaison. From Lévy-Bruhl, take a step (whether via Erich Neumann's *Mystical Man* essay or without it) back toward the mainstream, Jung's analytical psychology; then go back a bit more, to Freud, and still sticking to the "language + psychology" line, to Lacan, who noted that not everything can be symbolized and that the unconscious is structured like language.

... auxiliary glasses ... (stolen from A.D. It seems like everyone steals from him anyway. Zeus is up on Olympus. Prometheus is chained to the Caucasus Mountains.)

4.

"Kissing Agathon, I had my soul upon my lips; for it rose, poor wretch, as though to cross over."

Beautiful lines from Plato; when reading them aloud in a semi-basement cafe, however, I fell under suspicion of deviant desires from those who, on their way to maturity, had recoiled at the first trial of masculine courage. I parried with Al-Juneid's words. These awful projections ... "Everything is inside me." Whether according to Bernhard or Nasimi (did he study experimental psychoanalysis, too?). Not to search in order to find, but to remember. A newborn child knows everything, but an angel comes, closes off his wisdom, and the baby starts to cry. Only when reading and studying books does he recall the omniscience he forgot. According to Huizinga, "poet" in Arabian, "şair," means "multiscient." But don't become a poet, don't become someone who wanders across the valleys speaking of what he doesn't do. They are followed by those who have lost their way.

The sixth word should be translated as nəfəs/breathe—nəfs/soul.

. . . O, blue . . .

5.

She is one of those women who always need to believe in something. A friend of Justine. Gives a perfect kiss. "Sit, talk, have fun, but no lips touching lips. There has been an order sent from above." Durrell's Pursewarden is the "father" of Cortázar's Morelli. But who is Pursewarden's "father" then? Stephen Dedalus? Oh this thing that conceals a rigid structure in its depth, and preserves the seemingly chaotic surface when melting under careful analytical reading . . . "Kiss, kiss Molly's lips," the late Cobain sang on his incestuous album, not so rough in sound and mood as the first and the second ones.

6.

Knowledge leads to wisdom. Wisdom leads to faith. Faith leads to mystery.

Knowledge is unwinding.

Wisdom is winding.

I think that the late Lotu Bahtiyar[3] was a very clever and wise man. He wrote poetry in prison, read books, prohibited rape, did not allow swearing. He was fair.

Is oblivion possible?

7.

"Why do some guys wear an earring?"

"I don't know, Dad . . ."

"Must be fags. You know, though, I've seen dervishes in Tabriz, they also have long hair and rings in their ears."

Bu sözləri sırğa elə, as qulağından. Make a ring of these words and put it through your ear. This is a proverb, an Azerbaijani one. A passionate longing for breaking the cycle.

"Will I be in your novel?"

8.

All that should have been written has been written already. All that is written is interpretation. The limits of interpretation produce a numinous duality. The most difficult thing here is to choose the middle way. When it is impossible to interpret everything positively. Everything is already fine, it will just get better. Do you remember eating fruit off each other's naked bodies? Love thieves. How hard they rock at the end there ... But their recent stuff is worse. Where did all that techno-punk go?

I've told you already! It's the eyes that change, the eyes and the heart. What will be depends on what eyes you're seeing through.

... от храма к хоромам, хараму, к гарему и карману, вплоть до кармы ...[4]

Mama Roma, after a small break. How sincerely and precisely it reveals the provincial exceptionalism and isolation of youth, the suburban romance—concrete apartment blocks, wastelands, a golden chain for the one who eases your restlessness. Ettore looks so much like Carmine; if the former hadn't died he would have surely become a pimp like the latter. In some way, each of us was Ettore once. Christian parallels. Dark spots under Mama Roma's eyes, thin nose, shape of a face from an icon ...

"кино" — "икон" — "инок"[5]

From Kislov's afterword to *Exercises in Style*: "Reading Guénon in many ways predetermined the nature of his work" ... "In 1956, Queneau visits the USSR and goes as far as Tashkent and Samarkand."

In his journals, Queneau writes, "And yet, my religious perception (everyone does not give a damn about my religious perception, though) is not at all Christian. I am Muslim." ... *read a book, made a call to Tashkent, and that means you're stoned ...*

9.

"I'm getting better at understanding the structure of subconscious-
ness and the unconscious. My love for you is the purest, unalloyed
sublimation. Such was the love of medieval mystics and Hebrew
prophets for God. They avoided meeting Him even though they
longed for that meeting. But there's a question facing me now: do I
love you (why you?) or my love for you (a kind of supreme egoism)?
All this is at least interesting. Isn't it?"

"Yes . . . it is. And yet I would prefer it if you didn't avoid me . . . I
love you, too. You. Not my love for you."

"O, stupid white woman, I don't need pot to get high. The mere
thought of you is enough to turn me into a black God."

. . . the ideal should be either avoided or exterminated/humiliated . . .

I remember exactly the visual sensation of "getting high." Before that,
I had been watching reality through a glass, darkly (. . . a quote from
the New Testament . . .), and when it started to come on, the glass slid
softly off somewhere to the right. The air was like mercury and began
to vibrate. I felt one of my favorite poems, Mandelstam's "The Horse-
shoe Finder," as a physical sensation.

10.

One of my recurrent dream motifs: a hole in the plinth and just white
light in it. With no other characteristics whatsoever.

Her stupid habit of wiping her own and my lips with a napkin after kissing! After we slept together, her mouth smelled of wine and
tobacco, and that was the best of her.

11.

ghost
guest

These photographs attract me: the way the photographer and the
object look through one another, become transparent, ghostly, yet at
the same time remaining totally concrete. "Frames of life that saw the
life." (E.W.) His other words, which are doubtlessly a repetition of
repetition: "In many ways, there is no 'us' until 'us' has created its own
poetry."

12.
Smell of wet soil.
October is nowhere if not
in the skin of wrists
and in the fold of elbow.
A bird is hovering over the neighborhood.
Distant voices: a woman, a man, a woman.
The taste of mulberry jam . . .
and the continuity of light-brown, dark-brown,
slightly broad straight eyebrows of Turkic virgins.

It's half past midnight, another cigarette is smoldering, I should try to quit. I made a phone call to Turker[6] in New York. He finishes the last plum in the icebox, makes black tea and speaks about Crumb's *Ancient Voices of Children*. "Even in this city I can't shake heaven off from my shoulders," he finally says, smiling. I should really quit smoking; it's no use dying, there's no need to die, it's an unnecessary repetition (that's what Sayid said when we were languidly exchanging opinions concerning I hardly remember what at the inevitable cup of coffee in Imereti. "He's got such bad posture, are all of your friends like that?" Polina asked, meaning Turker, the day after he organized an *Eraserhead* happening for her at my request. The best minds of my generation. Now I'll take a walk, deep in Old Akhmedli, where I haven't been for a long time. Abandoned streets, potlatch is a magnificent invention. So is Polina. Dick Laurent is dead, but I can try to help him through the ecstatic repetition of this line: Dick Laurent is dead. Is it possible to picture New York as a desert with streets? Forty minutes more and it's time to go home, go to bed. A grapevine and/or golden sunflowers are unforgettable.

13.
Can all plots of world literature be reduced to the following?:
A man finds himself through a woman—mother, sister, wife, daughter, Anima.
A woman finds herself through a child.
A child finds him/herself through parents.
Man is in the most vulnerable position in this triad. "Man's blood

changes every seven years." Hadith say that all children are believers until the age of seven, and that Paradise lies beneath the feet of mothers.

Being born a man involves the serious ordeal of becoming implicated with four real women and one non-existent one. It might be symbolically related to the fact that Islam allows men to take four wives.

And here is the second meaning of the banal (all banalities are divine in nature, but "in order for the banal to reveal its secret, it must first be mythologized" (Rancière), another quote stolen from A.D. Oğrudan oğruya halaldır—to deceive a deceiver is no deceit) European saying, "A man is not a man if he has not known five women in his whole life."

To an inexperienced reader, Sufi poetry is homosexual and incestuous through and through. The sought-for is in our eyes and in our heart. A good thing is always a mirror to some extent. *What eyes you're seeing through . . .*

14.

That black mulberry tree was growing in the garden. Right beside the iwan. In a hot Absheron midday, following the playful instructions of the grown-ups, the boy would climb it and shake its branches, calling the saving wind by repeating, "Mən anamın ilkiyəm,/ağzı qara tülküyəm,/xəzri, gəl,/gilavar, gəl"—"I am my mother's firstborn, I am a fox with black jaws, blow, hazri, blow, gilavar." The tree was cut down later, but the boy still remembers it.

"Д(е)рево"—"древность"[7]
"Дремучий лес"—"дремучие времена"[8]

"Дрема"—"dream" = "бессознательное"[9]

"Корни"—"крона"[10]

"C o r n"

The Ancient Greek god Cronus = time

(only the sky/Uranus is higher than crowns/Cronus)

A tree is a symbol (for the unconscious and time) in those cultures, where the dead were buried/ХоРоНили like c o r n for the purpose of resurrection.

Thus, the crucifixion of Jesus (whose father was a carpenter, cultivating the flesh of wood) on a wooden cross is a symbol of a symbol, the literal merging of tree and body, the meeting of twins that leads to resurrection without burial—releasing explosion.

True Christianity emerged and disappeared right at the moment of crucifixion.

The figure of the crucified Jesus has the following meaning: to find release/salvation one must merge with one's other half, to find harmony with oneself and therefore with others. That's why love asserts itself.

Isn't orthodox Islam regressive in this context, representing instead a return to fear (of the unconscious)?

We must move to the "living void."

From L.'s letter on February 3, 2009: *Hi. I barely felt alive yesterday, I wanted to write to tell you that Odin crucified himself on the World Tree, to which Gods tie their horses; quantum physics sees the Universe as a tree;* pramatter *in Latin is "silva," which means "forest"...*

From L.'s letter on February 4, 2009: *The BODHI TREE in Buddhism is a tree, under which Shakyamuni achieved enlightenment (Bodhi) and became a Buddha.*

From L.'s letter on February 9, 2009: *I had a dream last night about growing from a pistachio seed (I felt so light) and I was woken by your question. Another tree for you.*

15.

The limits of interpretation. Projections detected and sent back. Is silence a part of symbolic exchange? Sun gods that die before or after the age of thirty. Fathers doomed to wisdom and fathers doomed to the gap between wisdom and experience. Both are prisoners of their own sanctity. "My sister is a garden locked," your ankles, feet, wrists are oozing endless reading, while outside the mother's lair, outside the resurrection, the mandala is melting on the steamy windowpane.

Paradise—Garden of Eden. According to the Talmud, there are four ways to approach the text of the Torah, **PaRDeS** (Hebrew.)—lit. "Garden." This is an acronym:

Peshat—plain (simple) or the direct meaning of the text.

Remez—lit. "hint."

Derash—interpretation.

Sod—secret (mystery).

Judaism sees Cabbala as the fourth and deepest level of understanding the Torah.

This is hokhma[11]—wisdom.

16.

An unpleasant feature of our consciousness: when it encounters something unknown and incomprehensible, it makes every effort to correlate it to accumulated personal experience, to pass it through the filters of established opinions and find a place for it on a dusty, recessed shelf.

to compare—to comprehend—to get rid of

Many difficult issues can be solved in the following way: you hold the problem in the consciousness for several seconds/minutes, focus on it, make sure of the improbability of a logical, rational solution, and then "forget" about it. In an uncertain amount of time, when a leaf falls from a tree or when you dance because it's raining, the answer comes as an illumination, satori, insight, from the place where it has always existed.

. . . when we are together, we create what created us . . .

17.

More than anything, I would like to have a cup of coffee and call Polina or be flying to New York and writing something that would probably begin with "Is it possible to picture New York as a desert with streets?"

18.

Speech (reconciliation of meaning and sound) is constant turning into the past, continuing oblivion, forgetting. Writing is continuing memory. Death as the total cleansing of memory. Death as roaming, turning into the past, slinging. Speech of oblivion, river of death. Peace is the center of everything, the place from which it is easiest to reach the rest. "I entrust you to burn me after my death and scatter my ashes in the wind. How precise am I, saying 'me' in the previous sentence? Wind is rose is wind." A search for reality and not the picture of reality is doomed to failure. Writing is listening with the eyes.

19.

İnsanın aqibəti birin bilib beşin bilməməkdir və ona görə də altı-beş altı-beş danışmaqdır. The destiny of man is ignorance and therefore speaking off the mark. "The limits of my language are the limits of my world," (L.W.) but "the map is not the territory." (A.K.)

20.

There's nothing we didn't do to each other in our dreams. And beyond them. Turning paradox into oscillation.

21.

The physical and metaphysical center of this short poem is the central word of the central fifth line, the only verb in the text, the verb "hovering." An excellent word, expressing both the idea of movement and immobility, peace and flight. The bird is both flying and not, I mean, it is surely flying but does not make any effort of its own to do it. This happens when one is in the center of a warm air flow, catching the wave. But for that to happen, you must first climb to a certain height. The problem of poetry as I understand it is as follows: when one fails to write a hovering text, a zero text, a void text, a text-silence, one has to write a disappearing text, or at a lower level, a text about hovering, zero, void, silence.

The "prose" part consists of nothing but American allusions.

A poem should be a kind of potlatch: during the act of donation/writing/reading, the donators should eliminate, throw away the gifts in their hands so that the main thing might happen—their hands touching one another in a friendly, fraternal handshake. "I cannot see any basic difference between a handshake and a poem." (P.C.); "the outstretched hand had to find response in another hand stretched out from the beyond." (J.C.)

22.

The heart J.D. speaks about in "Che cos'è la poesia?" is a place where the horizontal *nəfs* and the vertical spirit meet.

... *a dove perched on the boulder covered with moss ... both you and I were once the dove, and the boulder, and the moss ...*

23.

F.N.: "*How poets ease life*. Poets, insofar as they too wish to ease men's lives, either avert their glance from the arduous present, or else help the present acquire new colors by making a light shine in from the past. To be able to do this, they themselves must in some respects be creatures facing backwards, so that they can be used as bridges to quite distant times and ideas, to religions and cultures dying out or dead. Actually, they are always and necessarily *epigones*."

24.

In ancient India, only the one with *burning desire* could become a master of the sitar, not the one who had a good ear and talent.

From sitar to line/sətir, legend/əsatir, sutra/surə and Saturn with masculine psychological traumas, initiation, detachment.

25.

Diagnosis: schizophrenia. How do I understand it? Or how does I understand it?

Schizophrenia is a double-bound realization of "multiply and replenish" from the Old Testament. A double bind is a situation in which a man is doomed to fail, to lose, whatever he does. There is a theory that a man in the grip of a double bind can develop symptoms of schizophrenia.

"A double message in the context of problems of everyday communication can concern the difference between verbal and non-verbal messages; for instance, the discrepancy between the body language of a mother (expressing disapproval, for example) and her words of approval, which leads the child to form several methods of interpreting the parent's signals, and as a consequence, mental discomfort due to the discrepancy between the 'said' message and the 'unsaid but shown' one."

26.

Sonata, sonnet, sənət/art, sünnət/circumcision, son ət (lit.)—foreskin. Culture/mədəniyyət begins with the restriction of the original natural substance, due to which the latter can be included in the social context; it begins with the appearance of the Town/Mədinə and wells/mədən, which are vertical discourses. Architecture replaces nature, memoirs are composed.

27.

Die and do whatever you want. "Dead Man." I bought a book of his interviews in Batumi, where everyone's soul and body are beautiful. Abi, abi, small Gypsies were shouting.

Georgia fascinates with its texture, from the guttural overtones of its people, in whose eyes there is the dream of what can never come true, to the landscape itself that defines that yearning. Mandelstam was absolutely right, "The Georgian Eros is what attracts Russian poets."

28.

"Whithersoever ye turn, there is the presence of Allah." (The Cow, 115); "You shall recite what is revealed to you of the scripture, and observe the Contact Prayers, for the Contact Prayers prohibit evil and vice. But the remembrance of God is the most important objective. God knows everything you do." (The Spider, 45)

... *təşbehlərdən təsbeh düzəltmək, zikr etmək ... to make beads from metaphors, to pray and remember ...*

29.

Democracy is the possibility of reconsideration.

30.

... hoping for partial overlapping of routes of reading ...

[ENDNOTES]

[1] Meraj (Arab.)—1) place to ascend to; 2) ascension to heaven; 3) elevation.

[2] Vird (Arab.)—continuous repetition of one and the same (word, poem, prayer etc.); mentioning the name of God.

[3] Lotu Bahtiyar was a legendary Azerbaijani mobster ("lotu" means "criminal," "rogue," "thief" in Azerbaijani).

[4] Literally: "... from temple to palace, haram, harem and pocket, up to karma ..."

[5] Literally: "cinema"—"icon"—"monk"

[5] Turker Gasimzadeh, Tair Ibishov, Ayaz Gambarli, Sayid Ganiyev, modern Azerbaijani composers.

[7] "tree"/"wood"—"ancient"

[8] "dense forest"—"primeval times"

[9] "drowsiness"—"dream" = "the unconscious"

[10] "roots"—"crown"

[11] The word means "joke" in modern Russian.

TRANSLATED FROM RUSSIAN BY ESMIRA SEROVA

Alhierd Bacharevic

The Art of Being a Stutterer

I AM A STUTTERER. All these impatient, desperate words—such a huge number of words—that I keep inside, very rarely manage to leave my throat freely. I could have become a silver-tongued speaker, a brilliant lawyer or TV reporter, I could have changed even the most stubborn minds, punishing or pardoning—how I wish I could—but for this invisible, dysfunctional bit of my organism which thrums away inside me when I try to chase after the bus of the conversation—in vain.

What usually happens is this. Some capricious sound—possibly "k" or "l"—that is supposed to be pronounced at the very beginning of a well-turned phrase suddenly starts to resist, grabbing with its nasty paws at the sides of the throat, whining and croaking. The sounds that should follow the "k" or "l" crowd together annoyingly, backing up behind the wretched thing, but the damned sound doesn't give way! The harmonious train of words breaks off; the person I am addressing looks away or contrariwise nods encouragingly, waiting for me to get out all I have to say. But already his thoughts have stopped interacting with mine; he can concentrate only on my stuttering. I feel I cannot say what I have to in elegant, well-chosen words, and I start shivering in panic. Frantically I try to say the same things in different words and sometimes I manage it. But where have my brilliant sentences, my choice words, and the calm voice intended to captivate my interlocutor gone? The conversation gradually loses its sense, the person I am speaking to looks at me askance with his eyes full of pity and disdain simultaneously—and then off he goes, taking with him his gift of pronouncing every sound as easily and naturally as breathing, a great gift, though he will never understand how lucky he is to possess it.

"You're not ill, simply tongue-tied!" a friend of a friend keeps telling me. "Impotence is far worse!" says a distant cousin, smirking under

27

his mustache. "I'd much rather stutter . . ." whispers a blind man. "No one ever died of stuttering," says a woman I hardly know, putting her hand on mine. How I hate this sympathy!

I laugh along with the rest when I hear funny stories about stutterers. But at the same time all I want is to convince you all that my stuttering is only temporary, that I suffer from it only when I am excited, and all the rest of the time I can chatter away as easily as you do. But I cannot tell you a joke of my own. I tried it once and that feeling of shame even now makes my stutter worse. Sometimes I forget that incident and say: "Hey, listen to this joke." But as soon as I begin, a friendly hand touches my shoulder as if saying, "Better not try." The forced laugh they tried to produce after doing their best to hear my joke to the end put me off talking completely for some time. But my joke was really funny, really, very funny! But I belong to this accursed tribe of the stutterers, the people whose "l-l-l-language" is reflected in the little hyphens that divide one l-l-letter from the next l-l-letter. When our language is written down it really hits you in the face. Hack writers constantly pick on us to make some of their characters more "true to life." A hack thinks that if he makes one character completely bald, gives a second constant snuffles, and makes a third a stutterer, the reader will find this more "convincing."

I am quite sure that writing was invented for us! It is we who can get the most out of it! Here we are able to show off our sense of humor, our wit, our sensitivity to language. The written word is our broad field, our freedom, our realm. Surely it was a stutterer who invented the alphabet. But when it becomes a matter of reading our own texts aloud to a wider audience . . . however eloquent the lines we have created, within a few moments the audience will start making for the exit—even those who bear the same stigma of stuttering as the author.

No one ever died of stuttering . . .

Once I spent a whole year with my grandfather, in his shabby one-room apartment that always smelled of medicine. Grandfather did not mind my stuttering. He had become almost completely crazy by that time, hardly ever got out of bed, and did not want to answer any questions. He ate nothing but the mashed potatoes that I would prepare for him—which I have hated ever since, I had to make so much of it! I even dreamed of mashed potatoes: I saw myself lying on my couch in the kitchen, next to the fridge, unable to move my arms because they were cemented together by the mash; I saw some kind of iron pipes hanging from the ceiling with the same yellowish puree creeping out of them like sausages . . .

Grandfather had taken root in his bed like a weed. This impression was even stronger when he raised his arms under the blanket or turned his head, which seemed to be nailed to the pillow. The thing he most enjoyed was staring at the ceiling from under his Brezhnev-like eyebrows. I assume he found the meaning of life and the answers to all his questions in the cobwebbed ceiling. Or maybe he saw his future there, instead of in a crystal ball. Sometimes he talked to it in a special argot, the language used by crazy people all over the world. Whenever this happened, I felt like a senseless little cloud in the sky from which my grandfather was staring into the inner world of his existence. Nevertheless, I loved my grandfather. I was happy when the doctor said that he would live a long time yet, and that with good care he could even recover. But the doctor went away, leaving behind prescriptions and footmarks on the floor that had still not dried out the following morning. I felt they were the footmarks of Death, who had stopped by to see if the old man was ready to leave.

My days would pass as follows. At nine a.m. I would get up, give my grandfather an injection, look into his unblinking eyes, and go to prepare breakfast. Mashed potatoes for granddad, a sandwich for myself. I would put a kettle on the stove and look out of the window. We'd have breakfast, then I'd go to the post office to pick up the money my father sent, and then go to the grocery store. When I got home, I'd read until one in the afternoon, make lunch, give my grandfather another injection, feed him, and watch TV until evening. Around seven, mashed potatoes would force me back to the kitchen to cook the five spuds left from the fifteen I had peeled, and to open small round cans of meat pâté—the shelves in the vestibule were piled high with those cans—and then, trying to bear the tedium, stuff my grandfather with that dangerous dish. Sometimes I would sit by his bed for an hour or so after supper, feeling that his almost invisible lips and knotty, pale-spotted hands were trying to convey to me: "Stay, sit by me." I would sit there thinking that maybe I would prolong his life by doing so.

Grandfather, by the way, could get himself to the bathroom alone. Lost in my reading, I would always miss that mysterious moment when the old man would get up from his bed. Only the sudden, startling sound of the toilet flushing would break the paralyzing silence of the flat: as if a thousand glass statuettes all fell on to the floor at once. Grandfather would appear against the door, as if it were a TV screen, take a step and disappear. I would sink back into my reading, but would not be able to concentrate on the book anymore; I would keep going back and rereading the same two pages. Even after a whole year of living in the same apartment, I could not get used to Grandfather's unexpected, but completely natural excursions.

After our wordless conversation I'd return to the kitchen couch and start reading again. However, the looming of tomorrow's mash, the warm breath of the cave between my sprawled legs, the entrance to which was concealed by the book, the comfort of the couch, the warmth of the lamp, the hand approaching the fly of my jeans, the vision of a woman's hair . . . The sameness of all the days of this year would not let me concentrate, but simply made it clear that this evening would end the same way as all the previous ones. I would burst into the hall, hide my face in the deaf and dumb coats no one had worn since my grandmother's death. This was the only way to suppress my painful wish for Grandfather's death. Then . . . then I could spend the rest of the money on wine and meat, fruit and chocolate; and even if not on my own merits—being a weak appendage of my grandfather—as a one-off luxury, I would get some woman into the apartment and smell her carbon dioxide till it hurt. Ready to kill myself for such thoughts, I'd put a coat on and go into the city.

What was I counting on? On a random meeting? Someone asking me for a cigarette? (I always kept a pack of cigarettes in my pocket even though I never smoked.) Was I counting on a glove falling out of a small seductive hand? On a chatterbox woman in a half-empty bus? I counted on anything that could tie me in some kind of knot. I counted on a gloomy young student girl who had left home after a fight with her parents and didn't know where she would spend the night; on a wife who had been turned out of her home by her drunken husband; on a woman looking for adventures. I did not need anything special from any of them. I just wanted to see, feel, smell, lie down next to her—very close to her—on the kitchen couch, stroking my hand across the warm curve on her back, which I saw now in everything, even in the armrests of a chair. Grandfather would not notice anything; he was only interested in the higher spheres. I wandered the shining streets, got into streetcars going nowhere, I went crazy on steps that looked like piano keys and repeated the same motive over and over again. It's hard to imagine how my face looked in the light of street lamps or shop windows: thirsty and frightening. Around midnight I was ready to settle for any female: even these two fat women. I would lie between them with my eyes closed, and by dawn I'd have turned into a happy shish kebab. But during those evenings in town I never found the inner strength to talk to anyone. I'd come home alone and fall asleep.

Once, however, my grandfather started to speak. I was elated. I hadn't been so happy for about 15 years, from the time I saw the movie *The Return of Sherlock Holmes*, and 40 minutes into it I discovered he had survived. My grandfather came to life again. It happened at midday. I was pouring tea into a big mug when I heard his quiet voice behind my back: "I want cucumbers, fresh cucumbers." I turned around and my grandfather was standing near the door staring at me reproachfully. I started laughing, I held him so tightly that he nearly fainted. "He feels better, he is recovering!" I thought. I sat him down on the sofa and promised to come back with the freshest cucumbers in the world. The only problem was that, at that time, there was only one shop where I could buy cucumbers. I hate those shops where the customer is supposed to deliver his order to the shop assistant, I believe they were invented to humiliate people like me. I prefer to choose the things myself, without talking, and then pay for it at a cash desk. However, I had no choice.

All cheered up by Grandfather's resurrection, I tried for a long time to make sense to the shop assistant, trying to explain why I had come and pointing to the basket of cucumbers. I shall never forget that lunch. We ate mashed potatoes and salad with sour cream and talked together, understanding each other completely. Afterwards Grandfather wanted to lie down and went over to the couch.

In the evening he felt unwell. White and naked, he lay on the ironed cotton sheet gasping for breath—it looked like he had been painted there. I tried to help him, but soon realized I had to call an ambulance. It would be hard to phone the hospital, because of my stutter, but I felt it was possible. I dialed the number, but when someone answered I realized I could not say a word. I tried hard, hiccuped, paused, and roared into the goddamned receiver that kept repeating, "Hello!? ... Hello!?" I made three or four more attempts, I don't remember quite how many, but it was all useless. I tried to call my father, who could have understood my spasmodic speech, but, unluckily, he was neither at home nor at work.

In despair, barefoot and wearing only jeans, I rang at the neighboring apartments. But it was too early, everyone was still at work or in school. Only the door of the last flat opened when I rang the bell. A woman I did not know appeared on the doorstep, wearing a white terrycloth robe. "Better go and sleep it off, ducky!" she said, shutting the door. I pressed the bell again and again, but the peephole that had gleamed a promising yellow a few moments before now showed dark on the blue surface of the door. I ran downstairs but suddenly remembered that Grandfather was all alone at home. He could be feeling better now or he could have ... I turned around abruptly and hurried back, feeling pieces of plaster that had fallen from the walls sticking to my unshod feet. In a few bounds I reached his bed underneath the shabby ceiling, but my grandfather had already d-d-d-d-d-d ...

TRANSLATED FROM BELARUSIAN BY VERA RICH

MICHEL LAMBERT

Long Night

PATRICK WAS WALKING up the Boulevard Haute-Victoire when he spotted the Rubberman across the street, striding the opposite way in his usual, astoundingly springy gait and lost, as always, in his musings. This was his territory, the district extending from the Gare du Nord to the Place des Orphelins, and he crisscrossed it tirelessly. At all hours of the day, and often the night, there was a good chance of passing him on the sidewalk or catching a glimpse of his roving silhouette as it disappeared around a corner.

Patrick recognized him instantly. He did an about-face and kept pace with him. The Rubberman was moving along at a good clip. He walked alongside the botanic gardens without even glancing at the greenhouses that were reflecting the last rays of sunlight. He passed the Hôtel Méridien, the neighborhood landmark, sole survivor of its era, and he advanced as far as the glass pyramid that served as the entrance to the new convention center.

He crossed the street at the traffic lights, and the two men found themselves face to face in front of the Etoile shopping mall. The Rubberman gave a little chuckle tinged with surprise. He was drenched. His long blond hair was matted to his head in thick clumps, and his whole being gave off an odor of dampness.

Patrick glanced up reflexively at the sky.

Half an hour earlier, a torrential rain had pelted the city, but now the sky had reverted to a uniformly pale blue, and the few lingering clouds had the appearance of wrapping paper adrift in the air.

"I was looking for you," said Patrick. "Are you free?"

The Rubberman nodded in acquiescence.

"Then I'm giving you a job."

Side by side, they proceeded into the mall and took the escalator up to the cafeteria at the FNAC bookstore. An empty table near the bay window offered a bird's-eye view over the arcades on the lower floors. They sat down, the Rubberman looping his long, supple limbs over the chair back in acrobatic style.

After waiting vainly for the waiter, Patrick went to get two coffees at the counter. When he returned with the tray, the Rubberman was amusing an audience with demonstrations of his flexibility, turning his head alternately to the right and left in nearly three-quarter rotations.

"Are you planning to go to Jean-Jacques's tonight?"

The Rubberman's head stopped in mid-swivel, and he grinned affirmatively. His eyes seemed to probe the intentions of Patrick, who replied:

"We can go together if you want. We're going to miss him," he sighed as he opened his little portion of milk.

Jean-Jacques had been in their lives for the length of a dream. He was the local parish priest. His superiors had decided to transfer him to a suburban parish, judging him too close to certain members of his congregation: artists, hoodlums, druggies, hookers. By way of farewell, the priest was to celebrate mass, after which everyone would attend a party in the rectory.

Patrick added sugar to his coffee, stirred it with a plastic spoon, and took a sip. Then he lit a cigarette, took several drags and peered appraisingly at the Rubberman, who looked as if he were made of soft, pink, perfectly pliable wax.

With a barely visible movement, like a beating of wings, the Rubberman flicked away the smoky veil that separated them. Patrick smiled.

"You'll never guess when I took up smoking. It was at the beginning of my career, to give myself a deeper voice."

Above their heads, the glass dome was turning dark. Patrick checked his watch.

Casting a distracted eye at the streams of movement on the lower floor, he said, "In less than two hours, I'll be onstage. Chekhov's *The Cherry Orchard*."

The Rubberman waggled his eyebrows in a sign of interest, real or feigned.

For a moment, Patrick wondered if his companion was truly mute, or if he was merely ashamed of his voice, as Patrick had once been. Unless all along he'd just been toying with everybody.

After a pause, he resumed pensively, "Chekhov's plays seem simple, but they're the hardest to perform. As an actor, you have to remain constantly below what the character is supposed to feel, to simulate gaiety when you know he's profoundly sad. The emotion is entirely in the lines, raise the tone a notch too high and you kill it."

He finished his coffee and pointed at his companion's swollen cheekbone.

"Did you get into another scrape?"

The Rubberman frowned resignedly.

"Because you gave somebody one of your goofy looks?"

His companion smiled enigmatically. Patrick didn't press the point. All of a sudden, as if the Rubberman's misadventures were bringing them back to him, his own troubles began to occupy his thoughts again. No matter the time or place, he always ended up thinking about them: his overdue rent, the bills that were piling up, his son's child support, the malicious chatter that portrayed him as a ruined man, forever captive to his weakness.

He began to perspire, simultaneously panicked over the mess he was in and elated at the prospect of making a fresh start with the Rubberman's unwitting assistance.

"Let's go," he grunted.

Sliding back his chair, he got to his feet and discreetly tidied his companion's appearance. The two of them headed for the exit.

Outside, the night was coming on, its grayness already dense. The air was crisp. Patrick, still in a sweat, buttoned his raincoat and turned up the collar. The traffic was clogged and noisy. People were jostling each other on the sidewalk, and in the distance the Marlboro and Mercedes signs had begun the flashing that would keep lonely stragglers company until dawn.

Making their way through the crowd, the two men advanced into the Avenue Général-Gohy, once home to some of the city's most distinguished families, but more recently a sleazy artery given over to peepshows, strip clubs and short-stay hotels. Today, between two ramshackle, squalid-looking buildings, sprawled an immense construction site, illuminated by garish neon signs, where iron and concrete skeletons of future office buildings were rising out of the ground.

"I don't have a cent left," declared Patrick in a matter-of-fact, almost bemused tone, as if he were talking about someone else. He laughed. "Not even a cherry orchard I can sell to pay off my bills! Chekhov had some good gags. Imagine, a cherry orchard! But don't worry; I'll be able to pay you tonight. Do you trust me?"

As his only response, the Rubberman made a running start, sprang into a handstand and walked a few steps on his hands. Then he stood up again, straight as a sentry, and gave Patrick a quick look of allegiance.

Patrick mimed applause, while reflecting that in any case the Rubberman didn't really have much choice. Some time back, he used to supplement his welfare checks by walking dogs and running errands for the prostitutes on the corner. But times had changed. The gentrification of the area had made the girls unwelcome, and they were migrating uptown. Meanwhile, the dog owners were selling their houses at astronomical prices.

"Life is hard," murmured Patrick as he patted the Rubberman's shoulder.

* * *

After the performance, Patrick returned to his dressing room, where he began removing his makeup under the fluttering gaze of the Rubberman, who, seated on the radiator, was digging into a bag of potato chips.

"Here," said Patrick, handing him a bill. "Go get me a pack of Gitanes at the corner store."

In his stage costume, Patrick still rather resembled Gayev, brother of the beautiful and carefree Lyubov Andreyevna, and also a landowner who, for all his benevolence and his crushing debts, belonged nonetheless to the ruling class.

As soon as he found himself alone, he began to ruminate, lost in his stage gestures. The cherry orchard was sold to save the family from ruin, it will be cleared off completely and then divided into parcels, and on each one a dacha will sprout. Nowadays it would be an office building. The endless cycle of history.

Then his thoughts unraveled. Soon nothing was left but a vague dejection, and once again the inevitable feeling came over him. Once again the mingled panic and giddiness. Once again the quivering hands, the urge to put a bullet through his head. A day filled with dread. The familiar pattern. You drop your guard, a little space opens in your brain, and suddenly you're snagged, unable to get free. A few hours later you've been wiped out, not a cent left, and for weeks and months you make the rounds, hoping to land a small part in a play and begin rebuilding your life.

But then again, maybe this would be the day when he actually managed to make a new beginning.

He got up abruptly, left his dressing room, knocked on the door of the adjacent room, and entered without permission.

"My little sister, my sweetheart," he said, advancing toward the woman who, half an hour earlier, had pressed herself tightly against him. Both of them had sobbed silently in front of the audience, distraught at the idea that the cherry orchard had been, in essence, nothing other than their own youth carelessly squandered. "My little sister, my sweetheart, I have a favor to ask of you."

Patrick realized he was still talking like a Chekhov character. It was always like that when he acted in a great author's play. The role entered him via his diction, and for a while after he left the stage, his own manner of speaking was colored by it.

But here he hadn't been able to play down his emotions as he did onstage. His voice was too earnest and lacked nuance. From the first word, it had been too harsh, too insistent, almost imploring, when it should have been overlaid with derision or tenderness.

He felt ridiculous. Both his life and his profession were ridiculous. This bourgeois drama. Chekhov himself.

And to say "little sister," with such exaggerated flair!

She barely deigned to look at him, and mumbled a barely audible, "Ah, it's you!" She, too, had removed her makeup, and her features were drawn. She was in the midst of undressing. Paying no attention to his presence, she stripped completely naked and disappeared behind the door of the shower stall.

He waited, shifting from one foot to the other, listening to the flowing water, imagining her warm and contented, as her partner's body must be, as all the good things of this world must be for those clever enough to get hold of them.

When she reappeared, a soapy fragrance spread through the room. Without his knowing why, the smell reminded Patrick of his childhood. He felt a wild impulse to cry, caress the young woman's breasts, kneel before her and bury his face between her thighs for the rest of his life.

But already she was heading toward a metal cabinet, from which she removed undergarments, jeans and a sweater.

Patrick followed her feverishly with his eyes, waiting for her to look at him.

"You must help me, little sister."

A sigh.

A little later, he resumed his appeal in a pitiable tone.

"My son is sick."

Ashamed, he started over:

"No, I'm the one who's sick. I mean, you know what I'm trying to say..."

As she finished dressing in adamant silence, her face scowling, steps echoed in the corridor. They heard a door open, followed by faint noises coming from the next dressing room. The Rubberman had just returned.

"I beg you, little sister," said Patrick in a breezy tone.

At that moment she was redoing her hair in front of the mirror.

"I couldn't care less about the money," he murmured when she turned around.

And it was true. He would have been content with much less. With her smile. With a wink. With even less than that. At the same time, he needed the money desperately.

"This is the last time. I won't bother you anymore."

She slipped into her raincoat, shouldered her bag, and prepared to leave.

With a quick lunge, he planted himself in her path.

"In the play," he said with sudden exasperation, "Lyubov Andreyevna is elegant, classy, she's a generous, free-spending woman. She knows how to love, to live. To laugh and cry."

"But you," he said, pointing at her, "you're just a middle-class sheep, tight with your money and stingy with your affections."

She stared at him icily. "You're in the process of screwing up your life. And your career, besides. Out there just now, you almost stunk out the house."

"Oh, my life!" he sneered. "My career!"

He plopped down on a hassock.

"My feet are throbbing with pain!" he wailed, staring at the black shoes of his theatrical get-up in a bid to make her laugh. "Of course, you don't give a damn. What's that guy doing next door?" he added, jerking his chin in the direction of the wall. "Is he swinging from the chandelier, or what?"

* * *

When they arrived at the rectory, the party was in full swing. Music, dancing, streamers, confetti. The scent of marijuana. The Rubberman, the acknowledged neighborhood mascot, was welcomed like royalty. A group of men raised him over their heads and tossed him in the air several times in quick succession, accompanied by the cheers of the other guests, who formed a circle around them.

"You smell like a dog," yelled a blonde who regularly hustled tricks outside the Gare du Nord.

There was an eruption of laughter.

The Rubberman protested by shaking his head emphatically and flashing a look of feigned outrage.

After shaking hands and kissing cheeks, Patrick made a detour by the buffet table before entering the back garden, where a portion of the human menagerie had gathered.

He lit a cigarette, let his mind wander. How long had it been since he'd seen his son? His mother? Lived with a woman? Been interviewed by a journalist? When had he become such a loser?

He was deep in meditation when the Rubberman came to join him.

"Is it true you're rich?" queried Patrick in a weary voice.

More than a question, it was an observation, an allusion to a rumor that was making the rounds in the neighborhood.

The Rubberman smiled in his enigmatic way, but a faint shadow of melancholy appeared in his eyes before he quickly averted them. He moved away from Patrick.

Why, several hours earlier, had Patrick wanted to see him as a heaven-sent opportunity?

The priest passed in front of him. A very tall, very lean guy. He circulated from one group to the next, tossing out pleasantries, inconsequential wisecracks. His somber gaze, accentuated by the dark circles beneath his eyes, focused intently on each of his guests. The whores and junkies. The young toughs and the talentless artists. All children of a barely glimpsed paradise. In less than a week, they would disappear from his life. It was his own particular cherry orchard, and he was being expelled from it as punishment for having loved it too much.

Patrick went over to greet him, patted him sympathetically on the shoulder. The two of them remained silent for a long moment. Behind them, a young couple were negotiating their future. The girl kept upping the ante, and the guy seemed ready to concede every point. The priest burst out laughing in his accustomed manner, booming and faintly hysterical. There was no telling whether he was covering up shyness or despondency.

"By the way . . ." began Patrick.

Clutching the priest by the arm, Patrick took him aside.

"I need money."

"Can't this wait until tomorrow?"

"No."

The priest's prow-shaped face darkened.

"You're that far gone?"

From overhead they heard a roar. Patrick looked up. An airplane was blinking in the crystalline night sky, softened by the city's burgeoning lights.

"Yes," he said. "I am."

"Then take up a collection. Now is the time, they're all drunk."

* * *

Accompanied by the Rubberman, Patrick went to exchange his wad of bills for gambling chips.

"You stay right on my heels," he said to his companion, whose presence in these surroundings was so odd that Patrick couldn't help laughing.

With what remained in his pocket, Patrick headed for the bar, inviting the Rubberman to follow him. They sat there like perfect strangers, and without exchanging so much as a glance, each of them sipped a whiskey. Behind them, in the gambling salon, the conversations were muffled, the laughter subdued.

Taking advantage of a lull, Patrick got up.

The Rubberman immediately mimicked him.

Flanked by his companion, Patrick roamed the salon, hovering over each table, forcing himself to observe the other players. Borrowing the technique he used for overcoming his stage fright, he focused his attention on one person's necktie, another's chain bracelet, the pudgy fingers of a third. It seemed to him that all of them were singularly lacking in skill, nerve and luck. He and the Rubberman would do much better. Finally, he took his place, the Rubberman standing guard behind him. With a sign, he directed him to lean over.

"Pick a number," he whispered.

The other appeared to reflect intently. Then, assuming a grave, almost solemn air, he showed Patrick his two hands wide open, but with one thumb folded under.

Patrick played the 9. The wheel turned, the 9 came up. The next time, he decided to trust his own unaided instinct. His number didn't win, but because he had wagered on the right color, he recovered his bet. The next time, it was both his number and his color.

Patrick grew bolder and started playing combinations of numbers. At regular intervals, he turned around to ensure that his guardian angel was still resolutely at his post.

"Come closer. A number. Quick. What color? Are you sure?"

He won, he lost, thought for a moment he'd lost everything, but recouped with a series of three simple bets that earned him the silent congratulations of his neighbors, as well as a more penetrating look from the croupier.

The chips piled up. A feeling of omnipotence came over him. As if magnetically drawn, men and women, some unknown to him, but also quite a few regulars, old comrades in good luck and bad, had gathered around the table, hanging on his every move.

* * *

When they left the casino, Patrick wasn't rich, but he had enough to cover his bills and his overdue rent, to meet his child support payments, and even to send peace offerings to both his son and his ex. The dawn was filled with promise. The streets were bathed in an indistinct light that engendered agreeable feelings. The last of the night owls were wandering off like amiable ghosts. Exquisite cherry orchards blossomed at every street corner.

In a mischievous mood, Patrick prompted the Rubberman to ring doorbells. To hail a taxi and then flip off the driver. To clamber up to apartment balconies, tap on the windows, and scamper back down without being seen. His companion obligingly met each request with the dexterity of a magically endowed cartoon character. A loose-jointed robot. Activate his controls and presto—a pirouette, shazam—a headstand.

Patrick guffawed.

"You still have that soggy smell!"

He took several bills from his pocket and, without counting them, gave them to the Rubberman.

"You've more than earned these."

With a dizzying sleight of hand, the Rubberman made the bills vanish, likewise without counting them.

Moving at a leisurely pace, they walked alongside a wooden fence that displayed a model's winsome smile on a billboard. In the distance the Marlboro and Mercedes signs were still blinking hypnotically. The halo of the streetlights dissolved in the glow of the newborn day. A girl entered her apartment building.

Patrick began to weep silently as he had done during the Chekhov play, but this time he hugged only his immense fatigue. He sat down on a doorstep. The Rubberman came and sat beside him. The stone slab was cold. The first of the day's number 33 buses went by in front of them.

"Long night," murmured Patrick as he stared at an oil stain on the asphalt.

He would have liked to ask the Rubberman if it was true that he was the son of a leading industrialist and had once been a high-living sophisticate. And what it was that had caused his sudden downfall. And also what inner turmoil made him seem so distracted and forlorn to those who secretly watched him.

Above all, he would have liked to ask him why, even when they won big at the roulette table, it was never enough to buy back the cherry orchard of his boyhood.

But of course it was hard to put questions like that to a mute, even if the Rubberman was only pretending to be one.

Across the street, a pair of lovers were kissing passionately. They kept at it for a long time. And even when the kissing was done, they were still locked in an embrace, each of them looking out into the distance at the extraordinary moment they had just experienced.

"You see, happiness does exist," said Patrick.

He stood up, and the Rubberman followed suit. As they went along, Patrick talked enthusiastically about a play of Pinter's that he would soon begin to rehearse. The mechanical diggers were already at work at the construction site on the Boulevard Général-Gohy, the old Hôtel Méridien suddenly presented its noble and lofty profile. At the intersection they went their separate ways.

TRANSLATED FROM FRENCH BY PAUL CURTIS DAW

VLADIMIR POLEGANOV

The Birds

One:

If she just looks long and hard enough through the grimy pane of the southern window, she is sure to see one of them returning to its nest. That's what she's been told, though it is unclear to her how to make out the exact location against the towering mountain slope. She has been staring into the distance for several hours now, to no avail—not a single bird, not even a feather. Only the words flutter about in her head that she remembers from when she was a child, her grandmother's words probably: "Good birds fly south." If they were to ask her now, she'd tell them: not good, but dark birds, black stains on the evening sky with crimson in their beaks. She doesn't know what good looks like, feathered or not, but good these birds are not, she is sure of it. Then again, none of them ever leaves this place; they just fly to the mountain and back.

The empty room slumbers behind her. Further behind that: a wall. Behind the wall, in the other room: dust, drain flies, and the sound of words drying and shriveling. He's at his desk, his typewriter devouring the paper sheet, his wound probably bleeding again. She will take care of it later; just stay here for a little while longer.

The sky has nothing to give her. Nor does time, apparently. Minutes, then hours glide across the blue—those that fly high soon evaporate in the heat, the rest get ripped to shreds by the towers of the town. You can't say that time is standing still here—she wished she could, but she can't. Still, its infiniteness is reassuring—*sine terminis*, there's always some more of it left. There's some for her to take now, to sit here, watching. To get up from the chair, turn and face the room, to look around, fix her skirt, and move toward the door. To open it slowly and step through, into the dust, the flies, and his words. To dress his wound again and take care of his stomach. To take care of herself.

Time to figure out what's going on.

Two:

As she enters his office, the desk is unoccupied. He's lying on the bed, asleep. The window is open. There is a black feather on the sill. She closes the window, picks up the feather, and puts it in the narrow vase next to the typewriter. There are several others there just like it. He opens his eyes.

"*I wrote a little today,*" he says.

"*I can see that.*" She turns toward the typewriter and its half-chewed prey. The white is not enough, there is too much ink. It will always be too much, how could it not be—these words are eating her husband, day by day.

ENOUGH!

The bandage is torn, red stains creeping down each individual thread—barely large enough to cover the wound. The ointments, creams, and disinfectants she uses to clean and dress it have long since been moved from the bathroom to this room, on the shelf next to his books.

"*They took me by surprise again. Every single time. I had closed the window, barred it shut ... Do you see that cardigan? I was wearing it over another one, and a shirt ... I thought that the layers would slow them down, that ...*"

"*Of course they won't,*" she interrupts, telling him to keep quiet and sit still as she removes the dripping bandage and rinses out the raw flesh beneath it. "*Have they ever?*"

Never, he concedes.

In the beginning, they would both cry each time they had to re-dress the wound. Their nights have been sleepless since he told her he was meant to write. The fury of her screams and the blows from her fists on the day they delivered the typewriter seem distant now, inconceivable. The curt confirmation telegram that the Mayor's office had sent some days later is now but one of many scars.

He has resigned himself to this new life all too quickly, but she's not going to follow suit. Oh, he has no idea. One day she will knock the photographs off the wall, breaking their frames, letting all that has been flowing out of them flow out even quicker. What use is it to her anyway? Some pre-writerly past, paralyzed moments in time, impossible now under the tyranny of words.

It is all in her head anyway:

> The afternoon walks in the town's only park.
> The midsummer nights' concerts.
> The chocolate ice cream he never quite warmed up to.
> The yellow boat in the lake.

It's all in her head, it clawed its way into her open mouth and curled up in the darkest corner of her brain as she read out the telegram for the first time:

> *Builder of Society*
> *Category: Writer*
> *Starting date: March of the current year.*

They were making a writer out of him. They *had* already made him a writer. She read the telegram again, hoping the act would invert the meaning of the text, erase the words from the piece of paper, stop the world from turning, or at least make it take a step backwards.

His groans rouse her out of her thoughts. When did he manage to get back to his desk? Whatever happens, I can't let this moment pass me by.

The next day, when she finds him in a puddle of blood, with several pages of writing stacked neatly next to the typewriter, she decides she has to do something. But first she finds some time to take care of his wounds.

Three:

The woman upstairs lost her mind several years ago. As many years as the pearls in the necklace she never lets out of her grip, she claims, though her medical records probably say otherwise. The writer's wife visits often, for the comfort of their shared silences: the madwoman's silence is heavy, imposing, almost operatic in scale; the wife's: brittle, sinking to the bottom like residue. In the wordless haze of their afternoon silence, each of their heads is like a tower in a drowned city: seen a lot, knows a lot, but mute as a tombstone.

But this time it is different. This is an afternoon of words, unleashed like a cork being popped with the visitor's cry: "I can't take it anymore"—a tempest that neither of them is able or willing to end.

"*Let me tell you how I lost my mind,*" begins the madwoman. "*It was the very last thing I lost. I held on to it by my fingernails, clutched it till I was blue in the face, but it would not stay. We lose everything in the end, remember—even my mother told me that: that's the way the world works: all will flow out of you. You, young lady, you have no valves, no doors. But look at me, I'm like a sieve! That's what she told me and it was all true. I, the fool, went out looking for truth, found it and went mad. Everything you see of me now, every fold and every crease of my once smooth skin is a letter.*

"*But let me spare you the reading: it was finding out where he had gone that drove me mad.*

"*Wait, WAIT! Let me tell you about the birds first: you can't defeat them. Not the big ones, not the small ones either—they fly, while we only drag ourselves across the ground. All we can do is look up at them. That and curse them. And I cursed, oh, I cursed them for so long I ran out of words. It wasn't my voice that had gone; it was the words—as if I had squandered them, drank them away. I mean, they came back, of course—anger is what remains when all else abandons you. Still, I'm keeping my words to myself these days. And for you, I guess, on occasion.*

"*I hated you in the beginning, did you know that? I wanted to strangle you—wrap my hands around your delicate neck, there, in that corner . . . I could have done it too, I was stronger then. But because I had once lost my words, I was afraid I'd also lose whatever strength I had, so I let it go. And then you turned out alright, there aren't many decent people left living in this building . . .*

"*So let me tell you what I saw. I don't know what it was: salvation or just an escape; whether I should feel fortunate or just sit here and cry. I never figured it out, as much as I mulled it over in that ever-decelerat-*

ing windmill creaking in my head. I left it in the end, told myself there was no point in trying—I'm mad already, what is it to me to look for his reasons? We need to get used to the feeling of ending, we do, for the end is coming and it's all we have left to look forward to."

* * *

The writer's wife descends the stairs, replaying the conversation with the madwoman in her head.

"*You need to go to the other side of the mountain.*" The other side?

"*Of the mountain, yes.*" It sounds fantastical, somehow, like a fairytale bent out of shape.

"*It does, but it isn't. And you'll lose him, it is inevitable.*" Lose what, she thinks to herself as the ground floor draws near, or whom? Man or mind? And isn't it the same anyway?

She leaves the useless thoughts at the door and steps inside, the madwoman's presence following her like a trailing odor. What did you see there?

"*What I saw is only for me to know. Whether I remember it, however . . . It's still somewhere inside me, spinning and smoldering, simmering slowly until, one day, it explodes. I won't think about it till then.*"

* * *

She tells him there is something she needs to attend to, it will be no more than a couple of days. He is not to write, if possible, and should notify the neighbors, *any* neighbor, if he absolutely has to. She'll leave a key in the flowerpot next to the door, and really, he should ask his brother to tear himself away from his precious factory for once and come keep him company. Don't move too much, only short trips to the bathroom or the kitchen; there's soup, a pot of casserole, two loaves of bread, and some dessert in the fridge. She kisses him on the cheek. The wound weeps.

Four:

The road to the mountain is straight, tree-lined, and perfect. The wind's mischievous fingers sway the tops of the poplars, their shadows licking the asphalt's glistening skin. She walks straight down the middle, trying not to let them get her, as if they weren't shadows but holes in the pavement, as if she could fall straight through and into nothing. Her eyes are fixed on the mountainside in the distance, on the cloudy tapestry above it. She herself will soon be there, she will soon understand. Or the madwoman will turn out to be a liar, jealous, deceitful . . .

She doesn't want to think about it, now is not the time. She will just keep walking, up to the end of the paved road, on to the mountain trail and up to the cliffs, then down to the valley beyond. She will not look back, this is no place for regret. She will not look up at the monstrous beaks carrying pieces of her husband and god knows how many other people, which would only make her angry. Oh, how gladly she would set fire to their nests! Or no, not fire—they are already the color of dirty smoke. No, she will choke the infernal throat they fly out of and let them tear each other to shreds. Yes.

Five:

She's approaching the end of the road. She wants to go on, only a few steps more, but she can't. She wants to rest her eyes, for just a moment, but she can't. She wants to turn to stone there where she stands, a delicate calcified tribute to grief and longing, but she won't. She wishes she were already insane and hallucinating, but she is painfully lucid.

Then she sees it: the house in the forest,

white, beautiful, superimposed onto the landscape, out of place yet unthinkable anywhere else, timeless.

Spring, summer, autumn, winter chase each other around its pristine walls without daring to touch them, like bashful suitors uncertain of their paramour's favor. This house is the safest place in the world. She can move now, the paralysis has suddenly drained down her leg, slithered away like a snake, and hidden under a stone somewhere. She takes a few steps forward, slowly at first, then almost running, toward the bright wooden door with its shining brass handle.

The stern look of the windows stops her in her tracks: *we lead to the soul of this house,* they rumble, *you can't run toward the soul of any-thing. Souls are to be approached reverently, carefully, quietly.* Yes, of course, she nods, of course. She remains still.

How is she only seeing them now? There are several of them, perched on the roof, on the sills, one hops a few feet from the door. Their eyes are curious, their beaks full. Her movements have not alarmed them. Only the cold wind seems capable of ruffling their impeccable assembly of feathers. She tries to scream at them and realizes her voice is gone. She's not surprised, somehow it seems logical. One by one, the birds disappear into the house, through the windows, phasing through the walls, through the door, through the chimney, as if sinking into the reflected image of a house on the surface of the world's calmest lake. A pestilence wherever they go, she thinks, and takes a careful step toward the windows.

She sees them: the man and the woman.

He is lying on the right side of their bed. She is sitting on a low chair next to him, a wet cloth in her lap and a metal basin by her feet. Her legs are slender, elegant under a short, green dress, a shade of green that evokes autumn, dark and rich next to the hazel of her hair. The man appears to be naked, his lower body under a gray blanket that matches the bedroom's thin curtains. Gray like the carpet under her delicate feet. The writer's wife imagines his legs are as strong and muscular as his shoulders and chest, and just as specked with the blood of many open wounds. The pain he must be in is all too familiar. She lets out a muffled sigh and looks on as the birds fly into the room.

One by one they appear, turning their heads around to take in the surroundings, looking for a place to leave their plunder, in order to tear into his flesh again. But no, she is wrong—instead, they hop across the carpet, making their way to the basin. Carefully, without spilling a drop of blood, they empty their beaks into it, by the woman's feet. She leans down and soaks the cloth in the water, wrings it out and gently runs it across the man's heaving chest. The skin sizzles and slowly closes, not even a scar to blemish the flawless curve of his torso. The man looks at her. She smiles, then breaks into laughter. Both of them are laughing now. They look happy. They look familiar. The woman outside can't hear anything; she can only read their faces.

And then she sees the details:

50

Every single detail suddenly looms into focus. Every line around the man's eyes, every wrinkle in the white sheets, every speck of dust on the chest of drawers by the door, every spider in every corner and every nook, every color in the photographs of children on the walls, every letter in the book lying open on the bedside table, every intricate outline in the wardrobe's woodwork, every hair on his body and on the body of the cat sleeping on the left side of the bed, every key of the broken typewriter on the desk. The details wash over her, flow into her body and fill up the space left vacant by paralysis, rush up her veins and arteries and storm her head, devouring her thoughts. It is the details that make this world, this new, terrible world over the mountain, real. Real and impossible for her to be in. She can only stare, or read its signs, but never be of it. Even if she were to reach out, she wouldn't be able to touch anything. Even if she were to open her mouth, no sound would come out. Even if she were to leave, there would be nowhere to go. *You can't move in a place where you don't belong,* the windows tell her. And she doesn't nod, because she can't.

TRANSLATED FROM BULGARIAN BY PETER BACHEV

CLAUS BECK-NIELSEN

The Author Himself

I SAW PETER HØEG from the back seat of my parents' car, a sudden perception, like a revelation, an abruptly descended prophet, as I leaned forward between the front seats to take the piece of blue Sorbits chewing gum that my father, hidden behind his headrest, was holding out in the palm of his hand while we sped northwards through Jutland on the E45 motorway. He (the author, my future real self) was actually concealed behind a half-mask of leather, and his intensely, almost insanely bright eyes were gazing up at the sky from above an article on page 4 of Politiken's arts section, which my mother in the passenger seat next to my father held in her lap. "Who's that?" I asked, and my mother, who didn't have the courage to take her eyes off the road for fear that my father would steer us into a head-on collision with an oncoming vehicle, handed back the newspaper between the two headrests, and I took it and laid it out on my bare knees and read what from then on would be a holy scripture, a kind of personal genesis penned by the author himself and recalling the moment in his life at which he had become an author. Until then it had never occurred to me to write as much as a single line outside the confines of my school exercise books or my reports in physics or social studies, but from that moment on I wanted to be an author too, or rather I wanted to be Peter Høeg, a person of multiple talents and personas who would never need to decide, because he could do everything all at once: study drama in Paris, trek through deserts, speak Swahili, fence, ski, dance ballet, climb mountains, write novels, sail the seven seas (simultaneously!), give talks, and meditate and look like a monk, and *be* a monk, and play Johannes V. Jensen, and *be* Johannes V. Jensen with the aid of only a half-mask, and marry an African and have beautiful children, and live like a saint in ten square meters of space in an oasis in the middle of the city, and write his books on his lap in only two hours a day, in the evenings, even, when he's feeling at his most exhausted and breast-feeding, even though he's a man! I wanted to meet him. But where? How do you meet a person who seems to be everywhere all at once?

The only thing I had to go on was the novel that the article claimed was the center of everything, and which the caption said had been published earlier that year. But since I was only twenty-five or twenty-six and had read little more than adventure books, Troels Kløvedal's travel literature, and *The Clan of the Cave Bear*, the title *Conception of the Twentieth Century*[1] sounded like it might be heavy going. So to begin with I simply tore the page out of the newspaper, folded it up and put it in the back pocket of my sister's cut-off jeans (which I was wearing, and which she would end up giving me a few years later, because, she said, "those boxer shorts you go around in aren't shorts at all, they're underpants, and I don't want people seeing me out with a brother in his underpants!"), and after that I leaned back in my seat and looked out through the window at the Danish summer flashing by as I sank deeper and deeper into my own *Conception of Peter Høeg*.

It wasn't until a few years later, after I had gone back to the house by the sea and had finally got around to visiting the library in the little town that I discovered *Conception of the Twentieth Century* on the shelf along with the librarian's recommendation, and borrowed it and took it back home with me to read at once while lying on the coir mat in the shady living room. After that, everything happened so quickly. I was only six years younger than him, but the only thing I had achieved in my life at that point was ... nothing. As soon as *Tales of the Night* appeared in Arnold Busck's bookstore I took it down from the shelf and slipped it inside my windbreaker and hurried out again, pregnant with significance. I had read neither Marquez nor Karen Blixen, and so I found it to be both brilliant and unique. I immediately enrolled in a drama school in Vordingborg and stole *Smilla's Sense of Snow* from the local bookstore there. At the same time, in a kind of parallel life— or rather two, ten, or twenty parallel lives—I was accepted into the School of Journalism, attended ballet lessons at Det Fynske Ballet-akademi, worked out at the gym, took a course in Spanish, went to

Alpe d'Huez to become a skiing instructor, played the flute, toyed with the idea of applying to the Academy of Music, studied psychology at Aarhus University, Spanish at Odense University, played in a local band, took guitar lessons from Svend Staal, practiced tai chi under the guidance of Tal R, and applied to work on a development project in a village outside Managua in Nicaragua (a motor scooter came with the job), *all at the same time*. I was everywhere, doing everything I couldn't, and without success, but most importantly: without meeting him, the revelation my own Conception was all about.

But then at last, one day in the spring of 1993, the twenty lives converged into one:

I step through the door of the meeting room of the Danish Authors' Society at Strandgade 6, and in the midst of what looks like the entire teeming congregation of Great Authors, along with their mothers and stepchildren and publishers and worst critics, all with wine glasses in hand and faces turned toward the man giving the award speech, there he stands among them, singularly without wine glass in hand, seemingly unaffected by all his success and the leading of so many hectic lives in recent years, wearing sandals and airy, loose-fitting cotton trousers that are unrestrictive of the genitals, undamaging to precious eggs, and a casual, unironed, flax-colored smock, his tousled hair bleached by the sun, his skin golden brown as though, quite unlike any other Great Author, he has not stepped directly from a taxi cab but from a circumnavigating wooden schooner, an engineless vessel that near-silently, with only the gentle glug of water under its stern, slipped into the harbor with the first blush of rising sun to moor at the quayside some fifty meters away behind the Ministry of Foreign Affairs. He stands as one sits, or more exactly *stands*, in a saddle: back straight, legs apart, knees slightly bent, anus thrust forward into alignment with the spinal column so as to allow the free flow of energy and inspiration and to permit the soul to plume like a flame thrown from asshole into cosmos. His gaze is intense, almost manically attentive and yet calmly and indulgently directed toward the man who stands only a couple of meters in front of him, mumbling his award speech into an occasionally squealing microphone.

What happened then is something of which I have absolutely no recollection. It's as if the story grinds to a halt here, the picture freezes, and the only thing I see, and continue to see, as though it were in front of me right now, is the image of him, Peter Høeg, not the congregation of Great Authors, but Peter Høeg, picked out from its midst as though in spite of it, existing in his own dimension, in another world entirely, that of the Conception itself.

And in that world, from that moment on I am his shadow, or rather: his shadows, the countless shadows of Peter Høeg.

I follow on behind, doing everything of which I am unable, living nowhere and everywhere at the same time, on a sofa in the broadcasting corporation's radio documentary department, beneath an overpass north of Marseille, in the basement of New York's Grand Central Station, in Joseph London's front room, with an unmarried female schoolteacher in a suburb of Prague, with a Jewish glassblower and her Uzbek sister-in-law in their apartment on the "island of poets" in St. Petersburg, on the floors of a former ice-cream factory in Hannover and a villa in Maisons-Laffitte. On a daybed in the attic of a public transport director in Risskov I read *Borderliners* during the course of some nights of despair, a novel I actually *purchase* (albeit with money borrowed from a biscuit tin in the kitchen of a woman who was out). In it I encounter for the first time the author inside the Conception, and I believe it really is him, until I am told that things are not that simple. I sigh and read on. I read slowly and intensely, and yet I am manically attentive, as if I were searching for something. But for what? For Peter Høeg, indeed, but not only for him, which is to say me, and not only for the key to my own life. I am searching for something else, something bigger, a door leading out into another world entirely.

Years pass, I meet the Woman of My Dreams and propose marriage to her, and she accepts, and at the same time *The Woman and the Ape* is published, and she buys it for me as a gift and I read it (as if it were myself), but am no longer quite as certain as before. Nonetheless I go on, getting up in the mornings, performing my exercises, dancing, practicing my tai chi, doing my sit-ups and push-ups, and so on. Like him, I am still doing all I can to do everything under the sun, I really am, only now I no longer know why.

Then all of a sudden, one day he is gone. Vanished! Rumors abound, the way rumors do when a phenomenon such as he disappears from one moment to the next after having been at the center of everything for seven or eight heightened years, appearing everywhere, in all the media, in everyday conversations, in the reading clubs, bookstores and cinemas, even Hollywood. But the *reality* of the matter is that no one knows anything. The truth is that Peter Høeg has disappeared, not only from literature but from the world. At first I am puzzled, then increasingly with each passing day I despair, until at once I realize that this is no tragedy, on the contrary, it is the pinnacle of the conception, the greatest of all strokes of brilliance: overnight, Peter Høeg went from being everything, everywhere and everyone (at the same time), to being nothing, nowhere and no one, vanished and gone.

And I? I had never been more than his shadow. And now he was gone. I felt I had to follow him and disappear myself. But how? I took the books out of my moving boxes in the most distant of my wife's colossal en suite rooms in Frederiksberg and re-read the now complete oeuvre in the hope of finding the door through which I, in the way of the Messiah's shadow, could proceed behind him into his other world. But the books were as though transformed. What I had thought to be the key to my life and to my redefinition within a completely different world, now seemed merely to be an illusion. Even the oeuvre's tenderest of moments, when Smilla is reunited with her lover, the electrician, a scene I had read as though it were the primeval love scene, the very image of utopian devotion, revealed itself to be nothing more than deception, a circus trick, something that in essence cannot be done, and yet: "He did it!"; the world in reverse: Smilla sticks her clitoris into the slit of the electrician's penis and "fucks" him. Voilà! The jingle of cash registers! All over the world, readers rise to their feet and applaud!

It was over. I closed the book and put it back in the moving box with the others. What then? I have no idea. I suppose time passed. Years. I missed him. Not the conception, not the many lives, and certainly not the books. I missed *him*, Peter Høeg the person, whom I had hardly even met, only seen once, many years before. And yet I missed him. I walked along the city lakes and looked across at the school I knew he had attended, Bording Realskole, where *Borderliners* takes place, a fine and uncomplicated red-brick building of three or four stories. At the very top, on the flat roof, like a mirage, was a little house with a neatly enclosed garden. There it was, on its own, peaceful, as if situated deep inside a wood, among hills, or far out upon a plain. I wondered if all the other people around me—the dog owners, the jogging business women and art directors and cinematographers and lawyers and real estate brokers—could see the house too, or if it was only me. I kept wanting to ask, but I feared their replies. In my conception, Peter Høeg had moved into that house and was living up there completely on his own. What does a person do when he is no one? He does nothing. He waters the plants, trims the lawn with nail scissors, opens the curtains in the morning and draws them again for no one when night comes.

And then catastrophe. The 9/11 of this tale. "Where were you on that fateful day?" I was alone in the reading room on the second floor of the library that is housed in the Blågården community centre. I still had my windbreaker on and was flicking absently through the day's newspapers that lay spread all over the four or perhaps six tables that had been pushed together to form a single surface. Then at one point the front page of B.T. emerged from the heap, and on it was the headline: "This is where Peter Høeg is hiding." There are certain things in the world one ought never to investigate, inventions and discoveries that ought never to be made, for the sheer sake of humanity. But people don't understand this fact. At least the journalists of the B.T. newspaper don't. They had been looking for Peter Høeg, and they had found him. Not in the little house on the roof of the Bording Realskole. Not in a completely different world. They had found him in a modest single-family home in a suburb of Copenhagen. He was divorced, older, and worst of all: he was still writing. During the past ten years, in which I had believed he had been living the ideal life of no one, he had been working on the same great novel, which sooner or later would be published. There was no picture of him, only of his house. It was a black-and-white raster image on the usual cheap paper, and the photo had been taken from the road. Through a winter's or early spring's entanglement of bare branches, garden shrubs and a couple of evergreens of the kind found in cemeteries could be seen a low, whitewashed house and the black edge of its roof. It was an image of dismal gray, everyday life, the world exactly as it is, impossible to imagine anything else.

In the intervening years I had found my own way out of the world, now merely haunting it, a ghost, a shadow of no one. And yet I put down the newspaper and returned outside with a feeling not of despair, but rather of grief, a great and quiet grief.

A few months or years later the book came out. I tried to hide, not listening to the radio, not reading any newspapers, and when I ventured out into the Netto discount store to buy avocados and carrots I would avoid looking at the headlines, humming loudly to myself in the checkout line so as not to hear what the people in front of me were talking about. Only after several months, when *The Quiet Girl* suddenly appeared on the display shelf one day at the library, did I pick it up, almost in passing and seemingly quite without thought, and take it home with me to my flat (now, after my divorce, I was living but a pistol shot away from Blågårds Plads). I turned the key and went inside, tossed the book onto the kitchen counter, made some tea, ate a carrot, looked out of the window, and then, as I turned and passed the counter with the steaming mug of tea in my hand, I stopped and opened the book and began to read as I stood. Impossible. I grasped nothing. What I saw on the pages was at once regular and yet utterly chaotic. I understood the words on their own, of course, or at least most of them, and could even, as though through a dense entanglement of branches, make out a scene, or at least its outline, or perhaps more exactly a structure, and behind that structure another structure, and behind that one another, and so on. If it was a circus trick then it was of such virtuosity that one could no longer see the artist or the figure he was drawing, the illusion. It was like thousands upon thousands of da Vinci drawings layered on top of each other, so dense and so extremely complex there was nothing to see. It was the opposite of nothing. It was everything. And all too much.

Just the other day—or perhaps this, too, is already several years away in the future—I met Peter Høeg, or rather I saw him again, for the second time in my life. It happens like this, out of the dismal gray:

I am visiting my publisher, for like the other Great Authors of Our Nation I, too, now have a publisher, or rather my publisher has me, though what it wants with me I have absolutely no idea, I am certainly not good business, on the contrary, I am most probably Denmark's leading worst seller, even if, fortunately, no one knows it apart from me, and the publisher of course, my editor having just informed me after glancing at a screen that my latest book, unlike its predecessors that sold 128 and 329 copies respectively, has now just passed the 600 mark. I go out through the gateway and am walking along Pilestræde, the weather is very windy, the sky, I know nothing about the sky, I am looking down at the cobblestones, they are gray and glistening, slippery looking in the drizzle. I cross Landemærket and continue on past Aage Jensen's window display to glance in at the electronic keyboards and drum sets, the cymbals and hi-hats, the floor toms, the cheap Fender guitars made on license in China that you can now get in a "starter pack" along with a case and a holder and a little amplifier, when suddenly I sense a slight fluctuation, a dark flutter at the periphery of my field of vision, and I know he is there. I stop, my heart suddenly racing, and turn around slowly. He is walking some fifty meters further ahead on the other side of the street, passing the glass front of the Danish Film Institute, with the Kongens Have park behind him. He walks quickly and with energy, not at any consistent pace, but in little fits and starts, as though the wind were propelling him on, nudging him chaotically along the sidewalk, unnoticed, it would seem, by everyone but me. He looks at least fifteen years older, which is unsurprising, but nonetheless sad: at least fifteen years have passed since as a young man with at least twenty simultaneous lives within me I saw him emerge from the congregation of Great Authors, the very hope of another world. He twirls around the corner and down Vognmagergade, slight and sinewy, tense, almost quivering, like a muscle that after forty years of unbroken focus on complete calm and equilibrium has now succumbed to cramp. He crosses the street and carries on past the windows of the Egmont Group building, turning his head as he goes, as if trying, not to look at something in particular, but rather to at least direct his eyes at something and keep them there for a moment, however brief. Then abruptly he stops, though without halting entirely, as yet in some continuing sideways motion, staring with wild intensity through a seemingly random windowpane, as though after twenty years someone has now seated themselves in the high-backed chair behind the polished mahogany desk of L. Ron Hubbard's office display—but who? L. Ron himself?

And again I see myself reflected in him, the way I did twenty years earlier in the back seat of my parents' car while heading north along the E45 motorway, only this time not as the person or persons I so much wanted to be, but as the one and only no one I have become: divorced, homeless, restlessly roaming, staggering unsettled from one day into the next, with strained and jagged features, and a look in my eyes that is far too intense, desperately searching, focused to the extreme, though without knowing exactly what I am searching for, but surely it can't be L. Ron Hubbard?

It was like a video sequence, not a Hollywood movie, not even a cheap TV documentary, just a black-and-white clip from a surveillance camera, a recording that would certainly be forgotten, consigned to the endless fractal depths of the internet, seen by no one unless someone, like me, by chance happened to notice, like when you're standing in the checkout line in Netto and your eyes absently pass over the shelves of cheap German chocolate, and all of a sudden you see yourself in monochrome on the little monitor screen to the right of the checkout guy. It lasted less than a minute and concerned nothing, there was no story in it, no conception, only what remained of one: a man, a human being, twirling around a corner and down a street, then gone.

[ENDNOTES]

[1] The English language version of Høeg's novel was later published under the title *The History of Danish Dreams*.

TRANSLATED FROM DANISH BY MARTIN AITKEN

ILMAR TASKA

Apartment for Rent

LIDIA'S FINGERS STRENGTHENED THEIR GRIP around the handle of the flower-print parasol. Turning the corner, she saw the spot on Banny Street where the apartment black market took place. Then her eyes came to rest on a metal sign attached to the boarding, its bold print proclaiming: "Assembly of citizens to discuss apartment matters strictly forbidden. Proceed to the Apartment Exchange Bureau."

"No, it's not fear, it's just excitement," thought Lidia, feeling a strange shudder run through her shoulders. She knew very well that all she had to do now was unleash the mystical power of the words: "I'm renting a one-room apartment with all the conveniences!" and the clamorous crowd would seize her frail form in its embrace, dozens of pairs of strange eyes would start boring greedily into her, and she would be deafened by the avalanche of questions. But she wasn't willing to become an animal trapped in a cage, just to find someone suitable. And so she remained silent. She walked onwards, resolutely shaking her head in response to the propositions from the shadows on either side.

Lidia felt a metal rail under her feet and she knew she was in the danger zone. She had to push onwards. There was no sound apart from the monotonous, hushed murmur of voices. At first it was impossible to make out any individual words. No one talked loudly here—secrets and anticipation reigned. Suddenly, a red streetcar with a single carriage burst into the space, its bell ringing noisily. The sound of voices, like the bubbling of a boiling saucepan, was cleaved, and for a moment the crowd was cut in two. Then the streetcar disappeared from view, and the trade moved back onto the rails. People gathered in clusters, assembling in one spot for a while, before jostling onwards. Like a shoal of hungry fish, they looked for new feeding waters, ready to bite at any moment. Lidia stood huddled under her provocatively jolly parasol, holding it low over her head. She felt the smooth silk touch her hair. She stared at the legs in front of her, trying to find something among them, trying to locate some interesting detail.

"So many ugly shoes, and some of them are muddy, even though it hasn't rained for several days!" Lidia frowned, for neither the legs nor the appearance of the shoes inspired her confidence. She cautiously lifted the parasol a little higher. Directly in front of her stood two men from somewhere in the South. She noticed a gold watch and their garish ties. Their regard made her uneasy. Lidia turned her back on them and pushed forward into the throng. She stood on tiptoe, craning her neck to assess the scene around her. The people here were the same as on the previous occasions: military men in uniform, students with long hair, suspicious looking girls, speculators, adulterers, thieves, sinners, and swindlers. "All psychopaths, not a single psychoanalyst among them," noted Lidia sadly, and then her eyes rested on two tall young men. They stood in silence by the boarding, looking forlorn. There was something in their sad, phlegmatic appearance and distracted stares that drew her to them.

And so the decision had been made. Lidia stepped up to the young men. "You're looking for an apartment, then, young man?" she asked the boy with blond hair. "Do you have something to offer?" the young man replied, his eyes livening up and features tensing. "I've got a beautiful one-room apartment with all the conveniences," answered Lidia. Her tone was confident, but a worried smile immediately appeared at the corners of her mouth. Now she would have to rapidly find answers to thousands of trivial questions. But there was something electrifying in the presence of the young men. Lidia felt tongue-tied.

"I'm renting my apartment for an indefinite period . . . We can agree on the price when we get there . . . You should have a look first, to see whether you actually like it," she said, forming the words into sentences with difficulty. Now that the moment for meaningful communication had arrived, she felt paralyzed by her confusion. But her words had their effect: a thick wall of people began to form around Lidia. An ominous chorus of voices had been unleashed. "What do you want?" Lidia cried in a shrill voice. Anger and indignation were growing inside her. It was humiliating to be blocked in by the clamoring herd like this. "Go away, I wasn't talking to you or offering you any-thing . . . I'm having a private conversation with these young men!" Peals of laughter rang out. Someone's words cut Lidia like a razor: "Does the countess have any more spare rooms in her castle?!" What was that supposed to mean? Who did they think they were mocking? Where was the witch who had been tied to a stake?

"Let's go," Lidia said decisively, grabbing the young men by their sleeves. They followed her obediently, at a swift pace. "You see, young men, the unhealthy frenzy caused by just one apartment, and it's not as if paradise on earth were being offered!" The rush of difficult emo-tions that had overcome Lidia started to gradually abate, and soon she was breathing deeply in relief. Lidia was happy with her find: the young men seemed to be reserved and mild-mannered. But it was hard to read anything from their expressions, there were no signs of excessive indulgence nor excessive hard work in them. "You must be students, if I'm not mistaken?" The young men nodded. They didn't seem particularly talkative. "I don't live far from here . . . a couple of stops on the metro and then ten minutes walk," said Lidia to spur on the young men, and she upped her tempo. She pushed pluckily for-wards, beckoning to the young men with a wave of her parasol when they got caught up in the crowds. The swift pace made Lidia feel con-fident and full of life.

The doors to the metro station opened, emitting a blast of musty air. The ventilators would circulate that same air for eternity. Air that contained winter with its snow and flu bugs, spring with its dankness and cold wind, summer with its heat and fevered sweat, and autumn with its mud and overripe fruit. Lidia took a handkerchief out of her handbag. She raised it to her nose and inhaled: thankfully the scent of lily of the valley had not yet faded. Lidia was picked up by the hu-man current and carried in the direction of the man-made precipice. Soon the ground started to move under her feet. Standing on the es-calator steps, pressed tight between the other people, Lidia felt anx-ious: at this moment she could do nothing of her own free will. She watched the faces coming up the escalator on the other side.

"Just masks, plastic faces, rubber faces . . . Only the odd real per-son here and there," thought Lidia gloomily, nodding in sad realiza-tion. The elevator steps came to an end and the current carried Lidia toward the tracks. The edge of the platform was getting closer, but the pressure from behind did not abate. The moment had arrived to switch back on her free will. Lidia grabbed on to a marble column and pulled herself free of the current. Beside the column a bronze soldier was kneeling on the ground, a machine gun in his hands. Seeing the sculpture, Lidia froze. She realized that she couldn't let her guard down, not for a single moment. No one knew where the iron ended and the flesh began. After all, the human gene had long since lost its original purity.

The train arrived with a rumble and Lidia let herself be shoved into the carriage. "*Ostorozhno, dveri zakryvayutsya,*"* announced the familiar robotic voice. Lidia sat down in an empty seat to the right, the young men stayed by the door. They stood with heir heads close together discussing something between themselves. Lidia pricked up her ears, but the noise inside the speeding train muffled all the fainter sounds, swallowing up the world without trace. Lidia had faith in today's visitors: she liked young people. With the young, the sclerosis of the conscience had not yet had time to set in, the putrefaction had not yet penetrated into their organisms and their souls.

Lidia recalled Marusya: that girl had been her dearest and most generous visitor. She had looked through Lidia's drawings attentively, and uttered the word "talent," and then even another word, "Rousseau." Lidia wanted to meet that girl again. She had looked for Marusya everywhere, she had called the warden of the hostel, the dean of her college, and even the university rector. How much inhuman bureaucracy, with all its icy coldness and unapproachability, surrounded that wonderful child! The hostel warden could not find Marusya's name in the list of residents, the dean refused to return her call, and the rector had no idea whom she was talking about. How could they not know the children who studied there, not feel responsibility for them! In response to Lidia's question—how is it that you don't know where your students are living, or even whether they are still alive?—the brute simply hung up the phone. But Lidia called back, and would call again tomorrow, and the day after, and eventually the whole truth would come out. So what if every call shortened

* Russian: "Attention, doors closing."

64

the time left to her in her old age by at least five years. Yesterday, leaving the telephone booth, she had felt a sudden feeling of discomfort in her heart, and it didn't pass until she had stopped in front of the kvass vendor and drunk a small three-kopeck glassful.

The train braked, and they had arrived at their station. Lidia got up and left the carriage with the young men. Coming out of the wearisome metro and back into the sunshine, she took a deep breath, then she checked the surroundings and determined which direction to go. Asymmetrical apartment blocks loomed above them, punctuated by newer buildings and an elevated highway. "I'll teach you right away how you will find the way home in the future," Lidia addressed the young men. "It's not at all easy since all the roads here look alike, gray and half-asphalted. And it's no use following the street names or block numbers, they change constantly."

Lidia winked emphatically at the young men and then added in a half-whisper: "Yes, they don't just demoralize you, but dis-inform you as well. It's a fine state of affairs. It's all intended to muddle everything up right before your eyes, so you end up losing not just your apartment but yourself as well. I can easily walk three times around the neighborhood in the evening just looking for my block, until some familiar little defect reminds me how to get home. In fact these defects are generally the most reliable way markers, since they don't change as often as the street signs, and it's far cheaper to hang up a new street sign than to repaint a building or reglaze a door."

A slight froth had appeared at the corners of Lidia's mouth, and the young men tried not to look in her direction. They were bored by her talking, and held back a couple of paces. The path continued alongside a row of buildings bordered by dusty shrubbery.

Lidia felt an uncontrollable urge to talk. But about what? She looked at the young men's faces. They were young and foolish. The fair-haired one's face reminded Lidia of some amorphous mass, on which nature had bestowed no identity at all, on which neither thoughts nor worries had left the slightest trace. "What good fortune," Lidia reflected, "that this boy at least has nice hair, and an attractive, broad-shouldered physique." The other young man's face was defined by the high, jutting line of his nose, and his large gray eyes. But a soul was absent from those eyes.

"All my life I have looked for a soul in people," said Lidia with pathos as she cast a cunning glance at the young men, "two cultures have always influenced the soul: a noble culture and a low culture. But believe me, young men, today those two opposed cultures have melted dialectically into one. There is no longer any point in talking about the fall of a single soul, now all souls fall together *en masse*, in large collectives. For example . . ." The sentence broke off abruptly as Lidia started to lose her composure. She felt her heartbeat getting faster, and a deep sense of excitement came over her: the door of her building was now visible, just ten steps away.

"Everything will be fine," Lidia thought, trying to calm herself down, to suppress her growing agitation. Dankness and a stench of urine assailed them from the dark corridor. Lidia's feet climbed the steps briskly. She tried to move in such a way as to minimize contact with the filthy stone floor, to keep her whole being separate from it. At long last she felt the soft doormat under her feet. She unlocked the three locks, one by one, and pushed the door open with a shove.

A sweet warmth emanated from the apartment, a smell of order and cleanliness. The main room contained several oval mirrors, some Jugendstil vases, and a wealth of books. A buffet cabinet and dresser were crowded with porcelain statuettes, elephants, snail shells, corals, plasticine figures, and artificial flowers. Hanging on the walls were gaily colored pictures, looking out from them were smiling red lips, green trees, chubby-cheeked children, odd-looking animals, and brightly colored flowers, all depicted with a primitivist tenderness. A cautious smile flashed across her features. The pink light flooding through the red silk curtains brought a new shade of color to her face. Lidia stood like a queen in her treasure chamber, surveying her fortunes through strangers' eyes. She followed the young men's every reaction tensely, trying to decipher their thoughts.

"It seems as if they like it here," thought Lidia, although a shadow of doubt now played across her features. "My buffet cabinet probably looks completed outdated to them. And I know they don't like these old chairs. But why aren't they looking at my pictures?" She had been hoping to get at least a tiny bit of attention for her work. There was no longer any sense in expecting admiration: in the industrial age people had forgotten their primordial emotions, and laudatory songs and jubilation could only be heard on television now. It even seemed like people smiled less.

"It's too bad there's no writing table in the room," said the long-nosed lad. Lidia looked perplexed for a moment, then pointed at the coffee table. "You can write there if you really need to. Do you young men have so much time for written work?"

"Yes, we're studying at the Institute of Literature; we're in our second year," answered the young man with obvious pride. "My field is prose, my friend is in the poetry department."

"So you will be writers?"

The young men shrugged their shoulders.

"What style do you write in?"

"Realism."

"Ah, so you are socialist realists then," said Lidia livening up, "that must be terribly hard to write?"

The young men were silent.

"I like those socialist-realist books. The ones that talk about revolution, and the ones that talk about evolution. Though I prefer the latter, for sure," said Lidia thoughtfully. "They give the reader strength, they open new perspectives in life, and they inspire one to great deeds." Lidia smiled girlishly at the young men. "By all means, a coffee table is not appropriate for writing those sorts of works. Petit-bourgeois comforts like that might have a bad influence on you. I'll have to procure a decent writing table for you, if of course we reach an agreement..."

"Sure, why not? Your apartment would be fine for us," mumbled the young men, looking around the room.

"How nice of you, please do take a seat," Lidia pointed at the chairs and seated herself on the sofa. "Young talents like you need to be treated tenderly. And don't ever let yourselves be discouraged by criticism. True, it's not yet possible to decide the ultimate value of today's literature, although we have already sent all our Pushkins, Lermontovs and Yesenins to early graves, and we might just end up tripping over those graves..."

The young men looked up questioningly, but Lidia continued her train of thought unperturbed: "Mozart and Salieri are walking around unidentified in our midst, and it is impossible to know who is who. I recently went to a ceramics factory and showed my patent to the director. He heard me out calmly, secretly memorized everything I said, and then showed me the door without much ceremony." Lidia looked down and took a deep breath. A strange, resentful expression appeared on her face. "But after I die, tiny varnished plasticine figures will show up on the counters of thousands of shops. I see them clearly before my eyes, in large and small displays, on the glass counters, and in cardboard boxes. But I won't be around to witness that big day." Lidia turned toward the young men and pointed at the small, shiny figures on the buffet cabinet, "Look, the nail polish forms an extremely solid glaze on the surface of the plasticine."

The young men appraised the shiny plasticine animals. "Hm, nice dolls," said the fair-haired lad, "but shouldn't we get back to talking about the apartment?" The other young man was also staring at Lidia.

"Marvelous! Let's get right down to business then," said Lidia energetically, and took an old chocolate box from the buffet cabinet. "All my documents are here. You can confirm from my passport that I am registered at this apartment. I never play with hidden cards. You were lucky, young men, that you ended up with an honest person. Not everyone is lucky enough to find someone honest down on Banny Street, it's teeming with swindlers and impostors! I would never have set foot there if my son had not been asking me so persistently to come and live with him. Slava got married, and his job is providing him with a new three-room apartment."

Lidia looked down at the floor and a gentle flush of joy came to her pale cheeks.

"And I've been a grandmother for over a month now. It all happened so quickly. The little boy is so sweet, he has my daughter-in-law's face. Gloria herself is youth and beauty incarnate …" Lidia found two photos of differing formats and passed them proudly to the young men. They looked carefully at the photo of the daughter-in-law and exchanged dubious glances.

"But the little nipper is getting to be hard work for them, so I decided to answer my children's prayers and move in with them. That's why I'm offering the apartment to you, after all there's no point in leaving it empty. And what's more, my pension is not at all large."

Lidia took the rent book from the box and opened it up. "Everything is written down accurately in here. The apartment rent and the utility bills are paid one month in advance, although the stamps are a little hard to make out. The tapes in those cash-office machines haven't been inked, which is why the letters haven't come out clearly. I've raised that issue with the payment department and instructed them to put their equipment in order, to avoid any more incorrect figures. But those girls that work there haven't learned anything at their evening school classes apart from how to bark at customers. It's senseless arguing with people who are on a different intellectual level, you just end up sacrificing your health trying to bring order to the eternal chaos."

Lidia bounced on the sofa's loose springs and experienced a mysterious joy, a familiar feeling of contentment. There was a smile on her face, her eyes were shining, and her heart was beating evenly. She felt a fresh rush of energy and quickened her rocking movement. Casting a glance at the bookshelf, she addressed the young men: "If you ever have a spare moment, you could have a browse through my books. On those shelves I've got a rich selection of scientific literature dealing with all the new discoveries. One shouldn't be left behind by progress—like it or not, you have to keep step with ecological processes, to be able to intelligently analyze the origins of new phenomena and abnormalities . . . because after all, just like the sun in the sky, the history of our planet also comes round full circle. A new Paleozoic era awaits our grandchildren, future generations will witness both slavery and the stone age again . . ."

The young men shifted in their chairs and looked demonstratively at their watches. Lidia took the hint, and looked over at the ornate wooden clock on the wall.

"But it isn't late at all . . ."

"Your clock must have stopped," said the young man with the large nose.

"Oh, really?" said Lidia in amazement, and added apologetically, "I still haven't gotten used to the fact that my clock is regularly affected by magnetic waves."

Lidia continued in a confiding tone: "To tell the truth, the hands of my clock all too often show the wrong hour. Like yesterday, for example. After I had checked and seen that there were exactly two hours left before the German information technology exhibition was due to shut, my clock started going backwards at full speed. Of course I only got to the exhibition once all the lights were turned off and the doors bolted. They simply don't want to let me find out their secrets. What's the use of them being in charge if I can guess everything in advance!"

"How much do you want per month for the apartment?" the long-nosed lad interrupted, his large gray eyes boring into Lidia's face, demanding an answer. Lidia was still tangled up in her train of thought, and was momentarily overcome with confusion. But she smiled shyly and said: "Before we get down to the financial details, let me offer you a cup of cocoa. For now you are still my guests."

The young men started to object, but Lidia quickly silenced them: "No arguments, otherwise our deal is off. I have tired you out quite enough with my talking, and now it is my duty to offer you a little treat." She got up and briskly walked over to the cupboard, picked up three spotted cups and seven little candies with pictures of fairies on their wrappers, and placed them on the table. The young men's eyes followed Lidia's actions, coming to rest questioningly on her arms. Her wrists were now visible from under the lace cuffs of her blouse, and there were purplish scar marks on them. Lidia noticed the young men's stares, and she knew what it meant. Carelessly, she had laid bare the traces of an earlier moment of weakness. Lidia felt the pulse of blood in her veins, and an unexpected twinge of bitterness stole across her smiling face. She didn't look at the young men, but just started bustling about more hurriedly. A glass door led directly from the room to a tiny kitchen. Lidia opened the door, stepped into the kitchen, and took a liter bottle of milk from the fridge. She poured some milk into a white enameled saucepan and placed it on the stovetop. Lidia knew that the young men were still within earshot. There, from behind the stove, out of sight, she could tell them about her scars.

"At the beginning of the 1950s a baseless accusation was made against me and I was dismissed from work. After that I was expelled from university, where I had been in the first year of a correspondence course. Everyone became very suspicious of me. And so it happened that I lost my appetite for life. These scars on my arm are testament to life's ruthlessness . . ."

Lidia tried to remain calm, although she felt an ill-boding tension.

With measured movements she took the matchbox and lit the flame on the burner. But she was finding it hard to control her wayward emotions: the familiar monotonous clatter of the typewriter was reverberating through her head again. Lidia tried to muffle the awful sound with her own voice: "I was working as a typist, and all I did was type. I didn't know anything about the research institute or their papers. I didn't even read the words I put down on paper. But I was suspected of spying. How stupid!"

The metallic typewriter sound in Lidia's ears got louder, and the blinding light of a desk lamp appeared before her eyes. The pan of cocoa and the burner had become objects from another world. Lidia was walking down long corridors, afraid of losing herself. It seemed like the terrifying interviews would never come to an end. Incomprehensible questions, impossible to answer, were spinning around her head. Then the corridor was swallowed up in a white fog, and Lidia knew that everything would soon be over. She stood at a distance, alone in the fog where there were no thoughts, no voices, no music. There was only silence and a stinging pain in her arms.

The milk had boiled over and the burning smell quickly brought Lidia to her senses. She turned off the gas and grabbed the lid from the saucepan. It was hot and burnt her fingers. She dropped it and laughed awkwardly. The lid rolled across the kitchen floor and fell flat in the doorway. Lidia took the packet of cocoa from the cupboard and shook it into the saucepan. "Our Brand." The cocoa was ready. She emptied the contents of the saucepan into a porcelain jug and carried the drink to the table in the other room. One by one she carefully filled three cups with steaming cocoa.

"Sorry, but how much does the apartment cost?" asked one of the young men.

Confused, Lidia looked at them for some time and then asked in a quiet voice: "Do you like it here?" She paused briefly. "At my place?"

"We can't pay very much."

"How much could you manage?"

"The normal amount, forty to fifty rubles a month."

Lidia took a spoon and stirred the cups of cocoa. A darker layer rose to the top making ripples as it mixed with the lighter one. Lidia nodded her head sadly and put the spoon down.

"This apartment costs one hundred and fifty rubles a month," she stated with deadly seriousness, without raising her eyes from the cup of cocoa.

The young men started laughing awkwardly. Their laughter dragged on and got louder.

"I'm serious," said Lidia dejectedly, tightly piercing her lips.

A tense silence hung over the room. With a shaking hand, Lidia lifted her cup of cocoa to her mouth.

"You're crazy," said one of the young men. They rose with a noisy knocking of chairs.

Lidia looked up fearfully from her cup of cocoa and said: "Have just one cup of cocoa with me! You're probably not happy with me . . . Please forgive me . . ."

The young men walked across the room and out of the front door without looking back. They left the door ajar, and Lidia could hear their footsteps getting quieter as they got further away.

"Don't go yet!" she called out feebly, and looked at the untouched cups of cocoa. "You didn't even taste it," she added in a whisper, then burst into tears. "I had to trick you . . . because nobody knows . . . how good the cocoa tastes . . . at my place . . ."

Lidia slumped in her seat and covered her face, which was contorted in pain, with her hands. The crying lasted for what seemed like an eternity, but it brought no comfort. As she cried, Lidia could feel her loneliness growing to terrible proportions, threatening to completely engulf her. Time had come to a standstill, and she was surrounded by the silence, like an everlasting spell.

Lidia reached out and pulled the old chocolate box toward her from between the cocoa cups and flower vases. She opened the box and took out the familiar photos. One of them had "To mother on her birthday – Slava" written on it. Printed on the back of another one was: "Silent film star Gloria Swanson." Then Lidia found her son's wedding photo at the bottom of the box. It was taken eight years ago. Standing by her son was an older-looking woman; Lidia had always known that this woman would never make her a grandmother. She carried on rummaging through the box. Among the photos she found a postcard with a view of Peterhof Palace. She raised the postcard up close to her eyes, and carefully examined the fountains, gold against the green of the park. Then she turned the postcard over. The post-mark was from last month. Lidia let her eyes run over the familiar lines of handwriting once again:

"Dear Mother! Thanks very much for your letters. It would be bet-ter if you don't come visit us this fall. Nadya is ill, and you know how cramped it can be for us all in one room. When Nadya gets better and we are able to have you stay with us, we will write. Kisses – Slava." The characters turned hazy and started to dissolve before Lidia's eyes. She put the postcard and photos back in the box and resolutely closed the lid. Then she raised herself with some difficulty from the sofa and went to stand by the window. Outside, dusk was falling. Dark night clouds had appeared in the early autumn sky. Lidia looked at the win-dows of the building opposite. The lights were already lit in half of them and tiny silhouettes of people could be seen moving around. She stood behind the curtains in her darkening room and watched the shadows play.

TRANSLATED FROM ESTONIAN BY MATTHEW HYDE

CHRISTIAN GAILLY

The Wheel

IT WAS REALLY HOT, 35 degrees out of the sun. I didn't say in the shade, I said out of the sun. I suspected as much, mind you. Didn't surprise me. Just by living, you know, we get used to it, used to gauging the air temperature. Within a degree or two, you know. You can say how hot it is. I thought it was 32 or 33 till I went to check.

I didn't go just for that. I could've cared less how hot it was exactly. The old thermometer hanging in the shed read 35 degrees when I went to get the hammer. The toolbox was on the shelf under the thermometer, so I had a look. For what it's worth, I didn't feel any hotter. A big old hammer I never use.

As it turns out, I didn't need to use it anyway, my strength alone was enough. I say my strength as if, like I'm saying I'm—but not at all. Nothing special for a man my size, but still stronger than the woman. In any case, strong enough, because even more might not have been enough. It was. But I couldn't have known. So I went to get the hammer the woman wanted. She rang my bell to ask for one.

You wouldn't happen to have a hammer? she asked me. She was hot, her hair in her eyes. Her lovely white gloves were covered in grease, which made her look like she had some pluck. That's what I thought. Don't know why. She wasn't scared to get 'em dirty. That's pluck. And then the fact that she was wearing them in this heat, that she cared about old-fashioned elegance. I say care, I should say aspired to. I liked that.

At the same time, I thought, with her sort of snub nose she must be a pain in the ass. But when I think about it, it's especially because of her look, a frank look that hit you with its hardness, let's say its sternness, anyway there was a resolute look in her eyes.

Should have one with my tools, I said. What for? She looked at me. My question annoyed her. I was wasting time. She didn't have any to spare. She was obviously holding herself back from saying: Who cares what for. Mind your own business. Just get me a hammer.

So I go: The reason I'm asking, I say, is that with hammers there's all different sizes. All depends on what you want to do. Her: I need a big one. You got one? Me: Yeah, but what for? 'Cause, you see, I explained, there's big and there's big. If it's a sledgehammer you need, you gotta say so, and still there's sledgehammers and sledgehammers: what's it for?

She turned around and surveyed the surrounding countryside. Wanted to see if she had other options. She didn't. I was the only one around. She turned around again. She was hot. Me too. We were chatting in full sunlight. She was tired. The lock of hair hanging in her eyes was irritating her. She was afraid of touching her face with her dirty gloves. I risked irritating her further.

With the tips of my fingers I moved the hair out of the way, at least for the time being. It was windy. My audacity, that made her smile. I saw her front teeth. She calmed down and said: Got a flat, one of the front tires. I see, I said, and you can't loosen the lug nuts. Exactly, she said, but I was thinking that with a hammer. Do you have one you could lend me?

Wait here, I said. I had her come into the yard and rest in the shade. Then I went to look for the hammer. I found it. Came back with it. I might not have been able to find it. Let's go, I said. Then she says: I don't need you, just your hammer. Don't trouble yourself. I'll take care of it. It's really heavy, I said. Let me carry it at least. She sighed. What, I said, you don't want me to help you? Is it that awful? She shrugged her shoulders.

Her car was sitting on the road a few hundred meters from the house in the middle of some fields. Over the past couple of weeks the crops had turned a uniform ochre, a charred, let's say singed vegetable color. It hadn't rained in a while, and everything was getting cooked out there. Not a drop of water in three months. The ground was cracking. Animals were dying of thirst.

I was thirsty, too. I went to the kitchen to get a drink, and while I was drinking I put my head under the faucet. I wiped my head off with the dish towel, but not too much, so the coolness stayed in my hair. I was toweling my head when I looked out the window. I saw the car stop, a sliver of it. The roof, I think. I couldn't be too sure. Everybody has the right to stop, even out here in the middle of nowhere. That's crazy. Me, I'd be speeding up. But anyway, I went back to work without much hope. My story was going nowhere.

Half an hour later, not any further along, the front bell interrupts me. It hangs above the gate. Just have to pull the string. That jiggles it, and it rings. Someone was pulling. It was ringing.

Lily makes fun of me with my bell. Lily's my girlfriend. She says I really could: You really could get an electric doorbell installed. Yes, no doubt about it. But I like my bell. It sounds nice, not too high or too low, not too loud or too soft. It's pleasant, just how I like it. And it's far from the house. I don't jump when I'm working. To me it sounds like a vague summons, a distant church. I say to myself: Hey, it's the mailman. Or maybe: Hey, it's my sweet little Lily. I can recognize her by her ring. The mailman, too.

The mailman had already been by. The phone bill and a letter from my editor asking me to, well let's move on. As for Lily, she was supposed to stop by later.

Who's that? I wondered, leaving my work behind. Not upset to leave it behind. I was bored. Any distraction is good. Any excuse that comes along, I'll seize it.

I crossed the charred lawn (we weren't allowed to water anymore). I opened the high wooden gate. I had to open it if I wanted to see who it was, and it was the woman with the dirty white gloves and the hair in her eyes. A blonde in a yellow suit. The rest we know. So here we go.

She was walking on my left. The large hammer was swinging from the end of my arm. Her elegance troubled me. Next to her, in my work clothes, dirty shirt and jeans, I looked like a Neanderthal. It was the end of the week. I change my clothes once a week. Lily's the one who does my laundry. This way she's got less to do. Didn't want her to, but she did.

The hammer was weighing down my arm. I put it up on my shoulder. I looked like a worker, a real one, a working man, I mean who really works, not a guy like me who doesn't know how to do anything with his hands and is only good for writing. My plot was going nowhere. I was bored with it. I was sticking with the story just so I didn't lose all hope. She and I, we were walking down the road.

Country roads are all the same. A slight camber, blacktop in the middle, rocks on the sides, gravel that they spread over the still-hot tar when they resurface the road. Rocks becoming loose little by little, then eventually pushed to the sides by cars, trucks, tractors, and other farm equipment.

All that to say that the woman was walking on the side of the road. The heels and soles of her shoes were making the gravel crunch. Very expensive shoes, very delicate and fine. I thought the rocks might be hurting her feet. Especially the bits of gravel, which must be tearing into the soles of her feet. I thought about her poor feet, the only part of her body I let myself look at, walking with my head down.

You should walk over here. It'll be easier, I said, giving her my spot in the middle of the road. More at ease, she started walking faster, which reminded me that she was in a hurry. I sped up too, I had to. The road headed slightly uphill. Spots that look flat but aren't are deadly in this heat. And then there was this pain. The hammer was digging into my shoulder. I lifted it up again and let it hang from my arm. I even think I let it swing back and forth. Made it less heavy. Anyway it helped me. Propelled me along.

There was the car, right nearby, on the curve. I turned around. I said to myself: Now, if earlier I could see a sliver of the car through the window, then right now, if I turn around, I should be able to see a sliver of the kitchen, I said to myself. And indeed, from where I was standing next to the car I could make out my kitchen window, once again confirming that patently obvious fact of optics: there, from the point you can see, you can be seen.

Then I heard. There were words. Not for me. The words were not meant for me, couldn't at all be for me. Otherwise, I would've headed back immediately. I would have foregone the spectacle of my house and its kitchen window, where I had been before being here, where I no longer was because I was here. Such a momentous observation. Anyway I wasn't being spoken to, but I heard speaking, so I turned around and saw whom the woman was speaking to.

A man in a dress shirt, tie loosened, dark hair, a white handkerchief stained with grease in his hand, his jacket next to him on the grass in the ditch, he himself lying on the slope in the shade, his feet in the ditch.

He must have been saying to her: You sure took your sweet time. He, too, was in his Sunday best, but something was off. It was more than Sunday best, dressed up for a party, I don't know what, a baptism, a wedding, a communion, perhaps. And she must have been saying to him: Do it yourself next time. It'll be faster.

The man's hands were also dirty. He was rubbing them with his handkerchief, which was so dirty he didn't dare mop his brow. He, too, must have tried to unscrew the lug nuts, I speculated. You a mechanic? he said irritably, in an arrogant and haughty tone, without even bothering to get up from the ditch. He was just dandy there on the grass, looking us over, my hammer and me.

No, I replied. I'm a writer. Broken down right now. I'm counting on you to give me some ideas. A writer? he said. How interesting, he said. What's your name? Paul Cédrat, I answered. My name didn't ring a bell. Doesn't ring anyone's bell. Therefore I was not a writer, at least not an important one. An unknown writer? No such thing, you know?

I was thinking: That's an understandable point of view, and the woman was looking at us like: Whenever you two are done. She'd just learned my name, my profession. From that moment on her attitude was different. Where'd this change come from? I don't know. I seemed to pique her interest. Always like that, piquing interest. Even if no one knows you, just by announcing that you write. They all imagine you're constantly experiencing some rare kind of profound joy. Poor fools. If they only knew.

It was so hot I didn't want to use the big hammer. I said to myself that maybe I could try my turn at the lug wrench. That maybe I would succeed where the woman in yellow and the man in black had failed. The man's suit was black, like formal wear for some ceremony. Not putting too much thought into it, I go:

When's the ceremony? Just left, said the woman. Oh? I replied, pulling on the wrench. I'd positioned myself so I could pull and not push. I'd moved it so I could pull up. You've got more power that way. The nut resisted. I grunted like a tennis player from the base line, or rather like a weight lifter. The first nut gave way. The others, obviously intimidated, came without a peep. Emboldened, I go:

You were invited to a wedding? Me, yes, said the woman. Not him. Yet you're together, I said as I got up. I had been squatting down in front of the wheel now relieved of its four nuts. And while I'm at it, I thought, might as well do the whole thing. I'm going to change their tire.

So, he wasn't invited? I said, placing the jack under the frame. You've got to put it in the notch that's for the jack. He was, said the woman. Well, no. You can't say that the groom is invited to his own wedding. He's the inviter, not the invitee.

Okay, okay, oh that's what's going on, I said without turning around while raising the car on the jack, crouching down and pumping the handle: He was the groom, ah, I get it. Or rather no, I don't really get it, I thought. This story's starting to get interesting.

But then, I said, pulling the heavy wheel toward me then laying it down on the road: If you yourself were invited, I said to the woman after getting up and looking at her: You're not the bride? Do you think you could get the spare out? I said to the man who was now lying flat on the ground, looking overwhelmed.

Hearing himself addressed directly, he straightened up and looked at me. I perceived an understandable sadness in his eyes. I didn't push it. Besides, he probably didn't know where the spare tire was. I wonder if he even had the slightest idea what a spare tire is.

Obviously he did, but well, anyway, I said to myself, I'll take care of it. In fact I was thrilled. When my work bores me, as I already said, any distraction is good. Any excuse that comes along, I'll seize it.

However, I had no idea where the spare tire was. I looked around. I was starting to feel ridiculous. I asked the woman. She didn't know either. Finally I found it under the floor of the trunk. I had some trouble getting it out. It had never been used before and was stuck.

Well then, what are you to him, exactly? I asked the woman. I returned with the new wheel. I was smacking it to make it roll like a hula hoop. She answered me, and it surprised me that she'd indulge my indiscretions, that she herself would be indiscreet. Surely it wasn't in compensation for my efforts. Overall, her demeanor gave the impression of exhaustion, too. With perhaps a shadow of despair she answered:

I don't really know what I am to him, she said. To keep it simple, he loves me. I'm the one he loves, not her, not that other woman. I see, I said. I was adjusting the new wheel on the wheel base. I was aiming for the four threaded lug posts. I was able to line them up in front of the holes on the first try, and while I kneeled down to fasten the nuts I said to her:

So, if I understand all this correctly, when they asked him the famous question: Do you take this woman to be your lawfully wedded wife, he said no. Not even, she said, squatting next to me like a little kid next to her father. Watching me work she added: He didn't wait for the question, or rather yes, he did. He was waiting to be asked. He must have felt it was taking too long. Which I understand, she told me. The officiator's speech was painfully long, and I was watching them, she said, especially him.

I'm listening, I said, go on. I had asked her to get up and move out of the way a bit. I needed to lower the car on the jack, and that can be dangerous. So I had interrupted her:

Sorry, I said, I interrupted you. Go on, I'm listening. You were in the middle of telling me you were watching both of them, especially him, I said, tightening the first lug nut. She didn't kneel back down. She stayed standing next to me, leaning against the car. Don't do that, I said. You'll get dirty. She said: Too late for that now.

She'd taken off her dirty gloves. She was holding them in her right hand, and as second thoughts passed through her mind, she'd smack them against her hip, like an aristocratic lord, a rider with a crop. I was finishing tightening the lug nuts. I had no desire for her to lose her wheel. She'd stopped speaking. I thought maybe she'd had enough, that maybe she was upset with herself for having said too much. I was wrong. She said to me:

And then after a little while he turned around. He looked at me. He saw my face. I saw his. It was settled. He came to get me. He left his betrothed and came toward me. I was seated in the third row, away from the family. I was invisible. I was nobody until he looked at me again, till he walked over to me. Then he leaned over, kissed me, pulled me up. And the two of you got the hell out of there, I said. No, she said, not even. We calmly walked out of the city hall.

And here we are, said the man. And already broken down, he said. On a pathetic little country road. Not anymore, I said. It's fixed. He seemed to have recovered. He'd gotten up from the grass, left the shade. He was coming to join us in the sunlight. He was going to fry himself like we'd been doing.

He had found his arrogant look again, and that delightful sarcastic tone. Oh, I love that. Makes me laugh. A bit pitiful, a man who struggles like that. I've been like that many a time. Don't need it. Don't really need anything, just some ideas so I can keep writing.

To wrap things up, I wanted to put the flat away in the trunk. I couldn't get it open. Do you have the key? On the dash. The woman went to get it. She opened the trunk for me. I laid the wheel down inside.

I was closing the trunk. The woman was next to me, and I asked her: And you, do you love him? I had forgotten to put the jack away. I went to get it, opened the trunk again and put the jack back in its compartment.

The woman hadn't moved. When I looked at her again I saw she was looking at me. She said: Are you that interested? Yes and no, I said. Anyway, I added, it's a dumb question. The answer's obviously yes. Otherwise you wouldn't be here with him. Who knows, she said.

So, I didn't use my big hammer after all. I said good-bye to the woman. She shook my hand and thanked me for my kindness. We went our separate ways. Don't forget your hammer, she said while opening her door. The man was already sitting in the car. I wanted to wish them luck. I did it while watching them drive off. They were already far away. No chance they'd hear me.

Now, it's strange, but when I got back home, in the kitchen, I felt my heart sink. Fortunately Lily wouldn't be too long. I jammed my head under the faucet and cried my goddamn eyes out, and then, using the dish towel, I wiped it all away.

TRANSLATED FROM FRENCH BY ALEXANDER HERTICH

Tsotne Tskhvediani

The Golden Town

"MA'AM, THERE'S NOTHING I can do to help you. According to the state, this child does not legally exist. You have to listen to what I'm saying. Do you understand? He does not show up anywhere in our records. Therefore, you only count as the mother of three—your family is not big enough to qualify for aid. The only possibility I see is to somehow set the child up with some relatives and get him a birth certificate."

The social worker had such a sad face and tired voice as she explained all this to my mother that you would have felt sorry for her. She was probably around twenty, with curly red hair. She didn't look like the other social workers. When Mom passed her some beautifully cut and peeled apple slices, she readily helped herself. The other ones would never accept anything Mom offered.

"You are already struggling enough as it is," they would say. At these moments I would feel very embarrassed. I liked this girl, who took the apple without even thinking. My mother was happy too.

"Please have more," she insisted. "This blessed gold mine will be built and save us. We won't always have these dark days," she said, sadly.

"God willing, ma'am," replied the redhead.

"In this blessed earth, there is gold everywhere, my child. If used with kindness and generosity, there is enough for everyone."

"God willing, ma'am," replied the redhead.

The social worker collected her papers, threw them into a black bag, said good-bye, and went out. The door had not even shut before Gigo let out a terrifying wail.

"Mooom, why do I not exist? Did I die?"

In one arm, Mother held Niaco, who was sobbing quietly. With her free hand, she was preparing food.

"Gigo, at least you stop crying. Of course you did not die. You exist."

"You see me, right?" Gigo asked doubtfully.

"That's enough. You exist and that's it!" Mom answered, getting angry.

Gigo sat at a low stool by the stove. From time to time he would steal furtive glances toward Mother. It was obvious he still had a thousand questions to ask. Then he was talking to himself, but you could not distinguish what he was saying. Suddenly he turned to me and asked:

"Do you love me?"

"Don't be silly," I answered uneasily. No one had asked me that before.

"Tell me." He wouldn't leave me alone.

"Stop it," I said.

"Tell me you love me. If you love me, then I exist."

I wanted to tell Gigo I loved him. But until then I had never told anyone that, and I was awfully embarrassed. Even Mom never said she loved us. A loong, loong time ago, when we had a house, Dad would say that to Mom. Not anymore though.

It probably wasn't even eight o'clock when I woke up. We were supposed to go play soccer. Father, Mother, Niaco, Gigo, Grandma, and I sleep in one room. We also have one more brother—Tengo. He's in Turkey, gone for work. Before he left, he used to sleep with us too. So did Grandpa, who died a few years ago. Without them, the house seems empty to me.

Mom is a light sleeper. If Niaco wakes up, we're doomed. They won't let us go to the stadium. Gigo sleeps next to Father. Scared of waking him, I couldn't approach any closer. I could only watch and wait until Gigo opened his eyes himself.

I didn't even have to wait five minutes. When his eyes shot open, there was such a fear in them that I couldn't bring myself to let him lie there waiting, and gave an almost inaudible whistle to get his attention. He looked at me, and his eyes lit up so brightly that I could not help but smile.

We grabbed our clothes and ran into the yard. We dressed outside so the noise wouldn't wake anyone. It was October, but the mornings were already very cold.

"I thought you left without me," said Gigo. "Just so you know, I would have killed you," he added as he scrunched his forehead and looked up at me menacingly.

"What are you gonna do without sneakers, anyway?"

"What do I need them for? Am I going to run? I just stand in the goal. I can jump just fine in flip-flops," he replied, and immediately, he proved he could. He jumped, stretching his body in the air, and slammed back to the rain-soaked ground with all his might. He stood up straight and said in a convincing voice, "We definitely have to win this time. Last time, we lost because of their stupid arguing."

"We have to win," I agreed. "Just don't start whining like last time. 'Oh they're kicking too hard!' And then they complain that they can't go all out because we put small children in the goal."

"No, no, I won't say that anymore. You already taught me to spit on my hands, right? It's disgusting, but I'll spit on my hands. It really helps. My hands don't hurt anymore and I catch the ball better too."

"OK, enough already with the spitting. Why do you find it so repulsive? We're not spitting on you ... it's your spit. Make sure you do it."

"OK, OK, I promise."

We got to the stadium. All the neighborhood kids were there already. Last night's rain had left puddles here and there. Of course, the worst conditions were right in front of the goal.

"Looks like you're gonna be splashing around a lot." I looked over at Gigo sympathetically.

"It's nothing, I'll wash off in the well."

Meanwhile, Zaza and Rezi joined us.

"We're putting the baby in the goal again?" asked Rezi, disapprovingly.

"He's eight already; what do you want?"

"In eight months I'll be nine," Gigo added.

"They'll rip us apart," said Zaza, waving his arm dismissively.

"Yeah, if you guys shit your pants before we start, of course they will."

"Who? Us?" They both attacked me at once.

"Alright, OK. Stop it already. We really gotta win today."

"Still don't feel like spitting on your hands?" they turned back to Gigo.

Gigo didn't even let them finish the question before he spit, with all his might, first on one hand, and then the other. He showed us his palms and grinned ear to ear.

At nine, our opponents arrived. Rezi spotted one of them from far away and began his whining again.

"Oh shit, they brought Nodara. He'll destroy us again."

"Hey guys," the newcomers called out to us.

"Back for more fun, huh? Are we gonna shut you out again, or will you guys make at least one this time?"

"I brought my newspaper," called their goalkeeper, laughing at his own joke.

"You should have brought your lawn chair too," his teammates added, bursting into laughter.

"OK, enough. Let's go."

"Let's go!"

"Play to four."

"OK, to four."

They brought the ball into play. The one called Nodara was two heads taller than us. He got the ball and came at us with such speed that Zaza only followed him with his eyes. Then he slammed Rezi with his shoulder and also left him behind. Using all my strength, I sprinted and slid between his feet, sending us both to the muddy ground with a splat. The droplets splashed Gigo.

"I'll be a son of a whore! That's a penalty." Nodara jumped to his feet. The others joined him at his side.

If someone cursed like that, then it absolutely had to be a penalty. If you did not agree to it, that meant the curse really did count against their mother, and the one who cursed has the right to hit you then.

"It's a penalty," I agreed.

"It's a penalty," repeated Nodara, satisfied.

Then, from the goal, he took seven measured steps, leveled the dirt, and put the ball down. Gigo stood slightly hunched over, with his hands resting on his knees.

"Watch the ball, kid, don't let your eyes off of it," I called out to him.

Nodara took three steps back, rushed forward and smashed the ball from below. Gigo threw himself into the air, but the ball went into a very high corner. They scored.

Gigo stood up and made to leave the field.

"If you want, put someone else on the goal," he called out, almost in tears.

"You're not going anywhere," I answered, and looked over at Zaza and Rezi so they wouldn't say anything.

Then they scored two more times and we were down 3–0. The third goal was entirely Gigo's fault. The ball was already caught in his hands, but he dropped it over the line, adding another one for them. Rezi got mad, but he calmed his nerves and said to Gigo:

"Why don't you take a rest? Nika will take over for a while."

Before Gigo left the goal, he looked over at me, but I avoided his eyes. With his head down, he left the field and sat off to the side.

An hour passed, at least. We were already covered in mud. We could barely stand from tiredness. My sneakers had almost ripped all the way through; I couldn't run anymore.

A corner kick was awarded at their goal. Zaza passed the ball. I wanted to trap it with my chest, but I couldn't, and I had to help stop it with my hand. Then I kicked it. The goalie didn't even move.

"Yes, Goooal!" Gigo rushed onto the stadium and hugged me.

"Goal!" yelled our team.

"That was a handball, it doesn't count," said Nodara calmly.

"It wasn't a handball," I argued.

"Go ahead then, curse."

"I won't curse."

"So you're lying."

"I'm not lying."

"Then why aren't you cursing?"

"I never curse."

"Then swear."

"Swear on what?"

"Your brother."

I became quiet, and suddenly Gigo pulled me by the hand and whispered: "Go ahead and swear to him. I don't exist anyway, right?"

"I won't swear," I said firmly.

"OK then, it doesn't count and we keep playing."

We continued and they scored again. We lost again without getting a single goal.

We walked over to the well. We tried as hard as we could to clean the mud off our clothes, but it wasn't working. Gigo's feet were especially filthy. He had practically been barefoot in those puddles, and he had mud stuck deep in his toenails. We did what we could to clean ourselves. As soon as we got home, Father started roaring, and Mother began to cry.

Father called us filthy and beat us both. Mother lamented, I don't even have enough laundry detergent for Niaco's clothes, what am I supposed to do with all this?

There was mud stuck in our hair too, and we didn't have any shampoo.

Freshly beaten, Gigo went to go lie down in his bed, but Father hit him again for this. "What are you thinking, lying down on your sheets with so much mud on you?" he said.

Crying, he crawled under the bed. In whispers, he kept repeating: "I don't exist, I don't exist, I don't exist . . ."

We are from Kazreti. We used to have a house. I don't remember it well, but it was big and bright. Then Father went into debt and they took it from us. Now we live in a hut made of boards nailed together by hand, built where there once stood a sheep pen.

We don't have a legal address, so we can't get any social aid. Social Services came by at least ten times, but they could never help us.

We don't have anywhere to go, although even if we did, Father does not plan to set foot anywhere else. He says that here, on this plot of land, they will build a gold mine. This is not just his fantasy. The neighbors watch us with envy. They also know the deal with the mine. Our local official promised the construction of the mine would begin very soon in the future. The church pastor also said the same thing.

Even now, gold can be found in our town, but not much. They think that the gold ore is only in the mountains, but all the oldest locals know that you can mine gold practically everywhere in the town.

Especially the place where our hut is. There are some neighbors who think the whole thing is a big joke. They say that the gold ore does not exist. Sometimes they spend all day arguing about it. The younger ones are skeptical. The ones who do believe in the gold deposits see the nonbelievers as enemies. This gold business has divided the town into two sides.

I think all this talk about the gold mine is silly. Earlier, when I loved my Father, I believed it, but now I hate him and his absurd ideas. When I think about my father, I remember what Grandma used to say. Grandma loved birds more than anything. She would spend entire days sitting in the yard and observing them. She used to tell us a lot about them. Grandma told us that the majority of birds could not recognize their own chicks. Some instinct makes them bring worms back to their nest, and it doesn't matter if they find their own chicks there or not. She told us that she had saved countless orphaned sparrows like this, placing the chicks in other birds' nests where they would be fed.

Father looks like a bird, too. If some other kids were to find themselves in our house, he probably wouldn't notice anything. He'd come in like always, set food on the table, then throw himself headfirst onto his bed.

He doesn't even look at us; he doesn't love us anymore. It's been years since we talked about anything. Except when he's fighting with us, shouting terrible words.

Sometimes he's beaten us so badly, with his callused hands, that our faces burn like fire all day. When he's like that, I can always hear his teeth grinding together. He grates them together so hard one would think they would all fall out. He's already lost most of his back teeth. His gums are infected, and his mouth emits a smell of blood and rotten eggs. My stomach turns every time I have to sit next to him when we eat. There are only four chairs at the table. Father and Mother never sit next to each other. That means either Gigo or I have to sit next to Father. I always try to get there first and take the seat next to Mom.

Mother says that Gigo was born at home. She couldn't go to the hospital, so that's why Gigo doesn't have a birth certificate. Because of this, he can't go to school, and besides that, when he was six, we didn't have money to buy him clothes, a backpack, or books. Furthermore, he was physically small, so Father said it was better to start him at school when he was seven. He himself started school when he was seven. Mom agreed.

One year passed, but nothing changed, so we put it off again. After that, Mother was ashamed when she had to deal with the teachers. They would criticize and blame her, why didn't you bring him earlier?

I go to school, but very rarely. I help my father collect scrap metal. Getting food is a struggle, but somehow we manage. The worst thing is that there's always fighting in our house. Father's nerves are in an awful state. Sometimes he gets upset at the smallest of things, and he becomes unrecognizable. He smashes everything; he hits Mother, and us, too. Mother used to be more calm, but now she's always yelling. I hate fighting, but at times I have beaten Gigo too. I feel sorry for him afterwards, but right then, when he's making me angry, I don't think about it.

When they're not fighting and yelling, being in our house is like lying in a coffin. No one makes a sound. We don't really have anything to talk about. Sometimes I think we don't even know each other.

Once, my classmates were playing that game where you look at each other in the eyes without laughing. That's when I realized that I had never looked directly into someone's eyes in my entire life. Mother and Father don't look each other in the eyes either.

Grandma became completely mute after Grandpa died. The doctors said it was because she was sick, but I don't think there is anything wrong with her; she just doesn't want to talk anymore. That was the first time I saw someone who just wanted to sleep all day. She was almost dead. Sometimes, rarely, she would eat, but even then she wasn't really here. She used to be completely different. She was always reading us something or telling us stories. Most of all, Gigo and I loved the Greek myths. Grandma would read to us from an old, worn book which had all the gods and goddesses, alphabetically. We liked the myth of the Argonauts the most, of course.

Grandma didn't just know how to tell stories; earlier, she used to make medicines. She also used to say blessings. She said some of them so beautifully, that nothing was better than listening to her. That was really nice, but it's been a long time since she forgot all that.

Now she only cuts our hair. She used to do it every two weeks, but now it's less often. We sit on chairs out in the yard, she puts a white sheet on our shoulders and cuts our hair beautifully. Then she collects every strand of hair and buries it in the ground. This is an old local custom. Grandma believes that after many years, the hair will turn into gold. Especially golden hair. That's precisely what Gigo has. Me—a little darker.

We miss the old, energetic Grandma very much, but we have accepted that we will never see her again. She basically died along with Grandpa.

Everyone always respected Grandpa. Even after he had a stroke and wasn't all there, the way the younger people would still meet him in the street, you would think he was a religious figure. I've heard old stories about him many times.

Everybody praised his honorable behavior. He saved several people's lives. Grandpa was a kind man, but if you didn't know him well, he could seem very unsociable. Sometimes he would tell us something so rudely that you would think—this man definitely hates us and it's better to avoid him. The next minute he would be kind and caring, but you still couldn't get him to say anything nice. By the way, Grandpa believed that the gold existed, and no one dared to argue about this while he was still alive.

On the other hand, Grandma never let Grandpa get away with anything. The two of them were always bickering. Grandma always saw our Father as a small boy, and she blamed all our problems, hunger, and lack of money on Grandpa. Eventually, Grandma got sick too—her nerves failed her. After every fight, she would run out of the house. She would say, I don't want to live in this terrible place and watch these children die. She would pack up a few of her dresses, give me, Gigo, and Tengo each a kiss, and run off toward the railway station. We would yell. Grandpa would chase after her . . . Then they would talk in the street for hours. Eventually, they would return. We were very happy, and would hug them both. This sort of thing sometimes happened several times in one week. Grandma would run off and Grandpa would chase her. Because of this, Grandpa lost his longstanding authority with the neighbors. They would joke about it, quietly at first, and then loudly. Everything got worse once Grandpa became bedridden. Grandma still ran away, and it was Gigo, Tengo, and I who had to bring her back.

One time, when Grandma ran away again, Grandpa couldn't get out of bed, and started to yell. He was calling us. He was already crying when we got there.

"Hurry, don't let her beat you to the railroad station. If she gets there first, everything is over," he said.

We chased after Grandma. I pulled her elbow, hanging onto it. Gigo wrapped himself around her legs. We begged, we pleaded.

Grandpa came from the house, dragging a chair, and leaning on it from time to time. With great effort, he finally reached us and squeezed Grandma's hand tight. It seemed like he wanted to hug her, but was embarrassed in front of us. Grandma's hair was a mess, and Grandpa was carefully fixing it, and putting each hair back in place, one at a time.

"Marusa, where are you going to go looking like such a crazy woman? Come home, put on something warm, brush your hair . . ."

Grandma was crying and kept repeating:

"You never speak to me normally, you never speak to me normally . . ."

In the evening, I asked Grandpa:

"What would happen if Grandma reached the station? She doesn't even have money to go anywhere, and the commuter train only leaves in the morning."

Grandpa was silent for a while. Then he answered:

"If she made it to the station, she would realize she has no where to go and she will never run away again . . ."

"But isn't that what we want, Grandpa?"

"We want Marusa to want to be with us."

That morning, when I woke up, Gigo was sitting on my bed.

"Good morning," he said and grinned.

I could swear that this was the first time anyone had said that to me. Before that, I had only heard it in movies. In our house, no one says such things. I don't think our neighbors do either . . .

Of course, I didn't answer Gigo. I just lay there feeling awkward.

"You say it too, OK?" begged Gigo.

"What's your problem?"

"Just say it, OK?" He wouldn't leave me alone.

"Good morning," I said, feeling as though I had just said a silly poem on stage in front of the whole school.

On the other hand, Gigo was so excited, he could barely contain his happiness.

Then, sympathetically, he asked me:

"You're embarrassed right? To say nice words? You're a fool. Although you do say nice things when we play soccer . . . It's OK, you'll learn . . . Whenever I say nice things, I believe I exist."

In the evening we were sitting out in the yard. Gigo was sitting alone and whispering to himself again. You couldn't tell what he was saying, but it was clear that he was having a serious debate with himself.

I went over and asked him:

"Kid, what's with all this talk about not existing, not existing?"

"That woman said it, didn't she?"

"She meant something else."

"She didn't mean anything else, she said about me, 'he doesn't exist.' Why didn't she say that about you?"

"I'm telling you, she meant something else."

"Then explain it to me."

"I don't really understand either."

"If I really disappear, will you be heartbroken?"

"Yes, then who will stand in the goal?" I answered him laughing.

"I don't believe you, you wouldn't even notice."

"I would notice."

"Mom wouldn't notice, neither would Dad. Niaco doesn't even understand yet."

"Shut up, we'll notice."

"You won't notice anything. Remember last year when I was at my godmother's for a week? How was everyone here? Of course, everything was probably the same. If I completely disappear, nothing would change. In the morning Niaco will cry, Mom will wake up and start yelling. Then Dad will wake up and he'll start yelling too. Then you two will go collect scrap metal, and then you'll be yelling again. The days will pass as usual . . . months . . . pshh . . . years . . . No one will notice that I'm not there. You guys don't even need me for soccer, remember? You didn't even let me play that day."

After that, Gigo started doing such weird things, that I would blush from embarrassment. Every morning, in an exaggerated and artificial voice, he would tell each of us: "Good morning!" and give a big grin.

Then, almost every hour, he would repeat to Mom: "I love you, you're so beautiful . . ." Mom was totally confused. The worst to see was when he stood over Dad's bed and asked, "Would you care for some tea?" Dad swung a shoe at him.

I couldn't watch all of this. I had seen in movies how some family members say sweet words to each other. But those are different kinds of families. In our house, such phrases sounded ridiculous. I won't even mention how every few minutes he would throw down some hopelessly polite niceties, like it was nothing. Personally, I had only heard this sort of talk from the Jehovah's Witnesses who live nearby.

One time I asked Gigo:

"What's wrong with you? Why are you acting like this?"

"I am trying to love you all."

"You don't love us?"

"Yeah, but you guys don't know that. The day has to feel different when I am here."

"We have to beat up Nodara." Gigo told me calmly.

"Are you crazy?"

"We definitely have to beat up someone, and Nodara gets on my nerves more than anyone else."

"Why do we have to beat up anyone?"

"If we beat up someone in the streets, we'll get tired and we won't fight at home anymore. If only Dad would fight with someone else, then he would leave us alone . . ."

"We're not going to beat up anyone, Gigo."

"What, are you scared?"

"I'm not scared, it's just that fighting and hitting people isn't right."

"But you hit me just fine, don't you?"

"Sorry . . ."

" . . ."

"It's your fault. Don't make me mad and I won't hit you."

"That's a lie. You absolutely have to hit someone. Everyone is like that. That's why it's better to find someone bad to do it to."

"Fine, let's beat up Nodara, tomorrow, after the game . . ."

"You better not be scared though. If you want, I'll hit him first."

"OK, I promise."

We sat for a few minutes in silence. Then Gigo started up again:

"In five, ten, or twenty years, I wonder what we will be like."

I couldn't answer him. I couldn't even imagine how we would be. Maybe we had some dreams, but I knew well that they would remain unfulfilled. This wasn't anything tragic for us—as far as we knew, there wasn't anyone around here whose dreams had come true. I sat quietly and thought about Gigo's question. I realized that I always only had one response: "Like Dad."

I was very scared of this answer. I didn't know if Gigo loved Dad or not. Generally, when you're young, it's hard to say definitely if you love someone or not. Only adults know for sure if they love or hate someone. Gigo, like me before, had his love and hate mixed up. But as soon as he grew up, I knew he would definitely hate him. This made me feel sorry for Dad. If only Gigo loved him at least.

I decided then that no matter what happened, I wouldn't give Gigo the chance to hate Dad. I started telling him thousands of stories in which I painted our father as a kind and strong hero. When it was time to eat, I would even beat Gigo to the table and sit next to Dad, so that Gigo wouldn't smell his terrible stench.

Our days are all the same. Thinking about getting money for food, then fighting, and so on—in circles. We follow the current, fighting for survival. The one and only place where it's possible to break the cycle, to encounter the unexpected, and to move against the stream, is the soccer field. Here you have to run until you can't breathe anymore, and during game time you forget everything: sickness, problems, hunger . . .

That morning we silently crept out of the house again. We knew Dad would beat us, but we absolutely had to win that day. Plus, after the game we had to beat up Nodara. I promised Gigo that he would stand in goal the entire time.

We started at nine.

"Play to four."

"OK, to four."

Nodara's friends brought a new boy with them. He played better than everyone else. They made two goals right at the start. Gigo was unrecognizable—he was blocking shots so skillfully, we couldn't believe our eyes, but our offense wasn't having any success. And on top of everything, my sneakers ripped all the way through. I couldn't hit the ball with all my strength—it hurt my toes. The sole of my right shoe came off and was hanging off the back like an old rag. My bare feet were touching the grass.

"Stop for a minute, I have to change my shoes," I said, and threw the ball out.

"What are you going to change into?" asked Gigo, confused.

"I brought Dad's dress shoes," I whispered to him.

"Are you crazy? He'll kill you. He'll murder us both . . ."

"I won't rip them."

My bag was next to the goal post. I took my dad's black dress shoes out of it and put them on. They were one or two sizes too big, but I tied the shoestrings really tight and made them fit. I felt like I had grown a full head. I also felt more power in my feet.

They brought the ball into play. This time, I slid between one of their player's legs, without even touching them, and hit the ball with the point of my shoe. I smashed my hip on the ground while sliding, and thin droplets of blood seeped out. I passed the ball to Zaza. He struck it and we got a goal.

Then Gigo kicked the ball with all his might, with his bare feet, and sent it all the way to their goal. The goalie punched it away, but it came right to me. I was one meter away from the empty goal; wearing my new shoes I hit the ball as hard as I could, into the netless goal and out the other side, flying off the field and into the canal. 2–2. Usually the person who hits the ball out of play has to get it, but Gigo was so excited that he rushed out of the goal, retrieved the ball from the canal, and placed it before their goalie.

I made the third goal too. Zaza delivered a corner kick and I headed it right into the goal. Gigo was yelling like crazy, and he came out of the goal again to hug me.

Then they scored again. Nodara again. He hit it from far away. Gigo tried to jump for it but couldn't reach it.

It was 3–3 and Nodara got the ball again. He kicked it and Zaza caught it with his hands. It was a penalty.

"That's it, we lost," Rezi slapped his forehead.

"Quiet, we haven't lost," I told him, and looked Gigo in the eyes.

"Watch the ball, don't let your eyes off it."

Nodara measured seven steps from the goal and placed the ball in the chosen place.

Gigo stood with his back arched and his hands resting on his knees.

"Gigo, I love you!" I yelled out to him.

Everyone turned to look at me.

"Maybe he has to go pee-pee too? You should ask him," shouted Nodara.

Then he ran up and kicked it. For a second, I thought Gigo wasn't going to reach the ball; but not only did he reach it, he caught it in midair with both hands and fell back to ground.

Gigo was laying on the grass and wouldn't let go of the ball. Zaza, Rezi, and I piled on top of him. We almost crushed him.

"If you weren't here we would've lost!" I yelled.

"Without Gigo we would've lost!" yelled Zaza and Rezi.

After that, even if all the neighborhood kids had been standing in their goal, it wouldn't have saved them. I was running with my new shoes, and it seemed to me that all the opposing side, even Nodara, only came up to my knees. I ran the whole length of the field, passed the ball to Zaza, and we won.

Gigo was running around the entire stadium—"We won! We won! We won!"

I went over and said in his ear:

"Hey, so should we beat up Nodara?"

"Oh screw him, we won didn't we . . . ?"

We went to the well and spent a long time cleaning the shoes. Then we headed home, our feet dragging behind us. We were sure we were going to get a terrible beating. At the doorway, our mouths dropped open in surprise. We saw Dad holding Mom close to his chest, and happily telling her something. I could swear they were dancing. Niaco was lying in bed, crying. Mom was grinning and begging Dad—"Let me go, I need to check on the baby." Finally, she broke free and went to Niaco. At this moment they noticed us.

"My boys are here!" Dad shouted happily.

"What happened?" asked Gigo, flabbergasted.

Dad came toward us. Gigo raised his hands to shield his head, but apparently no one was planning to beat us at all. Dad took Gigo in his arms and kissed him on both cheeks. I was watching all of this in disbelief. But Gigo took everything in stride, and after a moment, he was hugging Dad back. He started talking about the game. Every few seconds he would turn to check with me.

"That's exactly what happened; tell him," he would say to me. "You should have seen this ball I saved. You would have gone crazy," he was telling Dad.

"Mom, what happened?" I asked.

"The governor was here, he told your father and some of the neighbors that they will start building the mine by the end of this week. First they will hire everyone to build it. Then, very soon, they'll start to mine the gold."

Then came the happiest days. Mom and Dad danced many more times. Grandma even came to her senses; she didn't sleep as much. One day, she unraveled a big pillow. From inside, she removed locks of her own blonde hair, cut when she was younger. In the evening, we buried the hair at the end of the street. First Grandma said the prayers, and then made Gigo and me repeat them. Gigo said:

"If you cut your hair now and buried it, it'll turn into silver."

Dad kept repeating what the governor had said:

"This place will become one of the most wealthy cities in Eastern Europe."

"One of the most wealthy cities in Eastern Europe . . ."

First, we took three months of Grandma's pension and redid the house. We bought new curtains and bedsheets. We baked an apple pie. We had the neighbors over for the first time. They were also excited. Dad drank and started bragging. He started counting each and every person that had ever argued with him, had not believed in the gold mine.

Dad came to the stadium and watched us play. We won that time as well. Oh yeah, we bought new sneakers with Grandma's pension too.

At the end of the week, the construction really began. They promised my father a salary of three hundred lari. We were very excited. Mom planned out what to do with the money up front. It did not fully cover our expenses, but we were still happy.

We didn't even complain when they didn't pay Father on time. The other workers didn't say a word either. We knew the mine would be built and then we would all be happy.

Meanwhile, the New Year came, as well as Christmas. We didn't have anything, but we were talking late into the night about the next happy New Year and Christmas.

In March, the mine opened. Visitors arrived from the capital. Enormous cars came to town in long lines. Until then, we had never had so many visitors. We too, without exception, gathered at the mine. Even Grandma came. She even brought her chair, which Gigo was tasked to carry.

They cut the red ribbon and smashed a bottle of champagne. They gave a special "thank you" to the workers.

In my childhood, when I believed they would build the mine, I would imagine a large golden building in front of my eyes. The real mine was completely different. A small structure and a haze of dust on the hills—nothing that looked very special.

On the other hand, the visitors who came to the opening looked pompous. One of them—the tallest, who, without a doubt, must have been some sort of important minister—stood posed on the temporarily built tribune and spoke of a million things. At one point, he raised his voice: "God has given us a great gift. Our land is filled with gold, but I know that the most valuable gold is in your hearts—in the hearts of honest, hard-working people. Maybe, over the years, a lot of worry and sorrow has settled on it, and it doesn't shine like it used to, but I, first and foremost, want to discover this gold."

Toward the end, he touched on several stories that Grandma used to tell us.

We are building the mythical Colchis, he yelled. He also mentioned the Golden Fleece and the Argonauts. He didn't know as much as Grandma about these things, but he knew a little. I looked for Grandma. She was sitting right there on her chair, and I have never seen her so cheerful. As I watched her, she removed the scarf from her head and lifted her hands to the sky. The wind ruffled her silver hair, and she looked like a Goddess drawn in the old mythology book.

Only some of the workers were hired at the mine. Father was not one of them. One day, they told him and most of the other workers to gather at the mine, and told them: for now, we can't take you all on, but we have your phone numbers and we will contact you when we need you. Most of them protested—we don't even have phones, where are you going to call us? The company representatives smiled sympathetically, and in a convincing voice, one of them started:

"That's nothing, we know your addresses don't we? We are already fellow citizens, together we will build a beautiful European city."

Most of the workers realized that they would never get the job, but my father was acting strangely. He never showed any disappointment, even for a second. He was still making plans on how to spend his salary and promising us millions of things. His dream had come true; they had really started to mine gold in our town. Father just couldn't comprehend it, that in the realization of his dream, he himself was left behind.

We too had such high hopes; I don't even remember when we finally understood that the mine would not bring us any fortune. Instead, the endless rumbling and clattering from the cargo trucks, and all the dust, transformed our town into an even more terrible place. Even the gold miners were not very satisfied with their work—they did not even pay them what they promised. They had to agree on a much lower salary. Those with their hopes dashed went to see the minister who had delivered such an exciting speech during the opening. But he found a million excuses, and finally even stopped answering the telephone.

Father no longer went to collect scrap metal. He slept all the time and never spoke to us. He became like Grandma—he didn't have anything left to say. Every day we were hungry. No one stopped us from going to play soccer, and Gigo and I spent our entire days at the field. If we didn't have a ball, we played with a Coca-Cola bottle.

One morning I woke up at eight o'clock. I stepped over Father, who was laying there on his mattress. I think I even stepped on him, but he didn't make a sound. I went to Gigo and woke him up.

"Come to the field," I told him quietly.

"I don't want to," he mumbled.

"Come to the field!" I yelled so loudly, that I woke Niaco.

Gigo wasn't planning to get up.

I grabbed his hair and yelled in his ear:

"Get your ass to the field, you son of a bitch!"

Gigo didn't even look up. He calmly closed his eyes and went back to sleep.

I went there alone, running with all my strength. I got there so early that no one was there yet. I was pacing back and forth. Finally, the others came. That day I played better than I ever had before; we were winning 5–0. Then suddenly, I felt my legs get very heavy, like someone had tied huge stones to them. Everything seemed so absurd to me—this foolish running. Everything.

All the strength left my muscles. I felt that the universe was very small, and there was no place for us there. Who needed us here? I just wanted to fall down on the grass and sleep. To disappear completely.

I laid down on my back and closed my eyes tight.

TRANSLATED FROM GEORGIAN BY GEORGE SIHARULIDZE

Krisztina Tóth

from *Pixel*

THE HAND'S STORY

The fingers on the hand are short and chubby, and the nails are chewed to the quick. The hand belongs to a six-year-old boy. The fingers help with counting and covering the eyes. The child sits on a stool scribbling circles in tailor's chalk on the tabletop, despite being asked not to a few times already. He draws the lines spiraling outwards, imagining that if he goes on drawing circles forever without stopping, the lines will gather on top of one another and rise off the table up into the space, like a physical spring. He had tried to explain this to the others, but no one would listen, so now he's working alone, his head bent to one side, covering the drawing with his arm. He found the chalk in a drawer where the grown-ups had hidden it. The little boy is called Dawid, by the way; he lives in the Warsaw Ghetto with his mother, Bozena, and her sisters. Someone kicks in the door and the three people in the room press into the corner. When Celina jumps to her feet she notices the chalk, but she can't say anything about it, because she's been shot. The chalk drops to the floor and breaks in two. Later, when some strangers are searching through the drawers for cutlery and linens, someone steps on it. Dawid isn't able to finish the chalk experiment, because he doesn't survive the war. He dies in Treblinka.

Sorry, wait. He doesn't die in Treblinka. And he's not even a boy, but a little girl. But sure, all these kids are so alike; nails all chewed down with pudgy, stubby fingers. So the hand belongs to a little girl and the girl's name is Irena. She's Lithuanian, from Vilna. Wait, I'm talking nonsense, I'm trying to tell everything at once. How could she be Lithuanian! She just looked blonde at first. Yes, she *looked* blonde, but her hair is actually rather dark and curly. In fact—and this is the truth—her name is Gavriela. She was born in Thessaloniki, and arrives at Auschwitz in February 1943. She survives the war but loses her mother and her home. Later on she settles in Paris and ends up as a French accountant. Yes. It can happen.

Her husband is a very nice, thin-haired official at the BNP Bank in Paris, but this has nothing to do with our story. Gavriela thinks in French, forgetting her Greek. More and more often she hears her mother's name, Domna, as if the French for "curse" were echoing within it. She speaks only French with her children and reads Greek literature in French translation. Her hand is remarkably ugly, her fingers short, so she doesn't even wear the jewelry her husband gives her. She keeps it in a leather case. Gavriela isn't happy, because even in Paris very few can manage that, but to be honest she's contented. She has a friend she goes shopping with.

This friend looks remarkably like her; when they sit beside each other on the metro, the passengers take them for sisters. Incidentally the friend is half-Romanian, half-Hungarian and has graying, curly hair as well. I know, it's getting more confusing by the second, but there's no way to smooth out the straying, tangled strands of reality into a shiny tassel. The friend's hands are just as ugly, but she doesn't worry about it anymore, being old.

Someone abandoned this hand a long time ago. It was the then-lover of her mother in Kolozsvár. When the news went around that the ghetto was going to be cleared, this lover got hold of two safe-conduct passes. The mother agonized for three days, then left with her lover and abandoned her four-year-old Cosmina, deciding that she'd rather save her own life. She put a parcel in the child's lap, then left without looking back. It was in the Iris district on May 13, 1944. The only reason any of this is interesting is because later Cosmina's son was born on May 13, and he was given the name David. Naturally this has nothing to do with the other boy by the same name seen in the Warsaw Ghetto, whom everyone soon forgot. This David wasn't forgotten. His Hungarian great-grandfather, who somehow survived the hell of war, but didn't survive Ceauşescu's Kingdom of Heaven, lived just long enough to hear of his great-grandson's birth. He thought the name David was a bad idea, but that's beside the point. The boy didn't learn this story of abandonment from his great-grandfather, though (and a good thing too), but from the other residents of the brick-factory ghetto who at the time, angry and horrified, had nursed the orphaned Cosmina.

That's a lie, but for some reason it seems correct. David was never aware someone had abandoned his mother's hand. In any case, there was nobody left who could have met him and explained to him how Cosmina's mother pleaded with her lover to give her both passes, and how the desire to live eventually won in her enamored and confused head. Gavriela doesn't know this story either, having heard a different story about the abandoned hand. She heard that all of this happened in far-off Lithuania, in Vilnius, and that the little girl was actually called Irena. Irena's mother had let go of the child's hand and left the child there. Gavriela also presumed that neither of them survived the war.

Naturally none of this is certain. The names drift around us, it would be difficult to follow up on each one. Most of the time we have to rely on assumptions. For example, the chalk experiment is feasible in theory, since the lines have extension. We can only assume that Dawid was correct. If someone were to endlessly draw circles on the same surface, then after a while the drawing would rise off the table in a cone shape, creating a tangible bulge different from the knots in the wood. You could even test it on paper, yet to this day nobody in the world has ever had the patience to do it long enough.

THE NECK'S STORY

"Mom, don't be stupid, you are *not* old!" The woman was standing in the corridor in front of the fitting rooms trying to shove her mother back in. The Germans waiting with dresses over their arms watched them uncomprehending; meanwhile, the older woman of the two just shook her head, she seemed unyielding. The problem was not that she had caught a glimpse of herself from behind in the double mirror—that she had seen the wide bra cutting into her back, and her tatty, gray hair. This could have been what the problem was, but it wasn't. It didn't even bother her that her daughter would pay for the dresses—her daughter was earning well and her German husband even bought his mother-in-law the odd trinket. This was a completely different story. The older woman had unexpectedly come across something in the fitting room and couldn't tell anyone about it. Her face was burning with shame but she couldn't say why. Her daughter could never hear the neck's story.

In seventy-eight she went to the West for the first time in her life. Not that she went so often later on, but that first trip had been particularly memorable. She'd been invited to a conference in Ulm. The girls were still small then and her husband was watching them. It wasn't customary for the doctors to bring X-ray assistants along, especially not for a five-day conference in the West. She assumed the head physician had arranged the trip, and she also assumed that he wanted something from her.

When they pressed up against each other in the corridor one night, she knew she'd end up following him into his room. Both of them had been drinking, and she was having particular trouble holding hers. Heads spinning, they fell onto the bed and made love until dawn, when at about five o'clock the doctor sobered up and quietly slipped off, as though he had been called to attend to a patient.

She didn't get up until half past eight. In the bathroom she noticed that he had given her a hickey on her neck. Nothing like this had ever happened to her before, and she began to worry that it wouldn't disappear within three days. She had her breakfast in the hotel, then set off into town with her travel allowance. She ended up in the women's section of a department store. The sex-filled night and the free morning ahead of her were liberating, and she didn't feel the customary, sudden pang of guilt that overcame her anytime she set about shopping for herself.

She stepped into the fitting room with a red low-cut dress. She would never have picked such a showy dress for herself at home, but here she figured she could wear it. She saw herself in the mirror and a woman's sky-blue eyes stared back, the type of woman who could easily wear red for a few more years.

She turned to have a look from the side, and that's when she saw the scarf on the hook. Someone must have forgotten it. The silk neck scarf was red and blue with something written on it. She had never stolen a thing in her life, nor did she intend to steal this, she simply wanted to try it on. It suited her, and it covered the mark on her neck perfectly. She took it off and put it back on the hook, so if the owner came back looking for it, they'd find it. She was just about to leave the fitting room when her heart started thumping wildly and an eddying desire came over her to go ahead and take it. The silk neck scarf for the red dress. She looked up at the ceiling, as though she were afraid someone might be watching, and then stuffed the scarf into her bag. At the checkout she felt like the cashier could see through her, like at any second she'd point to her handbag and have her take it out. Or some customer would pounce on her and interrogate her about what happened to the silk scarf they had left in the fitting room. But nobody even looked at her when she paid, and no one followed her when she left the store with the shopping bag in her hand. On the escalator, on her way down, her thumping heart finally subsided.

That afternoon she wore the red dress and the scarf to the conference, where she gave a slide show, their presentation. The scarf brought out her bright blue eyes. The head physician then gave a longer speech in German that she didn't understand, but she felt as though everyone were staring at her breasts throughout it, and that despite her two children people still found them enticing.

That evening she left the scarf on for dinner, and later she allowed the doctor to knock on the door and repeat the previous night.

Now, twenty-nine years later, as she was trying on dresses, she suddenly hesitated, and the usual depression came over her—what's the point, anyway. She peeled off the uncomfortably tight blouse and went across to her daughter's fitting room. She tugged back the curtain and stepped inside. Her daughter was in the process of trying on a sweater, and from inside the sweater she called out, is that you mom? Her head popped out at the top, but instead of her dyed-blonde hair there appeared a piece of bright fabric. At first her mother thought she had gotten tangled up in her slip. Then she saw that she was wearing a kerchief on her head that covered her face like some sort of veil. She pulled the silk kerchief from her face and hung it back up on the hook next to two others, exactly the same. "They put these everywhere," she explained, "or at least in the nicer places. It's so the customers don't muck up the clothes with their makeup when they're trying them on."

Without a word the old lady turned and left the fitting room. She recalled how, back in seventy-eight, she had stood there on the podium wearing that department store's kerchief and she was certain now that everyone had seen where it was from. There was that red and blue stripe across it, the same as on the company's shopping bags. And now she was convinced that they had spotted the purple mark underneath the kerchief, the stolen love, and her husband left at home with the two little girls, like how in an X-ray she could see things the patient would never guess.

"I don't need anything," she said to her daughter wearily, and beat a path through the people waiting in line, like she'd do in the hospital corridors with a diagnosis in her hand, hoping not to be accosted by the next-of-kin.

THE EYE'S STORY

She is sitting in the Budapest metro right beside the door on the end of the row. Exactly where Gavriela and Cosmina were sitting in a metro car from a different story. And myself, the narrator—or rather the voice you can hear, sometimes fading, sometimes perfectly audible, like during the radio broadcast of a theater performance—I'm sitting directly opposite her in the stuffy car of the present day. I hadn't noticed her until now because I was standing, but a seat opened up across from her. At times like this you can't help staring at people, at least not when it isn't crowded and the swarming clothes don't block your view.

She's clearly blind. Sat firmly upright with dark sunglasses. All kinds of packages by her side and the thin white stick beside them. Its little plastic nose for tapping the way rests on the floor beside her shoes. Wow! She's in high heels. A vain, slender, blind woman. She must be sitting beside the door because somebody offered her their seat when she got on.

The next stop comes and several people stand up, blocking the passengers opposite from view. Meanwhile I think about the blind, I have their cautious and gentle walk in front of me, always prepared for a sudden halt. That distinctly raised head. How they never look at their feet.

A lot of people get off. The space frees up again in front of me and

I can see the row of seats opposite. She's still there, perched stiffly in the seat. She could be around fifty-five or sixty. The kind whose age you can never guess. She's wearing a cute brown skirt and a similarly colored jacket. Her nails are painted. There's a remarkably large, odd-looking ring on her finger. Square-shaped with a sandblasted surface, and a heavy thing by the look of it. Could be a wedding ring but it seems too thick. Not your everyday piece of jewelry.

We're approaching the next stop and someone stands in front of me again. I think about the varnished, light-pink nails. It's difficult to paint nails, even for sighted people, it takes practice. She must not paint them herself. She gets them manicured, which means she wasn't always blind. It's a habit left over from her old life that she won't give up. Or rather she *lost* her sight. She must have a sad, aging husband who always compliments her nails. Or there's a manicure girl in the city who knows everything about her, she would even take her sunglasses off in front of her. She sets down her sunglasses on the little table while she soaks her nails in the little kidney dish. No. She has a daughter, ridden with guilt, who regularly paints her nails and they decide on the color at length beforehand. The girl hates her mother's veiny hands and the acetone smell makes her stomach turn.

I can see her again, and I look at her face now and her hair. It's been cut and dyed with care, she must visit the hairdresser at least twice a week. No doubt this is for her sad husband as well. She used to have gorgeous blue eyes but she lost her sight in an accident. A car accident. No. A tropical eye disease. Her husband is a diplomat and they were living in some exotic country when she was infected by an incurable eye disease. She was even treated in Switzerland, but they were only able to find a temporary cure, though they spent an enormous amount of money on the operations. No. She had gorgeous amber eyes once, that's what her husband really fell for back then. Then a few years ago, the optic nerve tumor was diagnosed and she lost her sight. She doesn't consider herself as blind, she's just adapted to this unusual and frankly outrageous situation. No. She has green eyes and she's only blind temporarily, like love. She's had a retina operation and for a few weeks she has to be careful of bright light, hence the sunglasses. She got the white stick at her husband's insistence, because it was prescribed, but she's ashamed of it. When she collected it, she kept picturing the familiar shop window with the mastectomy swimsuits and almost turned back. When she actually made it into the neighborhood medical supply shop her heart was pounding. In the end people walking by will think she has breast implants or something. She was still worried that maybe someone had seen her from the tram. Should have gone to a different shop, she thought, but she'd already known this one because she's been coming home this way for years.

A crowd pours in and the people getting on block her from view. Something's bothering me, but I can't quite put my finger on it. Like a detective I start piecing together the details in my head and I can tell there's an anomaly, something doesn't add up. Suddenly it pops into my brain and I see what's wrong. I smile like an inspector who's just figured out the one tiny frame of the story that doesn't fit the whole picture.

That's it! That's what's wrong! She's wearing a watch! Why would she wear a watch? She could just be wearing it as jewelry. Another habit left over from her old life that she's relentlessly clinging on to. The gold watch is hard to put on—she has to fiddle with the clasp. Her husband usually fastens it for her and gets frustrated because it's difficult. But he doesn't dare ask what the point in keeping it is. He's been too scared to ask anything for years, he'd only answer when she asks him things, but even then with caution. And any morning he's late he blames that damn watch, or his wife, because yet again *he* has to fiddle with the clasp.

The crowd drifts toward the door. I spot her high heels among the shoes. Apparently she's stood up. She's moving for the door and I can see her now from head to toe. She's got paper bags in one hand with a home furnishing store's blue logo across them. But the white stick isn't tapping the ground in the other hand. No, because the white stick is actually a plastic-tipped curtain rod. She's not blind.

And the watch she's wearing isn't from her son. She does have two sons, but this watch is from her daughter Helga, that's right! It's fake. It doesn't even keep time, because on the platform she sees the metro clock is twelve minutes ahead of her own. The watch cost five euros and the daughter got it at the seaside in Greece with her man, whatever, that's what she's getting, it'll do. She didn't want to spend more because they had already bought a load of stuff and anyway she doesn't even love her mother.

THE HEAD'S STORY

It all began during the Italy trip. His old tourist's reflexes were working and he did his best to see everything there was to see. A long time ago, the engineer had worked in the preservation of historical monuments, and during this trip he made a point of looking at every single façade worth seeing in the little Italian city, and the *palazzi* along Via Garibaldi too. But at the same time he swore he would never take on another lecture abroad, this was the last.

The next day, before noon, he was lying in the hotel room when the bed gave a lurch. It rocked back and forth, then slowly, it began to rise and fall. The logical explanation would have been an earthquake. With tremendous effort he pushed himself onto his feet and staggered to the window to look outside. He saw a peaceful morning square, with some old fellow walking a dog and a blonde woman heading by in high heels. But as he lay back down on the bed the tremors hadn't stopped. His last conscious thought was to grab the little gold key from the dark-stained wardrobe opposite.

If he'd woken up later with the key in his hand, then he could have been sure the quake wasn't a dream. When he came to his hand was empty, but his clothes were drenched with sweat. His shoulders ached, since he had been clinging to the bed with every ounce of his strength a few hours ago, when the room lost its solid outline.

After dark he strolled down to the ice cream shop across the square. When he looked up at the cashier girl, who was wearing a white top and hooped earrings, he saw a large, amorphous blotch where her face should be. He suspected it was just sunstroke, but he swore that he would get himself checked out as soon as he got home nevertheless. Normally, he would have to wait a month for the MRI, but he was bumped to the top of the list. They handed him a plastic pump and asked him to press it if he feels uncomfortable at any point during the scan.

Inside the thing it was like lying in some kind of coffin. The whole time he could hear this rhythmic knocking. As though someone were trying to dig him out from under the ruins of his life, and in the meantime using Morse code to let him know they were getting close.

The head physician presented him with the findings. She had remarkably big blue eyes. The remarkably blue pair of eyes sat in a sagging, mature face, but there was still something appealing and radiantly feminine in her presence.

At home the man distractedly watched the World Cup and decided not to say anything to his wife for the time being. What could he have said anyway? That recently he's been having strange hallucinations and a blue-eyed doctor has asked him to come in again next Tuesday?

That Tuesday they took a seat in the small office of the head physician. She noticed the ring on his finger, which he wasn't wearing last time during the MRI because he'd had to take it off in the changing room. It really was an interesting thing. His wife had it made by a designer for their thirty-fifth wedding anniversary. It was round on the inside and square on the outside with a sandblasted surface. He would never have worn anything like that himself, but given that he had long since stopped loving his wife, he wore it respectfully. The doctor chose to look at the ring rather than his face as she went through the diagnosis. She didn't tell him the truth, that is, she didn't say a single word about what the picture showed. She just mentioned he would need further scans and that certain signs might indicate a tumor. We have to explore every possibility, she raised her eyes.

Had she told the truth, she would have first explained that the tumor was on the brainstem. She would have continued by telling him that soon he was going to lose his memory, and most probably his personality as well. That presumably he would become paralyzed. She held the scans up to the light and pointed out which bits to look at. He thought they were like symmetrical inkblots and you could see all sorts of things in them. An owl, a Pekinese dog, a lion. True, she added, and a baboon, but he couldn't make out the monkey head. From time to time during the consultation she would look at his hand, trying to decide whether the ring was a wedding ring or not. She thought it was far too flashy, whatever it was.

The wife, on the other hand, was mad about unique pieces like that. While this very conversation was taking place she was strolling around an IKEA, and had picked out a large blue illuminated globe. Not for their own flat, but for their daughter Helga's. Helga was thirty years old and had moved into the loft space of a newly built apartment building. The mother knew she couldn't count on any grandchildren in the near future, after all, Helga had been a married man's lover for years now, but she had started furnishing the future baby's room anyway. She bought a white, plastic-tipped curtain rod and a few (in terms of our story) completely uninteresting bath mats.

Meanwhile, the brain tumor was also settling in, trying in its own way to make the occupied property, namely the man's brain, homier. Thoughts didn't revolve around his wife anymore in this brain, in fact let's admit it, Helga and the two sons had all been driven out together with the new flat. At nine o'clock that night, with the MRIs in his lap, he phoned the doctor from the bathroom and told her he could see the baboon.

She never found out whether the clunky ring was a wedding ring or not, but she did accept the invitation to his country house near Villány. The little cottage had a porch and was built from sun-dried clay bricks, so it stayed cool inside despite the summer heat. He reeled off a well-practiced speech about how he had salvaged the original ironwork and put in the wooden rafters, before tipping the blue-eyed doctor on the coarse, woolen throw.

The doctor's body wasn't remarkably beautiful, but he was still much happier to put his arms around hers than his wife's thin, forever cold-skinned body. As he undressed her layer by layer he noticed a deep and lengthy scar across her stomach. The doctor had given birth to both of her children by Caesarean and had told him a little about them on the road down, when they stopped at a small, musty roadside tavern. During lunch she had told him how one of her daughters, Edit, had married a man in Germany and the other (Ági maybe?) lived on Baross utca in Budapest and had just turned thirty. She's pretty miserable, the poor thing, can't find herself a normal man. The architect took out a photo of his three grown-up children and boasted to her that he had bought each of them a flat, but that he had put together this little house just for himself, and actually, he'd just bought a nearby wine cellar to go with it.

The whole time they were making love the coarse, woolen bed cover itched horribly. She ran her fingers up his back and thought about how a good designer really has to think of everything, that's what design is all about. The square-shaped anniversary ring irritated her throughout the petting, but she thought it would be rude to ask him to take it off.

In the evening they sat out on the porch of the little house, and she realized quite contentedly that the man's mobile hadn't rung all day because he'd turned it off. They sipped on the wine and stared into the falling darkness. Suddenly the man started squinting into the distance and pointed in surprise, saying wow, the water was rising, higher and higher waves were coming in toward the porch and he couldn't understand, when there aren't even any lakes around here. You're right, she said, look at how pretty the water is. How it reflects the Moon. The man could see perfectly well that there was no moon of any sort reflected in the swelling mass of water, plus he would have found the picture much too romantic, but he didn't want to argue. On the one hand, he had a splitting headache—from the driving, obviously. On the other, he had fallen in love with this stranger, this blue-eyed doctor.

TRANSLATED FROM HUNGARIAN BY OWEN GOOD

ROB DOYLE

John-Paul Finnegan, Paltry Realist

WHEN I THINK OF IRELAND, John-Paul Finnegan said as we stood on the deck of the ferry while it pulled out of Holyhead, I think of a limitless ignorance. And not just an ignorance, but a *wallowing* in ignorance, akin to the wallowing in filth of a pig or a naked, demented savage. Ireland and the people of Ireland wallow in ignorance much in the way that a child or a lunatic wallows in its own filth, smearing the walls with it, grinning and cooing loudly, smearing the walls and itself with its own filth, its own stinking self-made filth. This is definitely how the Irish people are, he said. This is their primary characteristic. Absolutely. Elsewhere in the world you can find qualities in people, both individuals and groups, which correspond to words such as spirit, life force, vitality, passion, and curiosity, but in Ireland you will find no such qualities. No such qualities at all. This is what John-Paul Finnegan, author of *Nevah Trust a Christian*, told me as the ferry, the *Ulysses*, began to move out of the harbour at Holyhead, propelling itself away from the British coast, towards Dublin.

Consider the name of this very ship, said John-Paul Finnegan. In fact, don't even get me started on the name of this ship, he said. But it was too late, because he had already got himself started on the name of the ship, which was *Ulysses.* Not a single fucking dickhead in all of Ireland has actually read *Ulysses*, said John-Paul Finnegan. Except me, of course, the biggest dickhead of them all. Yet everyone in Ireland pretends to have read *Ulysses,* or acts like they've read it, but none of them have. The last person in Ireland to read *Ulysses* was James Joyce, and even he only read half of it, said John-Paul Finnegan. Come to think of it, there were a few professors who came after Joyce who also read *Ulysses*, or rather, they didn't read it, they *killed* it, they killed *Ulysses* by James Joyce, just like they have killed almost every other

113

book that was once worth reading. And not only did they kill *Ulysses*, but first they mutilated it, subjecting it to the most mental forms of torture. And how did they kill it? he asked. I will tell you, he said. They killed *Ulysses* by rendering it as a desiccated literary relic; they wrote a slew of murderously dull articles about *Ulysses*, and thereby killed it. They killed *Ulysses* by making it seem to anyone unfortunate or depraved enough to read one of their hateful papers that *Ulysses* is the most boring and flaccid book in the world, when of course it is anything but the most boring and flaccid book in the world, it is in fact deeply subversive, scatological, irreverent, perverse, and above all, diabolically deviant. That is, the form and the content of the book are deviant: they deviate from good taste, from literary classicism, from the boredoms of morality and plot, and from sentimentality—in other words, from *all the shit of literature*, said John-Paul Finnegan, the typical and all-too-prevalent *shit of literature*. Like any decent author, said John-Paul Finnegan, Joyce ignored the shit, he sidestepped it, the *hideous shit of literature*, because he couldn't be bothered and he wanted to write a new kind of book, which is the only thing worth doing if you call yourself a writer of any description. Yet if you read one of the papers, *any* of the papers by those *unconscionable fucking dickheads* who write about *Ulysses*, you will soon if not immediately come to the conclusion that this book, this *Ulysses* is not worth reading precisely because, judging by how these *academic fucks,* these *sick, life-hating, evil, mental, and spiritually crippled fucks* write about it, *Ulysses* must be the least interesting of all books, said John-Paul Finnegan as the ship, the *Ulysses*, finally pulled out of the harbour and commenced upon open water.

I sighed. John-Paul Finnegan was right, I thought. But then again, maybe he wasn't right. Maybe he was entirely wrong, as he had so often been entirely wrong before, about so many things, nearly everything in fact. After all, *I* had read *Ulysses*, so he wasn't entirely right. Likelier he was entirely wrong. After all, I was Irish, and I had read *Ulysses*. What about me? I said to John-Paul Finnegan, suddenly indignant that he would so casually disparage the entirety of the Irish race, myself included, on the basis of such a truly sweeping generalisation. What about me? I said again. To which John-Paul Finnegan looked at me, clasping his hands as the ship cut across the waves. What about you? he said warily. I read *Ulysses*, I said. That's right, he said, I'd forgotten that. He seemed to be having a moment of self-doubt. So there's you and then there's me and then there's James Joyce, he said finally. We three have all read *Ulysses*. But no one else in Ireland has ever read *Ulysses*, he added. This I know. I know this simply because I know it, he said, his confidence returning. In other words it is what the philosophers call *a priori* knowledge, the kind of knowledge which we can possess prior to, indeed independently of, empirical verification. I simply *know*, as you know, as everybody knows, that everyone in Ireland, everyone except you and I, is too fucking dim-witted, too altogether stupid and moronic, and above all too terrified by the very word *literature*, to have bothered to read *Ulysses*. That's how I know. You think I'm fucking joking, he said, jabbing a finger in my chest. I am not fucking joking, he said. I am not even exaggerating, let alone joking. Irishmen are terrified of the word *literature*. I can guarantee you that if I were to suddenly turn around, on this deck, with these couples and old drunken builders and traveller families and whatnot, and if I were then to roar the word *literature* at the top of my lungs, the vast majority of these people would run to the sides of the ship and hurl themselves over the edge to be drowned. They would sooner drown than confront a man roaring *literature*. And the rest of them, John-Paul Finnegan added, would simply collapse on the spot, they would die of the sheer horror that the word *literature* provoked in them, the boundless sense of nausea, terror and repulsion it provoked in their Irish hearts, that is to say their *pig hearts*, their *flaccid dickhead hearts*. Some of them would have heart attacks, others aneurysms. Others would simply keel, causes unknown. For they know nothing of literature, of Joyce, and they care for less, these Irishmen, said John-Paul Finnegan, glowering at me now with a ferocity and yes, a hatred which I had done nothing to deserve, or so I felt. I may as well roar *Allahu Akbar*, added John-Paul Finnegan, as roar *literature*. I may as well wrap a towel around my head and roar *Allahu Akbar* while ripping off my shirt to reveal a suicide vest, as to roar *literature*, for the effect it would have on these Irishmen, in other words these cretins, these fuckheads, these unconscionable morons and idiots, these fucking heartless and mindless pricks, these pigs and sheep and rodents that call themselves Irishmen, when in truth they should call themselves sheep and pigs and rodents, if not total fucking spanners, said John-Paul Finnegan, who now had flecks of foam collecting at the corners of his mouth, and whose eyes had not left mine. But it seemed to me that the boundless hate had drained from John-Paul Finnegan's eyes, and what remained was a childlike fear, a pleading, a remorse even. I imagined that John-Paul Finnegan was flailing out in the sea, not the Irish Sea which our ship, the *Ulysses*, was cutting across at a decent speed, but the metaphorical sea, the Black Sea or the Dead Sea, the sea of loneliness, self-hate, and dread that is the fate not of all men, but certainly of all *thinking* men, as John-Paul Finnegan had himself told me, in one of his more vulnerable moments, when we had lived together in London, in a crowded and unsanitary house near Finsbury Park.

These pricks! he shouted. These unconscionable mental pricks! How I fucking loathe them, he muttered, shaking his head violently, too violently I thought, he might do himself damage. He drew sharply from his hip flask, neglecting to pass it to me. How low can you go? he asked. How fucking low? I will tell you how low: all the way to Ireland. That's how low you can fucking go. I let it pass, that inane comment, and fell to thinking about our lives in London, the lives we were leaving behind, standing as we were on the deck of this ship, this *Ulysses* that was cutting across the Irish Sea, the coast of Britain fading behind us. It was in the house near Finsbury Park that John-Paul Finnegan had written the last three volumes of *Nevah Trust a Christian*, his *novel in eleven volumes*, as he always called it, with bottomless perversity, the fact being that there were no fewer than *thirteen* volumes in his novel, if it even was a novel. I had moved into the house when John-Paul Finnegan was nearing the end of volume twelve, which he had titled *Who's Ya Daddy?* I write eight thousand words per day, he had told me on the night we first went out for drinks in the Twelve Pins pub on Seven Sisters Road. I replied that eight thousand words seemed like a lot, in fact it seemed like far too many words to write in a single day. Absolutely fucking correct, it is too many, it's far too many words even for the most deadline-haunted hack, let alone for a writer of literature, such as myself, John-Paul

Finnegan said, pouring a shot of whiskey into his Guinness, as was his wont, a concoction which he called *Guinnskey*. It was then that John-Paul Finnegan had explained to me his notion of *paltry realism*, the genre in which he claimed to write, and which he also claimed to have invented. Paltry realism means writing shit, he said. What I mean to say is, what is art, only a howl against death. Are we agreed on this, Rob? he demanded. I nodded my head. Good, he said. Then we are agreed that art is a howl against death and nothing more. Yet why is it, he said, that so much art tries to do the opposite, to ignore, even to deny death? Have you thought about this? he asked. Art, and especially literature, has a thousand clever ways of denying or ignoring death. One of these ways is literariness itself, that is, literary imposture, said John-Paul Finnegan. By which I mean the ceaseless attempt by practitioners of literature to achieve beauty and perfection, to write well, in short *to craft perfect and elegant sentences*. This is infinite bollocks, said John-Paul Finnegan. If you write slowly, carefully, then what are you doing if not indulging in vanity—the *vanity of writing well*. It's no different from wearing a nice coat or a frock or a shiny pair of shoes to a *bourgeois* dinner party—and I will tell you now, he added, I am not nor have I ever been the kind of man to attend dinner parties, *bourgeois* or otherwise. And death is no fucking dinner party. The point is, though, said John-Paul Finnegan, trying to write well is vanity and nothing other than vanity, and when I say vanity I essentially mean *the fear of death expressed in self-framing*, as you will have guessed. That is where the technique of paltry realism makes its stance. Paltry realism means writing rapidly, and yes, even writing badly, in fact only writing badly, and not seeking to impress anyone with your writing, with either its style or its content. Paltry realism means writing eight thousand words per day, he said. Eight thousand words—far too many for any *decent or tasteful writer*, but perfect for the practitioner of paltry realism, a school which, for the time being, consists solely of me, said John-Paul Finnegan, fixing another Guinnskey. I was intrigued by his theory of paltry realism and urged him to say more, though I needn't have bothered, as he was already talking over me, caught up in the swell of his own oratory, aflame with the zeal I was to observe in him many times over the course of our friendship, which began that night in the Twelve Pins and continued to the afternoon when we stood together on the deck of the *Ulysses*, which was now at full steam as it tore across the Irish Sea, the British coast-line having faded completely to the stern. Another indicator of the vanity and ultimately the self-delusion of literature, even in its so-called avant-garde, modernist, or experimental guises, is that its prac-titioners invariably display a craving, a very unseemly craving, to have their work published, John-Paul Finnegan had said that night in the pub, him downing Guinnskeys and me downing Guinnesses. All of them, the brazen slags, all they want is to be published, he said. They want an adoring or a scandalised public to read their works, thereby granting them a kind of immortality, or so they would like to think. This goes for Céline, Kafka, Pessoa, Joyce, Marinetti, Musil, Markson, Handke, Hamsun, Stein, Sebald, Bernhard, Ballard, Beckett, Blan-chot, Burroughs, Bolaño, Cioran, Duras, Gombrowicz, Pound, Eliot, and any other dickhead of the so-called avant-garde that you might care to mention, as much as it goes for McEwan, Self, Banville, Tóibín, Auster, Atwood, Easton-Ellis, Amis, Thirlwell, Hollinghurst, Smith, Doyle, Dyer, Franzen, and any other arsehole active in mainstream literature today, said John-Paul Finnegan. To them, the value of a work of literature is dependent on its being published. If it is not pub-lished, it has no value. There is an ontological question at work here, he added: if a book is unread by anyone except its author, can it be said to exist? More pertinently, can it be said to be any good? My re-sponse, and paltry realism's response, is simply to bypass the whole squalid agenda. What is the point in sending my writing out to pub-lishers, said John-Paul Finnegan, so that they might accept or reject it? What is the use in that? I will tell you now: *I* reject the publishers, every last one of them, even the ones I admire, the ones I revere, the good and the best of them, because I am a paltry realist, and publica-tion, Rob, is not among my aims, not among my aims at all, it is not among my aims, I am simply not fucking interested in being pub-lished, he said, slamming his Guinnskey on the table. I write for other reasons, he added, though he neglected to say what they were. On several occasions, while we were living together in the house near Finsbury Park, John-Paul Finnegan had permitted me to read sec-tions of *Nevah Trust a Christian*, his gargantuan work allegedly in the paltry realist mode. True enough, the writing was very bad, and obvi-

118

ously written in great haste (handwritten, that is—John-Paul Finnegan hated typing on a laptop.) The prose was utterly devoid of literary flair and displayed not the slightest effort to seduce or entertain the reader. Not that the writing was *hostile* to the reader, as can be the case among the severest of modernists; rather, the writing seemed *indifferent* to the reader, perhaps even unaware of the reader's existence. There were few paragraph breaks and no chapter breaks. There was no discernible story and no characters. The word *fuck*, or one of its variants, appeared at least once on every line, more often twice or three times, or more. The word *cunt* was almost as frequent; the words *bastard, dickhead, rodent* and *moron* riddled the text. Several pages consisted solely of *fuck*-derived words repeated hundreds of times, punctuated by *bastard, mongrel, cunthawk,* or *dickhead*. Others offered perfunctory descriptions of dusty towns and hurtling trams, giant mounds of waste and crumbling ridges, or glibly vicious references to contemporary events. I had the sense of an inner monologue; not exactly a stream-of-consciousness, more like a machine-gun-of-consciousness, or a self-bludgeoning-of-consciousness, or just an interminable, pointless spewing of language, a kind of insane vomiting of language, page after page of it, a dozen volumes stacked on the floor beside John-Paul Finnegan's desk, which was a backstage dressing table salvaged from a closed-down strip club.

But this is not even the worst of it, John-Paul Finnegan said suddenly as we stood together on the deck of the *Ulysses* as it bounced over the waves, away from Britain. This ship, this *Ulysses*, is not even the worst of it, he repeated. The worst of it is *Bloomsday*. Have you ever seen Bloomsday? he asked. What I'm talking about, he said, is the national day of celebration in tribute to a book that no one in Ireland has *even fucking read!* That is what I refer to, said John-Paul Finnegan. Until a decade or so ago, Bloomsday was merely a kind of minor national stain, a silly and moronic venture that no one really bothered with, and which you could safely ignore. But then the government, that gang of dribbling pricks, that *moron collective*, as I have so often labelled them, saw in Bloomsday a serious marketing opportunity, one which they, in their infinite hatefulness, decided was far too lucrative to ignore. There was more money to be squeezed out of Joyce, they decided, as if Joyce were a sponge or a testicle, and even though not one of them—this I know—not one of them had ever read *Ulysses*, or even *Dubliners*, or any of Joyce's books at all, said John-Paul Finnegan. In fact, these morons that I'm referring to, these are the kind of people who, if you suggested to them that they might read *Ulysses* or *Dubliners*, would laugh out loud. And I'm not talking about an embarrassed or a *social* form of laughter, he said, but a *bellowing, hearty, and spontaneous* laughter, from the guts, a laughter of delight at what they would consider the mad and uproarious idea of reading *Ulysses* or *Dubliners*, said John-Paul Finnegan. He drew again from his hip flask, then passed it to me. I drank. These morons, these dickheads, these unconscionable fucking arseholes decided to commercialise this so-called Bloomsday, said John-Paul Finnegan, the day when the fictional Leopold Bloom fictionally wandered around Dublin city, drinking, ruminating, chatting and so on. In other words, the sixteenth of June, he said. It would bring in the tourists, they reckoned. It would bring in the Yanks and Japs, the French and the Germans, the Swedes and the Slavs, the vulgarian Bulgarians and the roaming Romanians, and all those grinning tourists would spend their money admiring *the Irish people* and their literary heritage, even though the people of Ireland no longer read, are too stupid to read, let alone to read *Ulysses*, the book that this whole moronic fiasco of Bloomsday purports to celebrate. You don't need me, said John-Paul Finnegan, to point out that the two Irish writers widely considered the greatest of the twentieth century, even by people who have never read and never intend to read either of them, namely Beckett and Joyce, had nothing but hatred and disgust for Ireland, and for the Irish. These two writers spent a huge amount of energy *actively disparaging* the Irish and Ireland, said John-Paul Finnegan, in their letters and conversation, and frequently in their published work too. Yet here we have a situation, this so-called Bloomsday, wherein all the fat waddling morons on the island gather in the streets to celebrate a book by Joyce which they never bothered to read! Pink pudgy dickheads. Mindless flabby wankers, trailing their moron progeny. Useless bastards one and all. They celebrate *Ulysses* in the most nauseatingly self-conscious of ways, prancing about for the snapping tourists, dancing like twats, like true dickheads for these snapping tourists, who gaze on in a euphoria of mindless-ness, clicking their cameras, their smartphone cameras, their video cameras, recording the Irish, *this literary nation*, making absolute fools of themselves by aping the characters in a book they have never read, a book they never intend to read, for they hate books, they hate all books regardless of provenance, the only exceptions being *Harry Potter* and football biographies, said John-Paul Finnegan. Bloomsday, he said, shaking his head in disgust. Bloomsday. Fucking Bloomsday. Blooms-fucking-day. Bloom-fuckings-day. Fuck off, he said. Fuck right off. I mean it, fuck all the world. Listen to this, John-Paul Finnegan said. A few years ago I was back in Dublin, don't ask me why, I was back in Dublin at the time of *Bloomsday*. I went into town, not to partake in the celebrations of course, but for unrelated reasons. And while I was in there I walked up O'Connell Street and listen to this, it will sound like the stuff of broad satire or lunatic fantasy but it is neither, Rob, I assure you. I walked onto O'Connell Street and what did I see, along the pedestrian island running up the middle of Dublin's great thoroughfare, but hundreds of fat grinning idiots, together with their chortling wives and their chubby, shrieking children, all sitting in rows along either side of an immensely long dining table, said John-Paul Finnegan. I am not kidding you. And listen to this. Over their heads was a massive dangling banner, a dangling banner that read *Denny Sausages Celebrate James Joyce's Bloomsday*. Yes! *Denny* fucking *Sausages!* As if the sausages themselves were bursting in ecstasy. This because somewhere in the scatological sprawl of *Ulysses*, between its intimate depictions of flatulence, defecation, masturbation, blasphemy, and unbridled male and female lust, there is brief mention made of *Denny* fucking *Sausages*, said John-Paul Finnegan. So here they were, hundreds of these fat chortling twats, crowded around a long dining table replete with white tablecloth, being served plate upon plate of sausages, each of them *cramming their faces* with sausage, a veritable orgy of sausage gorging in honour of James Joyce, high-modernist and high-mocker of Ireland. *Here is your legacy, James Joyce*, John-Paul Finnegan roared over the waves, *here is your legacy— two hundred chortling fucks eating sausages! You have really left your fucking mark, James Joyce. Oh yes you have! You are the KING OF MODERNISM!* Presently John-Paul Finnegan produced his hip flask, swigged on it, and passed it to me. I drank self-consciously, for despite the roar of the turbines and the waves crashing against the prow, many of the other travelers on deck had heard John-Paul Finnegan's outburst and were looking warily in our direction. John-Paul Finnegan was oblivious to their gazes, or just indifferent. Fat waddling pricks, he muttered, more subdued now. How they waddle. Like fat, mental penguins. Fat chortling penguins, grinning like lunatics. Penguins of depravity, penguins of hate. Will I tell you what I did? he said, turning to me sharply. I will tell you what I did. I made it my business to at least attempt to fathom this unprecedented display of public idiocy, this linking of high-modernism to pork consumption. I walked along the rows of chortling, sausage-cramming Dubliners, through the gauntlet of snapping Japs, the lens-faced legions. Then I stopped and asked one woman who was sitting with a pile of sausages on a plate in front of her, whether she had actually read *Ulysses*, said John-Paul Finnegan. She stared at me for a long time, her expression conveying sheerest bewilderment and horror. Her child began to cry. Eventually the woman came out of her trance, and she said to me, very slowly, *Ulysses*. Just the word *Ulysses*, nothing more. I never saw a woman so afraid. Her little boy had his head in his hands now, weeping through his fingers, wailing. That was when the father turned around. He looked me in the eye, a long and disdainful look it was. Then he said, *I think you'd better leave*. What the fuck, said John-Paul Finnegan, recollecting the incident. What the fuck? All I had done was ask her if she had read *Ulysses*. They ran me out of there, he said. They'd have lynched me, that sausage-mob, if I had not made off with myself. A black day for Ireland, and a black day for me, said John-Paul Finnegan. And yet here I am, here we are, on a ferry, on the fucking *Ulysses* no less, gliding across the sea not away from, but *in the direction of* the accursed land, the steaming hole, the potato field, the literary and intellectual *silence* of Ireland. Would that it would crumble into the sea, he added. Would that the entire stinking mass, the whole abominable island would groan, keel, and tumble into the sea. Dissolve in the sea. Dissolve like a man who is made of salt, a man who fell into the sea, he said. He was silent for a time, looking out at the waves. I thought about London, about Dublin, about our position now, suspended between the two cities. We must be the only two Irishmen returning to Ireland rather than fleeing from it, I reflected, not for the first time. I thought about Irish pubs, the many of them back in London I had drunk in with John-Paul Finnegan, and it seemed to me now that they weren't pubs at all, but cages, or bear traps. I began to fantasize about climbing the rail and flinging myself to the sea, vanishing in the foam with a truncated yell.

The journey was nearing its end. John-Paul Finnegan was muttering away by my side, as if in tense dialogue with the waves, or the treacherous forms that squirmed inside his head. I sensed that the closer we got to Dublin, the less sure of himself he became. Very soon we would be at Dublin port. I could already make out the Poolbeg towers hazed on the horizon. I thought of all the time we had spent away, John-Paul Finnegan and I, and the hatred my friend bore within him, the hatred that is purer than any other, the hatred for where one comes from. And now John-Paul Finnegan turned to me, gripping the rail. I could feel his gaze on me. I turned to face him. What the fuck did they do to me? he said quietly, referring to what, I did not know. What the fuck did they do to me, Rob? The words had to them a tone of revelation. The coastline was expanding across the horizon, sinister and domineering. John-Paul Finnegan shook his head. What the fuck did they do to me? What the fuck was going on, Rob? What the fuck was going on?

I turned away, facing the coast. Neither of us spoke for a time. John-Paul Finnegan went to speak again but hesitated. I did not look at him. Finally he said, There is no healing. Writing changes nothing, it's an infliction. You inflict yourself on the page, and then on the reader, and on the world. Better to have no readers, better not to write at all. There was no worth to what I wrote, nor to anything I have ever done. Nothing in my life has had any worth. Writing has no worth. Nothing has any worth. Nothing. We were both silent as the ferry sailed into the mouth of the port, the twin red-and-white towers looming like sentries. Now John-Paul Finnegan seemed truly calm, self-possessed once more, neither raging nor afraid. I will not forgive, he said. Fuck it all. I have decided. I will not forgive them, not forgive any of them for what they have done, for what they have done to me. I will not forgive them, he said. I will not. No. Fuck it, he said.

MĀRA ZĀLĪTE

The Major and the Candy

A tailor sits on the rim of a well
Mending his Sunday tailcoat
Pretty Laura passes by
Tries to splash him with water!

Mama sings and rocks Laura on her knee. Mama is trying; it isn't as if Mama isn't trying. The next verse is the one Laura likes the most, the bit where Mama uses a different voice and shakes her.

Lassie have you lost your mind?
My tailcoat will get ruined!
I must go to church tomorrow!
What will I have to wear?

The tailor is dreadfully angry. Dreadfully! But all Laura wants to do is laugh. The tailor is hilarious after all! Laura laughs as if she were being tickled. But if Mama actually tickles her, then it's even more ticklish. Where Laura is most ticklish is under her chin. A person can be tickled to death because Papa has told Laura that the Chinese tickle all their naughty ones until they're as dead as doornails.

"Up-sy-dai-sy, up-sy-dai-sy, Laura's going home by train! Up-si-dai-sy, tra-la-la—Laura's going home la-la! Laura's going to Avoti, up-si-la! Up-si-dai-sy, upsi-la, boozy, woozy, splat!"

Now and then Papa also tries; he rocks Laura on his knee, grasping her under her armpits and throwing her up in the air until she gets tired, and both, out-of-breath, end up laughing. That's when Papa is happy. When Mama is happy. Those are the good moments. But when Laura has been whining non-stop for half the day, then Papa usually exclaims—"*dofiga*!"—That's enough! Then he goes to have a smoke.

At some train stop Madame Attendant opens the compartment door.

"Here you are. There's no other place, Comrade Major." Madame Attendant tries to make excuses for the compartment.

Today she has really made an effort: painted her lips a fiery red, blackened the arches of her eyebrows, and squeezed into a tight-fitting dress.

"It will do, Puss," the Major says as he slaps her soft behind.

Madame Attendant takes no offense. As the door closes after her, she leaves the compartment filled with a pungent and cloyingly sweet smell of lily of the valley combined with her own body odor.

"May I?" the Major asks, not waiting for a response. He takes off his army hat and hangs it up. It's a beautiful hat, blue-colored on top. This can be seen well from above by Laura who is settled on the baggage rack. His hair is graying. His broad face is brown like a cedar nut. Mama and Papa exchange worried glances. Why? But Laura is delighted at the appearance of the Major, at least something is happening.

After a while the Major begins a conversation. "Where are you young people off to?"

"To Moscow." Papa's response is abrupt.

Laura is hiding on the compartment's top baggage rack. Where the luggage should be. She's still debating if she should show herself to the Major.

"To Moscow. Yes, yes," mama confirms kindly, attempting to correct papa's abruptness, "*V Moskvu. Da. Da.*"

To Moscow? Laura freezes. What Moscow? What are they talking about? Isn't Laura going to Latvia? Have Papa and Mama been telling tales? They're talking in Russian and Laura understands Russian well, but sometimes when grown-ups talk nothing can be understood in any language.

"To study? Are you students?" The Major wants to know.

"No, no!" Papa and Mama are not talkative.

"Have some," the Major hospitably offers, putting out a half loaf of brick-shaped bread, hard-boiled eggs, streaky bacon, and pickles.

Laura is disappointed because they have the same sort of food themselves.

Always the same. That's why Laura is constipated, that's why her tummy hurts.

The Major busies himself, with a host's gesture of largesse he places a bottle on the table, tears off the green metal strip and pours into the cut tea glasses almost all of the bottle's contents. Three glasses, but one of these is Laura's glass! No way will Laura drink the Major's vodka!

"Comrades! What now? We've got *zakuskas*, got glasses, got vodka, and a reason to drink can always be found! What do you suggest?"

It seems that Papa and Mama don't know what to suggest.

"Let's toast our youth, comrades! To our splendid Soviet youth! A great future is yours, young people! The Party is leading you there! A toast to the Party! To you! To the future!" The Major, elated, empties his glass in one gulp, shakes himself, and avidly inhales the odor of the brick-shaped bread.

He smells the bread to be certain that Germans haven't pooped in the rye and contaminated it, Laura knows! Laura knows!

Papa drinks half his glass while Mama only raises the glass to touch her lips. Just a taste, the tiniest of sips. Laura wonders which young people the Major is talking about. Which young people are here? Only Mama and Papa. The major hasn't seen Laura yet. Or maybe he does see her after all?

"And you? Also headed to Moscow?" Papa has become more talkative.

"Only as far as the Urals. That's my usual route. *Sluzba*—duty calls! The enemy never sleeps. But tell me, what are you doing in Moscow? I didn't get an answer."

"Laura isn't going to Moscow!" Laura yells from above.

"Now, what have we here? And I was wondering where the third passenger could be? There she is! Ah, I see, I see. Hiding, talking in a strange language, probably a *shpion*—a spy! Hey! *Shpionka, diversantka*—spy, saboteur! I have something for you!" The Major smiles and hands Laura a candy.

Wrapped in a light blue paper, the candy is beautiful. Even more beautiful than the blue hat. And big! There's a picture in color on the wrapping. Two small bears romping among felled trees, while a third watches.

"What do you say?"

Laura knows very well what she must say.

What is most precious is the light blue wrapping. Because that can be saved. The paper wrapping serves as undeniable proof. Otherwise no one will believe that Laura has had such a candy, that Laura has eaten such a candy!

"Laura is going to Latvia!" she says, making sure it sounds forceful, loud, and sassy. Not so much for the sake of the Major, no, more so for Mama and Papa, to let them know that Laura won't go to any Moscow! Laura will get off the train! They can go on their own if they want, because Laura won't go to Moscow! And that's not being naughty!

"From Moscow we'll continue further to Latvia," Mama adds, because what else can she say now.

"Home. After fifteen years," Papa explains, immediately regretting what he has said.

He empties his glass to the very bottom, then pours the contents of Mama's glass into his. Mama looks at him reproachfully.

Mama's afraid that when Papa is drunk he may talk too much.

"To Tallinn? I was there during the war. In the town of Paldiski. Do you know it? No, you're too young. Besides, the facility was secret!" The Major begins vigorously, but quickly falls silent and seems to be contemplating something.

He pours the remaining vodka into his glass and drinks it in one go. He doesn't shake himself as he did before, maybe he has forgotten to shake himself, and he doesn't smell the bread anymore, because why should he do it twice.

"No, Tallinn is in Estonia. We're going to Riga," Mama clarifies.

"Ah, yes! I still confuse that *Pribaltika*—the Baltics. Latvia. Lithuania. Estonia. Then you must be Lithuanians?"

"No, Latvians." Mama has to be the one to speak, because Papa has grown glum.

"Yes, yes. Latvians. The Communist politician and Latvian writer Vilis Lācis—his book *Sin ribaka* about the fisherman's son. Right? The Latvian Riflemen! Right? How so—after fifteen years?" The Major doesn't let anything slip by.

"That's how it's turned out," Mama is frightened. Laura senses this with every cell of her body how very much Mama is afraid.

"How old are you then, girl?" the Major asks Mama, but Laura thinks she's the one who has been asked. Where, after all, would there be another girl here?

"Laura is five. Going on six," she announces.

"My wife Anda is twenty-four," Papa says and, in a protective move, draws Mama closer to him.

"And you, young man??"

"The same."

"Well, well, a real pre-school bunch we have here, what more can I say! So I've been plying virtual adolescents with vodka!" The Major pulls out another bottle of vodka.

"Laura, Anda. Aha. And what is your name? Hans? Fritz? Fine, fine, I'm just joking. *Da.* Sit down! Sit! What the hell ... ? Sit down. I already said, I was just joking, besides it was stupid, I know, I know, I'm sorry." The Major holds out his hand to Papa.

"Jānis," Papa replies, not noticing the Major's hand.

"Aleksandr Ivanovich. You *pribalti*, don't use your patronymic, I know, I know. But it's foolish, *zrya*—a shame, because a father's name is important. Ah, that's why from the very beginning you seemed so odd to me! I enter and see—two young people sitting here. But where is that spark of Soviet youth, where the fire in the eyes? Pale, stiff. Frightened. I think, maybe I've caught them making love? No such thing—*Nye figa.* The fruit of their love wails from above, just look, what a big kid she is, legs right to the floor! Good for you, you started early. Early. Oh my, my—*Yomayo!* Deportees? Going home? Freed! Happy! Betrayers of the people? *Kulaks*—rich farmers? Bourgeois nationalists? Children and grandchildren of the enemies of the people?" The Major, now totally animated, mocks them openly and refills the glasses.

"We've been rehabilitated—you could say exonerated." Papa tries to remain calm.

Mama is frightened again. Mama is always worried that they may be sent back to Siberia.

"Johnny, Johnny," quietly she whispers a warning. But the Major has heard her.

"*Prekratyity*—That's enough! What kind of a name is that—Johnny? John? What kind of an *amerikanskiy, burzhuasniy, imperialisti-*

cheskiy outrage is this? Is a Soviet person, even if you are Latvian, allowed to call himself by that name? John! *Prekratyity!*" The Major is commanding an invisible army.

"That's just a nickname, just a nickname!" Mama begins to cry.

"A nickname? Aha, maybe a *klichka podpolnaya*—a code name? Latvians! You can't be trusted at all. *Vot*—see now how you've revealed your true, rotten Western nature!" Having uncovered their nature, the Major calms down. Time for a drink. The Major no longer offers any to the others. He turns to Mama.

"Anda, tell me your patronymic," the Major insists.

"Edmundovna," Mama whispers, sobbing.

"Anda Edmundovna! Are you afraid of my epaulets? Yes, you're afraid. But don't be afraid! You're a beautiful woman!"

"Leave my wife alone!" Papa jumps to his feet.

"Sit down wimp! Anda Edmundovna! Are you afraid of my medals? They're not decorations, although I deserve them, no, they're just shit medals! I see how afraid you are. Don't be afraid! But under the medals I have, do you know what? Can't you guess? A heart! I've got a heart there! Let's drink! Let's drink this *charka*—toast for Maima! Maima was my Estonian girlfriend. Fifteen years ago. Listen, Anda Edmundovna! Mai-ma! Mai-ma! Like a wolf I howled for her— Mai-ma! But I don't know her patronymic and didn't know it then; I couldn't find her on the list of scheduled deportees to cross it out! I had the opportunity, but I couldn't save her. See here, that's what happens when you don't use your patronymic. That's why I say a father's name is important. Maybe Maima is also returning home, also rehabilitated?" the Major asks Mama.

He clutches Mama's arm. How should Mama know? Laura also doesn't know, how should Laura know?

"Of course, she's also returning, and she too has some son of a bitch beside her, some John, *yebitvayumaty*—motherfucker. *Da,* I wouldn't even call a dog by that name! And he's also produced similar brats and hellions with her! Let her return, I don't begrudge it, let her return, the bitch—*blyad,* let her return. Mai-ma! Mai-ma!" The major howls like a wolf and pounds his chest so that the medals clang and jingle.

"Hey, you!" The Major turns to Papa. "Let's drink to beautiful women! Drink, John Adolfovich, drink, Fritz Hansovich, ha, ha, ha! A kick to your ribs! Anda Edmundovna, you too have a drink, *davai, davai*! Reap while there's still dew! Eh!" The major empties his glass in one gulp.

Papa also empties his glass. Mama too empties a glass! Right down to the bottom. What will Laura do with three drunken people?

"Rehabilitated, bastards, rehabilitated. Rehabilitated, scum, all of you rehabilitated! Innocent as lambs? Free as birds? Happy as pigs? Just think. Going home, the little shits! Is that just? Is that honorable? When will I, when will I go home? Who's going to rehabilitate me? Who'll rehabilitate me? Who? When will I return home? When?" The Major, head bent, talks to the floor. He sobs, moans, with snot flying in the air, screams at the ceiling, tries to get to his feet, still wants to say something to Papa and Mama, to Laura and to Maima, tries to pull his revolver out of the holster but fails, and finally his body slumps limply down on the seat.

"Thank God! He could have killed us!" Mama is still trembling.

"Killed us?" Laura exclaims in disbelief.

"No, no! He gave you a candy, after all." Mama takes her words back. How can words be taken back, Laura wonders.

"Stupid me, couldn't I have just held my tongue, did I have to tell about the fifteen years? A KGB Major is the perfect person to unburden my heart to! Anda, I'm an idiot! Forgive me! It's my fault. Why did I even have to talk? He's got a Nagant revolver. Do you think we should take it from him?"

"No, are you insane? He's drunk as a pig, Johnny. He'll sleep like a corpse and won't remember anything in the morning. He'll get off at the Uralskaya station. Please, please just calm down."

When Laura wakes up, the Major is no longer in the compartment. Laura's tummy hurts because she hasn't gone potty the whole time on the train. Laura needs to go, but doesn't want to go out to the toilet, so Laura will try to restrain herself.

"We're past the Urals," Mama says, overcome with joy.

"We're in Europe, Laura," Papa says proudly.

For Laura these are strange and empty words. Some kind of Urals, some kind of Europe. The same as Moscow, some kind of Moscow. For Laura many words are empty. Words that only have an outside, and nothing inside. A word that has an outside, a word that has a taste and a fragrance, a word that has color and fullness, Latvia is just such a word for Laura.

"Is Latvia still far?"

"It's closer now."

"How much closer?"

"Much closer."

"How much?" As usual, Laura persists and then immediately backs off.

Fine, alright, fine. Laura has something to do. Laura will eat the candy the Major gave her, and afterward she will carefully fold up the wrapper for safekeeping. She'll eat the candy slowly, very slowly, and also very slowly fold the wrapper. But where's the candy? Has Laura in her excitement not noticed that she's already eaten it? It's nowhere to be found. Laura searches her crumpled sheets, until shame rises and scalds her like a great heat wave—shame! Shame tumbles over Laura like a rockslide, shame! The sheets are soiled brown. Lara has gone potty in her bed! Oh awful, awful! The sheets are covered with stains, darker and lighter brown. Laura has shit herself, the big girl; humiliation drives Laura into a black corner, horrified. What will Madame Attendant say? She's going to yell it out all over the train! Laura will die from shame, she'll just die! Her despair escapes from her mouth as a scream.

"Mama!" Laura sobs, terrified, and Mama reads her thoughts. "Sweetie, it's only chocolate! Laurie, it's the candy! It just melted in the heat and spread over the sheets, look, the wrapping paper also got torn into pieces. It's alright, it's nothing, calm down, there, there. It's just a candy! Honey! My poor little baby! It's the melted candy, just the candy. Smell it! Well, do you see now, are you calm now?"

"We'll buy another one in Latvia," Papa says, trying to pacify Laura. "Many, many more. We'll buy lots of things in Latvia. Lots of candies, better ones, so don't cry for the sake of one measly candy. We shouldn't have taken anything from that bullshit Major!"

Papa doesn't understand anything! Because of a measly candy? Laura isn't crying because of a measly candy! It's fine that he doesn't understand. But it's true that the sheets don't smell of poop, they smell of chocolate. There is a difference after all.

Calming down, Laura notices that the Major has forgotten his hat. It's still hanging there where he hung it up. She could bring that to Grandpa! Grandpa surely doesn't have a hat like that! The blue color is beautiful. Grandpa would like it. Does Papa want the hat for himself? No, he throws it out of the window. Why did he do that?

Madame Attendant enters looking grumpy. The red lipstick has disappeared, the eyebrow arches have faded, her eyes are puffy.

"Has Comrade Major left his *furazhka* in the compartment?"

"I really don't know, but you can have a look," Papa says.

"I didn't see any *furazhka*." Mama says, appearing surprised.

"What is that—*furazhka*?" Laura asks.

Madame Attendant angrily slams the compartment door.

"Sour puss," Mama says.

"That's for sure," Papa says.

TRANSLATED FROM LATVIAN BY MARGITA GAILITIS
EDITED BY VIJA KOSTOFF

ARMIN ÖHRI

The Interrogation

November 23, 1947

Colonel Malek was always surprised by the disparate reactions of the condemned. Some trembled and whimpered, while others struggled with all their force, hitting out wildly and needing to be physically restrained, either with rope or with punches. Some wept in despair, letting out sharp, intermittent sobs. Others remained calm, as though they had long since come to terms with their fate.

With these latter convicts, whenever the colonel looked into their eyes he sensed an unexplainable peace, which sent chills through him, even though he wasn't the one who was going to die. As for this doctor, whose turn it would be in just a few minutes, Malek felt compelled to put an end to his frenetic lashings, with the help of his rifle butt. The screaming had been unbearable, but the whimpering that followed the blow wasn't much better. The colonel let out a sigh, and reached in his pocket for a handkerchief to wipe off the man's forehead. At the very least, this traitor should be able to look death in the face. The sentenced man's knees were limp, only the handcuffs behind his back held him upright against the tree trunk.

"Alright Polotsky, it'll all be over soon," the colonel said, and the man was spitting blood as he tried to respond.

Malek took two steps backwards to give the firing squad room. His eyes scanned the surrounding area. He noticed the iridescent light coming from the sky, which seemed to announce a storm's imminent arrival. The air had gotten cool, there was a cutting wind. The colonel turned up his jacket collar. The forest would have been quite beautiful, each detail full of enchantment and charm, if the atmosphere hadn't been poisoned by the presence of this absurd moment of execution.

The firing squad had taken their places. Malek cleared the shooting line and positioned himself a few meters behind the men, who were standing with their rifles raised. He wanted to wait a few more seconds before giving the command to shoot: with traitors, he always tried to stretch out the fear of death, to let it intensify to the limits of madness. This was his personal method of punishment. He lifted his hand and counted quietly to ten. When he dropped it, the sound of gunfire pierced the silence.

November 22, 1947

The detention room was run-down, and brought to mind the dingy dens and offices described in the American hard-boiled novels that were fetching nice prices on the black market. This was the first association that colonel Malek made as he entered the room where the traitor was waiting. The man was sitting on a chair behind a desk, his face stoic, hands slightly trembling. "May I have something to drink?" he asked politely.

Malek ignored the request and began.

"You're a doctor?"

"I've done nothing wrong," the man replied calmly. "What are you actually accusing me of, anyways?"

"Are you a doctor?" repeated the colonel irritably.

"And what if I were?"

Malek took a deep breath. "You've come to request repatriation, is that right Herr Polotsky?"

The man on the chair examined him closely. Malek looked down at the photo that was included in the intelligence report. The description fit: height and weight, hair color and eye color.

"Yes, I'm a doctor," the man responded hesitantly.

"And you've been working with Holmston-Smyslovsky?"

"Who?"

Malek tried to control himself. These interrogations were always tiresome, monotone, following a preset order that eventually became unbearable.

"Holmston," he repeated sharply.

This time the man shook his head.

"Holmston," the colonel raised his voice. "Holmston-Smyslovsky, Boris Holmston. Better known as General Holmston."

"I don't know anyone by that name."

"You were in the 1st Russian National Army."

"No. I don't know any general and I was never in any army."

"Where were you in April 1945?"

"Somewhere outside of Berlin, then later in the city proper."

"Nonsense. You were in Nuremberg and Eschenbach and who knows where else . . ."

"Good heavens, no! I was in Berlin! How many times do I have to say it?"

Malek stood up, walked around the table and hit the man across the face with his open hand. The blow came so surprisingly, and with such unexpected force, that the chair tipped and fell backwards. The colonel set his foot on the man's chest, leaned down and spoke with cold composure: "Let's start from the beginning. You have a document that was issued by the Liechtensteinian government?"

The man nodded, breathing heavily.

"Then you're Grigory Polotsky, doctor of the Russian National Army."

"No, damn it! The document isn't mine! I stole it at the customs office!"

Malek laughed. The absurd stories some of the detainees told him were too much. This time he went with his foot, and a lengthy scream announced the breaking of two ribs. The interrogation could have gone so smoothly.

November 21, 1947

For months, the hordes of those attempting to return had been practically unmanageable. Some sat in groups, most were entire families, or at least the surviving part of a family; others squatted in corners and tried to make the best of their situation. The few benches in the waiting room were occupied by the quickest and the strongest, while the pregnant and elderly were left with nothing. Thieves circulated through the confusion, trying to steal passports and travel documents, in order to cross back over and start a new life. But gradually, as the weeks passed, the stream of refugees diminished, fewer and fewer people passed through customs, and the situation seemed like it would soon return to normal.

Colonel Malek stepped through the room collecting travel documents in a battered cardboard box. After gathering around thirty or so, he returned to his office. He was always happy to close the door behind him, shutting himself off from the noise of the waiting room. He spilled out the contents of the box onto the table and began his tedious task. Grabbing a document, checking the date and stamp, comparing the entry with the official registration, and then putting it aside. It had all become so mechanical, so automatic. Malek yawned.

Ten minutes later, he was wide awake.

He picked up the telephone receiver, dialed a number, and for five minutes he was concentrated, tense, absorbed in conversation. He replaced the handset, and finally took a deep breath. He looked over the document in front of him, reading over and over the name that stood there: Polotsky, Grigory.

November 20, 1947

All the waiting had really done a job on their nerves. Every muscle, every tendon felt tense. The seats were uncomfortable: hard and without backs. Grigory stroked Sylvia's hand while his eyes incessantly scanned the room.

"There he is, over there," he whispered. "I noticed him yesterday. He tried to steal a passport three times, without success."

His companion looked in that direction. "The one in the gray coat?"

"Yes. Now pay attention, here's what we'll do . . ."

She observed the stranger wandering through the rows of seats, his face directed downwards. Just before the closed-off area, where the customs offices were located, he turned around. After a few steps he stood still and wiped his nose with a filthy handkerchief.

"He's the right height," Sylvia said.

"And my hair color," remarked Grigory.

"I'm scared," she said softly.

"It's going to work perfectly."

"I'm not worried about that," she said, "but it's just not right. They might kill him."

"Quiet," he grumbled. She remained silent.

The man was three rows away from them. The doctor reached in his pocket and pulled out a passport, which he placed on his chest, in plain sight. He pulled his companion toward him, and she closed her eyes and lay her head on his shoulder. Grigory leaned his head back, opened his mouth slightly, and let out a few snoring sounds.

He felt almost nothing as the stranger stole the passport.

Polotsky waited two more minutes before opening his eyes. The thief had disappeared. The doctor nudged his lover. "It worked," he said. "Soon a man by the name of Grigory Polotsky will cross into the Soviet Union and be arrested as a traitor."

"It's not right," Sylvia mumbled, thinking about the unlucky thief. "It's just not right." Nevertheless, the trace of a smile came across her face as she imagined their future, a future in their homeland, free, under new names.

TRANSLATED FROM GERMAN BY NATHANIEL DAVIS

Paulina Pukytė

FROM *A Loser and a Do-Gooder*

PIGEONS AND LIONS

IMMIGRANT: But I'm on my way to work! I need to get to work!

OFFICER: And what is your job?

IMMIGRANT: I work with pigeons.

OFFICER: With pigeons? Where?

IMMIGRANT: In a large square . . . you know . . . the one with the lions.

OFFICER: Trafalgar Square?

IMMIGRANT: Maybe. I don't know.

OFFICER: So what is your job?

IMMIGRANT: The pigeons sit on my hands and people take photographs.

OFFICER: Uh . . . That's not really a job.

THE LOSER AND THE DO-GOODER

"You see, when I first came to this country I met some bad people. They took my passport and I had to slave for them a whole year, but finally I ran away."

"To slave for them? What do you mean by 'to slave for them'?"

"I had to do everything ... For nothing. But I ran away from them."

"And where do you live now?"

"By the palace."

"What palace? Buckingham Palace?"

"I don't know. By the large one. Where the demonstration was yesterday. A lot of people were there."

"What sort of demonstration? The Tamil one?"

"Who? I don't know, there were a lot of people there."

"Was it by the Houses of Parliament?"

"Maybe. A beautiful, large palace."

"Who's going to let you sleep by the Houses of Parliament? They'd move you immediately."

"Well, not right by the palace ... I know a place there, on the grass, it's a great spot."

"I need some information about you. Do you have any illnesses?"

"I'm not ill. The only thing is I had my stomach removed, you see, I had three operations—they were very good doctors—they inserted some kind of tube, and I had to relieve myself into a bag. But then some good people took pity on me and did something so that I wouldn't need those bags anymore, and instead ..."

"Do you have any mental health problems?"

"My skull was split here when a bomb exploded."

"What bomb? A terrorist bomb?"

"What terrorists? This was a long time ago."

"Was this during your revolution?"

"What revolution? No, no, it was a German bomb."

"German? What year was this? I don't understand."

"There were lots of those shells lying around. Left over from the war."

"Which war? The Second World War?"

"I don't know, probably. From the last one. We found a grenade and threw it into a bonfire. And then: bang! My friend was torn to pieces, and I injured my head here ... Since then I always see these sort of arrows along the edges of plates, but considering how long it's been since I last ate off a plate, they—"

"Listen, I don't have a lot of time. Where were you born? In Lithuania?"

"Both of my parents were deported. They met in Siberia, where they got married. I was born there but grew up in Lithuania . . ."

"So they were deported to Lithuania?"

"Actually, I really only wanted to ask you about getting my clothes back."

"Yes, you keep asking about your clothes. But believe me, your clothes are not your biggest problem right now."

"But what will people think if I go back to Lithuania dressed like this?! How am I going to enter the country looking like this? I don't have any other clothes. I don't have any money to buy any clothes."

"Well, alright, what clothing was there? How many items, a lot?"

"No, not a lot. A pair of track suit bottoms, a black leather jacket, and a t-shirt . . ."

"And that's it? That's all?"

"Yes, but you have to understand, those clothes are very important to me because . . ."

"Let's get back to the matter at hand. You're suspected of having stolen a carp. A very large and very expensive carp that recently disappeared from a lady's pond. Worth a thousand pounds. The police were looking for the culprits and came across you in the street. They say that you had a very strong smell of fish on you, and for that reason they thought it was you who stole the carp. Since they didn't find the carp on you, they suspected that you had eaten it."

"I didn't steal any carp!"

"So why were you smelling of fish?"

"Well, I met up with some friends—they also collect scrap metal. We wanted to get warm, we were drinking vodka in a park, I think we were eating herring . . . we had to chase the vodka down with something . . ."

THE THEORY OF PROBABILITY

"It says here that last night you were drunk and yelling loudly in the street. Would you agree with that?"

140

"Yelling? I don't remember, I was drunk."

"It says that you were shouting. Were you shouting?"

"I don't remember."

"I understand that you don't remember, but could that have been the case?"

"I don't remember."

"I'm not asking you now if you remember or not, I'm asking if that's possible. Is that possible or not? Yes or no?"

"Well, no, it's not possible. Why would I be shouting?"

"So it's not possible?"

"No."

"So you're saying that last night you weren't yelling in the middle of the street?"

"Well, I don't remember anything."

"But you agree that you were drunk?"

"I was drunk."

"In other words you don't remember."

"I don't remember."

"So it's possible that you were yelling."

"No, that's not possible."

"I understand that you don't remember—when I drink, sometimes I don't remember everything. But if you don't remember, it means that there is the possibility that's how it was."

"Well, no, it couldn't have been like that."

"So you say you weren't yelling?"

"No, I don't remember anything."

"But are you saying you really weren't shouting? That that's not the truth?"

"It might be the truth. But no, it couldn't have been like that. Why would I shout?"

PLEASE COME QUICKLY

"Hello, I need the police, my husband's been beaten up, come quickly!"

"Hello. What happened?"

"My husband was beaten up, he's covered in blood, come quickly!"

"What's the surname?"

"Marcinkevičius."

"Muscavities?"

"Marcinkevičius."

"Nickaveshees?"

"Mar-cin-ke-vi-čius!"

"Mersintevikeys?"

"MAR-CIN-KE-VI-ČIUS!"

"Perhaps you could spell it?"

"M."

"N?"

"M!"

"M as in mother?"

"Yes."

"And after that?"

"A as in alfa."

"Alpha."

"R as in rocket, C as in citrus, I as in ... I as in ... Icarus!"

"What?"

"Alright, I as in ... India, then Namibia ... Kuwait ... India ... Canada ... India ... Uruguay ... Somalia."

"Got it: Martinkinkykiss. Does your husband have the same surname?"

"That's my husband's surname, my husband's!"

"I was asking for your surname. Is it the same surname?"

"Yes, Marcinkevičienė"

"So it's not the same?"

"It's only the ending that's different, only the ending, it's the same surname, or, to be exact, it's the same surname but only the ending is different—"

"So is it the same or different?"

"It's a bit different ..."

"Maybe you could spell it?"

"Let's say it's the same! Come as quickly as you can, he's been beaten up, beaten up!"

"Who beat him up?"

"I don't know. Friends!"

"So was it friends or don't you know?"

"Well, they're not my friends, they're his friends."

"Your husband's friends?"

"No, not his friends, they're our neighbor's friends. Come as quickly as you can, I'm begging you!"

"Your neighbor's friends? Where was he beaten up?"

"Here, in our house!"

"Your neighbor's friends were in your house?"

"A friend came in and . . ."

"Which friend?"

"Well, not a friend, the neighbor!"

"Where does this neighbor live?"

"In the same flat, in the same flat!"

"In the same flat as his friends?"

"In the same flat as us, as us!"

"So you live together?"

"Well, not together, not together, he's in another room!"

"And his friends?"

"I don't know where his friends are from, what's the difference, come as quickly as you can!"

"Miss, don't get upset now, I need to get all the information first and only then will we be able to come and assist you . . . What did they use to beat him with?"

"Everything, hands, feet—"

"Did they use any weapons?"

"Yes, they did, yes, they did!"

"What kind?"

"Well, those, golf sticks—"

"Golf clubs?"

"Well, baseball sticks, what do you call them?"

"Baseball bats?"

"Well, yes, golf bats, I don't know—"

"The ones they play golf with?"

"Well, yes, yes!"

"The ones they use to hit a ball with, on a green, yes?"

"Yes, yes, a ball! They're made of wood!"

"They're made of wood? Golf clubs are metal!"

"OK, then, maybe they were baseball clubs!"

"So were they golf clubs or baseball bats?"

"How would I know, how would I know, what's the difference, isn't it the same thing, why are you asking these stupid questions?"

"Please, Miss, don't yell at me. I need to get the information from you so we can help your husband."

"OK, OK, but he's bleeding, a lot, please hurry!"

"Where is he bleeding?"

"His head's bleeding, please hurry!"

"His head? Which part of his head?"

"I don't know, the temple and the back of the head, it's bleeding in five different places!"

"Five places? And where else?"

"I've just told you!"

"You've mentioned only two places."

"Well, maybe four!"

"You said five."

"Well, I don't really know, I can't see, there's so much blood, from all the different wounds on his head!"

"Is he bleeding anywhere else?"

"His head, his head!"

"Is he bleeding anywhere else?"

"I don't know, I don't know! How am I supposed to know?"

"I need to know where else he's bleeding."

"Please hurry, he's not speaking anymore! He's losing consciousness!"

"I need to know where else he's bleeding."

"I don't know, I don't know, why do you keep asking me, please come quickly!"

"Miss, the quicker you give us the information we need the quicker we'll be able to come. So please don't interrupt ..."

"Oh, God, he's collapsed. Oh, no!"

"Don't you need an ambulance?"

"Yes, yes, the police and an ambulance!"

"So why haven't you called for an ambulance?"

"I have, I have! I'm calling you now! I've already called!"

"You called earlier? So have they arrived?"

"I don't know, I don't know!"

"Where are those friends now?"

"What friends?"

"The ones who beat up your husband?"

"They're not my friends!"

"Alright then, your neighbors."

"They've left the house!"

"They've left?"

"They've driven off!"

"So they've gone out of the house or driven off?"

"They've driven off."

"In what?"

"A car perhaps, I don't know, I don't know! Please hurry!"

"What's your address?"

"Favcit Road—"

"What?"

"Fakit . . . Fuckwit—"

"There is no need for that. Give me the address!"

"Faceit or perhaps Favcheat—"

"Perhaps you could spell it?"

"F as in factory."

"Yes. Foxtrot."

"What?"

"Carry on."

"A as in alpha."

"Yes."

"Two V's."

"What?"

"V as in . . . V as in . . ."

"W?"

"What?"

"What's the letter?"

"As in water maybe? C as in circus."

"Carry on."

"E as in … E as in …"

"As in echo?"

"Yes!"

"And after that?"

"T as in tango!"

"T as in tango."

"T as in tango!"

"I've already got that."

"And again!"

"What again?"

"T as in tango!"

"Two T's?"

"Yes, I think so! Or maybe one. What's the difference? Why are you asking me these ridiculous questions?!"

"Fawcett. The number?"

"Whose number?"

"The house number."

"Four – ten."

"Forty?"

"Four, dash, ten!"

"Four, three, ten?"

"Not three, dash!"

"Three dashes?"

"One dash."

"One, dash, what?"

"Four, dash, ten!"

…

"There's no such address."

"What do you mean, there's no such address? No such address? We live here!"

"According to the information I have there is no such address. What's the post code?"

"The post code? How would I know that?"

"How could you not know your own post code? Everyone knows their post code."

"Quickly, quickly, come quickly, he's collapsed, he's already unconscious!"

"How can we come to you if we don't know where to go?"

OWN LIFE

"A man died in your room."

"So I heard."

"What was his name?"

"I don't know."

"How did he die?"

"I don't know.

"He had a lot of injuries, it's obvious that he was beaten for a long time."

"I didn't see anything like that. Everyone at our place minded their own business, and I didn't stick my nose into other people's business either. I'm not the sort of person to stick my nose in other people's business."

"Who else, besides you, lived in that room?"

"Oh, lots of people lived there ... One, two, ... plus the Poles ... fourteen people. But I don't know their names."

"How long did you live there?"

"Two or three months."

"For three months you lived in a twenty square-meter room with fourteen people and you don't know their names? How's that possible?"

"Well, I was introduced to them, his name is this, his name is that, but how are you going to remember them all?"

"Are you saying that you didn't know any of them?"

"Not really. We would just say 'hello' and 'good-bye,' that's all."

"But you slept on the same mattress with one of them, pressed up against one another."

"Yes, but not like a man with another man!"

"But still, right next to each other."

"So what? I had my own life."

EPILOGUE. DEATH OF A POET

BOY: Listen! Can you hear the rejoicing? Do you know who's rejoicing?

MOTHER: Who?

BOY: The grasshoppers! The grasshoppers are rejoicing!

MOTHER: They're not rejoicing. They're chirping.

TRANSLATED FROM LITHUANIAN BY ROMAS KINKA

NICO HELMINGER

FROM *Luxembourg Lions*

then we rode the revanche de la flèche du sud route. we rode the revenge of the revenge. by bike, over the sidewalk. the winner got to kiss sus. lorang always won. except for once. once i won. i was proud to win, but they laughed because they had let me win just so they could see how i would kiss sus. i was ten years old, and she was eleven or twelve. and already into the dirty stuff, they said. with lorang and with mertens too. a cousin of his. or maybe not. the only girl that always went along with us to war. people said she wasn't a real girl. a tomboy, some said. sus stuck her tongue into my mouth. i remember exactly how it felt. the taste of the cigarette that she'd smoked in secret. i didn't know what i was supposed to do.

—look at him, he looks like a fish, one of them said, and they all laughed. i acted like it didn't bother me. i just went along with them. in mertens's gang. in the war against venanzi. in the war of the border. in the war on the prinzenring. in the hiel, where mertens senior had his garden. with the garden shed. that's where we dragged little delé. the mascot of venanzi's gang. sus was there and also one of sus's girlfriends.

little delé had been strolling along the rue du brill with a loaf of bread under his arm. there were six or seven of us.

—don't touch me, the italian's gonna smash all your faces! said little delé.

the italian, that was venanzi.

—you're coming with us, said mertens.

little delé tried to run away, but one of us tripped him. he fell down and his nose started bleeding.

—he was already bleeding before we even touched him, said mertens.

—well, come on, then! said lorang, who was mertens's first officer.

i was the second officer. even though i didn't hang around with them much and mostly stayed on the sidelines. but mertens liked me. his father worked in our company and maybe that's why mertens thought it was a good idea to treat me nicely. it's possible his dad had said something to him.

i was in the gang. in brill you had to be in a gang.

—come on! said lorang, and grabbed little delé's arm. delé stopped resisting and walked with us toward hiel like a prisoner. the barrier was down in the rue jean-pierre bausch. in front of the barrier mertens said to delé: try anything and i'll throw you under the train.

—got any money? asked lorang.

little delé didn't answer. lorang turned out his pockets. he still had a few cents left over, change from the bakery.

—we can't buy much with that, said mertens, and sent lorang off to buy some gum. as lorang ran off to old mrs. turmes's shop, we walked on ahead. mertens had picked up a birch switch from the ground, and now and then he would whip the back of little delé's legs. delé cried out. his nose had stopped bleeding, but when he wiped a tear from his eye he smeared some blood over his face.

—faster! said mertens and cracked the switch again.

lorang came running up with three pieces of gum.

—you want a piece? mertens asked delé. when delé hesitated, mertens said: i'm not like that. even the little ones get something from me!

when delé reached for it, mertens yanked the gum away and laughed:

—ha, i bet you'd like some!

in the garden shed mertens said, alright, twerp, tell us where your treasures are hidden.

treasures. a bag of spoils from the second world war: two nazi helmets, a bayonet, pieces of a uniform, and a great big swastika flag. no idea where venanzi managed to get all that stuff. in any case his dad didn't want him showing it off in the street. didn't want him storing it in the house either. that's why venanzi had it hidden somewhere else.

delé didn't say anything, just whimpered.

—we're waiting, said mertens, taking a bite of delé's bread.

—stop it, i'm gonna get in trouble, said little delé.

—you hear that? asked mertens, he'll get in trouble with his mommy.

and everybody laughed. sus laughed loudest. mertens liked that.

—doesn't she have a nasty laugh, he said.

then sus's friend also gave a nasty laugh.

—you're not going home till you tell us, said lorang.

—i don't know anything, delé said.

—that's what they all say at first, said mertens, but later, after we rough 'em up a bit, they suddenly remember.

—but i really don't know, said delé.

—i'll bash your nose in, said lorang.

then little delé really began to cry. sitting there, pushing his tears out like he had a cramp in his belly.

—that's not gonna help much, said mertens, tell us where the stuff is and you can go.

—but i really don't know, he whimpered. broken voice, every word choked by tears.

—we'll make you talk, said mertens and whipped the switch. he signaled to lorang, who grabbed his nose, dragged him down slowly, and when he was bent low, let the tip of his nose go and smacked him right in the face with his open hand. delé gave a little cry. when he looked up his nose was bleeding again. his whole body was trembling. if he really knew where the hiding place was he would have told us. but he just whimpered. mertens whipped his legs a few times with the switch. delé crumpled to the floor and cried. eventually even mertens realized that delé didn't know anything.

—what do we do with him now? he asked. he was still chewing away at his gum. this guy was ready to attack at any moment. when nobody replied, he ran the switch over delé's fly and said: undo it!

delé's eyes were full of fear. he looked at each of us, one by one, to see if there was somebody who would say to mertens: that's enough! let him go!

but nobody moved. delé's lips were quivering. he looked like he was going to beg for mercy.

—go ahead, pray, said mertens.

delé wouldn't pull his pants off. so lorang did it for him. delé struggled one last time and got a kick in the ribs from one of us. he lay bowled over on the ground and his bum was showing.

—show it! said mertens.

behind me sus and her friend were giggling.

—show it! mertens repeated.

lorang forced delé to get up. he was holding both of his hands in front of his prick. lorang pulled them away.

—oh la la! said mertens, i've never seen such a massive dong!

and everybody laughed. delé instinctively covered himself again and got another whack from mertens's switch. he was red in the face, red from the blood, and red again from shame.

—you have to yank it, said mertens, yank and rub it, then it'll get bigger.

sus's friend was laughing like crazy. mertens stood there, fiddling with the garden shears. suddenly delé made a strange sound. his stomach burbled out of fear. he made a horrible face, clenched his teeth, his mouth twisted and his eyes rolled back. for a second it looked like he was going to have an epileptic fit. and then the burbling sound again, this time much louder. and already the shit was running down his leg. a thin, brown streak that stank like a trailer of dung. delé cried away. the crying pulsed through his body. he couldn't control himself, standing, quivering, crying, and he defecated some more. sus gave a horrible cry, whether thrilled or disgusted, it was hard to say. mertens laughed, like i'd never heard him laugh before. when he laughed himself out, he was overcome by a sudden rage and screeched like a crazy man at delé, who stood there, tiny, wretched, and sniveling: you pig! is that all you can do? shit over everything here? delé looked off into the distance. he'd run out of tears and he just sniffed back a glob of snot. he stood there like someone who had lost all hope.

—clean it up! said mertens, and threw a rag at him. delé obediently wiped up. then mertens shoved him out the door, naked, and threw his clothes after him.

—you sure smell like shit, he said, and laughed again. we all laughed. we laughed like crazy. delé piled his clothes together and ran off, clutching them under his arm. he ran to the other side of the garden, to where the woods start. he hid himself behind a hedge to get dressed. we were still laughing.

—this calls for a beer! said mertens, triumphantly.

i despised little delé. and i despised mertens too. and i especially despised that pig venanzi with his two nazi helmets who, i found out later, beat up little delé again just for letting himself get caught by us.

TRANSLATED FROM GERMAN BY JASON BLAKE

Rumena Bužarovska

Waves

THE MORNING WE LEFT, I remember my mother woke me very early. I didn't want to get up, so mommy put my orange coat on over my pajamas. She put some socks on my feet and had such a hard time pulling on my boots that she twisted my ankle a bit. Then she picked me up and carried me to the front door, where a big man in a thick coat and a black turtleneck was waiting. "Let's go," my mother said to him, and he picked up the two big suitcases leaning against the wall and followed my mother to the main gate. I wanted to ask where we were going and whether my mother had remembered my teddy bear and my diary, but I just couldn't open my mouth or unglue the eyelashes of my left eye.

It was dark and cold outside. One of my pajama legs had ridden up and I felt the air rush in like a jet of cold water, and the little hairs on my legs stood on end. My mother whispered something in my ear, but her words disappeared into the air and all I heard was a "shhh." In the parking lot, the man opened the back door of a big black car—it wasn't one of ours—and we got in. The leather seats were cold. My mother covered me with her coat and put my head on her lap. The car shook when the man got in and closed the door; then I heard the hum of the engine, and finally I could feel we had started moving. The city lights passed above through the fogged-up windows and slowly became milky white spots between my eyelids. I couldn't see my mother's face very well because she was looking through the window without wiping the moisture off it. Then she tried to draw a woman's eye but accidentally smudged it in the right-hand corner. She erased it and drew two mountains next to it, with a sun in between. Slowly the car warmed up, and the sun and the mountains started running down the glass. Suddenly, I was all soft and warm and fell fast asleep again. I remember waking up after a while and seeing that my mother had changed me from my pajamas into my brown corduroy pants and yellow sweat-er. The light was purple outside and the moon looked like a sharp sickle wedged in the corner of the window. It followed us, overtaking the telephone poles and the naked trees. Then I fell asleep again.

The driver of the black car took the two suitcases out of the trunk and put them in front of the café where my mother and I sat down to have breakfast. I heard the people around us speaking Greek, and I saw the sea. I remembered the summers when we used to come here on vacation. But this place didn't seem familiar. When we sat down, my mother told me we were in Greece, in a small town, without tell-ing me which, and said we were here on vacation. Then she ordered toast and orange juice for me. She just drank coffee and smoked four cigarettes while I ate.

"Why are we going on vacation now?" I asked my mother. I knew she'd be upset even more if I asked about my father right away, so I de-cided to wait a bit.

"Because it's very cold in Skopje and there's a lot of hassle," she told me hastily, through the smoke coming out of her mouth and nostrils.

"What kind of hassle?" I asked her.

"Oh, all sorts," she said, stubbing out her cigarette and opening her cigarette case to get out another. Her nails weren't as pretty as usual. They were broken in a few places and the golden nail polish was chipped.

"Is daddy coming?" I asked a little uneasily. I knew she wouldn't like it.

"Yes, he is," she answered in a sharp voice.

"When?" came out even more quietly and shyly.

"Probably next week," she said and took out her cell phone. She al-ways took out her cell phone and pretended she had text messages to read or write when she didn't want to talk to me anymore. Then she began typing a message.

"Who are you writing to?"

"Frosi, I've told you a hundred times: that's my business, and it's impolite of you to ask."

"Where are we going?" I kept on with my questions. I also drank the last sip of my juice.

"To a beautiful little island where you'll be able to swim in the sea and have a nice time," my mother said and tried to smile. She stroked me on the head with her hand holding the cigarette and left ribbons of smoke floating around me.

"Which little island?"

My mother sighed. "Frosina, you ask sooo many questions. How about you let me get some rest too, huh? You slept in the car, but I'm dead tired."

"What about me missing two tests this week and not going to school at all?"

My mother sighed again impatiently and kept typing on her phone. After a short pause, she said, "Don't worry. You just enjoy yourself."

"Can I have some more juice?" I asked, looking at the empty glass.

My mother got up and left some coins on the table. "Not now. We'll miss our ferry. Come on, get your coat on."

"But I want some more juice."

"I'll buy you some on the way. Come on, hurry up! We'll be in trouble if we miss the ferry," my mother said and took the suitcases by their handles. I grabbed onto her coat, but she pushed me aside because she had to pull the two suitcases along behind her. Her face went red and she started breathing through her mouth. We walked for five minutes before reaching our ferry, and there a man ran up to help my mother carry the suitcases on board.

"If you look carefully, I'm sure you'll see some dolphins," my mother told me when the ferry cast off. I was glued to the porthole after that. It was dirty and scratched, and I had to look very hard so I wouldn't miss a dolphin jumping between the waves. I peered through the porthole for the whole trip and hoped to be lucky enough to see at least one. And maybe I did, but I couldn't be sure if they were dolphins I saw in the distance or just small white waves. I tugged my mother's arm so she would come and see them, but she was asleep with her mouth open and her head leaning against the back of the seat.

I seized the chance to rummage in her handbag and check her cell phone messages to see if daddy had happened to write. When he wrote messages, they always came from unknown numbers.

156

Thinking of you.kiss frosina

That was the last message, sent that morning at nine o'clock. It made me feel warm inside, so I put the phone back into my mother's bag right away and leaned back in my seat to enjoy the feeling. I closed my eyes and thought of my father.

My father had left home almost a month before us and said he was going away on a trip. The last time I saw him, he was crouching at the front door to say good-bye to me. His unshaven cheeks scratched my face, but I always liked that. I pressed my cheek against his glasses and made them all sticky. "Ouch, cutie, that was more like a strangle than a cuddle!" he said laughing, and took off his glasses to clean them, but what could he wipe them with? He held his tie, then looked at his jacket, and in the end he grabbed my blouse with his left hand and held his glasses up to my mouth with his right: "Puff!" I wanted to know when he was coming back, and he said "soon." "In a week?" I asked again. He just kissed me, and I took that as a yes.

My mother had locked herself in the bedroom. She was probably crying, since the radio was blaring inside. Whenever she and my father quarreled, she went into the bedroom, slammed the door, locked it twice, and turned the radio on loud. Sometimes my father banged on the door and yelled "Meri, open up, Meri," and then "Meri, don't make a scene, open the door," and in the end "Meri, open the door or I'll break it down!" Once he really did break it down. After that, my mother started opening the door if my father started knocking on it. Through the radio noises I heard muffled yelling, mostly my mother's. When my father got mad, he talked through his teeth in a low voice. He only emphasized a few words and phrases: "break it down," "stop it," "you'll see," and "impossible." My mother mostly yelled, "Why?"

My parents had been fighting more and more often in the few months before we left, when my father started being on TV a lot. First he was fired from the position of director, and then he was often in the news. When they talked about him on the news, I wasn't allowed to watch and had to go to my room. No matter how hard I pressed my ear to the door, I couldn't hear the TV very well or make out what the newsreaders were saying about my father. I realized it couldn't be anything good because no one talked about it when I was around. One day, when my mother and father had gone out, I turned on the

TV to watch the news. There was a report about him and some bank accounts, and then they showed our cars, our house, my grandmother's renovated house, and the apartment where we used to live a few years ago. They also showed my father sitting behind a desk and talking to another man who used to come and visit us, and at the end they showed my mother going into a store in the shopping mall. She looked very pretty, but when the woman with the microphone came up to her, mommy got angry and turned away.

Then the phone started ringing a lot. Sometimes both my mother and my father were home, but they didn't pick it up. Several times my mother answered the phone and started yelling at the caller, and there were times when she would just hang up and ask my father to come into the bedroom so they could fight. Once I picked up the phone, even though I wasn't allowed to. I was at home alone, and the phone rang more than ten times. My father had bought me a cell phone so they could call me on it, so I wouldn't need to answer the normal phone at all—but I really, really wanted to know who was calling, so I picked it up and said hello. I heard a rasping woman's voice at the other end, almost like a whisper. "That father of yours is a swindler, I'm telling you, a damned swindler!" and she hung up. I didn't know for sure what a swindler was, but it had to be something bad, so I didn't want to ask mommy or daddy what the word meant. Fifteen minutes later, the phone rang again. I didn't want to answer it, but I was dying of curiosity, so I picked it up again.

"Hello?" I said. I hoped it might be my grandma. I could ask her what a swindler was.

At first I heard only a crackle and breathing. "Hello?" I asked again.

"Your mother is a slut, and you're a little bastard," a deep, hoarse voice told me this time, and hung up.

I knew "bastard" was a bad word, but again I didn't know what it meant. I went and lay in the armchair in the living room and cried a bit. Then our housekeeper came to make lunch, so I decided to ask her about the words.

"Gotsa, what's a swindler?"

Gotsa stopped in the middle of cutting a bloody piece of meat. With the top of the hand that held the knife, she brushed an imaginary lock of hair from her forehead. She always did that when she was thinking what to answer. "A crook," she finally told me. "A crook?" I repeated, amazed. "Yes, a crook," she said and went on cutting the meat.

"And what does 'slut' mean? And 'bastard,'" I asked her, although I expected she would tell me off, or not answer at all.

Gotsa stopped cutting the meat, but she kept looking at it and didn't raise her head. "Those are very bad words. Where did you hear them?"

"At school. Please tell me, Gotsa. I promise no one will find out you told me," I begged.

"Those are not words for children," Gotsa said and turned on the little TV set in the kitchen so I couldn't ask her any more questions.

Still, some children used those words, especially the boys. Nikola, for example, often chased Darko around the classroom, and then he would call him "bastard," which had to be a rude word. Also, once I overheard two teachers talking, and one told the other, "Maya's a real slut," and turned her head in disgust and looked down. Then she saw me and blushed. That's how I knew it was also a very bad word.

No one at school called me a "bastard" or told me my mother was a slut. But ever since they began showing daddy on TV, I noticed other children whispering behind my back. Bilyana was the only one who still played with me in the lunch break. A few days before my father left, Bilyana and I wanted to play with the other girls from our class. Milena had a new phone and was showing it to her friends. When Bilyana and I came up, Milena hid her phone. All the girls fell silent and looked at us. "Bilyana can see it, but you can't," Milena told me. Christina, Milena's best friend, looked at Bilyana and told her, "Don't you know she's a child of crooks."

"Child of crooks, child of crooks!" several girls chanted quietly. I ran away and waited in the classroom for the lunch break to end. Bilyana didn't come in to see me, as I hoped she would. Not only did she not come in, but she didn't talk to me at all anymore, so I stopped going out during the lunch breaks. Instead, I sat in the classroom and looked through my notebooks.

Two days before my mother and I left, while my father was away on his trip, someone smashed my bedroom window at night. I woke up scared and started to scream. That's why I didn't feel too bad about my mother taking me to Greece. I was sad only because I didn't know when my father would be coming.

Although at first my mother wouldn't tell me the name of the little island we were traveling to, I read it on the ferry ticket anyway. When we arrived there, my mother crouched down and looked me straight in the eye. She said that when we went back to Skopje I wasn't allowed to tell anyone where I'd been. I was to lie that I'd been visiting my grandma in the countryside. I nodded.

We stayed in a hotel near the harbor on the little island. They gave us a room on the top floor with a great view of the sea, the waves, another little island a bit farther from ours, and the ships that arrived every day. The sun set behind the hotel, so every evening the island opposite our room became pink, purple, and then dark blue, and in the end it disappeared. My mother and I sat on the terrace every evening and guessed what the next color would be. We played cards every day. There was a small sandy beach near our hotel, but it wasn't warm enough to swim, so sometimes we sat on the beach instead of the terrace and played without swimming. I didn't mind because the hotel had two indoor pools. I could swim and play in the smaller one, and my mother swam in the big pool in the mornings. We watched TV, went to breakfast, lunch, or dinner, went for walks on the beach, or read books my mother had brought from Skopje. She also bought some magazines with pretty women in them. We looked through them together, although they were in Greek and we didn't understand a word.

Those were the nice things about our little island. But there were bad things, too. For example, mommy sometimes cried into her pillow at night when she thought I wouldn't hear her. Sometimes I cried too, quietly so she wouldn't hear me, because she'd stopped comforting me when I cried and just started to get angry. A few times she slapped me in the face, and all because of daddy. After she slapped me, she explained that I shouldn't ask her so often about when daddy was coming because he had work to do and she didn't know when to expect him. "But he will be coming soon!" she said. The slap stung my cheek, but it felt good because it hurt just as much as I missed daddy. I also missed the teddy bear I used to sleep with, which my mother had forgotten to pack. I missed Gotsa's meals, too. Every day I got more and more bored. The second time my mother slapped me in the face she said it was for "being a pain in the neck" and for "whining too much." She said there was nothing more we could do, "the situation is as it is," and I shouldn't "hassle her" so much. The third time she slapped me was when she saw I had been reading her cell phone messages. Daddy was sending messages, and mommy didn't tell me or do the things daddy asked her to do.

I don't know.problems again.kiss frosi for me.

This message arrived; my mother read it, pursed her lips, and went to the bathroom, leaving the phone on the table. I waited until she had locked the door and let the water run in the basin, and only then did I take the phone. I quickly opened the last message to see if it was from daddy. Then I started reading the other messages, too. A lot of them were from unknown numbers, just like daddy's messages.

I miss you. The city is empty without you.

This one didn't mention me, and that made me feel a pang in my chest. So I started looking through the other messages from unknown numbers, and I was in one of them:

I'll call you some day soon.tell frosi-wosi that daddy loves her.

I had a lump in my throat and felt like I was about to cry. Mommy never told me that daddy loved me, nor did she ever say that he sent me a kiss. My eyes went blurry with tears, but I kept reading until my mother came back in.

When are we going to meet? I can't stand it without you any more. I need you.

Just then, my mother came out of the bathroom and caught me holding her phone. I could have lied to her that I'd wanted to play some game, but I got such a fright when I saw her that I jumped and the phone landed on the floor. My mother's nostrils flared in anger. There was also that wrinkle between her brows that only stands out when she gets really mad. She knelt down, picked up the phone, and saw that I'd read the last message. Then she slapped my face twice and said, "Shame on you! *Shame* on you!"

I didn't dare to read mommy's messages from then on, but daddy came soon afterward anyway.

Daddy came while I was asleep. When I got up, I found him on the terrace. He and my mother were sitting in the deck chairs, drinking coffee, smoking, and not talking. My father was playing with the cigarette box on the table, and my mother had her sunglasses on. I ran up to him. "Boy, I missed you!" he yelled and hugged me tight.

"I'm not a boy, I'm a girl," I said in a baby voice and pressed my face into his neck. It smelled of cologne and wasn't prickly.

"I know you're not a boy, cutie, it's just a saying," he explained playfully and then started kissing me on the cheeks. My mother stared out to sea and didn't smile. I was sorry she didn't want to hug and be happy with us. Maybe she'd already been happy that morning when she saw him, I thought.

Then we all went inside, and I showed my father the games mommy and I played, the drawings I'd done, and the two books I'd read. My father said I was very clever and stroked me on the head. He seemed fuller in the face and had soft bags under his eyes. His hair had gone completely gray. Meanwhile, my mother was in her room the whole time. She said she had a headache, so my father and I went for a walk along the small beach near the hotel and talked. While we were sitting on the sand, my father gave me a bracelet made of very small blue glass beads. He told me it would protect me from bad luck and that he brought it for me from Turkey. He said he'd have to travel a lot in the few months ahead, but after that he'd be home with me. I asked him how much longer my mother and I would be on vacation. "A little longer, cutie," he answered. I also asked him when he would be leaving, and he only said he'd be here with me for a little while. I wanted to ask many more things, but he quickly suggested a shell-collecting competition, shouting "one, two, three," and we both started running along the beach.

My father had come in a big white car. He said he'd borrowed it to drive around Greece, and we drove in it to the other side of the island to eat at a nice restaurant where they served fish. On the way, we saw places my mother and I didn't know, but she kept quiet and didn't react when I pointed to things and said, "Look, mommy, look." She just asked me to leave her alone because she had a headache. We got out of the car, and I went on ahead of my mother and father.

"Please don't make a scene," my father said to her quietly so I wouldn't hear.

"I'm not making a scene, I have a headache," my mother answered loudly. My father was about to say something more, but I jumped in between them and took them both by the hand. My mother's hand was limp, cold, and sweaty. Then we sat down at the restaurant on a big terrace overlooking the sea. In front of us there was a lovely small beach with pebbles in many different colors, and there were a few puppies running around the terrace that my father told me not to pet after I'd washed my hands.

My mother sat with her arms crossed and looked at the sea. When she took off her sunglasses, she had bags under her eyes like my father. The waiter first brought us salad in a big bowl and we all got down to eating. My mother chewed slowly. Then she turned toward my father:

"And? How long is this going to go on for?" I noticed that her nostrils were wide and flaring.

My father looked at her over the rim of his glasses. Then he finished his mouthful of salad and wiped his mouth, which was greasy from oil.

"Meri, please," he said irritably and gave her a pained glance.

"*Please* what? Tell me how long we're going to be here because I can't take it anymore. Frosina's bored, too," my mother said.

"I'm not bored," I decided to butt in, so my father wouldn't be offended. I felt sorry my mother was attacking him.

"Frosina, please don't interfere," my mother said. She looked at me with contempt and let out a puff of disapproval. Just then, the waiter came and brought two huge red lobsters. In front of me, he put a plate of small fried fish, just the kind I liked.

"Meri, I'd like to have dinner like a normal family tonight, and then we can have this conversation in private, if you like," my father told my mother calmly and, using a pair of pliers the waiter had brought him, broke open one of the lobster's claws.

"You can't pretend we're a normal family, because we aren't," my mother said while cracking the lobster's armor in several places with the pliers. Her chin began to quiver and her mouth winced. "We simply aren't," she repeated, and this time her voice trembled. "We haven't lived as a *normal* family for a long time." My mother's voice trembled ever more and became louder and louder. A young woman at the next table took a sip of wine and began looking at us. Our eyes met. My mother dropped the pliers onto the plate with a loud clang. My father kept eating in silence, breaking his lobster calmly and eating the meat inside.

"We've been living here like boarders for a whole month now. I can't take it anymore. Do you think I enjoy it?" my mother scowled and tried to light a cigarette, but her finger slipped off the lighter a few times. When the cigarette was lit, she threw the lighter onto the table.

Now even the young man sitting with the woman at the next table turned toward us and looked at my mother. But she continued: "We've been hanging around here for days, and on top of that I'm supposed to keep explaining what's going on and when you're going to come. What am I supposed to do?"

My father kept eating in silence, looking out at the sea. His cheeks went slightly red.

"Why don't you say something?" my mother yelled. I touched her hand to stroke it, thinking it would maybe calm her down, but she pulled her hand away angrily and reached for the ashtray.

"Meri, please don't go on like this, particularly in front of the child."

"In front of the child—," my mother repeated with a trembling voice and took a drag from her cigarette, "In front of the child, huh? Well, don't you think for a minute that the child doesn't realize what's going on. Of course she does. Frosina knows and understands everything. Don't you underestimate her!"

Since they were talking about me, I tried again to calm my mother. I got up from my chair and hugged her neck, but she didn't move. I felt like I was hugging a tall, cold statue. "OK, Frosina, OK," my mother told me and waved for me to sit down. "Are you perhaps going to say something now?" she asked my father, this time a bit more calmly.

"What do you want me to say?" he answered, looking at her and shrugging.

"Tell me what you were thinking! Did you think it would all pass just like that?"

This time, my father's forehead went red, too. He took a piece of cucumber, put it in his mouth, chewed and swallowed it, and was about to speak when I called, "I've finished," and pushed away the fish plate.

"Frosi, darling, if you're finished, why don't you go and play on the beach for a while, OK sweetheart?" my father told me. I was glad my father asked me to get up because a heavy feeling was growing in my chest. I got up and tried to hug my mother. This time she just bent her head a bit, but she didn't turn her face toward me. "Go on, Frosi, go," she said. Then I went and hugged my father, and stroked his cheek. He gave me a few kisses and then pinched my nose.

I went down the small flight of stairs to the shore. When I got close to the sea, I barely heard the voices from the restaurant anymore, and couldn't hear my mother and father at all. Instead, my ears were filled with the sound of the little waves breaking on the beach, their white bubbles bursting, and when the waves retreated I could hear the hissing of the pebbles rolling down, returning toward the water that was running away from them. Every now and again there came the clink of a fork on a plate or the barking of one of the puppies on the terrace. A gull was circling in my view, and then it suddenly flew down and landed nearby. It looked at me and took a few steps toward me. I smiled at it, but it took off and headed out to sea again, and only then did I notice that the sky had turned pink.

TRANSLATED FROM MACEDONIAN BY WILL FIRTH

Ion Buzu

Another Piss in Nisporeni

IT WAS BACK when I was a part-time student and rarely visited the university building. I only had classes two weeks a term, plus five days of exams. Apart from that, I had no reason to get up at, say, twenty to eight in the morning, as I had done for the twelve years I attended lyceum. I was always telling myself to find something worthwhile to do with my time, or at least something that would give me a reason to go outside, apart from trips to the outhouse in the backyard.

I had very few contacts with people. Everyone I knew had gotten into university, and they all had their own set routines now, their own roles that they played in their own social circles. Each of them had an internal motivating force, a motor of sorts. I had a hard time convincing them to go out with me, even just for a cup of tea. They would say that we weren't that close anymore.

I came up with the idea of going to the library and reading the authors I had always told myself I should read: Deleuze, Foucault, Jung, Nietzsche, Schopenhauer, Heidegger ... The idea really appealed to me: getting up early in the morning and catching the bus just to read Nietzsche. But most of the time I would fall asleep at the table where I was reading, wake up with a painful jolt, then nod off again. For two, three hours I would be in agony, caught between sleep and waking, unable to lay my head on the table for fear they might throw me out. I would fall asleep with my chin resting on my palm, then with my head lolling to one side, and would wake up with awful pains in my face, neck, and forehead, like someone had given me a thrashing. Every time I jerked awake the other people in the reading room gave me long stares.

I couldn't afford to spend much on food and brought along the cheapest sweets from the nearest supermarket, plus a couple of apples in my pocket; that was more or less my food for the day. Sometimes, when

I only had enough for bus fare, the two apples plus my own detachment would suffice. Usually I would leave the reading room to eat, but sometimes I would move all my books to one side, place the apples there in front of me, take a knife from my coat pocket and cut each apple into eight segments, which I would then eat slowly, with my eyes closed.

My life in the library lasted for about three months, maybe longer. I always took several books from the philosophy section, even if I only read five pages of each. I kept expecting one of the librarians to tell me that I was one of the few people who read such authors, or that she hadn't seen anybody touch those books for a long time, or that she admired me and would like to get to know me better, or to ask me why I kept coming every day and why I only read books from that shelf. But those unpleasant women just chattered away all day long, disturbing my reading and my painful sleep, and tried to prevent me from eating my two apples the way I liked.

During that period I felt like I had lost all my willpower, that it had been crushed, and had died at the muscular level—that is, as if it were dead even to the physical organs that would be able to reanimate it. The entire idea of willpower had become alien to me. My own internal motor that used to make me go to that particular shop or that particular building, to recite my homework to the biology teacher, to tell the guy next to me what time it was, to pick up that mug or that fork—after twelve years of school, during which I had learned nothing save how to study for exams, that motor had been exposed as a bitter illusion.

It was a period when nothing happened, and I mean absolutely nothing. I ended up losing any notion of holidays or days off. I would lie in bed and wonder what day it was, whether it was Saturday or still Friday; but I didn't wait long for an answer, just turned over onto my other side and tried to go back to sleep.

I was always waiting for the phone to ring or to get a text message from somebody, but all I got were stupid announcements and special offers from the mobile phone company. It wouldn't have been the worst thing in the world if somebody had come in to check whether I was still alive, whether I was still good for something, whether my mind was healthy enough to allow me to go outside, whether I had forgotten that "outside" still existed.

I thought about my schoolmates, who would now be laughing their heads off at me and saying something like: "Look at the state he's in, he used to be top of the class, he even used to read books after school and do other people's homework for them, he always wrote my exercises during the break; I can't believe it, I thought he'd be studying engineering or medicine at university, that he'd go far, but look at him now!"

It was back then that I took those two pills, without having any idea what they were for or why I'd swallowed them. I had found them in a pocket. "Something's got to happen to me," I told myself. "I have to give this here corpse of mine a shake, whether it kills me or just tumbles me out of bed." I felt I needed to ingest something new, to have some different substance enter my organism—and so I took the two pills, which I had found in a dusty jacket in a barn. After taking them I got a strange feeling, like I wanted to look for more pills to neck down, any kind of pill I could find, so that I could experience more and more strange new states.

I wondered whether that was what would happen. I decided to make a wager. Could two unfamiliar pills really kill me? Could my swallowing them be my final act? Tomorrow I would see. But before losing consciousness a thought came to me, the faintest glimmer of an idea: that it was time to repair my life.

It was close to noon when I woke up at my desk. I stood up, the lamp was lit, a mug was lying on the floor, but it wasn't broken. I went to put some water on to boil for tea and tried to remember why I'd woken up at my desk and not in my bed, how I had fallen asleep there, and why I had a headache and, more worryingly, a stomachache. Then the image of two red pills flashed to mind. Yes, that's right, the challenge. The two mystery pills I'd swallowed. Well, it seemed that they hadn't worked after all, damn it. They hadn't managed to kill me, they were just as useless as I was. And then the thought returned: that I had to repair my life.

I decided to go back to sleep and wake up a day later, that is, at six thirty on Monday morning. When I awoke I had an awful headache. I said to myself: "All right, I understand, you want to repair your life, whatever that means, but this isn't the way, getting up at six thirty after months of waking up at ten or eleven—take it a bit more slowly!"

I splash my face with water, but the headache doesn't go away. It's still dark outside. It's not often that I see this part of the day, quarter of six—in fact this past year I can only remember getting up this early maybe five times. After getting dressed, I took the bus to Chişinău, intent on dragging my corpse to the polling organization to see whether they had any work for me. I'd worked for them about eight months earlier, doing a day of fieldwork for a survey about pregnant women. When I entered the building this time the manager greeted me with upraised arms. "Hey there, Ion, I'm glad you're here, hey, we urgently need a fieldworker, are you in, what do you say?"

"Yeah, all right."

They gave me some questionnaires for an opinion poll about the crime rate in the republic, which I was supposed to conduct in a far-flung town, Nisporeni.

And so here I am in the administrative capital of the Nisporeni district, a place I've visited once before on similar business. Yes, I say to myself, there's the town hall, there's the lyceum. Look, there's the bar I went into in despair, cursing this town so rundown that it doesn't have any street signs, not even rusty, dusty ones in Cyrillic letters. I had come in and asked for a strong drink to give me courage, but there were some guys at the bar who started asking me questions: where I was from, what I was doing there, whether I was trying to pull off some kind of scam, what was with that blue coat of mine, and why was it blue; I got annoyed and left. Well, since I'm already familiar with the dangers of the place, I should be able to get out unscathed. You'd be surprised how well a guy like me knows the ins and outs, a guy who thinks, optimistically, that everything might work out, that he's not being led on a wild goose chase.

I set off with fifteen questionnaires in my bag, each one twenty pages long and packed with ridiculous questions that would make me laugh if they were addressed to me; I'd send the pollster packing if he tried a survey like this on me. However, to my good fortune or misfortune, I'm the pollster in this case. Well, I say to myself, I wish you the best of luck, my man, you who has chosen to repair your life this way. The questions were all about the crime rate in the community, how safe people felt, how well the forces of law and order did their job, what institutions they felt to be the most trustworthy. Questions like: have your animals, items from your home, car, motorcycle, bicycle ever been stolen? Have you ever been physically, sexually, or verbally assaulted? Have you ever been threatened, with or without a weapon? Did you report it to the police? Why? . . .

I walked around aimlessly in the cold for more than two hours, up and down the muddy streets, without coming across a single soul willing to do a questionnaire. Céline was right when he said that villages are always sad, with their unending mud, the houses with nobody home, and roads that lead nowhere. What the hell! Where is everybody? Where are you all hiding? Huh? It was like the villagers had made a pact among themselves to keep anyone from filling out my questionnaire. They probably talked about me after the last time I was here: "Hey, listen, if you see a short, slouching boy in a blue coat, with a bag slung over his right shoulder, walking around aimlessly as if he were lost and didn't know which way to go, don't let him see you! And if he creeps up softly and starts talking to you strangely, tell him to get lost!"

And they were right. All day long I kept thinking: "What am I doing here? How did I end up in stinking Nisporeni again, when I swore I'd never set foot here again, no, no, never again!" But finally I found it. It was well hidden, the doorbell. Hanging from a gate. Ah, dear doorbell, you can't imagine how much I love you. I approach it, I touch it as delicately as can be, and zrrrr, zrrrr, a woman of about forty-five comes out. I launch into my spiel: "My name is Ion Buzu, I'm conducting an opinion poll for the Soros Foundation about the crime rate in the Republic of Moldova, how safe people feel, and how satisfied they are with the legal system, the police . . ." Then I read off the questions on the form. I ask her what she thinks about the local judges and she says she's never had anything to do with them and can't answer.

"All right, but in your opinion, how well do you think they perform their duties?"

"I don't know, I've never seen one in my life, so how can I talk about a man I've never even seen?"

"But don't you have an opinion about it?"

"No, I don't. There's something burning on the stove!"

And she closes the door.

It's one o'clock already and I've only filled in one of the fifteen questionnaires. And even that one is incomplete. Everywhere there are huge chains and locks hanging from people's gates, as if to spite me, taunting me: "Nyah, loser, screw off!"

I'm sick of schlepping past these houses. All I can do is hope to come across somebody working in his yard, or try shouting for the owner. But I don't know what to shout. "Mister homeowner?" Or should I shout out different names until I hit on the right one and somebody comes out of the house? Or should I try "sir," and then quickly explain that I'm not begging or peddling religious or political propaganda, and that I'm after something else entirely. Fuck this village. I head off toward the tenement blocks. There'll be a lot more doorbells there. I'm in love with them now, after all. At least there won't be any more chains and padlocks laughing in my face.

But it wouldn't be long before the doorbells deceived me. Seeing all those padlocks on the gates made me realize that most statistics are lies. The representative segment of the population, that is, the sample selected for the poll, is either not at home, or don't have time, or simply don't exist. The ones left over are the pensioners, the unemployed, the depressed, and those on holiday. And so this becomes the representative voice in all the statistical studies. The numbers I'm trudging after now, trying to find anybody to answer my questions, are really not worth the effort.

Finally I reach the tenement blocks. I enter a building, press a doorbell, and zrrrr, a guy opens the door with his mouth full, chewing something or other, a trail of food-juice dribbling down his chin. "Whaddya want?" he says, spraying crumbs from his mouth. I say my thing: "I represent the sociological polling company, which, at the request of . . ." He stops chewing, looks at me in amazement and at the same time bewilderment, looks down at my feet, measures me up and down, blinks a few times, looks at the sheet of questions I'm holding, blinks, and says: "Get lost and leave me alone!" Then he goes back inside, slamming the door behind him.

I had to write down all the refusals and the reasons for them. And they started coming thicker and faster, refusals and the sound of slamming doors. "I don't have the time." "I don't want to." "It's not worth it, you're wasting your time." "What? Nah, no way, can't you see it's got nothing to do with me." "I don't understand a word you're saying."

"All right, I get it, now get lost." Just some of the things I heard over the course of the next two hours.

By then I'd stopped writing them down, it was getting tedious, and they no longer made me laugh. I felt like sitting down somewhere and crying, because I was a sucker for having got up that morning, and at half past six no less. As Céline says: "When things start turning sour, the only choice is to retreat." Why don't I just get on the damned minibus, go home, get my hands on every kind of pill I can find, swallow them and pass out?

But before that, I'll try one last door. I ring the bell and a man in a brown shirt opens it. I give him my introduction and he says: "Come in, it's not nice to stand outside like that. Have a seat. I'm sure you must be tired. Your feet must be killing you." Completely taken aback, I think to myself: "What's going on? Why has he agreed to answer? There must be something wrong with him. I'd better be careful, ready to make a quick exit." I start reading the questions.

"Do you have a gun?"

"Yes, of course I do. A hunting rifle. A Winchester 1300. I'll just go and get it, to show you."

"No, no, there's no need. Please let's continue with the questionnaire," and I see the thick butt, I see the trigger, I see the barrel, I see the bead of sweat dripping off my forehead onto my hand, I see my trembling legs, I see my chest rising and falling quicker and quicker.

"Look, it's a pretty nice gun. Here's my permit, it's all legit, write it down on your sheet of paper there, that it's all legal, go on, write it."

"Ah, yes, OK, thank you very much, I've written it down."

By then I was half-paralyzed with fear. The guy could have a screw loose. You never know. I mean, he invites me into his house and is more than willing to answer my ridiculous questions—I wouldn't wonder if he were a bit loony.

At the end of the interview I ask for his telephone number, as instructed. He goes back and reopens the safe where he keeps the rifle. Shit! He's maybe more than a bit loony, he's about to get his rifle and bang! my brains will have redecorated his apartment. You never know how and to whom you might come in handy, but I never saw myself decorating someone's apartment, let alone like this. Maybe the guy is basically like me: nice, decent, articulate, friendly, pleasant, but suddenly he just loses it and bashes my skull in. Then he'll sit back down, light a cigarette, look out the window, then look at all the blood on the floor, take a drag, check what brand of cigarette he's holding, take another drag, examine the cigarette lighter, look out the window at the children playing and singing songs they've learned in school, look at my body, my blood having formed a puddle, get up, shake his head in puzzlement, and say: "What happened?" But the man just takes his ID card from the safe and hands it to me:

"Here, I don't want to give any false information, so just write down whatever you need."

When I stand up to thank him, he says: "I haven't got time to make you coffee, but take some apples. Snack on them on your way back. You must be hungry. I know what it's like to be hungry, it's hard."

"Thank you very much."

"Thank you very much too, for dropping by for a chat. I enjoyed it. Not many people come by here. The doorbell hasn't rung for quite a while. I thought it was out of order. That's why I didn't open the door straight away when you rang. I couldn't figure out what that buzzing was."

"Yes, I know what you mean, I'm familiar with that feeling. I enjoyed it, too. Maybe I'll stop in again next time."

"Take care now."

I went downstairs thinking about how lonely he was. I admired him. I kept looking at the apples he gave me and couldn't get over my amazement. Suddenly it was like the gods started to smile down on me, and the rejections held off. There was a young couple, who said: "Alright, we've got the time. Come on in, don't be embarrassed." I go into their kitchen and do the questionnaire with the husband. I get to the question about whether the interviewee has ever experienced sexual aggression, but I say "physical" instead of "sexual," so as not to spoil the interview by using that word. The man says that yes, he's experienced physical aggression. Shit, he took it to mean whether he's ever been beaten up, and I have to tick "yes" for the question asking whether he's ever experienced sexual aggression. I don't dare explain that "physical" in this case means "sexual." That would have been even more embarrassing.

"How many people were involved?"

"Three."

"Where did the incident take place?"

"In front of my building."

"Did you report it to the police?"

"No."

"Why?"

"It wasn't serious."

"Ah, hmm, OK, I understand, I understand. Thank you."

Then there was another kindly old man who invited me inside. He even switched off the television set and turned down the gas cooker. By that point I'd done eight questionnaires, but it was getting late, and I risked missing the minibus back. I started running, but got lost between all those apartment buildings. I run and run—shit, more buildings. I run in a different direction—I don't get it, what are these bushes doing here? And then more buildings, obviously. Hang on a minute, what's going on? Where's the main road? I look at my watch: 17:06. Is the minibus at 17:30 or 17:00? Oh, please, Lord, let it be at 17:30, otherwise I'm screwed. Nisporeni is eighty kilometers from Chișinău and I only have 24 lei in my pocket, just enough for the bus ticket. Who could I ask to drive all the way from Chișinău and back just to pick me up? I'm running around in circles, darting between buildings, when suddenly I see a man emerging from the darkness, his hands in his pockets, whistling.

"Excuse me, how do I get to the town hall?" I ask.

"Turn left, go straight ahead, take another left, and then straight ahead."

"Thanks," I call as I run off.

By then I was out of breath and had a sharp pain in my side. It's a quarter past five already and I'm not sure whether the last minibus is at half past or not. But finally I get to the bus station and see the minibus, it hasn't left, I'm saved. I stand for two minutes to catch my breath, then I realize I should probably find a toilet or some bushes or at least a crumbling old wall, it doesn't matter what, since it's a two-hour journey and Christ, I've been holding myself in all day, all the while sipping the coffee I poured into an old Pepsi bottle for myself. No wonder the tenants kept giving me dirty looks, they were probably thinking: "Look at the little bastard, drinking Pepsi, without offering me any, how am I supposed to answer his questions when he keeps drinking Pepsi at my expense, getting money for the questionnaire he's doing with me, and I don't get so much as a taste? No way. Get out of here!"

After boarding the minibus I open my bag and see the apples. I pick one up and take a bite. The apple of a lonely man who keeps a gun in his safe along with his identity card and driving license.

The next day, at half past six in the morning, my eyes were open, or at least I was trying to keep them open. I still had seven question-naires to do, but I was dreading it. So many refusals, so many people not home. Nisporeni puts up quite a resistance to pollsters: how was I supposed to overcome that? I didn't know if it was better to get out of bed or forget about the whole thing. Nevertheless, I got up and walked to the station to catch the next minibus to Nisporeni.

I get to Nisporeni and decide to take a different route than the one I took yesterday. Maybe this time it'll be easier. But once again, not one house with any sign of life. I walked and walked, looking and praying for somebody to come out. I continued like that for more than three hours without filling in a single page. I kept thinking: "Christ, what's going on around here? Where is everybody? Have they agreed with each other to hide? How did they manage to or-ganize themselves overnight? Or maybe I'm deranged, maybe I have some kind of undiscovered mental illness. Maybe I should turn my-self in to the authorities before I do myself any more harm." Then I spotted a small building. I figured there wasn't much chance of any life inside, since it looked like it was due to be torn down. I go up to the door, but there's no doorbell, of course. I bunch my fingers into a fist and knock a few times. And then it happens! The door opens and a young guy shorter than me appears, looking down at the ground. I explain to him who I am and what I do and what information I need-ed from him. He opens the door wider, moves back a few steps, still looking at the ground, and says very quietly: "Come in."

I start with the questions. "Age?"

Still looking down, he hesitates for almost thirty seconds and without lifting his eyes says: "Twenty."

He kept staring at some fixed point on the floor, or maybe he wasn't looking at anything, but whatever it was, he never got tired of looking at it.

"Do you think the level of crime in your town has increased, stayed the same, or decreased?"

Sometimes he would make a slow movement of the head, without looking up. "Stayed the same," he answered.

He hesitated for about half a minute after each question. Could he be autistic? He answered with difficulty and didn't move his eyes from the floor. I thanked him, he nodded, and answered softly, his head still lowered: "You're welcome. Have a safe journey."

He turned around and went back inside, very slowly, as if he were measuring the distance in paces.

I went into a tenement block, rang a doorbell, and a woman appeared, saying: "No, no, we can't answer questions like that, crime has nothing to do with us, no, we're simple folk, we can't answer your questions, try across the hall."

I ring the doorbell of the flat across the hall and a man of around twenty-six comes out: "Sorry, I don't have time, I'm eating and after that I have to go straight to work. Try across the hall,"—the flat of the woman I just spoke to—"they've got plenty of time. I've never seen them go out. Sorry."

I go into another building, ring a doorbell and a man comes out, yawning, his eyes half-closed with sleep. I tell him I'm doing a survey for the Soros Foundation and the rest of the spiel. He keeps yawning. I give him the pitch once more and he says: "No, I'm no good at that kind of thing. I thought you wanted something to eat, I even had a one-leu coin in my hand to give you. But surveys, no. There's hardly anybody left in this building. Upstairs there's a guy like me, but I don't think he'll want to answer either, so . . . "

Despite what the man said, I found somebody who shrugged and said: "All right, if it only takes ten minutes, come on, out with it." How I loved those people! You couldn't say that they loved me in return, because they kept shaking their heads grudgingly and saying: "I thought you said just ten minutes, but you've been here twenty-five minutes already, how many pages is that thing?"

A girl who lived with her mother invited me into the hall of her flat. Reading down the list of questions, I ask her if she has ever been threatened. In a quiet voice she says that she has.

"With or without a weapon."

"With."

She signals to me to talk more softly, so her mother won't hear. I move closer. She tells me that the threat wasn't serious; it was an ex-boyfriend that had waved a pistol in her face. He was crying and threatening to kill himself if she started seeing anybody else. I finish the questionnaire and leave.

I ring a doorbell and a fat Gypsy woman comes out. She immediately starts swearing at me. A man comes out and bustles her back inside. From within I hear: "Chase that idiot away, can't you see he's trying to con you?" The man answers: "Shut up, woman, go back inside and shut up, because I happen to find this kind of thing interesting."

I ask him what the punishment should be for a young person who commits a theft—stealing a color TV, for example—but who has never stolen anything before. "Community service would be appropriate. Prison would be too much."

I ask another question. "Have you ever been sexually harassed?"

"I should be so lucky. No, I'm stuck with—well, you saw that mound of flesh—and I've never had the happy occasion to be sexually harassed on the street, no."

I finish the questionnaire and look for another flat. It's four twenty-five. A bald old man the same height as me opens the door and invites me in, smiling.

He gives me his telephone number without hesitation. I have to take down the telephone numbers of all the respondents so the people at the office can check that I've really spoken to them, and haven't been forging the questionnaires. I start by asking him about crimes: "Do you think the crime rate has increased in the last five years?"

"Look, I served in the German army. I got a medal. I can show it to you. That's all I can tell you. And now Igor is in Italy. Yes, Italy, and I'm all alone. Not quite alone, actually, there's another man here, I don't even know him very well, he sits around in his pajamas all day. But Igor came back to visit not long ago. He sends money. Igor is my son."

"Yes, but what about the crime rate, do you think it has increased or not?"

"I told you I served in the German army, but now I've turned to drink. I'm a drunk, I spend my days at the bar on the corner there, see it? That's where I go to drink every day, and I feel all right with that."

He coughs and then says: "I'm sorry, but you have to understand that I drink, and I apologize."

He smiles at me and coughs. I ask him another question: "Do you have a bicycle at home?"

"Yes, I'll show it to you. I've also got two grandchildren, Vasya and Anișoara, I'll show you. I use the bicycle when I go to buy booze. Couldn't do without it."

He takes me into the living room and shows me some photographs.

"These are my grandchildren. Look, this is me before I went bald. Look, here's the bicycle, too. Ha ha!"

We both smiled. He kept coughing and apologizing and reminding me that he drank, that he served in the German army, but that now he was a drunk, that he didn't do much and felt all right about it. I shook his hand and thanked him. I left, almost joyful, astonished. It seems like the only decent people around here are the nutcases, I thought.

I ran for the minibus, worried that I was going in the wrong direction. But I soon arrived at the bus station. Before boarding I went over to the crumbling wall, unzipped my fly, and pissed. I felt like at long last I was ridding myself of something rotten. The two pills, my broken motor, the madness of the last two days: at that moment nothing had any more importance. The world made sense. I had managed to arrive there on time and relieve myself, and I felt like nothing else could make a fool out of me after that.

TRANSLATED FROM ROMANIAN BY ALISTAIR IAN BLYTH

ILIJA ĐUROVIĆ

The Five Widows

THE FIVE WIDOWS is not a bad neighborhood—quiet and safe, without being manicured and sterile. There are a few benches, some greenery, and these five modernist high-rise buildings looking toward the river and one of two hills, depending on which direction your balcony and windows face. The five buildings once stood stark and alone on this street in Podgorica, thus their name. I'm on the northeastern side looking toward the larger of the hills and the river—the pretty green river and the hill of conifers. It's a nice view, and I'm fond of my window. I don't have a balcony.

I sit alone by the window, usually with a cup of tea in hand, and look out at the hill, the river, or the big white bridge with ribs, which reaches from one riverbank to the other. People and cars cross the bridge and continue along the street that separates these five high-rises from the river and the row of buildings constructed too close to it. They could end up in the water one day. When that happens, I hope I'll be by the window with a cup of my favorite tea.

The colors I see in the city change depending on which tea I'm drinking. My favorites are hibiscus and ginger. When I drink dark-red hibiscus tea, the ribs of the bridge become red as if they've been torn out of some huge carcass and wedged there to join the banks of the river, while the cypresses on the hill take on a murky color, a mixture of coniferous green and dark red. When I drink ginger, everything is a pretty yellow. When I drink Reiki, everything is greenish. I have fun like this when I'm looking at the city from the window. I'm high enough that no one sees me doing it. People could see me from the bridge if they knew when and where to look. People from the buildings across the road could see me too, but they rarely go out. I'm well camouflaged up here.

I moved into the apartment five and a half years ago, a few months after my music theory and counterpoint teacher threw herself out of this window. She jumped from right here, on the eighth floor, and landed on the pavement in front of the building. She wasn't all in one piece when they found her. Afterwards, her parents, whom she had been living with, moved to their house in the country and rented out the apartment. The rent was very reasonable for this part of the city. They could have charged quite a bit more because of the two university buildings nearby, but they just wanted to get rid of the apartment. I kept track of developments and contacted them as soon as the ad was in the paper. Just a week or ten days after my teacher's suicide I drank my first tea by the window she jumped from. I didn't find it unpleasant. Why should I have?

My music theory and counterpoint teacher was very attractive. Even the people who picked her up off the pavement probably noticed. She had big green eyes and wavy red hair. There's no need for me to conceal that I was in love with her for my four years of high school. I thought she loved me, too. That was my main misconception.

We got along wonderfully well together. She became aware of me in the first classes of music theory in my freshman year. It took me a long time to summon the courage to go into the classroom when she was alone after a lesson. I don't remember anymore how I struck up the conversation. It was awkward, that's all I know. I probably said something about music, or asked a question, and she invited me to come in and I sat down at my place. I always sat right in front of her. After that, we began to exchange CDs. She brought CDs and I listened to them at home. A good slice of my early collection of classical music came from her, plus a lot of twentieth-century music and some twenty-first. We talked a lot.

We soon got to talking about our private lives. Mine, to begin with. Her private life wasn't a complete unknown: she wasn't married, she used to have something going with my then homeroom teacher, who taught English, and her partners from school included a young piano teacher, who told me she was the most screwed-up woman he had ever met. They were together for as long as he could stand the torture, and then they split up. From her stories, I was able to deduce that she traveled to Italy several times a year. She may have had a lover there, but she never said anything to that effect. I heard from fellow students that she had had relationships with boys in the past. They also said she often mentioned me, so some of them thought I would be her next affair. Unfortunately, that's not how things turned out.

What really disappointed me, if only briefly, was the story I heard about one of the affairs that my music theory and counterpoint teacher had with a student. An unconfirmed source told me that she had been together with a real idiot a few years before I enrolled at the school. As a boy, he had become popular at a festival for young singers. He capered about on stage, and one of his songs ended up topping the children's charts. Later, as an adolescent, he remained an idiot: he gave up capering about, played the trumpet badly, and mumbled when he spoke, under lifelong trauma because of that childhood hit. This was the jerk they said had once been in a relationship with my teacher. I didn't want to believe it, so I never made a point of verifying the story. Instead, I just tried to forget it.

I began getting closer to my music theory and counterpoint teacher when I discovered the dramas of puberty. When we finished talking about music, I would tell her about my problems at home. She said she understood me. She persuaded me not to drop out of school, although I sometimes wanted to. It was thanks to her that I finished high school. I did the third year externally because I didn't have any classes with her that year. After I don't know how many sessions in the classroom between or after lessons, I confessed to her that I was also a composer. And it was true, I did—I composed terrible music. In any case, my love of music, the crises of puberty, and my drive to compose were her reasons for liking me. And she showed it openly by telling me I was different than the others; I wasn't like my age-mates or my parents, and therefore I had to figure out a way of relating to them more amicably, or at least with less friction. That's what she told me. But she spoke about me to others in a less restrained way, telling them I was wonderful and very talented.

Several times I heard her compliments second hand. I seemed to have made a good impression on her. Often I thought that a different boy, one less shy than me, would make a move during an intimate moment. Perhaps a kiss. Or a request to go up to her apartment. Any of the tricks known to the Romeos at music school, some of which were known to me, too. But although I knew the tricks in theory, or thought I knew them, I never attempted a single one in practice. I just didn't have the balls. All cerebral.

My music theory and counterpoint teacher also helped me when I started skipping a lot of classes. She used her influence over my home-room teacher, and wrote excuse letters for me when I was spending whole weeks at a time in the forest, up on the hill I'm now looking at from the window. She helped me with my other subjects, too. She never told me when she intervened in my favor, but I always felt the results. Sometimes people even told me that my teacher was in love with me, and I noticed a smile on their faces, which I interpreted as a sign that they also knew about her affairs with younger men, her students, and that they predicted something similar for me. But they didn't realize how shy I was. That's how I was back then, and later too: shy and retiring, with occasional flashes of brilliance. This behavior produced a large group of people who considered me a loony recluse, and a small group who believed I was interesting and had potential. But even among them, there was no one I really hit it off with in the same way as my teacher.

I often imagined what it would be like to sleep with her, and she figured in almost all my masturbation fantasies. I would do her in all sorts of different positions and places, to the best music. When I found out where she lived—in the middle tower of the Five Wid-ows—I would go to the building and look up to the eighth-floor window; I imagined being there with her, with the lights dimmed low, fucking her like crazy. My teacher was my greatest high-school love. Even today, masturbation sessions with her in the main role are among my favorites.

During my "external" year, things seemed to fizzle out between us. Life seemed to have gotten more serious. She was fast approaching her fifth decade and I believed she had stopped having relationships with students. I felt like I had missed the last train. I had. And then my teacher committed suicide. It didn't happen right after my gradu-ation from high school. Even though I already felt at that point that something in her had changed forever, she lived for several years more.

So I gradually withdrew and awaited the end of school, with no great rapport left between us. Without saying good-bye, I went away to another city to make an attempt at studying. I came back after several months of trying. Half a year later, I saw her again at a concert of my old high school's jazz department. I was still fresh in everyone's mind as the one who had given up music, only to return to our small city after two months away studying. But they didn't stare at me like a freak or anything. I met my music theory and counterpoint teacher in front of the entrance to the auditorium. When we walked up the stairs together, she asked if I was waiting for anyone. I told her I was there alone, and she laughed and said she was, too, so we could sit together. I felt her uneasiness when we turned up together amid the floodlit seats—many people knew us, and yet no one had expected to see us there together. The uneasiness soon passed as we went in and took our seats. We chatted on and off. I couldn't concentrate. During the concert, our elbows touched and I smelt the eucalyptus chewing gum on her breath whenever she turned and spoke to me. We felt comfortable with each other.

After the concert, we headed into town. I suggested that I accompany her as far as the bridge, whose ribs I now look at every day. She agreed and said I didn't have to if it wasn't on my way. I told her it was. I don't remember what I talked about during our walk, but somewhere around halfway—when we could already see the Five Widows, which we would head toward once we crossed the river—I suggested that we get a drink. She gave me a look as if her battered sensitivity was weighing up whether our provincial society allowed her to be out with a student after eleven o'clock on a midsummer's night. Finally she agreed. I was no longer a student, but that didn't mean I would get what I masturbated over as a high schooler. That evening or any other. I was still equally unable to take that plunge.

It was a warm night that demanded refreshment, and we found the ideal spot round the back of the building across from the college. There was a bar with a patio enclosed by a tall hedge. I told her everything, from my departure for university until my return, and everything that happened in between. She liked the sound of it all, although I felt like even she didn't quite understand. But I didn't try to explain things. Then we got to talking about her. She still lived with her parents. Her father was ill and her mother was boring. Her sister, a pianist, had an orderly life: a job at the Music Academy, two children, and a husband—an idiot who taught cello at our high school. My counterpoint teacher was different to her sister, and her mother couldn't forgive her for it. She often fought with her mother, and her father was slowly dying. The three of them lived together in the apartment on the eighth floor of the middle Widow. It was unbearable for a woman like her.

She told me how much she enjoyed watching television. TV was the only good thing when she was at home, in her room. For the first time in the four years we had known each other, she spoke with me like I had spoken with her during my high-school crises. Now she herself was in crisis. She told me that she had her own room and lived in it, and that she only felt like an adult on weekends, when her parents were away at their house in the country. This was a Saturday.

It was hard for me to listen to her description of her mornings, drinking coffee in front of the television before going to work. She said she didn't watch nonsense, just Discovery Channel, National Geographic, and History Channel, but I knew those programs were for absolute suckers. I mean, what could be as brain-dead as watching oil rigs and derricks in Scandinavia for hours on end? She obviously wasn't well, even though she tried to be lucid like before. What made this easier for me to take was that we were the last to leave; I had downed several mini bottles of white wine, and she had had a few liqueurs with ice. When it was time to pay, I went toward the bathroom and asked the waiter if it would be alright for me to bring the money the next day because I had invited my teacher for a drink but didn't have my wallet. The waiter was a good guy, so the night behind the hedge ended without embarrassment.

What I would otherwise have considered the climax of the evening—strolling through the balmy night with the person I love, between the buildings still radiating the heat of the day—was spoiled by a misunderstanding about food. We were both hungry: my dearest teacher wanted a hamburger, while the scrawny vegetarian in me proposed the bakery. She responded awkwardly, apologizing for having suggested dead animal and laughing, but still acting like she'd put her foot in it. So she accepted the bakery idea, and we set off toward her high-rise with a paper bag full of rolls and pastries. She said I didn't have to walk her all the way. But I wanted to, and I told her so, saying I was used to walking a lot. And so we kept going toward the middle Widow. That was probably the perfect moment for me to make an attempt, with both of us moderately drunk and her parents away at their house in the country, but it wasn't enough. I accompanied her to the bench in front of the middle Widow and didn't even manage to ask her for a little kiss on the cheek. She reached out her hand, said she was glad we had met, and I mumbled a few words. Then she headed for her entrance and I walked back toward the ribbed bridge that I now see from the window. That was the last time I saw her, before the death notice in the paper.

After our good-bye, everything went very fast. I returned to my life, and my teacher went back to her mornings spent watching the pumpjacks. One season of Discovery Channel, National Geographic, and History Channel programs passed before my teacher jumped out of the window and landed on the concrete in front of the middle Widow. That was the end of any possibility of a relationship.

A few weeks later, I had the good fortune to move into her apartment. Her death didn't come as too much of a blow to me. It seemed like the natural continuation of a lonely morning in her room, when her parents were at their house in the country, and her coffee by the windowsill, where I am now holding my cup of tea. Perhaps she had an argument with her man, if she had one at the time. Perhaps she had finally found someone who was able to torture her, like she used to torture her men. Maybe she jumped out of the window because of him. I could imagine that. Perhaps she had a bad morning and her parents were not there to manage the meltdown. They were away, and my teacher was living out her adult weekend in front of *MythBusters*. Then she drank her coffee, watched the sunset from the window, and jumped to her death on the pavement between the benches.

I know that she finished her coffee before jumping because the music-school people talked a lot about her suicide. Everyone was surprised by the event, and for some time everyone talked about her last sunset. Somehow they found out that an empty coffee cup had been found at the window of the apartment. She drank her coffee, watched the sunset, and jumped. It was the fifth of January, a time that tends to be cold in our city. But it was a cloudless day, so her last sunset must have been dazzling. Now, every fifth of January, I enjoy reconstructing the setting of my teacher's sun. But I discovered something strange when I watched my first sunset from the new, eighth-floor window: my former teacher's window, now my window in her parents' apartment, faces northeast, which means that the sunset—the real sunset—cannot be seen from our window.

Instead we have the reflective glass on the building opposite, one of those buildings on the riverbank that are sure to be claimed by the water one day. The building's windows are mirrors for us in the northeast. I don't know if any of the neighbors have noticed it too, but I'm sure my teacher did. The setting sun in the west can be viewed perfectly in the upper left-hand corner of the mirrors, with small spills seeping out at the window joints. Sometimes the last moment of the sunset is magnified across the entire glass facade, and then the sun looks like a giant egg yolk impaled on a fork. Maybe my teacher saw just such a sun before she jumped and made a mess down on the concrete. On the fifth of January, the light is different. The city is particularly ugly then.

TRANSLATED FROM MONTENEGRIN BY WILL FIRTH

Justyna Bargielska

FROM *Born Sleeping*

I'd Like to Tell You about the Last Time I Gave Birth

My Caesarean section was scheduled for May the 9th at nine in the morning. The date had been determined after comparing four calendars: mine, the obstetrician's, the anesthesiologist's and the District Office press officer's. Our chief aim was to ensure that this date coincided across all four calendars. It did, although the day before I had serious concerns in—pardon my French—*my womb* that I'd miss the deadline. In the end I didn't. I was supposed to submit an entire piece by the evening, and it was already half done (I'm a pro, after all), and that successfully kept the contractions at bay.

On Friday I got up at one thirty a.m. and went to the bathroom to clean the grouting. Five hours later my husband and our older child got up and we set off. We dropped off our son at the babysitter's on the way.

I was given a room painted a motivating orange, and they gave me a blue gown with appliqué designs. I mistook a certain fuzziness for concentration, which became most apparent after a series of friendly inquiries (HIV, STDs, Hep B, etc.), when the doctor asked me: "Where did you have your previous C-section?" After an interminably long pause, during which I could have traveled to Vega and back—where I must have come from, since he was asking me questions like that—I answered: "In my belly." The doctor looked to my husband for a translation, so he obliged, saying it was in the hospital in Praga.

Then they came to take me to the operating theater. They weren't able to explain why I had to remove my panties, but I decided to give way to their irrational arguments, since it might have been my last chance to give way to irrational arguments when it came to the removal of panties.

And then on the operating table, my gynecologist said: "Oh dear, I forgot to examine you."

At this point it turned out I'd been in labor for quite some time, actually I was almost near the end, but I'd been distracted by the grouting and hadn't noticed.

Then everything happened in a flash: they got my baby out—he looked like white sausage—they took him to the cubicle next door to be measured, the pediatrician whistled for my husband to go with them, and the anesthetic stopped working. I told the anesthesiologist I thought the anesthetic had worn off, to which he replied: "No way!" And that's the precise moment I fell in love with him.

The pediatrician popped back in for a minute with my husband to tell me the baby's measurements. "fifty-six centimeters," he said, at which my husband pointed out that surely the doctor had got it wrong, and after that they both went back into the other cubicle.

Then the anesthesiologist, the obstetrician, and the midwife left the room, after first saying "thank you" nicely. "And thank *you*," I said.

Then it was just me there with the other midwife, me crying, the midwife washing me. The tiles were colored a faded caca brown.

Next time I'd like to tell you about how my cat Paweł met his death falling from the balcony.

How It Seemed I Had Time

I sat down, and for once there was no one hanging off my boob, no one a-poking me with the beak of a sippy cup to give them juice (or with any other protrusion for me to give them something). I just sat there. Kubica hadn't become champion yet; the Polish Euro Cup squad, not yet plunged into total apathy, were tucking into bread rolls and bananas. I could watch a thunderstorm over the distant outlines of the city with no chance of it reaching my village, the white meadow, the pheasants, the washing safe on the balcony. I sat there and it lasted maybe two milliseconds before my husband came to talk about the book.

Winnie-the-Pooh in the sing-along pop-up book series—Play-a-Song—published by Egmont, batteries included. A pop-up picture on every page! Ten push buttons to play! Sing along with the music.

You want to pause it? Press the star!

My husband flicked the balloon button and showed me the words marked with the same red balloon: "Bouncy, trouncy, flouncy, pouncy, fun, fun, fun, fun, fun!"

"Could you sing the words to this tune?"

Unfortunately it didn't work. Maybe the translation was bad or I didn't have the right educational qualifications, but there was no harmony of words and sounds. At my husband's request I sang "How Sweet to Be a Cloud" to the tune blaring out from Winnie-the-Pooh, or "Up, Down, and Touch the Ground" from the Eeyore button. And it was all very jaunty, but still sounding somewhat like the ancient hymn *Mo-o-o-ther of God,* when he gave me a sly look: "The buttons are mixed up," he said. "You see where it's a balloon there, you have to sing along to the umbrella, and Piglet is actually Tigger. I figured it out."

And now it's very early morning, I'm sitting in the kitchen and looking for the star you have to press to make everything stop.

How My Cat Paweł Fell to His Death from the Balcony

Paweł was with me and my husband from the beginning. My husband brought him over in a carrier bag with his toothbrush and some other stuff and asked if they could move in with me. Yes, they could, and at the time Paweł was twenty to thirty centimeters long and had one black whisker and one white one. Paweł then appeared regularly in various family photos up until the last Friday in May, when he met his death falling from the balcony.

My sister and her son had just come over.

I'm not blaming her, because I now know it was my inattentive subconscious that killed Paweł, but for the purposes of synchronicity I'd like to emphasize that they'd just come over and created their usual air-sign whirlwind, which I and my water-sign children watched from along the fine line between a shrug of the shoulders and a nervous breakdown. I had to open the balcony door to get some oxygen, and I need to own up and say it: I did slightly lose control of the situation, and Paweł got out—who knows when—and fell—who knows when, but we do know what he fell onto. Concrete.

But I didn't see it, so I looked for Paweł in the wardrobe, berating him, because he wasn't allowed in the wardrobe.

Then my husband came home from work and it became clear Paweł was not on the premises in the narrowest sense, so my husband went to see if he was lying anywhere on the premises in the wider sense. He wasn't.

And later on, a little numb, still hoping, we stood on the balcony late into the night, after the children had gone to sleep, and we talked about how maybe Paweł hadn't yet met his death, maybe he'd climbed over to the balcony next door, to the neighbor whose wife and seven-month-old daughter had died in a car crash, because the neighbor's window had been open for a while that afternoon, although it was closed now and he was hardly ever at home. I was always glad he was hardly ever in, because I hoped I'd never see him. At the notary's, when the previous owner told us about this neighbor, I knew already I didn't want to see him. Once, when we were loading the kids into their buggy in the hall, someone came and entered our neighbor's apartment. But my husband said it wasn't him, because he's taller and a bit more stylish. But through the crack in the door I saw bags of sugar in the corridor.

So we were looking down and sideways at our relatively new home and its bald patio, when I saw a black spot, something like a trash bag, near the communal rubbish area.

"Is that Paweł there?" I said to my husband.

"Nah, can't be," said my husband.

And in the morning he phoned me from work—he works in the wooded area just beyond the city boundary of Warsaw—and said:

"So anyway, I've buried him."

And Once Again the International Pizza and Pasta Acrobatic Eating and Beat the Clock Eating Championships Are Taking Place in Our District, and I Have a Notion to Tell You about It

But that's next Saturday, last Saturday I went to the cemetery to clean the graves.

"Do you know how to clean graves?" my mom asked, wrenching away the watering can and the skein of glass wool, which in our family

190

it's traditional to clean graves with. So in the end I didn't clean them, I just carried water, careful not to drip on my shoes, being as it's cemetery water.

"Mom, where do you want to be buried?"

The best spot would have been with Granny on my dad's side, since no one else has ever aspired to lie there with her. But it turned out Dad skimped on her the way she skimped on him all her life, and Granny's buried in bare earth, not in the tomb, and you are only allowed to add bodies to the tomb. A corpse has to remain in bare earth for seventy years before you can billet anyone else there. So Granny's grave, though distressingly occupied, proved of no value to me. I quickly made a note to check prices and take the necessary steps.

"Are you writing a poem?" asked my mom. "I don't know how you can write poems. Who d'you take after?"

Maybe my dad. I pushed the children's buggy back sadly, while Mom walked behind us, placing half zloty candles between the terrazzo headstones, for under each one of them lay somebody's special patron (my mother chose them): mine, my children's, my husband's; even all my younger sister's boyfriends had patrons, often young suicides or tragic deaths. A grave with two surnames flashed past, here lay Janina, under her first and second married names, and an anonymous soldier, clearly added in a hurry to Janina during wartime operations, when there was no time for courtship, let alone hygiene. The property market, I thought to myself, is a battleground. I'll just add myself to somebody when the time comes and I'll tell the kids to do the same. Besides, by then death will have been abolished, especially decomposition.

Back at our house, Uncle was waiting, and he came to the gate to meet us.

"What do slaves have on their shoulders and backs? Six letters, third one 't'?" he asked.

I thought slaves didn't have anything on, that's the whole point of them.

"A litter," said Piotruś's fiancée, who drew different conclusions from having nothing on.

"How are you feeling?" she asked, seeing my double buggy from New Zealand and the sleeping children. "I've heard you're a She-Ra, you don't feel pain, don't feel tiredness. Piotruś told me. Oh God, they're waking up," she added, peering inside the buggy.

They were indeed waking, like a July dawn rising over Stalingrad, hazy but vaguely threatening. The phone rang and a friend asked me what I was doing tomorrow.

"What do you think I'm doing? Sitting at home. The nearest decompression chamber is in Gdańsk," I said. "Come on over."

Back in the Days When Watchmakers Made Hair Pins

I got up early and decided to go swimming, as by now I had a real urge. The pool is for residents only, so at the reception you have to show the same proof as when you first moved in, some ID card preferably. But I still have my old, out-of-date ID, so I had to produce the deeds to my apartment and a record of registration. I brought my daughter with me, so just in case I took her birth certificate and her vaccination card. This dossier proved satisfactory, and we were just about to make our way to the changing room when they pushed another notice at me: a subscription to pay 300 zloty toward election campaign funds for the political party that uses the pool. Party members draped in towels looked out at me from behind columns, across the unruffled surface of the water.

And then I really woke up, and my mom came over with my daughter, though possibly it was a bit later and it was me who was coming back from my son's immunization, and they were sitting on the curb by the gate waiting for us. My daughter gave me some chamomile and thistle flowers, Mom whispered something in her ear and my daughter said, "I love you, Mommy." At home, a spider crawled out of the flowers and my mom said not to go in the kitchen, just to give her a piece of toilet paper. Afterwards she said she'd never seen such a beautiful, pearly spider.

Finally, early that afternoon, I felt I really had gotten up, or at least that I was awake. Wanting to describe it all, I opened my computer while my daughter sat on my lap, shrieking: "Quick, quick!" and: "Running away, running away!" Also: "Eight, nine!" We wrote a shopping list—juice, little cookies, frankfurters—and a second list of everyone we love. But not wanting to write names down like that in case they die, I opened another window and quickly explained death using a balloon as an example. Then my daughter sniffled: "Oogh no, I've got boogers," she said with despair.

We went to clean out the boogers. My son was asleep, Australians were checking if anyone needed rescuing. Like net curtains in a June draft, like peony petals I fell for the Corpus of Christi.

Rain Of Course

So I look out the window and everyone's better than me. Someone is even riding an ATV! Instead of working I'm cooking ham in Coca-Cola and drinking something from the bottom shelf. The bottom shelf is where we keep the booze my husband gets from my family, the top shelf is what he gets at work. No, he's not a doctor. I'm only allowed to drink the stuff from the bottom shelf because it's poorer quality, although the labels are more fanciful. In this way I'm referencing my femininity, since I need a drink as soon as I'm left at home on my own.

I had a dream about one of my sister's boyfriends, and I feel strange about it now. He asked me why I'd been talking about him to a girl from the foundation at a local association picnic. Actually I'd been dissing his old ass because he'd convinced my sister she had a genetic defect, which had supposedly caused her to miscarry their shared pregnancy. He even paid for the tests, then scanned them in and emailed them to G. He is, as he put it, "firing on all cylinders." I swear I didn't fancy him before those tests! But when someone is prepared to go to such lengths to prove they're "firing on all cylinders," that makes him a hard player, and I sure go for those, mowing down everyone in my way. Obviously the hardness of such a player subsides between the sheets, but for epidemiological and ideological reasons I consider this medical fact irrelevant.

The floor of my balcony is bathed in sun. The scrap of sky I can see from my computer is completely covered by a sullen steel-gray sponge. There's a challenge! Just put the laptop in a rucksack and get out there, enter the fray, the war of light and dark, not caring how it ends. It's just that I'm waiting for the postman to bring my new rucksack.

I'm waiting, waiting. Beautiful flowers on the balcony, husband at work, children healthy.

Why, remembering I've got one life which will end sooner than I'd wish or plan, do I put on a medley of baroque hits instead of playing the whole *Art of the Fugue*? Why don't the mitochondria in my body cry out, "Moron! Play the whole thing! You've got time!"

Because I haven't?

On Spewing out of Your Mouth

Jehovah's Witnesses with folders full of the kingdom of heaven came by, and I thought it was social services coming to take my kids away from me for wandering about in my nightie until noon. When they were gone I phoned my husband and said, after all there is medication you can take, so maybe I should take it. I live in great fear because I've lost the list of twenty-five wonders of the district I'm supposed to have described by the end of last month. I tried recreating them from memory, but I couldn't get past the first half dozen. Apart from that I'm obsessed with death. Of the species and of the individual. Bronka has it too, and she quotes some eighty-year-old writer: "Even as a child I felt that forcing someone to come into being was a preposterous abuse. Everyone should be asked if they'd rather simply not be." If grants for NGOs were easier to come by, I could spend my life asking everyone, before they were forced into being, if they'd rather they simply weren't. Lovingly, I'd lean over each unborn person and pose the question.

I've also recently attended an infant blessing.

When a child dies without being christened and it's still very tiny, like under thirteen centimeters, you give it a special blessing instead of a funeral. It's one option available to you. At the infant blessing there were about three-quarters of a dozen people, who watched the box containing the to-be-blessed child from a safe distance.

The father had painted part of the box a jolly color, the mother's part was muted. The father's part showed a silver Saab and a line of people lifting their hands in the air, while the mother's part had violet and blue swirls that looked like intravenous anesthetic. The Dominican monk took off his hood, recited the formula, and we all cried, all of us who had kept our distance. I wish I had a Dominican like that at home for crying. The gravediggers moved aside the slab with the aid of a rounded pole placed underneath it, and I thought, I wonder if that's how the wheel was invented—one day some alien civilization gave us a grave with a slab, and we thought, how can we move this slab, and we invented a rounded pole and climbed into the grave and flew down to Earth in it. The gravediggers put the box inside, covered it with earth and then with the slab, but whether my nephew who'd been blessed flew off anywhere I don't know. I left him some white flowers belonging to the gentian family, but when it came to the sad trip to a café I made my excuses.

*** (Granburying)

We buried Gran on the eve of All Saints. Baby girl, my baby girl looked like the princess of darkness, and of course danced in her cherry-red slippers for most of the funeral. Halfway through we had to go over to the Sunday School for a pee, but we came back as a host of angels was taking Gran to Paradise. To make sure we didn't leave before the end of the show, the organist moved without warning to the Chopin funeral march, and my baby girl performed an interpretive dance called "sliding on your tummy across a pew in time to the music." The emphatic way the organist produced sad notes with his gnarled hands suited her, since it enabled her to show the holy congregation the panty area of her little white tights.

The sun shone openly and, given the date, the cemetery looked like everyone was going to everybody else's funeral in an orgy of mourning. Nowadays you bring the body from such strange places, some mortuary or some chapel of rest. At one time the house where you mourned was a house of mourning. Gentlemen who specialize in the laying of wreaths on graves laid our wreaths on the grave and we went to Gran's house for the wake. As the woman who does the cooking in this family, I had decorated the table with violet napkins and was going to scatter some violet heads from the garden to amplify the effect, but I remembered that in this house of mourning Gran had already been rouged up, and I felt abundance had already been achieved, even an excess of the beautifying efforts relating to the worldly partialities and needs of my Gran. In the end, the table was decked out with violet flowers in my head, which entirely satisfied my needs at the very least. Here too, members of the family took turns telling stories from Gran's life, with either her or those of us present starring in the principal roles, which either ripped the soul to its tassels or soothed it.

First to speak in my head was my mom, who told us about when Gran was on her way home from market with two baby pillows, and word reached her that the teacher had hit my uncle, and she stopped off at the school office, transferred the two pillows under one arm and with her free hand she split the office desk in half, also shattering the sorry soul of the teacher sitting at it—a man who hit small boys not in anger or for their lack of educational progress, but simply because he was grappling with his drinking problem. Next, Auntie stepped forward to remind us how in Gran's family there was a lot of that postwar type of romanticism and did we remember how it was Auntie herself who carried Aunt Marysia's bridal veil during her wedding to Uncle Stasiek, and how during the vows a candle on the altar near Auntie Marysia's side went out, and some small while later she was killed by lightning. The postwar nature of this romanticism could be justified on the grounds that Auntie was peeling potatoes and listening to the radio when she suddenly stood up and went out into the field and was killed. I stepped forward in turn and asked whether the remaining grandchildren remembered Gran shouting "Prayer time!" Next, Ania appeared in my head saying she didn't think she'd be able to get through the mourning process properly and she was sure this business with Gran would bring on her post-traumatic stress disorder.

"Do you know what Gran's last words to me were?" I said to my husband that evening in our marital love-bed. "Go with God."

"What, seriously?" said my husband.

No, they were the second to last. Her last words were: "What are you doing up so early?"

Aimez-moi, Caron

I'm writing in a notebook stolen from Gran and I'm writing very small so it lasts me a long time. And then eleven years later I'm sitting in the kitchen in the middle of the night, children and husband asleep, and suddenly it hits me that when Dr. O. played us Josquin's "Mille Regretz," her wakeful gaze from beneath her fringe at the words "a thousand regrets at deserting you" may not have meant she felt sorry for me on account of Student A saying good-bye before classes because he was hurrying to catch a train home.

Then, but still eleven years earlier in relation to what happened eleven years later, I dream about Student A, and he tells me how he spent his holidays (he was in central Bulgaria, then Florence for a bit) and shows me a miniature Inferno, two centimeters by two centimeters, which he brought back from warmer climes. I ask him how he feels about my proposition, to which he replies that when he understood what I wanted he took it greatly to heart. I ask what his final attitude is toward the matter, and he says, "Positive."

Then, but more or less at the same time as Florence and the middle circle of hell, I read in Aristotle that apparently even a sponge appears to possess some sensory perception, so Student A and I eat some unassuming noodles on a sofa in the apartment my friend has lent us, and we stay the night. This takes place in an area once annexed by the Russian Empire, because there's no shower or bath in the apartment; instead, there is a tiled wood stove and a small radio. Anyway, toward morning I say to Student A that he should leave, just because. After he's gone I cry a bit and then I sort of eat my friend's chocolate, which turns out later to be the only memento her boyfriend left her before he went off and met someone else. This ages me. I start writing a novel with a plot about lesbian love, Nervosol tincture, snow, and the value system my sister and I shared: love, friendship, music, crap, God in everything we do, and by way of summary point sixteen: "I don't have any more values, do you?"

Student A wanders around the college with a sword, because he's a knight. Eleven years later, I'm a little sorry that he didn't flip out and hack our year to pieces, because maybe I'd have copped an explanatory scratch, some kind of first blood.

Then, eleven years henceforth from the time of the non-occurring bloodbath, St. Paul visits me in the kitchen and reminds me that I should act as befits my calling, suffering others unto me with love.

"Verily, verily, yeah." I take liberties. "For they have eaten and are sated."

About My Publisher

Once every quarter, on the first Martian Friday of the month, my publisher remembers me and writes me an email: "Send me a nude photo of yourself." Sometimes I send him one, other times I ask if I can send him a picture where I look like the Virgin Mary. But sometimes I turn the tables on him and demand to know why he doesn't love me anymore. I learnt this trick from Basia.

Basia has a grandmother who weighs about two hundred kilos and barely moves from the bed made up in the living room. Near the bed there's an antique dresser which also weighs about two hundred kilos and doesn't budge either, but nobody makes a big deal out of this. Basia's grandmother makes dark cakes, the kind grown ups eat, and in the center my mom sticks a violet rose and my birthday candles. The first time Basia's grandma sees me in a push up bra she says: "You've changed greatly to advantage." Apart from Basia's mom, Basia's grandma had another child, a boy, who sat on the kitchen stove and died from the burns. No one in that family could forgive anybody else. When Basia's grandma sets off to join her son, I wonder if they'll find a square coffin.

In their recently sold house, Basia is primping her hair in front of the mirror: "I'm going to do it like this for my man."

"But what for?" I ask.

"To lure him."

"But he'll already be yours."

"But he might be writing something."

Basia's "but" is always one better than my "but." Basia is an expert in sexualizing church property and retaking Maturas on the Poland of the Jagiellonian kings. Basia likes to bellyache when men leave her. When this happens we see each other more often, and Basia always asks me: "Film me singing 'I Love You, Life.' Go on." Sometimes in the middle of the night we call the veterinarian's office, where a vet I adore works, and we record our interpretations of children's TV bedtime songs on the answering machine. We know my vet is there and can hear us. How do we know? Because we do. My vet is dumber than that fox terrier of his, but it's passion and I have to sing.

I go and get married, Basia goes to some party and meets a Japanese guy. For a long time they speak to each other in the language of love, which sounds kind of like Italian, but when you listen closely it turns out to be a mix of English, Japanese and figure skating sports commentary-speak. Basia's Japanese guy grows more beautiful and takes up more and more of the bed. And then they move with this bed to Minneapolis.

"I dreamt about you," Basia says to me transatlantically. "I dreamt I wanted to tell you something and you told me to shut up because you wanted to tell me something."

"If you like, Basia, I'll send you a nude photo of myself where I look like the Virgin Mary."

About My Son with Bond

I have a son with the new Bond. He's not in the cinemas yet, but I've already had his baby.

The grandmother of my son with Bond, the father of my son with Bond (my husband, that is), everyone sees milk and honey in my son, peace and comfort. Though it's blue milk. What do I see in him? A glinting knife and a black gun. But to keep up appearances I talk to my husband about my son with Bond's future. Maybe he's going to be an athlete.

"His head's too big for an athlete," says my husband.

"But what about a shot putter? For a shot putter it would be good," I say.

"What's he supposed to do? Putt with his head?" asks my husband pityingly though it's me who pities him, since I haven't told him who I've had his son with.

"How'd it happen you have a son with the new Bond?" Bronka asks.

"Well I was just standing at the window, you know, and he came by on horseback, jumped up off the horse, hung in the air at my eye level and asked if I would come over. 'Now?' 'Now.' So tell me, wouldn't you have gone, too," I ask, "for a five o'clock rendezvous?"

"I see," says Bronka. "So you mean it happened by imprinting."

That's not true. All through the pregnancy with my son I tried to focus on one image: my neighbor's five-year-old daughter splashing in her wading pool. It's the middle of summer and above her head, flapping about on a sisal rope, four silver foxes are being aired. Collars. When this image was out of order I sat and waited, cutting and pasting yellow flowers. But I must have missed something, and now I have a son with the new Bond.

I carry him with me everywhere, I tie him onto myself and off I go, because you should always keep a knife and a gun close, next to your body.

But at nighttime, somehow my son comes less from Bond, more from an angel in heaven: he calls me so softly, and sometimes he doesn't even call, just scratches the quilt with a tiny nail, an eyelash rustles against the pillow and I'm already running. I bring him to my bed, put him on my breast and laugh as he kicks his feet in time to each gulp and falls asleep, still kicking. I fall asleep too, walking barefoot through snow.

TRANSLATED FROM POLISH BY MARIA JASTRZĘBSKA

João de Melo

Strange and Magnificent Powers

ONE MORNING I AWOKE EARLY, well before seven, which is unlike me, but I felt perfectly rested. Most days I allowed myself to linger in bed wrapped in the warm covers for an hour or more, listening to the sounds coming from both inside the building and from the street, or listening to my majestic Beethoven collection, reading a book or luxuriating in the warmth of the bed with closed eyes and a calm heart. Thus I was surprised by the burst of energy that made me jump up, without even stretching with grunts and yawns, or even snuggling down in the warm sheets for a little longer (I'm given to staying up late and am not at all fond of useless early-morning rising). I even forgot to gaze with tenderness at the photo of my departed wife, and to kiss it, which I did infallibly each morning when I got up, taking it from my night table and remembering, with sighs of love and longing, her eyes, her smile, the life with her that continued to impregnate my memories.

I felt—I can't say it any other way—endowed with strange and magnificent powers. A very unusual wave of optimism swept across my mind and my spirit, expelling the dark thoughts that come to us at dawn and ruin our poor days, painfully etched into our souls by the loneliness of our flat and empty Portuguese time that moves along monotonously, marked by the same daily routines, taken along by the inertia of a lack of feeling for everything that happens to us and around us.

On an impulse, very hungry and buoyed by the will to live, I took care of everything I had to do and more: a good half hour of gymnastics to stretch my body and delay aging; the daily cold bath to stimulate the functioning of my brain; the careful trim of my beard in the magnifying mirror; scrupulous cleansing of my skin, eyes, ears, and mouth. I ate a large orange, almost as big as a full moon on a summer night, and a plain yogurt; slowly and conscientiously, I chewed a piece of toasted bread with a crust as hard as a nut shell, smearing it with honey and cinnamon; I drank my hot mint tea, without sugar. And I smoked the first cigarette of the day—serenely, in the blessed quiet of my home, still thinking of nothing, without regrets or worries about ailments or health setbacks, nor even any complaints about having been left a widower. In a short time, dressed and groomed to my standards, as always, I was ready to go out. I was content with life, I wish to stress, as I had not been in a very long time.

But it was too early to start the routine of my morning rounds. This being the case, I distracted myself by tidying up the house, moving about for more than an hour, listening to classical music, aware of the stirrings of the neighbors next door and above me, following their sleepy movements with my imagination. I was familiar with their daily rituals by which they prepared themselves for twelve hours of daylight spent in the streets, at their jobs, strolling in the sun, or sitting for a chat with friends on the stone benches of the only public garden in the neighborhood.

When I finally left the house, it was full morning with a pendulous light, already high in the sky, announcing spring weather. Lisbon glistened under the curve of a clear firmament that illuminated the colors, the great river estuary, the reliefs, and the landscape of the city. Just as I had closed the door to the street behind me, a young Roma gypsy approached. She was selling calendars to passersby, and she asked me for money for food, saying she had not yet eaten anything that day. Even though the year was half over and I had plenty of calendars, I didn't hesitate to give her a five euro bill for one of the wall calendars—which, by the way, was somewhat garish and in bad taste—to hang in my kitchen. But it was with a rare feeling of inner peace that I saw her run along happily, incredulous, skipping, in the direction of the bakery on the corner, where I was also going for my morning coffee. Walking in behind her, I heard her order a rice ball and a coffee with milk, which she ingested on foot at the counter, to the distaste of some of the customers, who openly demonstrated their dislike of the Roma, and who didn't tolerate any gypsies in their midst. I noticed that she was famished, feeding a centuries-old hunger, visible in those dark eyes, on her not very clean face, and even in her lusterless braided hair that she tied at the back of her neck with an elastic band.

Attentive and fascinated, I kept watching her eat, sitting at my regular table in the corner, waiting for the young man to bring me my order: a double espresso, a bottle of sparkling mineral water, the paper with the morning news. The waiter who attended me greeted me with the joviality of someone seeing a family member. He knew how I liked my coffee, which papers I read, and which was my favorite table— he always reserved it for me for the time I usually showed up. His name was Adérito, he was from the north of the country, and he could never resist starting a conversation with me. He loved to talk about the weather and the forecasts. He used a lot of diminutives. For example, the cold was always "a little cold"; the water bottle, which he let me touch with the back of my hand to test if the temperature was all right, was the "little bottle of water." Adérito bestowed all his rituals of serving a table on me: a discreet, affectionate greeting, two or three pithy remarks or asides, the mutual courtesy between two gentlemen who sincerely respect each other, a familiar smile to begin and end our daily protocol. Afterwards he'd walk away at a determined clip, very professional, to attend to other customers.

Then it was my turn to place my attention on stirring the sugar, emptying the cold water into the glass, unfolding and opening the paper on the table, and running my eyes over the tragic headlines in large font that took up the entire first page. Yes, in fact, the world was turbulent and dangerous, a badly written and poorly staged tragedy, day after day mired in wars, earthquakes, floods, accidents, and political slogans that announced epidemics and economic catastrophes. There was talk of crisis, of a difficult time of austerity that threatened to trample and unravel our lives, brandishing opinions like weapons in a duel. As impressive as this was, there was one fact to console me: this violent, nefarious world was far away, very distant from my door, usually happening on the other side of the planet. I wasn't obliged to ruin my day or my already short time to live with so many fearsome things that were happening far from my home, my street, the sheltered and unreal country in which I still believed. I therefore turned the page of the newspaper and moved on. Consoled, I turned my attention to the inside pages where they didn't talk as caustically about the world as on the front page, and where there were color ads, photos of beautiful half-naked women, and the deliciously banal stories of telegenic people, and above all my beloved crossword puzzles. I do them with the greatest concentration, absenting myself completely from the voices and everything else going on around me—taking distracted sips of coffee and brief gulps of that pure water that hydrates my skin and nourishes my physical and mental health every day. It's not just a way of passing the time in my incipient old age and retirement, but a way to pass on to the world my knowledge of general culture and my mastery of the Portuguese language in each crossword puzzle.

And it was from the depths of that admittedly deaf absence from the misfortunes of the outside world that Adérito, the waiter, calls me and brings me back to reality so that I see what is going on in the street in front of the entrance to the cafe. There aren't that many people who want to come in to see me at my table, it could be little more than a large family. But it's sufficient, in any case, for the waiter to describe it hyperbolically as a stampeding throng. In the lead is the young girl from a little while ago, the very dark little gypsy with the braids, to whom I had given the money for breakfast in exchange for the horrible calendar with its cheap, garish designs, too cheap even for the already loud colors of my kitchen.

"They insist on talking to you, sir!" insists Adérito, walking toward me with a barely contained excitement, and in a state of indignation at those sordid and inopportune people from Romania who were never welcome or tolerated in their workplace: the street. Around us, heads nodded in agreement, supporting and underscoring Adérito's opinions, just because he had been the first one to speak and to say out loud what the others were thinking. I know that the Portuguese hate some foreigners, not all of them. But they need someone to take the initiative to express their hate for them in a loud voice, and to then look around and reap the applause of the eyes and mouths that until then pretend not to be there, distracted, and thinking only of their own lives.

The growing crowd threatens to force its way inside, to destroy the cafe and rain blows on anyone who tries to impede the people from coming to me, talking to me, listening to me, touching me, even if just with a finger. I promptly agree to receive them and talk with them without reservation, but outside on the street. This was an attempt to avoid provoking more anger or rancorous looks from the customers who don't want to have any association or contact with the gypsies! They are a starving, disenfranchised people, a foreign European folk who still cannot find housing or work in Portugal. They have certainly come to ask me to spot them for the first meal of the day to kill their hunger. "If that were the only problem! I'd find a way to cover the cost," I thought. I'm not a rich man, not even close; I live honestly in the comfort of a pension and the survivor benefits from my late wife. But we have to help our neighbors, especially in the case of such poverty-stricken people, who are so hungry early in the morning at our doorstep, while we drink coffee and read about dramas and tragedies in the papers that will be tossed in the garbage the next day.

So I walk to the entrance of the cafe. The girl I had encountered earlier points at me. Jumping and shouting, perhaps a little too excited for my taste, she says to her followers:

"It's him! The man who saved my day by giving me something to eat!"

Immediately a huge clamor rises around me, something resembling a sob in a language that is unknown to me, interrupted occasionally by an order from the little gypsy so she can translate for me what each one of them is trying to say, all the things they are requesting of me. I am surprised that no one complains of being hungry, or cold, or living homeless in the wet streets, day in and day out. Or of being the object of social and labor discrimination by the Portuguese. I listen to them, I understand them, I sympathize with them. But what can I, a poor retiree, do for them? They answer me in chorus that I can very well give them a word, a simple magic word that will encourage them and save them from the misfortunes of this world. I immediately start to tremble with panic at the thought that I may not be up to their expectations or desires. I am not a revolutionary or a prophet. I was never a political man. How could it occur to them that I have special powers, a mystery that is mine alone, an influence that people don't recognize? They are really crazier than I had supposed; they believe in miracles, in false redeemers and demagogues who appear by coincidence in their lives and promise to save the world. But it suddenly occurs to me to say the word "revolution" to them. And immediately they start jumping up and down, erupting in a sudden collective fury, as powerful once again as they had been before in their poor, distant lands, finally recovering their dignity after many years of silence and humiliation outside of their country of birth.

I watch them disperse, each one headed for his own destiny, only to see them return a short while later bringing more and more people with them. Now some hold up a lame man with an atrophied leg: he extends a hand to touch me and it's enough for him to start jumping and dancing, proclaiming that his leg seemed to be giving off an electric charge, gaining shape and volume, and becoming perfectly functional. Then they bring a blind man to my presence: I look him in his blank eyes. And suddenly he is astonished to see the very blue sky, the trees draped in green, the birds flying here and there, public transportation stopped or in motion, the buildings of all shapes and colors around him. Behind him come two junkies with teeth the color of lead and purple gums, gray hair, skin, and clothing, miserable human detritus. Suddenly the unbelieving eyes of these forgotten beings light up and they feel free of the cursed dependency and its social slavery.

The worst is that all who are saved and redeemed by my strange and magnificent powers of this day leave to proclaim the miracle, the marvel of the great metamorphosis that I have performed on their lives. They go out to find others, always others, many, many others. They bring them at a run, dragging them or pushing them like living dead, so that none of them misses the great and unique chance of their lives at a time when there is no pity or mercy for any of them in this land that belongs to others.

There is even a moment when the people take the entire street by storm and block the traffic in both directions. I can't see the whole crowd, even after climbing on a chair and then on one of the cafe tables. I know that now I have hundreds, thousands, even millions of poor and indigent people waiting for me outside on the street. They finally ask me to climb a tree or to stand on a balcony. They need to see me, and above all be seen by me. Without this, they say, they will all return again to their miserable condition, to the nameless misfortunes of the sick world they came from, persecuted and rejected. They shout, they murmur things that are impossible to believe. Someone even tells me that there are more and more people with eyes glowing like embers in the crowd, eyes of healthy people who had come to beg me to resurrect their dead—and that this was promptly granted to them by my powers. The lost and absent return; they reappear at their homes, in the bosom of their families, unfaithful husbands and wives who left in search of invented or illusory love, along with children who disappeared into the ugly worlds of perdition that block their way home and make them forget their desire to return.

Many are reconciled who thought themselves incapable of forgiving. The poor and the starving finally feel their stomachs full and at peace. The depressed, looking around suddenly, meet my serene, beatific face, and smile at me with the happy demeanor of those who feel cured of the soul's infinite ills. The old people cease being sad as the saddest night of the world; they no longer have pains in their backs, in their joints, or dizziness caused by problems in their spinal columns. Even cancer patients venture to believe that the poisonous snakes and scorpions of their disease have died inside them. The hopeless unemployed proclaim me a miracle worker for having helped them find the job of their dreams. And the failed and desperate give thanks to God for having sent them a divinity, an earthly messiah, a new redeemer of the world who will also save them from shame and disgrace in public, in their homes, and in the bosom of their own families.

There is so, so much human happiness around me that it doesn't take long for a war to break out between those who hail me as a prophet and those who feel inconvenienced by the traffic gridlock, the crowds, and the excessive noise in the habitual tranquility of the neighborhood, and other hateful little disputes. They all want to see me, to approach me, to touch me even with a fingernail, or to exchange a brief look of supplication and salvation with me. Deep down, they need as much to believe in me as to believe in the faith that they have in me. They don't take long to break the dike, to smash the windows of the cafe where I used to come every morning just to read my paper and look out at the people of the city, on foot or in cars, passing by the café windows on their way to work. Now the sirens wail in the distance, and the strident whistles of policemen sound closer, followed by the blue lights flashing on the security forces' fast cars. The rioters take positions on the street corners and try to raise barricades to block the authorities from invading my bunker, from arresting me and dragging me away in handcuffs, to who knows where.

Adérito, the waiter, whispers to me that they're coming not just to arrest me and take me away, but to kill me on the spot, in front of all of them, the gypsies and the others, certainly with a bullet between my eyes or in the back of my neck, making it look like an accident, exterminating my poison in one blow. In an instant I had become suspected of social agitation, he says; and I had empowered the people not with order, or religion, or morals, or laws, or the political dogma of the State, but with the idea of human justice and decency. In the popular heart, nothing was more explosive than the dream of a new ideal for the future.

The best plan, he suggests, is to crouch down and follow him on all fours, crawling between the legs of the tables and chairs of the cafe, so that we can escape out the back entrance, where the merchants and cleaning ladies and bakers come in at all hours, starting early in the morning. Then he asks me to run ahead of him, to run far away and never look back. According to him, there are extremely envious people in this world and in this Portuguese city, people capable of the worst treachery in the kingdom of God, who would force me to reveal the secret of such strange and magnificent powers, on this single day of glory and joy that never again returned, except in my thoughts, in my vision of what is good, in my modest and innocent dreams— the dreams of a poet.

TRANSLATED FROM PORTUGUESE BY ELIZABETH LOWE

Marius Daniel Popescu

from *La Symphonie du loup*

THEY WERE NOT YOUR FRIENDS, they were there like characters on a stage, and the backdrop was the scenery of an entire country. You are one of those witnesses to the misfortunes of the world, you have lived and you live to see, to hear, and to tell.

You were a boy of thirteen and you sniffed people out and sniffed out their habits. You used to come on foot to this ruined factory over the fields that linked the city suburbs and the highway.

They were relics of the Party era, they were the have-nots of the new system. You let them treat you as their "boy." From time to time they would send you to do their shopping.

The people who benefited from their services were, for the most part, people like them, poor and on the margins of the world, people that lived off scrap. They all wore the same bottom-of-the-range sneakers. The laces of their shoes were stained with the same grease that stained their hands. You sensed in each of them a will for revenge, a desire to smash their fist into someone else's face, or against a wall.

You noticed their kindness, their concern for the child you were. When you asked questions about the ghost factory, they explained everything you wanted to know, to the smallest detail. You would notice the softness in their voices, and their knowledge of a skill they could no longer use.

They were like sailors obliged to continue living on a disused naval base. You had become aware that the world you perceived through your five senses was much more complex than the world of your dreams. You dreamt of your outings to the forest accompanied by your friends; you dreamt that you flew over your grandmother's town, flying like one of the swallows whose nest hung from the eaves above the lamp on your grandmother's patio; you dreamt of the fish caught during the day; you dreamt of your uncle's company car that you had already driven alone at the wheel; you dreamt of your girlfriend. But never did you dream of the hardest, the most extreme, most shocking, the most unexpected encounters in your life.

Between the twelve of them, they occupied several of the factory's hangers; they were at once the fictive owners of two clashing worlds and the employees of a carnival God, made of pulped cardboard, his veins drawn on his body with lipstick. You spent long hours there with them.

You made comparisons between the world of your homework and this world belonging to them, you compared secondary school equations with scrap merchants' gestures. You thought about forming an equation out of gestures and spoken words. You felt that looks and physiognomies could be put into an equation. You realized that equations could not contain the vibrations in your body, in your voice, when you saw these people, who welcomed you, reeking of distress, incomprehension, ignorance.

They were cloistered between the walls of a moldy cathedral, they swam in the waters of words without roots, you experienced these men as one might experience snails one sees crossing the road, being squashed one by one by the wheels of cars, by other people's feet.

They had families to feed, each of them had children at home. They were at once angels and brutes, you knew them down to their slightest mannerisms, you knew they were capable of cradling babies in their arms, you knew they were capable of killing.

You had your own kingdom there, built of smells both delicate and foul, of images of saints and devils, the taste of petrol and plastic, the noise of metal saws, the feel of steel plate. You were a king. Because your great-grandfather was the administrator of the king's forests in your region, because I had narrated scenes of my father's life, at the age of thirteen you sometimes took yourself for a king. In your mind you transformed these twelve workers into your subjects and you gave them tasks to accomplish, duties, rewards, and medals.

They didn't pay you much attention, they thought of you as an innocent that strayed into their world, they saw you as a child without ties, they thought you clung to them and this thought was not altogether untrue. To some extent, all they thought about you was true: you wanted to live, to get to know the world outside of your family universe, your home, your street. You had ventured outside of your neighborhood, outside your town.

They were on the outside. They were living the drama of a bruised country. You were a boy of thirteen and smelt the odor that came off their trousers, you breathed their breath, their blunt words, their way of living with their backs against a wall much bigger, much more impenetrable than any physical wall: a wall of solitude.

You were the only one among them who brought a flicker of nostalgia, of *joie de vivre*, or a desire to cry. When you cried because your string bow made of high tension electric cable broke, three of them came to you to ask what was wrong; you told them, they listened, and then they made you the best bow you would ever have: with this bow you could go hunting deer in the forest of your childhood.

You always thanked them for their help, for their advice, their kindness to you. They sensed that you were not one of them, they sensed that you were not of the potential enemy's camp either, they loved you as one loves a kid that crosses the street with his head held high, they loved you and you loved them as one loves whatever one happens upon in life.

The cast-iron stove factory was no longer operational, and the orchard that surrounded it, which was several hectares in size, had not been kept up for years. The ground beneath the apple trees was covered with tall grass, the trees were no longer cut back, no one worked the land, the harvest was slender, and the wooden posts that marked the edge of the farm property were rotting at the base and leaning to one side.

You spent hours in the workshops and in the orchard that surrounded them, the change from the smell of rust to that of the earth took place gently, like drifting asleep with your eyes open. You used to play Red Indians between the overgrown trees, or you would while away time watching the flowers, the blades of grass, the lizards. You scraped at the earth with sticks you found by your side, you lay on your back and watched the sky. You saw grasshoppers bustling around your immobile body, you heard the crickets and the cracking of branches that mingled with the far-off voices of the workers.

They knew you played in the orchard, they had gotten used to seeing you running between the trees. You picked apples for them and carried them over to the factory.

One day, when you arrived in one of the factory's hallways at around four o'clock in the afternoon, you saw through the window a horse in the orchard, and you knew it was the Gypsy's horse. You recognized the horse that belonged to the Gypsy that lived a few houses down from your grandmother, you were happy to see it there, free amongst the apple trees, it wasn't tied up and it moved around slowly.

This horse was another witness to the dead factory and to its last twelve workers. Its master had spotted the orchard when walking past, along the road, and he brought his animal here every morning, early, then he came to take it away in the evening, at sunset.

The Gypsy was a man of small stature, his back and arms were muscular from the labor he did every day in the town's freight railway station. He wore a mustache and the rest of his face was well shaven, he had a small brick house without any paint on the outside, where he lived with his wife and his four children.

Most of the workers did not like the Gypsy. They began to talk about him, saying at first: "That one with his horse, he's got no business being here!" then treating him as a chicken thief, as "jobless," and as a member of a "filthy race." You heard their unkind words, you noticed that their eyes sparked when they talked about the Gypsy in the black hat, they criticized him mercilessly, little by little this Gypsy became one of their biggest obsessions.

They considered the orchard their own, the Gypsy and his horse as intruders, undesired and lawless. They could not bear seeing the horse grazing on the tall grass in the orchard, they spat on the ground insulting a world they said was "badly made."

You did not know how things were going to turn out with the Gypsy, his horse, and these twelve workers, you sensed a hatred that exuded from them each time they spoke of the horse. This hatred was a sort of fog that coated all the scrap metal in the deserted factory, it transformed the hallways into a labyrinth, which made you think of a disused cemetery.

They wanted to fight against someone, against something, they wanted to revenge themselves on some enemy or other, they hated politicians and priests, they hated their poverty, they hated the Gypsy and his horse, who represented one of the roots of the ill.

The fog that came out of their bodies, their words, and their gestures got thicker and thicker, you noticed how they had begun to walk as if blind through the objects that made up their day-to-day world, they exhaled fog and cloaked it around themselves like a thick blanket one might wrap oneself in completely, they could no longer work without glancing out at the horse that lived in the orchard. You felt the heavy treading of their boots. Crossing through this fog made your eyes and ears sore, they spoke less and less to you, the fog coming out of their guts solidified itself on the walls and on the scrap metal strewn about, like the green plaster stage decorations for a battle scene or a suit of camouflage.

You entered the large hall to look for some ball bearings to use to make a scooter, and the horse was there. They had dragged it into the enclosure with a rope, they had positioned it on a large slab of steel plate, and they had welded its hooves to the metal.

You stopped a few steps from the animal, immobile on its hooves. It wanted to move, it wanted to leave the place, it could move nothing but its neck, its head, its tail, and some muscles in its thighs. Most of the workers were drunk, and they mocked the horse, crying: "Go on, go on," laughing as the animal attempted to detach its welded hooves from the slab of metal, they were sitting around the metal slab and they passed around a bottle of liquor that they lifted to their rough mouths. The fog was total. You could no longer move. One of them noticed you and said, "Come here boy, come and do some riding!" Despite their apparent good humor, they were all frozen stiff, like the empty bottles you often saw on the side of the tracks you took across the fields. They were proud of their deed, the horse had become their living trophy, they were enjoying themselves in this fog heralding death and mourning, they wanted to show they were strong, invincible. They were fighting their own fog.

You had gone silent. Your words remained somewhere in your throat or escaped from your neck and your face in a wave of heat and perspiration. For the first time in your life, the world had become a theater whose stage you had to cross.

Enveloped by the horse, the twelve workers, the Gypsy, the orchard, and the scrap metal, you turned your back on it all, you turned your mind toward home, you took refuge in thoughts about your schoolbooks, then you were able to say a few words, you said, imperceptibly: "He must be hurting!"

When the Gypsy arrived in the hall, the sun was no longer in the sky, he saw his horse covered in a whitish froth and welded by his hooves to the slab of sheet metal, and he wailed. His wailing, his eyes looking up to the ceiling, his arms spread wide, and then his hands falling to his head made each of the twelve workers step back, back up against the wall. There was a silence in which only the breathing of the weary animal could be heard. Your childhood tumbled inexorably into a world previously unknown. At this moment you knew you were the freest and the most lonely of men. The twelve workers had not finished their massacre, you watched them circle the Gypsy and threaten him with death. They pushed him toward the door and, using the welding tool, they sawed the sheet metal around the horses' hooves. The horse now had enormous, stinging, cutting hooves, it walked trembling, with difficulty keeping its balance, the workers screamed with joy to see the Gypsy crying for his animal.

You had no weight, your body became a memory, the horse fell sideways onto some cast-iron ingots, you saw its blood, you saw it get back up and move on toward the orchard, then it fell again.

The twelve workers formed a sort of procession around the animal and the Gypsy, who was trying in vain to hold up his horse; they walked on the traces of blood spilling onto the tarmac, they were saying "Get the hell out of here!" Their faces were clenched and their eyes were bulging out of the sockets, like gangrenous wounds.

The horse died in the tall grass in the orchard and the Gypsy watched over it for the whole night. Its corpse decomposed beside an apple tree. The stench it gave off lasted for weeks, forcing the workers to leave the place. They never returned to the old cast-iron stove factory.

In autumn, apples fall on the horse's skeleton and on its hooves soldered to the sheet steel slabs. You are now nearly forty years old, your memory no longer sleeps, you often dream of the Gypsy.

TRANSLATED FROM FRENCH BY OLIVIA HEAL

SRĐAN V. TEŠIN

Where Is Grandma, Where Do You Think She's Hiding?

Even when someone nameless dies, I'm broken with sorrow;
But, I cheer up: I still breathe!
　　　　　—Bai Juyi (translated from German by Slavko Jezic)

1.

She buttons up her frilly silk blouse, zips the zipper on the long wooly skirt, the one with the fake belt attached to it, pulls on her suede ankle-high boots, puts on the double-breasted tartan coat, ties a flowery scarf around her neck, arranges a lock of gray hair across her forehead, adds a bit more blush, pulls on her old netted gloves, picks up a canvas bag and her aluminum cane, almost soundlessly unlocks the door and leaves the apartment.

She passes an overturned garbage can, where stray dogs, cats, and other unfortunates had taken out everything that could be eaten and digested. With her cane, she moves the torn black garbage bag aside and takes the stairs to the path that leads to the promenade, bordered by a row of young bare-branched chestnut trees. She walks slowly, one foot at the time, hunched over, eyes downcast. At the end of the promenade there is a rundown shop, no more then a metal container plastered with various posters and advertisements—handwritten, torn, and sun bleached. She puts down the canvas bag and hands her grocery list through the small, half-opened window, to a drowsy shop girl. Two loaves of whole-wheat bread, five cans each of sardines, canned meat, and beef pâté, two boxes of pasta, half a kilo each, potatoes and onions, three packets of instant soup, two fifty-gram containers of cottage cheese, a liter of milk and a liter of yogurt, two cups of sheep's-milk yogurt, and three bags of frozen chicken meat. She pulls the neatly folded banknotes from her large red vinyl wallet and pays for her groceries, to the exact dinar.

An envelope sticks out of the mailbox. A retirement check. She almost tosses the bag and cane to the floor as she unlocks the mailbox, grabs the envelope, gives it a shake with both hands, kisses it, and tucks it into her coat pocket. Outside her apartment the cleaning lady is unhappily thrashing the doormat with a broom. The older woman gives a little cough and lightly taps the other woman's leg with her aluminum cane. She starts and jumps to the side. Without a word, the older woman approaches the door and unlocks it, not even glancing at the cleaning lady. After her door locks with a metallic click, a loud exhalation could be heard from the hallway.

2.

Morning on Mars always smells of the heavy fumes discharged by the neighboring factories. On weekday mornings, one hears the roaring of motors from the cars of the few residents that have jobs to rush off to, delivery trucks drone, cab radios blare, wooden and plastic blinds open and close, small children cry out, forcefully awakened and dressed by their parents, the shouts of night-shift workers returning home. On the weekends, the voices of drunken revelers resound like metallic bells, breaking the nocturnal calm, loiterers drink beer at daybreak and argue amongst themselves, sitting on dew-drenched benches outside the tenements, whose tenants, rudely awakened, curse at the drunkards to drive them away, empty beer bottles shatter on the building facade, police sirens wail in the distance, overloaded fruit and vegetable carts clatter down the uneven road, ungreased bike chains squeak. Seated upon discarded, broken concrete blocks, an impoverished stew of immigrants, vagabonds, and pensioners gathers, vaguely resembling the Campus Martius of the Romans.

3.

He shaves with a dull razor. Trims his mustache and sideburns with care. Using tweezers, he plucks solitary hairs from his cheeks. With the scissors, he neatens his bushy eyebrows. Legs shriveled like prunes, he stands barefoot on the moist ceramic tiles. The soap leaves a film on the ceramic and glass of the shower stall. He removes a clod of long gray hair from the shower strainer and gives the stall a quick rinse. He wipes the glass shower wall and the basin, opens a small single pane window to let the cool air in. He hastily ties a towel around his head, puts on the bathrobe and slides his feet into his slippers. He sits on the armchair and picks up a pension check from the coffee table. The amount is just the same as the previous months. It's going to be plenty to survive until the next check.

He glances over at the chest freezer covered with a lace doily and smiles faintly.

4.

—I'm coming!

. . .

—Who is it?

—We're from Social Services, ma'am. We're conducting a survey about the needs of the elderly.

—But, I'm not dressed properly. Can we do it at the door, through the chain?

—Do you not trust us? Here, our identification and official documents.

—There are all kinds of shysters out there, you know.

—We understand, but . . .

—Say what you have to say, I'm standing here in the draft, I could catch a cold.

—OK. Do you live alone?

—Yes, alone.

—Since when?

—Since forever.

—How old are you?

—What kind of a question is that?

—I'd say you're about seventy-five, not a day older.

—Add fifteen more, and, you guessed it.

—Have you been married?

—Yes, I have. My husband passed away fifteen years ago. A stroke. The same as his mother. It's hereditary with them. He was a good man.

—Do you have any children?

—A daughter. She also died of a stroke.

—Was your daughter married, and did she have children?

—Who knows? She ran away when she was sixteen, then just appeared after ten years with a little boy in her arms. She asked for money, and I gave it to her, but God knows what it was for. Never saw her again.

—And the grandson?

—My grandson appeared one day to bring me the bad news. He was the one who came to tell me that his mother died in the public hospital. Where they were and what they were doing—I never asked, nor did it interest me. For a while, he visited me regularly, fetched my groceries. Then I caught him stealing from me. I kicked him out and disinherited him. A leech and a bum. Never in his life did he lift anything heavier then a spoon. Nothing better could come out of such a mother. God, what have I done to deserve such disgrace?

—He doesn't come around anymore?

—No. And there's no need for him to try. He'd get this cane on his head if he showed up on this doorstep. Let him stay as far away from my sight as possible.

—But, who is taking care of you now?

—Nobody, son, nobody. I support myself now. And, if you have no more questions, I would like to go get dressed. I'm chilled to the bone.

—That's all we have to ask. Take these pamphlets. Everything you need to know is in here. If you need anything, give us a call. We could send you home-care workers from the gerontology department, they could cook something for you, do the laundry, or check your blood pressure.

—That's all right, thank you, but that is an unnecessary luxury, and there might be some wily crooks among those home-care workers, I've heard it all.

—Don't think like that . . .

—Go now, go now, good-bye, see you again.

—Good-bye, ma'am.

5.

She buttons up her blouse, zips up the skirt, puts on the shoes, puts on the coat, ties the scarf, arranges the lock of hair over her forehead, adds some blush, pulls on her gloves, takes her canvas bag and cane, unlocks the door and leaves the apartment.

Somewhere along the promenade bordered by the chestnut trees, there, adjoining the boxwood hedge, is the park with the concrete fountain in the shape of a frog. Across from the park, urban planners have installed children's playground equipment. In the park, strangers sit and read on the benches at irregular intervals—never glancing up from their books—strangers who not only do not talk to each other, but do not give two hoots about the existence of anyone else there, something that can be seen even from the height of an airplane. As nobody is using the playground, the equipment looks abandoned and unnecessary.

She sits on an unoccupied bench. The green paint peeling off the wooden crossbeams sticks to her clothing. From the canvas bag, she pulls out a book. She leafs through the pages and then begins to read. Although it is a dry summer, secret and suspicious looks fall like summer rain upon her.

6.

—Excuse me, ma'am, may I?

—If you must . . . I can't stop you.

—I see you are reading Singer's *Selected Stories*.

—Yes, I like this book.

—Me too. My favorite one is "Old Love." The part where Harry Bendiner says: "Once you pass eighty, you're as good as a corpse."—simply divine!

—I prefer what Ethel Brokeles says: "A man is never old."

—That's true!

—We haven't introduced ourselves. I'm . . .

—No need. We know each other. From the same tribe, so to speak. Our slogan is: Careful observation of small things reveals big things. Like recognizes like.

—Do you know the children's song that goes something like this: "Everyone has a granny, hidden in the cranny?"

7.

I have suggested to my so-called *colleagues* that we set up a citizens' association to better organize ourselves. We gather in the Mars park anyway, so we could create a forum to exchange the knowledge we've gained from experience. I could gather together, in my helter-skelter way, a list of ideas and techniques and have them distributed on little slips of paper. We could form a guild for all the grandchildren who hide their grandmothers in chest freezers, closets, cellars, attics, wine barrels, cabbage vats, rolled up in carpets, or hidden in linen chests under the bed, with a guild hierarchy of the bravest ones, those who have buried their grannies, theirs and others', in secret locations at night, or those who've had them preserved and mummified using various techniques, or those who cut them up into pieces, cooked them, and distributed them as food to the poor of Mars. In this guild, novices could be taught cross-dressing techniques, make-up, camouflage, and how to forge documents and signatures. We would collect donations for those whose covers were blown by the police and Social Services. The donations would pay for lawyers and defense teams.

My suggestions were rejected as redundant. The final decision was that the occasional meeting in the park, for now, is just fine. Nobody knows anything about anyone else—not their gender, name, or place of residence. That's the way it should stay. The majority was of the opinion that anyone who wants to socialize can join the Retiree's Club.

My experience has shown me that a human is born, but does not necessarily have to die. For no particular reason, people see aging and death as God-given things. Don't grannies live forever?

TRANSLATED FROM SERBIAN BY NADINE LINTON
AND ANICA TESIN

Veronika Simoniti

A House of Paper

Ride la stella Aldebaran, ride e fa:
to be, to be, to be or not to be
ride la stella, ride e fa: trallallà
to be, to be, to be or not to be
—Paolo Conte, *l'Orchestrina (Nelson)*

It was back last summer that I noticed I was shrinking. First by my clothes, by my long sleeves and pant legs, by my skirt falling below the knee rather than just above it, then by my shoes, in which my toes could suddenly not just wiggle up and down but Charleston left and right. This summer, my feet are swimming in their sandals, tripping me up as I walk down the summer pavement, with the greasy white lines of pedestrian crossings turning to bright dashes, exclamation marks, hyphens, the clouds stretching out at times into revision marks, unspaced, bold, italic, change the word order and the weather will change. All this meddling of alien hands and eyes with texts is changing the atmosphere, delaying the regular comet arrivals, undermining the psyche of translators, let alone authors.

As a translator, I bear my share of the guilt as well. With my own perspective and idio-whatever, I interfere ("grossly interfere" is the most common phrase) with authorial creations, counterfeiting them in another language. Perhaps this shrinking is my punishment for defacing all the books I have translated—over the last fifteen years mainly the works of a single author, the famous Janus Carta. I am the one to sift each of his words, turn it around, inspect it from all sides, sniff at it, even correct it with a faint twinge of conscience, that is, find a better equivalent when the rush of the narrative dulls the author's sensitivity to detail. But we, dissecting them to the bone, we drudges know every one of their weaknesses, we know where the blind fool has repeated a word for the third time on the page, we contract "she is cooking, and when dinner is ready" into "when she has cooked dinner," smiling maternally in our bitter solitude at each improvement. All writers should be proficient in another language and translate themselves into it—then they would see how thankful they should be for our hair-splitting *acribia*. After all, they can't expect us to shoulder the blame for their own shortcomings!

And now, having noted for some time that I am shrinking, I wonder if it might be a visitation of St. Jerome for my translator's sins. At first I blamed it on the sun and took to keeping in the shade, then I settled on clothes that were a size smaller, and on shoes that were two. I did not panic until I dreamt one night that I had shrunk almost to the point of disappearance. Frightened, I sent Janus Carta a postcard: "*Dear Janus, I have just translated your* House of Paper *and am now enjoying my holiday. The publisher assures me that it will come out by the end of September. Best wishes...*" I was one of the few who knew his real address, everyone else had to contact him by fax. It was his clever way of evading the pests who badgered him daily with three-hundred-page novels, asking for recommendations.

I had only met Janus a couple of times. His sharp nose sniffed out at once that I was single. A woman who could devote much of her time—all of it, in fact—to transplanting his oeuvre to another language. A woman with no other self-affirmation in her life. A woman perhaps secretly in love with her translatee. Paper eroticism, platonic pedestals, repressed elective affinity. A woman with a life unlived, with just the devotion needed to transfer his greatness intact to readers in her own language.

It was Janus who suggested a blood test in his letter, after I had complained about my perceived shrinkage and my fear of it. *It does not flow through our veins for nothing*, he wrote in his slanting hand, which pressed on toward a pathetically yearning future, *it carries secret messages under the parchment-like epidermis*. Strange that he did not use the more poetic verb *course*. Anyway, I mustered up courage and went to the health center, holding the author's imaginary hand in mine. Watching blood drops oozing into the test tube like wine lees, I agonized over what those young lab assistants would learn about me: decoding from the blood molecules and chemistry formulas who I was, what I wanted, and where I was headed, they would give me sage looks and most likely never tell me the truth. I would leave feeling stupid, with no more knowledge about myself, while they would look after me, joining their heads together and shaking them in disapproval. But in fact the doctor admitted that he was puzzled by my reduction, *reductio corporis* was how he put it technically, the first perhaps to have introduced this medical term. He told me to have my height measured at his office every month, and promised to pay particular attention to my case—to give lectures on it to his students, perhaps even at an all-important symposium in Tokyo, to which he aspired to be invited in five years. What I hope is that I am not reduced to a Thumbelina by then, accompanying him to Japan in a glasses or cell phone case, like a showcase Lilliputian.

What I feared was losing not only my size but my memory as well: losing my memories, knowledge, skills. What if the reduced size of my brain robbed me of my full self-awareness, what if my language knowledge cocooned in an imperceptible pore within some microscopic curve of my brain, never to be teased out again? A midget, I would squeak out sentences which could never hold or know a subordinate clause, let alone speculate on the simplest structural feature of another language. Janus Carta, partly concerned that the numbing fear might hinder my intensive translating, and partly, no doubt, fed up with me, tried to dismiss all my worries with: *My dear lady, if you are to remain tall, you must hold up your head.* It was easy for him to talk: I was the smaller one in any case.

Even after his death. Yes, soon afterwards rumors spread that he was ill. Worried as I was, I didn't dare ask him outright, hoping that he would reveal more in his letters, in his replies to my questions about what the hell he had meant with a word that could have several meanings in our language. And before I had gathered the nerve to inquire after his health directly, news came from his country of the unexpected demise of a great artist, matchless aesthete, and candidate for, or winner of, several prestigious international literary prizes.

On hearing the news I seemed to shrink even more. My summer straw hat began dancing around the circle of my head, its brim slipping over my eyes. Where is the disappearing part of me going? Perhaps I am evaporating in the white sun, the growing vacuum around me licking at my own edges, as fire licks at paper. I had always believed that I was doing something meaningful, something great in its smallness, that I was a Vestal Virgin of literary truth, a dictionary priestess in the service of Our Lords the Authors, a pious servant shuffling the carefully considered words that were engraved in books for all eternity. I had always wondered what it was like on the other side, in the world of a fool's freedom, where you can build yourself a house of paper written all over and simply live in it, and if you have built well, others come respectfully knocking on the door of your paper home, curiously peeping in to see if the writing inside is the same as outside. I had always wondered how it feels to be an author, how it feels when, halfway between your idea and your recording hand, a great fraud happens at the world's expense. Do you sleep peacefully, counterfeiter? Are you haunted by illusions, fictions, dreams? Are you real to yourself, or are you fading away into the white page, from whose milky light you can always emerge to reveal yourself in hazy outlines?

After Janus Carta's death this summer, there was no bookshop window that did not display his books. In my translation, naturally. He was discussed in cultural features on the radio and TV, in newspapers and their literary supplements. He sold like hot cakes, to be served with all kinds of tea. Disseminated in death, his sentences were blown like dandelion clocks to the City and the World: now he was heard of where he had previously been unknown. I, for my part, went on shrinking. The advantage was that it gave me a good excuse for a brand new summer wardrobe, especially a swimsuit. I followed the hot summer's cultural news on holiday at the seaside, my first real holiday because there was no more steady work for me to do; I had translated everything of Carta's there was to translate, so I could take a break now. And I was no longer pestered by anyone wanting to contact him. No one was interested in his fax number anymore.

I was sitting under a night sky in front of the pension, talking to people I had met at the seaside: to a historian uncovering the massacres after World War II and his wife discovering the pangs of post-forty aging, to a chatty cyclist who rode his bike to the beach every day, and to an elderly couple—to him, with his hair dyed a new color this year, and her, who had replaced the gentleman's escort from the year before. They were flattered to know the translator of a famous author they had not heard of until two months ago. We were sitting under the dark olive trees facing the sea, and the talkative cyclist said, *It looks like Taurus has shrunk: if we could see his eye in the summer, the star Aldebaran, it would certainly crumple up on itself, though it would go on giving an intense light.* He was the most perceptive of the bunch, the cyclist, the others were just nodding, bluffing their way through. Every now and then he would glance at my diminished breasts.

The evening and night were lit up by fireflies, whose cool, constant light is produced by a chemical reaction. As with glowworms: I saw a documentary on them once, worms hanging like stars from the ceilings of black subterranean caves, lowering deadly sticky threads to trap spiders and other unfortunates wandering into this Hades. That evening and night were the most peaceful in my life.

Autumn in the city, just as dazzling as the summer, was more eventful. Soon after arriving home, I had a phone call from a Mr. Henk, who introduced himself as Carta's lawyer. He claimed to have found some things, some notes to do with me. I was annoyed by the prospect of more hassle with Carta, who wouldn't let me rest even when he was gone. Still, I journeyed to the neighboring country to see Mr. Henk, who peered at me sagely from behind his mahogany desk. *This portfolio is for you,* he said, *papers and such, and also this key—before he died, you see, he told me to give you the key to his summer cottage, which is hardly bigger than this room, to straighten things out. By Carta's orders, I used to send a boy from a technical firm there to feed paper through the window—all he had to do was open the shutters and undo the lock on the window frame—into the house, or rather into a device inside, endless paper, but don't take it literally, it's just a phrase, paper can never be endless.*

Paper could never be endless? Hm. And I should go there to straighten things out? That was a good one. How could Carta expect anything more from me now that he was dead, even if it was death that had made him eternal and endless like his paper? How could he expect more than the faithfulness I had already bestowed on him?

The day was brilliant, the summer was Indian, and the cottage of Janus Carta on the hill was white—how much lovelier it must have looked in the black northern gale. I trudged uphill, my feet blistered from my new shoes, again a size smaller, and from the distance the house seemed encrusted, as if held upright by cardboard, or salt, or invisible threads running up to Aldebaran, the invisible star from the cyclist's conversation. Winded, I reached the door, fished out the key and tried to unlock it, but it seemed to be stuck or else forced into place by an unknown power, the natural force of air or water or vacuum. I went on pushing with all my might, and suddenly a multilayered lava of paper sheets slid out from behind the door. I tossed them aside, not minding at the time that they could be blown away, so eager was I to see what lay inside. Trying to clear a passage for the door, I removed a fair amount of paper. Machine-typed pages. Tired, I sat down in front of the house and picked up a few. All of them were headed by a date, a strange code, and the sender's name.

All had been faxed.

The fax. Carta's fax. His one means of receiving unwanted mail from the pests. Requests for an interview, for a feature in some magazine or other, for a recommendation; letters from budding writers eager for publication; texts by potential talents, by never-to-be literary stars. Anything that would have distracted Janus from his creative work had been channelled into this cottage where he had shut away the outside world. And as the lawyer had said, someone had regularly come to feed paper into the fax machine. Endless paper.

There was no stopping me in my zeal. It was morning and I had the whole day left to burrow my way to the answer.

In the red glow of evening, having emptied enough of the cottage to make sure that it contained nothing else but a little table for the fax machine and two old thesauri, I sat down, sweating, on a patch of grass still bare of paper, and opened a can of beer. The wind danced among the pages, playfully mixing them in an insoluble rebus. I smiled and raised the can in a toast toward the sky, *You are there, Janus, aren't you?*

The answer arrived like a paper airplane, folded in class by a schoolboy and sent flying into the teacher's face. I am being eroded by the outside world through the epidermis, the magic circle of my skin, and you, you packed that world into a cottage to grow rampant in its interior, to fill its guts like a tumor while leaving you untouched. You were alone in yourself to the last, while I am dwindling to nothing, running out, running out of words to describe it all.

I phoned Carta's lawyer, asking him to order a truck to take away all that cellulose, written all over with the desires and pleas and dreams of people I would never meet. Take the whole pile to the dump, or else shake it from the truck bed into the backyard of some zealous Carta biographer. But Mr. Henk would have none of it: for him, he said, *In re Carta* was closed. I switched off my phone, alone in the waning light with the layers of letters and words and sentences struggling for expression on the white paper, the only bright spot left in the twilight. I struck a match, bent down, and felt the mellow warmth of the pages which were slowly being consumed. The fire roamed across them as if to read every single one and take it along into the sooty sky, reddened by the transient light of the flames. Surely there would be a final full stop to this oeuvre, too.

TRANSLATED FROM SLOVENIAN BY NADA GROŠELJ

Harkaitz Cano & Andoni Aduriz

FROM *Mugaritz: B.S.O.*

LOS ALEJADOS

"We're not advancing much," Aurelio Malanotte complained.

"It's the stones, Señor."

". . ."

"The stones slow us down, Señor."

". . ."

"I warned you, Señor."

Aurelio pretended not to have heard the guide and whipped his horse hard, as many times as he'd heard the word "Señor." The horse redoubled its speed for a short stretch, but soon slackened its rhythm again. The guide rebuked him with a gesture—the rims of both their hats helped them avoid each other's eyes.

After midday the horses started to whinny and became frantic, greatly endangering the riders. They had to stop by a stream to cool down.

"The stones, Señor. In the heat of the sun the stones burn their hoofs: I told you it would have been better if the horseshoes . . . Besides, my mare is about to . . . They're going to collapse if we don't stop soon, Señor."

"Quiet!"

"Yes, Señor. As you wish, Señor."

"The stones. Damn stones. You should have eaten them all up. You and the rest of your tribe . . ."

The guide thought Aurelio Malanotte was arrogant and disrespectful. But he refrained from sharing his thoughts. He wanted to arrive before nightfall. It would be preferable to arrive before nightfall. He knew it was impossible to arrive before nightfall.

Sweat flooded Aurelio Malanotte's forehead. His thin eyebrows were not a strong enough dam to protect his eyes. Román, the hardened guide, much better equipped for the environs, was also suffering from the midday sun, but he wasn't momentarily coming undone like his Señor was. Aurelio Malanotte's pride didn't believe in making stops, couldn't read the landscape. Román had come to terms with the idea of going along with that arrogant fool until exhaustion did him over. It was taking longer than he thought. "Arrogance rides alone," he thought at one point, and felt certain that he, Román Expósito, would never visit Europe. He had no desire. What for? To be at the service of thoughtless, useless men like Aurelio Malanotte?

When it became clear that they wouldn't reach their destination they set up camp near a cliff. There was scarcely any wind, but they took shelter in a cave all the same, to be able to light a proper fire.

"There are snakes, Señor."

"And in the caves?"

"In the caves too, but fewer."

For the first time since leaving the camp, Román thought he saw a splinter of fear on Malanotte's face. Where did those splinters of fear come from? From a spiritual ax wound? Or were they, on the contrary, shrapnel from the threat of earthly reality? There was no way of knowing it. He found the white man's fear amusing at the beginning, but then he felt pity for him.

"Don't worry, I'll keep watch while you sleep."

Román threw two pieces of meat on the grill. There were pebbles all over the ground of the cave. Stones under the embers. Stones everywhere.

"The sun beats down on the rocks all day here and come nighttime the temperature is quite good."

The fire crackled and the meat breathed its flavors. Aurelio Malanotte had to admit it: it wasn't so bad in there.

"Are you all right, Señor?"

"Yes Román, thanks for asking."

Román took a wind instrument made of clay out his leather pouch. He played a joyful tune while the meat cooked.

"Do you have children, Román?"

"Three, Señor. Two girls and a boy."

Malanotte let a few seconds go by.

"Linda was all I had."

Román didn't answer. He dug his knife into the meat and cut it up on an aluminum bowl better suited for boiling liquids than serving food. He then passed the meat over to him with a very old fork he kept with his flute.

"Eat some, it'll do you good."

"I'm not hungry."

"You have to eat to keep sadness at bay."

"When will we reach Los Alejados?"

"Tomorrow around midday we'll be close."

"Is the road less steep from here on?"

"It's all downhill from here, but not easier. The stones, you see."

They could hear cicadas and other insects. The starry sky, a cricket for each star.

When he saw the tears fill Malanotte's eyes, Román told himself that not having eyebrows under the eyes, on the cheeks, was a great pity. Eyebrows like those would impede tears flowing all the way down the chin of an arrogant man, wrecking his composure. Román felt embarrassed for him. Was the manliness of the European male as feeble as all that? He flogged the horse in fury and, moments later, collapsed to the ground. Román was disappointed. He offered him a blanket in silence and discreetly retired to sleep.

The wind sneaked through the gaps in the red clay flute abandoned on the stony ground, voicing disquieting whispers. It took Aurelio Malanotte a while to fall asleep. He didn't see any all night, but he couldn't help thinking about snakes.

The following morning they left at dawn, before the blast of the sun started hitting hard.

Going downhill was worse. The path was narrow, barely wide enough for them to ride single file, even. The horses slipped on the rocky path; again and again, they scrambled and crashed against the stones. It was hard to hold the reins in the circumstances. Aurelio Malanotte was incapable of taking his eyes off the path. Stones and more stones, he saw nothing else.

Long before midday they saw a village in the distance.

"Is that Los Alejados?" Malanotte asked, trying to hide his nervousness.

"No, Los Alejados is further south. But they'll give us hay for the horses and water to freshen up."

Aurelio Malanotte delighted the village children. Never before had they seen a man *so* white. They offered him food that tasted strange and delicious at the same time. Everything tasted of potatoes. A woman—the mother of *all* of them?—smiled at him with curiosity, turning her neck this way and that, as if trying to observe him from every possible angle.

"Much longer before we reach Los Alejados?" he dared ask his guide again.

"A bit, not much."

Aurelio Malanotte started missing the metric system, kilometers, highway signs, round numbers, prime numbers, all numbers, anything that was a bit more concrete than "not much." Suddenly, an old, undeclared love returned: mathematics.

Malanotte heard his guide speak to the village men in a dialect he didn't understand. They talked and laughed. He imagined the dialogue: "Yes, that's him, the mad scientist's husband." Without waiting for his guide, he climbed the stirrups and took to the road again. He avoided looking behind him for a while but, when he did, he saw Román following him closely, in silence, without reproach, at a safe distance. He wasn't even mumbling "arrogant, arrogant fool" anymore.

The sun radiated molten lead again. Aurelio realized that he would reach Los Alejados—if he ever did—with his mourning completed: he had sweated out all his tears.

Román stopped his mare at the edge of a crevice.

"There it is. Los Alejados."

Barely three homes, all of them made of stone, right there where the rocky path ended. They couldn't see a soul from where they stood.

Aurelio Malanotte galloped toward the village. Out of respect, Román decided not to follow him.

At the entrance of the one-horse village he saw a mound of pebbles that looked like it had just been piled together. He tried to jump over the pile, but the horse failed the jump and they both fell on top of the mound.

Aurelio Malanotte turned over the pebbles with annoyance,

pushed them away with his arms, tried to stand up and didn't succeed. He lay face down on the bed of stones and, sinking his hands into it, started digging down.

He exposed a lifeless hand. He immediately recognized his wife's wedding ring.

Half a dozen farmers surrounded the woman's grave. They were surprised to find her husband there, holding the hand of the woman they had just buried.

They decided that white men must have strange customs and maybe he hadn't liked the fact that they, in Los Alejados, had buried her without waiting for her husband. Right there, under pebbles. Under pebbles and nothing else.

Pebbles without a river. Pebbles for Linda. Did they even know her name? Did they call her by her name or had they never gotten past "the mad scientist"?

The farmers stepped aside to let an elderly man with long straight hair pass through. He inclined his head softly, with true warmth, and with a quiet smile said:

"Welcome to Los Alejados."

EDIBLE STONES

Ingredients (serves 8)

The coating mixture:	60 g kaolin (white clay)
	40 g lactose
	1 g black vegetable dye
	0.5 g table salt
	80 ml water
The boiled potatoes:	16 small Cherie potatoes (32-35 g each)
	3 liters water
	24 g salt
The garlic confit:	500 ml Arbequina extra virgin olive oil
	1 garlic bulb
The potatoes coated in clay:	The boiled potatoes
	The coating mixture

The aioli: 40 g garlic confit
1 egg yolk
60 ml Arbequina extra virgin olive oil
6 ml water
Salt

Extras: Skewers, polished river stones

The coating:

Place the kaolin, lactose, black dye, and salt in a bowl. Mix it together while gradually adding water. Although the mixture may initially seem very dry, simply let it stand for 12 hours to become more fluid and acquire the appropriate texture to bathe the potatoes.

The potatoes:

Gently clean the potatoes with a soft brush. Do not peel. Bring the salted water to a boil in a large pan, then add the potatoes. Boil for 8-10 minutes, depending on the size of the potatoes. Drain them and place on a tray.

The potatoes coated in clay:

Pierce the flattest side of each potato with the tip of a skewer. Remove the skewer and insert its blunt side to approximately the center of the potato. Stir the kaolin mixture until thoroughly combined and of the correct consistency. Dip the potatoes into the mixture, completely covering them. Insert the ends of the skewers into the holes of a perforated baking sheet so that they are held in a vertical position. Place the sheet in the oven at a low temperature—50°C (120°F)—for approximately 30 minutes or until the coating has dried out to a crisp texture. This will contrast with the smoothness of the potato inside, which will be tender and creamy thanks to the protection of this "shell."

The garlic confit:

Pour the oil into a deep saucepan and place on a griddle or a low-intensity fire, without allowing it to reach a high temperature. Heating the oil can also be done over the edge of the cooker top so that it is done as gently as possible. When the oil is warm, place the separated, unpeeled garlic cloves in the oil and poach them gently for approximately 2 hours. At the end of cooking, the garlic will be tender, easy to peel and completely impregnated with oil. When ready, drain the oil, peel the garlic gloves, crush them, then pass them through a chinois and set aside.

The aioli:

Put the garlic confit in a tall beaker, add the egg yolk and combine with a handheld blender until the mixture forms an emulsion. Meanwhile, slowly drizzle the oil in, being careful that the emulsion does not lose stability. Once ready, add salt to taste and set aside in a covered bowl.

Finishing and presentation:

In the oven, heat a few polished river stones the same size as the potatoes coated in the gray clay. The stones will add the finishing touch to the presentation and keep the potatoes hot for longer. Serve the potatoes in between the stones. Serve a heaped portion of aioli in smaller, individual dishes. The potatoes should be eaten with the fingers and the first bite should be taken without sauce. This emphasizes the boundary between the texture of the coverage and its contents. After that, the potatoes should be dipped into the aioli.

IN THE HERD

In the beginning it's the sound of bells. An awakening just like any other. My heart keeps an even beat, but it's too fast. It's a drum without an echo. Too regular to be my own heartbeat. So regular it frightens me.

Yes, but no. I am, but I am not.

Am I crouching? Not exactly.

It's more like I "move forward" crouching. They push me. I see only the ground, weeds; chunks of earth dislodge and sink under my hooves every now and then. Acrid, milky smells are mixed in with the day's dampness. I want to scan the horizon and so I try to stand up. Soon I realize it's going to be impossible to do such a thing. My nature impedes it: I walk on four legs.

There is no time to think. I imitate my fellow beings. I am one of them. I bleat meekly. It comes out of me as if it wasn't the first time. No one looks at me. No one seems to pay any attention to me. Someone takes advantage of my lapse in concentration and head butts me away to nibble on a few square inches of grass I thought were mine for the taking.

It is then that I begin to remember that it wasn't always like this. A crazy confession and a rejection turned me into what I am. "I just want to crawl under a rock," the figure of speech. The fainting. And immediately after, the waking: turned wooly and docile. I look around me and see other scorned lovers that have been turned into sheep. Sheep like me. Sheep like us. I understand it very quickly; we are all the same.

I head butt one of my companions. I hump her. I eat grass.

I follow the others, wondering if it'll be a cabin or a sacrificial altar that awaits us at the end of the road. Not knowing if I've been condemned or released. If this is a temporary state of things or if it will be like this forever.

A faceless shepherd slits my throat in my nightmares and uses my blood to warm up his hands while he sings a sad song.

Afterward I see him blow a horn and it sounds like bagpipes. He covers the holes in the instrument intently, as if he were afraid that if he lifted his fingers an evil spirit would escape through the orifices.

It happens then. I wake up startled. And, even though I'm still a sheep, I'm relieved to be alive.

BUTTERY IDIAZABAL CHEESE GNOCCHI
soaked in a broth of salted meats of Iberico pig, served with vegetable contrasts

Ingredients (serves 4)

The gnocchi: 100 g semi-cured D.O. Idiazabal cheese
300 ml water
Salt
25 g kuzu

The Iberico broth: 40 g pork belly (side)
500 g fresh white pork meat
40 g chickpeas
30 g chopped carrot
40 g chopped leek
60 g chopped onion
Arbequina extra virgin olive oil
1.3 liter water
Salt

The vegetable contrasts:

Red shiso "Perilla frutescens var. crispa f. purpurea"
Green shiso "Perilla frutescens var. crispa"
Purple fennel "Foeniculum vulgare purpurascens"
Fennel "Foeniculum vulgare"
Anise "Pimpinella anisum"
Arbequina extra virgin olive oil

The gnocchi:
Cut the cheese into 1 cm cubes and place in a food processor with the salted water. Crush at 55°C (130°F) and at medium speed for 10 minutes. Brew by decanting through a very fine mesh strainer. Pour into a saucepan the 250 ml of cheese juice obtained and add 25 g of kuzu. Cook the mixture gently on the cooker top at 200°C (400°F) stirring constantly for 15 minutes until the cream becomes glutinous and gradually gels. Leave the dough tempering for a few minutes and put it in a sleeve pastry. Put the sleeve in a bowl with water and ice. Squeeze out small sausage-like pieces of the mixture into the water. When they come into contact with the water, they will acquire the shape of small oval gnocchi.

The Iberico broth:
Gently clean the pork belly (side) in water to remove excess salt. Cut the fresh pork meat in cubes and place them in a roasting pan in the oven at 170°C (340°F) with a drizzle of extra virgin olive oil. Once golden, re-move from the oven and remove excess fat. Place the pork belly, chickpeas, chopped vegetables, roasted meat, and water in a container. Leave to hydrate for 2 hours, then cook the mixture over very low heat and avoid boiling to ensure the stock remains as clear as possible, until it is reduced to half its volume. Strain through a chinois and filter paper. Salt to taste and set aside.

The vegetable contrasts:
Rinse the shoots and set aside in a mixture of ice water and vegetable disin-fectant. Then rinse them with abundant running water and keep them be-tween wet papers until it is time to use them.

Finishing and presentation:
Cover the gnocchi and place in the oven without removing them from the brine. Heat the Iberico broth in a saucepan. Do not boil. Drain the gnocchi

from the brine and place them on absorbent paper towels. Place 5 gnocchi in each of the warmed dishes, which should be deep and high-sided. Pour a generous serving of Iberico broth over the gnocchi. Support the plant contrasts on the gnocchi and sprinkle everything with a few drops of extra virgin olive oil.

SEA-URCHIN THERAPY

Although there is no consensus on the subject, it seems that sea-urchin therapy can be dated back at least to ancient Mesopotamian civilizations, although its origins, according to some experts, might extend even further back in time.

Sea-urchin therapy might be simply described as "brushing but not touching," or "feeling without the sting," all kinds of prickly creatures, be they sea urchins or hedgehogs, with healing intent. The prickly shells of chestnuts can be used for this purpose too, in case of extreme necessity, but they are not nearly as effective.

Although initially this type of traditional therapy was associated with the treatment of strictly circulatory and neurological problems, recent studies demonstrate that it can be used in cases of anxiety, ADHD in children, stress, and so on. Improvements have also been shown in patients suffering from Alzheimer's and Parkinson's diseases, although the studies carried out in the last ten years by the Magnetic Theremin Edge Fields University are not completely conclusive.

The technique required to apply a caress—to use the very contentious equivalent of the word quoted in Persian manuals—to a sea urchin demands arduous training: the success or failure of this therapy depends on maintaining a minimal distance between fingertips and the said sea urchins, or hedgehogs. This distance is difficult to quantify in that it isn't always the same, depending on whether the sea urchin or hedgehog is caressed by fingertips, proximal phalanges, or the palm of the hand.

Under no circumstances must the creature come into contact with any part of the skin beyond the patient's wrist.

Those who learn to caress sea urchins or hedgehogs properly have an untold advantage when it comes to knowing how to caress a lover.

SEA URCHIN
dressed with roasted vegetable tears and garnished with long pepper grains

Ingredients (serves 4)

The onion broth: 8 kg onions

The sea urchins: 1.5 kg sea urchins
1 liter water
30 g salt

The onion gel: 200 ml onion broth
2 g table salt
10 g kuzu

Long peppercorns: 2 long pepper catkins

The onion broth:
Prepare a good amount of vine shoot or vegetable charcoal embers on a grill. Cut the onions in half and place them cut-side down on the grill rack at a height of 15 cm above the embers. Keep them on the grill until the exterior turns completely black. Turn the onions and keep them at the same height until they begin to "boil" on the cut side. Take them off the grill and strip them of the burnt part to leave an exposed inner layer, which should be a nice golden color. Put the roasted onions into a heatproof bowl and cover them with ovenproof cling film (plastic wrap). Place the bowl in the oven at 70°C (150°F) for 6 hours. Remove them from the oven and place them in a fine mesh strainer, gently applying pressure until the juice strains through. Chill this broth and set it aside.

The sea urchins:
Gradually cut open the sea urchins with scissors starting from the mouth until you make a circle that allows you to remove the roe. Prepare brine with salt and water. Collect the roe with a teaspoon and immerse them in the brine to wash them, then place them on greaseproof (wax) paper and refrigerate.

The onion gel:
Put the broth and salt in a container and hydrate the kuzu in it for a few seconds until it is well dissolved. Put the mixture into a small pan and place it over heat. Stir the mixture with a silicone spatula and cook it until the starch

gels and the mixture looks translucent and smooth. Cover it with plastic wrap and store in a warm place.

The long peppercorns:
Grind the pepper catkins in a mortar and recover the peppercorns.

Finishing and presentation:
Carefully place the sea urchin roe on a large plate. Do not pile them. Bathe them with the onion gel, until they are covered. Finish it off by placing three long peppercorns over the roe.

STORIES BY HARKAITZ CANO

RECIPES BY ANDONI ADURIZ

TRANSLATED FROM BASQUE BY AMAIA GABANTXO

EDGAR CANTERO

Aesop's Urinal

IT ALL STARTED (to go down the toilet) when they changed the weather forecast into the weather critique. This emerging intellectualoid fad, added to the demand for parasitic jobs, couldn't lead anywhere else. The new breed of weather guy doesn't predict the meteorology for the coming days. Nope, he limits himself to reviewing the previous days. He writes scathing critiques like "Last Monday the sun barely let itself be seen, listlessly warming a populace disheartened by the deplorable air quality," or even better "Yesterday's relative humidity stole the lead role from the winds originating in the north, which were visibly exhausted after a European tour." It quickly became apparent that, in the matter of climate too, our country is a third-rate power compared to the capitals of cumulonimbus culture. Nowhere does the sun shine more boldly than in New York, and no storms ever blow like those in London. God is a has-been of the genre, sort of like David Bowie, who even on the wane is capable of generating the odd apotheosized storm, although lacking any point of comparison with his radical statements in antiquity—like the universal flood, sadly never to be repeated.

As soon as I extract a date from the girl I've been pursuing for months, I see from the balcony how the rain starts falling just when I hang up the phone, and who bobs to the surface of my memory but Jonathan Lipschitz, author of the renowned monograph on the gay friend syndrome who was likewise surprised by a torrential downpour in similar circumstances. Lipschitz maintained that, contrary to Freud's opinion, a woman doesn't become enamored of a penis but rather dates, is courted by, copulates with, gets engaged to and marries a penis without ever being enamored—either of the penis or of the person attached to it. Since the conditions a man must assemble to enamor a woman have nothing to do with the genitals and consequently

240

are asexual, the woman can make a man the depository of her esteem and trust without coming to understand him in his sexual dimension, thus condemning him to chastity. The stereotype of the gay friend, therefore, confidant and confessor of the urban heroine, guarantor of an intimate and disinhibited friendship, masculine container of feminine sensibility and empathy, is reinterpreted by Lipschitz as an unassuming suitor of that very girl, often declared and always refused, who is labelled gay in order to obviate any scrutiny of his true yet troublesome sentiments. The way to avoid these "misunderstandings of the sexual contract," the text advises, is to display sexual desire from the start or, in the author's words, "Never open the heart before opening the zipper." Nonetheless, like all provocative sages, Lipschitz was far from taking this tack in his private life. He still believed in the classic courtship, and the clearest proof is the occasion when he visited his beloved at Canet de Mar with a bouquet of red roses as his credentials. While he waited for her at the portal, a heavy shower fell so violently that, despite his determination to endure the rain, he couldn't withstand the floods that swept him down the street and into the sea. He turned up two weeks later on a beach in Corsica, still alive, but not for very long, since in the interval he had to derive sustenance from fish and roses. The bones of the former and the thorns of the latter had left his esophagus like a colander. He died days later, and they buried him in a swamp.

Quite like Jonathan Lipschitz, I have to meet a girl on a corner in Barcelona; I am holding a rose in my hand, and the rain is pissing down. Sorting out the corner proved to be a chapter in itself: she randomly proposed two streets in Eixample, Muntaner and Aribau, and before leaving home I realized both those streets run in the same direction. I reasoned as follows: if parallel lines run straight till they cross in infinity, according to Euclidian geometry, you need only walk down one street and in infinity it will form a corner with the other. Happy with this resolution of the paradox, I chose Muntaner and decided to follow it in a northerly direction, more than anything else because the sea lies toward the south and I don't want to get wet—a really absurd precaution, given the circumstances. As for the rose I carry in my hand, it's as anecdotal as the fact of carrying nothing in the other.

I'm a staunch follower of Elizabeth Schneider, who even in the nine-
teenth century, in London, declared herself opposed to umbrellas because they embody the fatuous human tendency to cold-shoulder
natural phenomena. "Rain falls from the sky," she argued, "and people
leave their houses with a mobile roof, aiming to adhere to the same
old routine. If dragons vomiting fire descended from the sky, they
would go out wearing neoprene suits and act as if it were nothing."
To be sure, the umbrella has become the identifying mark of civilization. The collective morality demands that one stay dry. Humankind
is obliged, in a Rousseauian sense, to grab an umbrella on rainy days,
carry it around everywhere, give up a useful hand, fight against the
wind with it, poke out the eyes of other umbrella-toters, and wind up
soaked regardless. If every time people grab an umbrella they grab a
rose instead, they would get wet just the same, and the world would
be a nicer place to live in. Especially for roses, if it's true they can enjoy
water after they've been snipped from their bush. I suppose they can
because when we give a rose to a girl, she immediately puts it in a vase.
Obviously, when you think about it, a rose can't enjoy anything, because the central nervous system of a plant, if it exists, wouldn't be in
the flower, which in reality is a sexual organ (like a penis). And this is
the reason (we return to Freud) why women like roses so much.[1]

As I make my own sweet way up Muntaner, the scenery changes, the
façades, but not the platitudes or the slow, constant rain. I'm leaving behind Eixample, and the street climbs through an upper-class
neighborhood, equally gray and monotonous, with more sumptu-
ous portals and fashionable boutiques and brand-name accessories.
Unpleasant ladies with fluorescent skin come out on their doorsteps
to watch the rain. At the sight of me passing by without an umbrella,
they point and shout, "Dissident!" A French Enlightenment thinker once wrote that people should stay inside on rainy days. The problem is that we don't know which thinker wrote it, or in which book
he wrote it, or if he really wrote it. Still, the fact is that a threat to the
capitalist world is hidden behind this innocent advice: the image of
a civilization subjected to weather, brought to a standstill by rain and

[1] Curiously, this argument occurred to Freud in his last years, but he didn't manage to put it
in writing because he lived tormented by repeated nightmares of giant spiders.

functioning only when the sun shines. Like snails, although the other way around. This prospect of a world shirking before the slightest climatic adversity makes those at the top tremble. Of course, this utopian context is not ideal either: the girl I've landed a date with, for example, could adduce this unexpected storm as a reason to stand me up. I imagine she'll have followed the same logic regarding the parallel lines that cross in infinity, and to bolster my hope I evoke the memory of Elizabeth Schneider, who one day, at Figueres, withstood a downpour of 133 liters per square meter in the middle of Carrer Esperança, singing an opera of her own creation. I also imagine that at this point the storm can't be described as unexpected, because the weather critics possess the extraordinary faculty of forecasting every phenomenon when it is already happening. With the rise of meteorological critique, the techniques of climate prediction have fallen into disuse, whether they rely on high-tech instruments or the interpretation of natural indices. As for the instruments, a week doesn't pass without the earth witnessing the fall of some of the many satellites that drift in orbit, forgotten by the very scientists who launched them. This morning one fell on the head of George W. Bush, who continued reading his speech as if nothing had happened. As for the traditional methods, nobody besides me seemed to notice that rats were evacuating the sewers. En masse, all of them forming a single line, with open umbrellas. Rats are not notable for their intelligence.

History contains many celebrated cases of women with gay friends. For example: Oscar Wilde and Lady Elizabeth Schneider. Another: Gustave Flaubert and Madame de Gravencourt. And that other Frenchman as well, who sang "Il pleut dans ma chambre," or perhaps there were two songs, "Il pleut" and "Dans ma chambre," I don't remember. Meanwhile the upper-class neighborhood has given way to another with old single-family dwellings and fixed gardens. The villas have green shutters and painted tiles at the entrances. Amid the drizzle you can hear birds and some crickets. This entire part of Barcelona, which really tends to infinity, doesn't show up on maps, on electoral posters, or in Woody Allen movies. On maps, this area appears as an empty green-colored space, and until recently it included dissuasive drawings, like pre-Columbian planispheres, which fill oceanic blues with illustrations of gigantic fish and crabs to discourage adventurers. Here pizza joints belong to franchises unknown in the city center, and in a bodega they sell strawberry Fanta. I know I'm reaching the end because the symbols multiply. Past a square there's an equestrian monument of a captain of the Republic, a sentry sculpted in a stone portico, an anemometer, a graffiti mural, photos of combination plates, an inscription in marble with the name of the French Enlightenment thinker I mentioned earlier, a statue of a pregnant Virgin Mary, two paired windows, a rose seller, a flattened rose, a convertible, a Seat 850, a telephone, a patio with black and white tiles, a plaque with the Francoist yoke and arrows, a black cat, a sundial, and the sun, oblique, amid the rain clouds. I hear a voice singing. I look at the street signs: the one above me says Muntaner, but the one over the opposite sidewalk says Aribau. Beneath it, leaning against a wall of reddish brick, stands the girl waiting for me. She is not holding an umbrella. A lock of drenched hair crosses half of her face, and in the other half, white and clean, daylight shines. We greet each other, and I hold out my hand, offering the rose. I could let it fall in a puddle on the ground, and it would be as if the city were an enormous vase, which in fact is what it is. In reality, we have pushed so far north of the city that we're not in Barcelona anymore. I'd say we've reached Figueres, and now that we're together, we'll continue walking in the rain, searching for Liza Schneider, whom I believe I hear intoning an aria.

TRANSLATED FROM CATALAN BY LAWRENCE VENUTI

BESSORA

Voyage Under Narcosis

All my attention was focused on this cup of yogurt, approvingly born from my imagination.

Its recyclable paper packaging was on display to my mind, indicating a natural raspberry flavor, while its aluminum top specified an expiration date long since passed. But it was still consumable: like us, yogurt has a life after death, a supplementary existence of about 21 days. After that, it needs to be incinerated. Like us. But not exactly. We at least have a choice. And we don't always opt for cremation. It is recommended by numerous cultures, however. In any case, the incineration of expired yogurt is an environmental necessity, and a legal obligation.

But this dairy product hadn't entered my mind to be incinerated. Nor to be eaten, to my own risks and perils. It had appeared to me, in extreme close-up, to extricate me from certain journeys that I'd been involuntarily undertaking in my sleep.

Indeed, big traveler that I am, I travel also in my sleep.

I can assure you that this is quite unpleasant.

This particular instance took place on a sticky July night filled with the fragrance of unseen linden trees, shaking off their odor like wet dogs in some nearby park. I wanted to sleep, simply to sleep. Was that too much to ask at four o'clock in the morning? But invasive dreams were preventing me. To find relief, I had to concentrate on an image, and this image was supposed to keep me out of the dreams. And so, this expired yogurt cup. Commanded into my consciousness, it was my second, maybe third attempt at evading my dreamtime nomadism.

That is to say, from voyage under narcosis.

Voyage under narcosis is a serious sleeping sickness, chronic and considerably more detrimental than a bite from a tsetse fly. Of course, the tsetse fly can be fatal, but voyage under narcosis doesn't even allow you this escape. You lose your memory, your notion of time, and you sometimes convince yourself of having lived through events that never existed. In the most serious cases, you forget your true identity and substitute it with another (often of lesser merit).

Now, on this sticky July morning, the tyranny of voyage under narcosis had begun around one o'clock.

I thought I'd nodded off twenty minutes earlier, but then, in a dream, I discovered that I was completely awake. With eyes open wide, I found myself in Abidjan, capital of an Ivory Coast. There was no indication, but I knew I was in that shimmering city. Standing in a sweltering heat at the precise center of a fish market, I looked over my surroundings in search of my bed.

No, I didn't want to be here, dazzled by the ivory sun (the sun had the texture and color of an elephant's tusk, but it was rounder, of course, and much brighter).

No, I wanted nothing to do with this place.

I wanted my bed, my bed in Paris, Paris and my bed, which were waiting for me and were probably worried sick about me, because of our sudden separation. They didn't like to be left alone, especially at night. But in the Abidjan where I was sequestered (narcotically speaking), there were so many people, so many amassed individuals, most of whom were vendors selling little beignets, that my view was completely blocked. I suspect they were doing it on purpose, making it impossible for me to extract myself from this horribly lucid, ivory dream, which smelled more like fish than beignets.

After some time had gone by in Abidjan, yearning for nothing more than rest, I watched helplessly as my legs began to run. Without my permission, they burst into a sprint like two people endowed with their own wills, which were contrary to my own. It seems that they had seen three policemen just behind me, hot on our trail. From that moment forward I was running to escape them, while behind my back I could hear them shouting.

They were screaming that I didn't have a visa for my stay.

I must return to my home country without delay.

My legs, already covered in sweat, went on running, and I could feel myself getting short of breath, but still I screamed back to my pursuers that I wanted nothing more than to go back home. Only I'd lost my bed. How can you go home when you don't know your own address?

I heard shots. Someone was firing at me. The policemen, no doubt, trigger-happy, swift and snappy.

As I painfully struggled with a perforation in my right lung, pierced by at least two bullets from a Kalashnikov, I wondered why narcosis had dumped me off in this country, at this exact hour, in a fish market sitting under a sun that could melt an atom. I was still running, though less effectively, of course, because my right lung was no longer functioning. The lack of oxygenation led me to several metaphysical considerations: Who? Where? Why? Did my imprisonment here have something to do with the fact that I'd spent my afternoon writing?

Indeed, I am a writer. Or at least, that's what I call myself today, though I'm not sure that it's my original identity. It's possible that I was someone else in a different time, but that I've forgotten who. It's possible, as well, that I stole my present identity from some poor, unsuspecting stranger.

Whatever the case may be, I write.

And you can be sure that the price I pay isn't slight.

After lunch, I mean to say earlier that day, well before going to bed, at a moment when I wasn't sleeping, I sat myself down at my writing desk. Indeed, every writer worthy of the title has a desk, preferably purchased from Ikea. This writing session took place in real life, in true, tangible time. A palpable time. However, I had temporarily left that time to plunge myself into my current story, a novelistic sequence in which I was shoving a plantain down the throat of an elephant hunter. This literary anecdote was unfolding in the 19th century, in a Congolese forest.

You will agree, of course, the Congo is not the Ivory Coast. And the 19th century is not the 21st.

So why had narcosis sent me off to the Ivorian capital, in the 21st century?

In this horrible dream, where two policemen had just punctured my right lung, my blood had begun pouring out in great torrents. I watched as it left my body. This caused me a great deal of sorrow. It's sad to watch your blood abandon you. I was so sad, and so bloodless, in fact, that my heart soon stopped beating.

And so, I was dead.

Would I, like a spoiled cup of yogurt, be forced to undergo cremation?

Not at all, or not yet, at least. Barely dead, narcotically speaking, I rose to the heavens, which are the color of an eggplant, not blue as we imagine them to be. Blue skies are a legend, I can assure you that, in reality, they are mauve. Up above, I was welcomed by the muscular arms of Morpheus. Himself. Note as well that Morpheus is also the color of an eggplant. Nevertheless, he stands out quite distinctly from the azure background. This Greek divinity, of Lithuanian origin, lifted me up by the armpits and set me onto his right wing.

And thus we flew in a meditative silence, though my silence was more tense than meditative. I anxiously watched the horizon, fearing that an incinerator's chimney would soon appear, and that I would be duly rushed there like a commonplace cup of spoiled yogurt. I was dead, but I didn't want to suffer.

Death doesn't interrupt suffering. Otherwise, word would get around.

But to my great surprise, and even greater joy, Morpheus carried me back to Paris, my heaven, and set me down in my bed, which is in some sense my Garden of Eden.

I fell asleep. I experienced a moment of peace. A short moment of grace.

Because a new dream tore me out of my blessed garden, and dragged me into a second unwilled dream.

This time I found myself seated on a small, cherry-red plastic chair, located beneath a large circus tent, I think in the Île-de-France. Île-de-France is in the exact center of the center of France, which I believe to be the center of the universe. It's a proven fact. The smell of manure, I think a pony's, was plundering my nostrils. Standing near me was a tall fellow, paunchy and hairy, I think a unionist. Taking into account his potbelly and militant hypertrichosis, I assumed that he was an author, probably of comic strips. I love comic strips. Because I know neither how to strip nor how to draw comics. So I admire anyone capable of doing both at the same time.

Anyways, this artist was saying something to me. At great speed, he was setting out his thoughts in sign language, which was then translated into speech bubbles. The animated bubbles told the story of how a minister had cut into his pension, he would now pay eight percent of his social security contributions, sometimes twelve, and that's not even mentioning value-added tax (an absolutely discriminatory tax), which had doubled, all while he was making two times less than the monthly minimum wage. I was in complete agreement with the artist, and with his speech bubbles: of course, the solution was higher employer contributions. Clearly, it was necessary to cut off the head of Louis XVI, and then drink the blood, which is known to be extremely rich in nutrients.

But I was so tired . . .

My weary eyes sought out Morpheus, or any charter flight that could whisk me off to the heaven of my bed, to my Garden of Eden. My cartoonist companion soon noticed that I was looking elsewhere. He assumed that I wasn't listening. He took me for an enemy of the cause, perhaps even a reincarnation of Marie Antoinette. And so, cartoonists being a species easily overcome by their male hormones, he didn't resist the temptation to slap me, strongly enough to unscrew my head.

But I survived this attempt at decapitation.

I'd managed to keep my head securely on my shoulders.

Masterful though it was, his murderous slap triggered Morpheus's return. The divinity of prophetic dreams landed beneath the circus tent, just beside my chair. A little staircase unfolded before me so that I could climb up into his muscular, Greek arms. We took off and flew far away from that hormonal-unionist trap, toward the cotton heaven of my duvet.

After a whirlwind journey through a dilated space-time, Morpheus set me down onto my balcony.

Liberated from my second narcotic voyage, I still hadn't reached the sleep that I was so desperately yearning for, but rather the wet tiles of my terrace, which were moistening my foundation (I mean to say my butt, but I'm no fan of vulgarity, so I say foundation, which to me seems preferable to ass).

And so I sat on the balcony, chilled to the bone.

Above my head, the laundry I'd hung up that evening was dripping down on me. I'd taken care of this household chore well before going to bed, at a moment of the day when time was still a tangible, undeniable reality. The clean laundry should have been almost dry. But there was a slight drizzle. And it was drizzling on my laundry, damn it. Despondent, my bottom flooded, I looked over the panties, socks, shirts, dresses, and bow ties as they took on rainwater, becoming saturated with that anonymous and radioactive smell which was in turn wiping out the lavender scent of my fabric softener.

I raised my eyes toward the heavens to call for help. A huge nail hammered into the sky taunted me. I think it was the moon, although I can't confirm that with any certitude, because it had taken on a red tint, a red not at all expected from the moon.

Awake in this painfully tangible night, otherwise known as 3:10 in the morning, I resolved to busy myself with something. I thus went to check the locks on my front door, securely bolted, the gas valve in the kitchen, securely tightened, the electric hotplates next to the fridge, securely cold. I came to the obvious conclusions: no evidence of a break-in, no prospect of a fire. Short of ideas, and having no other recourse, I went back to bed, dreading the sandman named Freddy Krueger. This serial killer dwells in your unconscious, but there's nothing imaginary about him. Patiently, he waits for you to fall asleep so that he can plunge you into blood-filled dreams from which there's no return.

He who sleeps dies.

We already saw the blood I lost in the Ivory Coast...

I didn't want eternal rest, I wanted it temporary, at most.

But sometimes, to get some rest, you must not fall asleep.

In order to avoid Freddy Kruger's nightmarish claws, I focused my thoughts on a meaningless image. I wouldn't sleep, I would have no more dreams. It was the cup of yogurt, relatively expired, with a natural flavor of raspberries.

But this object, at first sight devoid of symbolism or significance, was no savior. Barthes (a guy by the name of Roland) was right: everything has meaning, nothing is empty.

And so I was off again on another voyage.

This time I was in indistinct surroundings and an uncertain era, nonexistent even, where there was no sign of any Freddy. I went forth to meet other specters, the ghosts of my own past, I suspected. And so it was. Their smell, their voice, their face and hands: they were perfect incarnations of my father.

My father looks nothing like Freddy Krueger, even if, like him, he'd supposedly disappeared.

"My dear daughter," my father said to me, "be sure to play this Friday's Super Lotto."

In my dream, I asked myself: how can someone have nothing else to say to his daughter when, after a long separation brought about by death, he's found her again around a bend in a mirage? If my father had really been dead for two years, upon his return, even in a dream, he would have surely found something more intelligent to say to me.

Distracted by these unseemly thoughts, I didn't notice the shape that was materializing slowly in the spectral fog. Suddenly, it swooped down to abduct me from my father, my father who had so suddenly left us two years earlier.

It was Morpheus . . . This Greek, directly involved in the drama of public debt in his home country, removed me from the dream that, for once, I would have liked to prolong. This Greek, whose mistakes had threatened the European Union and its anchor currency, forcefully returned me to reality and its lies.

5:13, the moon had wandered off. The rain had gone with it. The air was dry, and daylight was timidly seeping into the night.

As a preventive measure, I commanded the yogurt back into my mind.

This time, I decided that the cup was empty, someone had eaten the yogurt, and so no more meaning, no more raspberry flavor, no more symbolism, no more expiration date. Into this lactic void, I poured out the memories of my nocturnal voyages: the foul-smelling market in Abidjan, the hormonal unionist, the gaming advice of my father, the muscular arms of Morpheus the Greek.

And when at last the recyclable yogurt was filled with my fantastical torments, a new pang of distress forced its way into my mind: and what if, now, there's nothing left to eat in the fridge?

Soon, I would have to get out of bed to go shopping: it was Sunday and the supermarket opened at 9:00.

So don't fall back asleep, or you risk missing the opening of the store.

It will close at 12:00.

So don't fall back asleep, or you risk waking up at 12:03.

I was screwed, my night screwed, sleep screwed.

I turned on the light, took a small notebook from my night table, and began a shopping list.

4 raspberry yogurts.

Stick it out . . . Day was already beginning to erase the night.

4 Reine-Claude plum yogurts.

In 2 hours and 37 minutes the store would be open . . .

A light bulb, not the kind you screw in, the kind with the big cap, for the bathroom.

And I concluded my list with this nota bene: *don't forget to play the Super Lotto like papa spectrally recommended.*

And so it was finished, I'd reached the end of the list, feeling so, so tired.

Soothed by the feeling of having accomplished this task, and also by the birth of day, in which there were no ghosts to be found, I let down my guard.

Toward 7:58, I sank into a deceptive sleep.

It was so pure and so deep, this sleep, so perfectly devoid of dreams, of voyages and ghosts, that I didn't wake up.

I was screwed, my day screwed, screw the supermarket.

TRANSLATED FROM FRENCH BY JESSE ANDERSON

MICHAEL FEHR

The Apparent Fisherman and Real Drunkard

And at the same time
by the brisk
and so: friendly and amicable and swift and feisty river
its edges frozen over with thick firm ice
these frozen edges on the surface followed below along the river bed
      by a very fine and
very gentle countercurrent
that rippled a little
so: emeried
over shingle
so: small fine stones
and rubble
so: coarser stones
and pebbles
so: coarse stones
rummaging a bit in the shingle and stirring it a bit and making it
      swirl
making the small stones ripple against each other and against the
      coarser stones
so: rub and pretty much crunch
the acoustics though with the lid of ice at the margins were different
      than usual
that is: the icy lid gave the amicable crunching
coming from the river bed
a friendly damper, repressing it
so: suppressing it and so: keeping it down
crunching all the while itself and louder
this under the pressure of the current
which was strong

and so masked the sound

the small stones below made as they rubbed together because of the
        countercurrent

and so its gentle nature meant the countercurrent lost its courage

so: lost its weak-as-it-was

so: weak-anyway

opposition and its own other direction

so: gave up

so: gave in

so: subsided

came out from under the ice

now bent on

following the general path of the current

and so strove for the middle of the river and fell in with the current

became absorbed in the brisk current

gave up

handed itself in

surrendered

let itself go

joined in amicably

went along with it

matched its swift pace

conformed with the current

only then to show opposition again

if a gentle

good-natured

weak

variety

and to find the courage

not to join in after all

not after all to go along with it

but to push weakly for the outside

toward the edges

to break out of the current

and cheerfully push beneath the ice

in order to resist again and to assert itself and as the countercurrent
        cope against the

current again
and it did indeed cope and again was non-compliant
the night meanwhile really was completely and utterly compliant
        and right 'n' bright
so: monotonously and quite unanimously ultramarine
and the moon really was completely and utterly pale gold a huge big
        moon and full
and the river was wide and like the quiet night sky
not a star up there in the sky
and so it was a stark and so: bleak ultramarine up there apart from
        the lonely
bare
so: spartan
so: naked
so: bright
full
so: ample
so: plump
so: bulging
so: heavy and firm
so: huge
tired
so: dull
so: lazy
so: languid
so: pale
so: pallid
so: white gold moon
the stars though it seemed had fallen down onto the river and were
        juggling and rocking
and twinkling and glistening all shiny white gold
on the floaty
so: swiftly flowing
soft
ultramarine waves
it seemed the stars had fallen down onto the river
but not fallen into the river

so hadn't sunk
which was why there was no light in the river
no ultramarine and no gold
not in the middle
where the strong current was
not at the edge beneath the ice
hence the deep blackness there
and in such a blackness a lonely
heavy hook with no nothing on it
now whirled up now whirled down now rummaged at times in the
    little stones on the
river bed and emeried over stones
a hook on a line
that in turn climbed through the deep blackness and came back up
    into the ultramarine
night
and there
in such a blue night
by the river
on the ultramarine lid of ice
with a fur cap on his head
with a part at the back that could be let down well down and warm
    as down covered his
ears
in a heavy
quilted
soft jacket
and in proper
so: heavy
padded boots
in anthracite-gray woolen trousers
his long rod in one hand
its thick rear part jammed under his arm
a little metal bottle in the other
silver with a screw top
the lid hanging down it on a little chain and the hole in the neck of
    it up at the gob of the

guy the two hands belonged to
listening to the oddly muffled and suppressed because of the ice
      sound of the river and
hearing the bells of the coarse cathedral strike up
and reach him from the distant town
as many dainty high
as deep primitive ones
snuffling constantly
so: sniffing through his cardinal-red nose
that in the dark was ultramarine-ish
so on the whole looked purple
a nose no one could see though
as no one was in attendance
so: no one was nearby
feeling the cold brew
that gave him a nice'n' hot feeling
reach his fat gut
so: stomach
the brisk
and so: friendly and amicable and jovial apparent fisherman and real
      drunkard
lost in contemplation of the icy current and the crunching ice be-
      neath his boots
and hit by the
heat
flowing through him with each swig
raised
his raw
stricken voice in the night, melodying and modulating
Hallelujah
Hallelujah

TRANSLATED FROM GERMAN BY DONAL MCLAUGHLIN

ARTEM CHAPEYE

Son, Please!

Things had gotten harder ever since her old man died.

Kolka, her grandson, who used to at least be afraid of Grandpa, was now totally out of control. He came over almost every day.

"Gimme a bottle, Grandma. I know you got some."

Then she had no more. God knows she only had the dozen bottles for neighbors, in case she had to ask them for help. Now she was out of vodka, and Kolka started demanding cash. She had to dip into the money she had put aside for her own funeral. Grandma Nadia was a small and timid woman.

Kolka took the money and went drinking with his friends. There were no jobs in the village.

"Grandma Nadia, don't supply him," her neighbor said. The neighbor had a big mustache and a big belly. He was about fifty years old. "Or do you want me to sit him down for a man-to-man talk?"

Grandma Nadia was silent. She smoothed the folds of her skirt.

"He's completely out of line," the lady neighbors would say, shaking their heads. "But who else is gonna look after him? His Dad hasn't been back from Russia for over a year."

Kolka's mother passed away long ago, and he now lived by himself in a dirty hut. His friends came to visit him there. The woman who ran the village shop felt sorry for Grandma Nadia, and she tried to avoid selling vodka to Kolka. In those cases Kolka went to Mikhail, who lived in the last hut and sold liquor at night. His father rarely transferred money from Russia, and it wasn't enough for Kolka. Grandma Nadia supported him with her funeral funds.

She needed more money.

Her sister from Baryshevka had gotten lucky, finding work as a concierge in Kiev. She took the train there every three days, earning 57 hryvnia for 24 hours' work, guaranteed, she said. But she was younger than Nadia, only sixty-five, and she used to work in a factory. No one's gonna hire me, Nadia thought, an old, uneducated grandmother.

Grandma Nadia went out to the shed to retrieve the old *kravchuchka*[1] handcart her old man had made. She wiped the layers of dust off the frame. The *kravchuchka* was big, almost bigger than Grandma herself. The wheels were solid rubber, taken from two wheelbarrows, and the platform for carrying the sack was a piece of dark-brown plexiglass.

When her old man was still alive he was always building things. Their children made fun of him for it. Once he made a hand plow following some blueprints, but the plow ended up being so hard to pull that it was easier to just dig up the whole orchard with a spade. He had also built a two-wheeled wheelbarrow, but it wouldn't fit through the wooden gate separating the yard from the orchard. Later he created a special device to dig holes for potatoes, but in the time it took him to move the thing from one hole to another, Grandma could make ten holes with her mattock.

Grandpa made the *kravchuchka* when half the village was going to Kiev to "make some deals." All the old ladies of the village admitted that Nadia's *kravchuchka* was the best. Grandma was silently proud, and she even forgave her old man for sometimes beating her. It's true that he became much calmer in his final years, after that heart attack. Not long before he died, he greased the *kravchuchka*'s wheels again. He liked order.

Nadia used to enjoy it when everyone was going into town together. They were all young then; some had just retired, and others were still of working age. But after the collective farm was divided into shares, there were no more jobs. They traveled back and forth, several women at a time—and they were mostly women. There were some old men among them, but very few. The first train of the morning left at three forty-seven. Free for retirees.

They all worked together to load the sacks quickly into the train. One, two, heave!—Some had cucumbers, others had milk, cream, and cottage cheese; load it all into the train doors. And it's an hour and a half to Kiev, so you could get a bit more sleep, lying horizontally across the bench with your legs bent. Or if you didn't want to sleep you could play cards, or just talk—also a good thing to do.

They stuck together when they got to Kiev, so they could help one another. The stout Luda, may her soul rest in peace, knew all the policemen.

"That one's nice, he has pity. If you say you didn't sell anything yet, you can give him money the next time, or he might even let it go. And with that one, it all depends on his mood. And that one—look how pompous he is—be wary of him, you'd better have money on you, so you can give him something in advance. But even then, he might take the money and still chase you away."

At the time, they would give two hryvnia to policemen. Then it was five hryvnia. Nowadays, the big-bellied neighbor told Nadia, you have to pay twenty. And sometimes they don't even take it, and just chase you away. You have to know where to go to sell now.

"Twenty rubles?"[2] Grandma Nadia said quietly. "What if you haven't sold anything yet?"

The neighbor shrugged.

"They'll probably just chase you off."

He was breathing heavily because he was overweight, and the sun was making him sweat.

The *kravchuchka* ladies were no longer the center of business. This mode of trade had become almost extinct. Nowadays, most did the same as her neighbor: he drives his little Lada sedan, pulling a trailer with a load of potatoes to sell in town. But you needed to already have money to get started in that kind of business.

Grandma Nadia sighed and went out to the orchard. She unlatched the wooden gate and closed it after herself. They had put up the gate to keep the chickens off the orchard, but after her old man died there were no more chickens—Nadia didn't have the energy to take care of them.

She pulled up some spring onions and shook off the dirt, knocking the roots against her dark-green rubber boots. She found several cucumbers hidden under the leaves. If she had known they would do so well, she would have planted more. Well, maybe next year. Now she has to gather the potatoes. They're heavy, and her back has been giving her all sorts of pain lately. Her feet feel as if they were gradually getting bent out of shape, look how crooked the big toes have gotten.

Grandma Nadia pulled her *kravchuchka* with the black-and-white checkered sack over to the shed, holding her right hand on her lower back. The shed still smelled of chickens. She bent down to the little chest where she kept some potatoes, so as not to have to go down to the root cellar each time. She picked out the better potatoes and placed them in the sack. The air was dusty, and she coughed several times.

She'll have to ask the neighbor how much potatoes cost in Kiev these days. She'll sell them a little bit cheaper, then people will buy them. She has to hope some kind soul will help her lift the sack into the train, which only stops for three minutes in the village.

"Grandma Nadia, are you there?"

It was her neighbor, the big-bellied one. He was looking into the shed from the outside, narrowing his eyes and trying to see Nadia in the darkness.

"My wife told me you're going to town. You don't have to drag your sacks on the train. I'm also going to Kiev tomorrow, so I could bring you."

Grandma felt uneasy accepting, but the neighbor persisted.

She didn't know what neighborhood she needed. She didn't know where people do business now. She decided to just go where he was going and find herself a spot.

They left late, at half past six the next morning. Grandma Nadia wore her newest headscarf, the yellow one with green and red flowers. She's going to the city, after all. She was sitting in the back seat, her hands folded neatly on her lap. She wore a dark-blue blouse and a long, straight skirt made of thick, brown cloth.

The neighbor didn't talk much, and Nadia looked out the window. As the trees and fenceposts and bushes and fields moved past, her thoughts passed unnoticed: about her husband who was so quiet in his last years, about her son who works in Nizhnevartovsk, and her daughter who lives in the nearby town and has been an alcoholic for a long time, about Kolka, the bad egg, who might do well if he could only find a job, but who's gonna take him, and about the money for her own funeral. Every once in a while she would readjust her headscarf and then return her hands to her lap.

"Look, some people set up over there," the neighbor pointed to the sidewalk near an intersection. There were already some women with cottage cheese and cream, vegetables and flowers. "There's some shade, you can take cover from the sun. I'll come back when I finish."

He parked a little farther down the road. He had a megaphone, and walked between the apartment buildings yelling: "Potatoes! Get your potatoes! Fresh Vinnitsa potatoes!"

He sold them by the sack, delivering direct to people's homes. He was still a strong man. Today he wore old clothes, so he didn't worry about getting covered with dust. He wasn't actually from the Vinnitsa region, of course, but everyone thought that Vinnitsa potatoes were the best, so that's what he advertised. He actually bought the potatoes from the neighboring villages.

People bought up Grandma Nadia's onions and cucumbers, but no one wanted her potatoes, even though she set the price at two rubles. The husband of the lady who was selling cream came back from the automobile bazaar, and they drove home together. The gypsy woman took her unsold flowers and went away.

"Maybe people will buy potatoes on their way back from work," the saleswoman from the candy kiosk said to Nadia.

It had gotten quite hot, and Grandma Nadia dragged her *kravchuchka* into the shade of the kiosk. She asked the saleswoman to help her move the heavy sack, thinking she could sit down on the platform of the cart to rest her feet. In the end, however, she remained standing, afraid that if she sat down it would be too difficult to stand up again.

The neighbor came back at around four o'clock.

"Grandma Nadia, shall we go?"

"I think I'll stay a bit longer," she said quietly.

"But you'll have to take the train. You'd better come with me."

She looked at her sack, still half-full of potatoes. She thought about how the train was free for retired people, and then she thought about her funeral and her grandson Kolka.

"Thank you, son. But I think I'll try and sell the rest this evening."

"Well, as you wish," the neighbor shrugged.

His cheeks were wet with sweat, and he was breathing heavily, his belly moving up and down. He wiped his forehead with his sleeve and looked up at the sky.

"Sure is hot today, hard work dragging sacks."

He got into the Lada and drove off.

After six o'clock there was a steady flow of customers, and they bought seven more kilos of potatoes. Grandma Nadia was glad she stayed. Maybe they'll buy everything and then she can go home. Three hours remained until the last train.

The stream of people began to trail off, and she started saying to passersby: "Who forgot potatoes? Who didn't buy potatoes yet?"

People hardly heard her quiet voice.

And then they arrived. The patrol sergeant had spent the whole night drinking at the police headquarters, because of that bitch. She had stood him up again, just like last time.

He was past the hangover now, having sweated out all the alcohol through the armpits of his uniform, which had grown too tight since he started gaining weight. The sun seemed like it was shining into his eyes the whole day, no matter what direction he looked. In the evening, tiny gnats appeared and swarmed around his head.

The patrol sergeant was trying to figure out if the bitch was screwing that long-haired fruit he sometimes saw near the stand where she worked. Why else would she keep brushing him off like that?

The sergeant's partner, a very young private who had just been accepted to the police force, was walking a little behind him and looking at a flock of pigeons feeding on the public lawn. He thought about chasing them for fun.

"I'm gonna go get some cigarettes," the private said.

"Go ahead."

At that moment, the sergeant caught sight of a babushka in a yellow headscarf, standing on the dusty lawn in the shade of a kiosk. Next to her was a *kravchuchka* bigger than the babushka herself, and a huge black-and-white checkered sack. She was moving her hands nervously, rubbing them against her dark-brown skirt. The sergeant moved toward her. The sun was in his eyes again.

"Can't you read?" he said.

Grandma Nadia had seen him before he saw her, but she couldn't get away because the sack wasn't on the plexiglass platform of the *kravchuchka*. Her feet continued to hurt, but she hadn't dared to sit down. Now she tried to lift the sack.

A few meters away from her there was a dirty metal sign, wired to the trunk of a poplar tree, about two meters off the ground:

IN CASE OF UNSANCTIONED STREET TRADING
PLEASE CALL THE PATROL REGIMENT OF THE
DNIPRO PRECINCT OF THE KIEV MINISTRY OF
INTERIOR AFFAIRS: 559-63-62

Grandma Nadia hadn't seen the sign. Everybody was trading here. The sign had grown rusty around the edges.

Nadia was trying to decide whether to give him the twenty or not. It would be half of her day's earnings.

"Come on, pack up your stuff!" the sergeant said.

The babushka started making a fuss.

The sergeant was standing above her. She was moving and bending down and pushing her sack from different sides, but she wasn't going away. The sergeant exploded, venting the anger that had been accumulating over the course of the day while he sweated in the sun.

"Or do I need to force you?" the sergeant said, stepping toward her.

"Son, please . . ."

She said it so quietly that he could hardly hear it; he had to bend down toward her to listen, and this irritated him even more.

"Move! Move!"

Grandma Nadia fought with the huge sack, trying to lift it onto the platform and failing. The thin rope handles cut into the woman's dry palms.

"I'm f– . . . freaking fed up with all this!" the staff sergeant said through clenched teeth as he approached her. The sun cut into his eyes.

Maybe he wanted to hold the handcart or help her lift the sack to speed things up. Or maybe he was just trying to move past. At any rate, as he stepped by the sack and the handcart, both fell over.

The private who was buying his cigarettes at a kiosk heard metal bang hard against the asphalt. He turned his head and saw potatoes jumping in the dust. Several potatoes rolled over the curb and under a four-by-four parked in the street.

No one was around to see it happen.

The old woman was standing, her hands smoothing her skirt, and she was repeating:

"Son, please . . . Son, please . . ."

"Goddammit!"

The sergeant lifted his right hand and rubbed it hard against his cheek, gritting his teeth. He stepped away from the old woman, turned around and said, "You better be outta here in five minutes." He hurried away, stepping over a potato.

"Huh . . . What's up?" the private called out toward his back. He started gathering potatoes, but then thought it was inappropriate for his position. He dropped the potatoes, adjusted his uniform and hurried after his partner.

That evening, Kolka came to ask for money, and he was already drunk.

[ENDNOTES]

1 Kravchuchka, "Kravchuk's lady": the common ironic name for a handcart, named after Kravchuk, the president of Ukraine during the depression of the 90s, when Ukrainians were forced to take handcarts, go to bazaars and sell whatever they could.
2 Older people still call a hryvnia a ruble, a habit that has lasted for twenty-five years, from Soviet times.

TRANSLATED FROM UKRAINIAN BY ARTEM CHAPEYE

HUW LAWRENCE

Restocking

I poured myself a glass of whisky and threw another log on the fire.

Yesterday at the reception everyone kept bringing up my future.

Glyn had suggested I go to Coleg Ceredigion for some kind of qualification, something that had never crossed my mind.

"You're free now," he said.

I shrugged. "I don't know. The will hasn't been sorted."

Although it was true I wasn't sure why I said that, because Gerwyn had told me what was in his will.

"I'd study forestry, I would, given the chance," Glyn said. "Management. And then come back to an office job and never touch another bloody tree."

"I like what I do," I said.

He shook his head. "It's finished up there, Emrys. Finished years ago. You know it is." He was tall and his sad brown eyes were level with mine. "Llinos has a good job and you'll probably have a tidy deposit for a house now. The old crowd are all settling down, Ems. Find something that pays."

Titch had joined us during Glyn's last remark, in his shiny shoes. He was shaking his ginger head. "You need a work record these days," he said, talking to Glyn, not me. Titch worked in the Council Tax Offices.

"Doesn't farming count then?" I said.

Neither of them said anything. Maybe it was because I'd always signed on and had never been on the books. But what books? Old Mr. and Mrs. Jones Pengarreg just had a couple of nails to stick receipts on.

"Do you want to see the sheep all gone then?" I asked Glyn. "'Habitat enhancing'? 'Rewilding'? Is that what you want to see?"

He didn't answer.

"Restocking is what we need," I said. "Not bloody rewilding."

Although Gerwyn had kept to himself most of his life, Pant-y-Ffynnon Chapel had been full and the village hall was full afterwards for the reception. We'd have held it in the Red Cow, the only place Gerwyn ever came down to, except it closed seven years ago and the nearest pubs now were miles away in Talybont, or Aberystwyth if you took the other road. "Flat land, flat people," Gerwyn liked to say about life down there, but that was an old saying that applied to yesterday, because these days it was all incomers by now and none of them farming, or even working, and there weren't enough of them anyway to keep the pubs and post offices from closing. Still, we are so high up in Nyth-y-Gigfran that the change hardly reaches us. Few people come up this far.

Nothing grows tall up here. It's all wild grasses and bracken and heathers, with sedges and reeds around the lakes. The trout make good eating. Gerwyn's old side-by-side hammer gun gets us rabbits and the occasional small, grey hare if we get up early enough. We talked about a new pup to train, the springer getting too old now. Talking about getting up early, though, you should see the heather just after dawn, all covered in shining spiders' webs like billions of silver necklaces! Gerwyn's finger followed the track down through that silver: "Down there the danger lies, Emrys," he said. And now everyone is expecting me to leave and go and live down there.

Chucking that log on the fire made me wonder what Gerwyn would think of me drinking whisky with the money from his chest of drawers and throwing so many logs on. Hell, should I be cold, while thinking what to do next? What I've been doing all my life till now is all I know, and the truth is I was glad to get home to Nyth from that reception. The dogs and Pengarreg's sheep are all the company I need. However much Llinos says the place is a dump I always feel cosy by the fire.

Not that I can say Llinos is wrong. Gerwyn thought propane gas was living with a bomb under your arse, so the cooker, for instance, is paraffin, and I doubt there is another like it in Wales. Gerwyn's father bought it in the nineteen forties. It still works. That was Gerwyn's answer to everything. "It works, doesn't it?" Pengarreg is on the mains, but close though we are to Pengarreg our electric comes off a generator, and, in any case, because we always preferred the quiet we always used paraffin lamps instead. The toilet was only inside insofar as we'd built a covered way to it. The water came from a tank fed by a stream. The floor was flags with a couple of mats. I have no argument to put to Llinos when she says that Nyth ought to be condemned.

Pengarreg is sheltered from the wind by a row of spruce planted when it was built, which is a very long time ago. Nyth has just one twisted mountain ash that got here somehow on its own. Gerwyn made his walking stick from the only straight bit he found on it. Yet the druids made their staves from this wood, according to the tatty encyclopaedia that Gerwyn fetched out once when I noticed the different butterflies the tree attracted. Gerwyn's father told him that the devil had hanged his mother from a mountain ash. His father had fixed a cross of two twigs to the back door. At the end of winter Gerwyn would say: "*Mae'r hen wraig yn deffro*," meaning "The old woman is waking." Then the tree would bring creamy-white flowers and later a crop of red berries that the birds always came for. Gerwyn used to say: "When the last berry is eaten we'll know that winter is here." The 'old woman' with all her white flowers and berries would have to go if there was an extension built to the house, like Llinos suggested to Gerwyn once. Gerwyn ignored her.

Sipping whisky, I can picture his gnarled old face and hear his gravelly voice. I remember him showing me how to work an otter board, how to lay snares, work ferrets and nets, make a whistle out of hazel . . . Lambing was the important thing, and carrying food to the sheep in extreme weather. Llinos tries to make out I wasn't born to this, as if upland farming isn't in my blood because I'm from Nant-y-Pistyll four miles down, where the land is green. But I was always coming up here on my bike to help out. I was working out in Pengarreg when I was still in Primary School, and did more and more after Dad went off and times got hard. Mr. and Mrs. Jones never had children and they needed the help. We ploughed thirty acres and put good grass down for hay back in those days. It's all slowly gone to seed. The tractor mostly stays in the barn now. I did almost everything after Gerwyn got too old. In the end I had to help him to the commode. Even then people were telling me I was wasting my life. But how could I have left him? He and Mr. and Mrs. Jones were all I'd had after Mam died.

None of the family that moved down to Aberystwyth did anything for me.

My mam was a real character. When I told her I would be all right and for her not to worry because Glyn and Titch and me were going to run away from home, she went straight to the row of cups holding money for the baker and milkman and the others and gave it all to me, telling me not to forget to send a postcard. I was ten. I told her I couldn't take it. Gerwyn laughed his head off when I told him.

He took me in when Mam died. I was sixteen, not earning enough to pay the rent on Mam's house down in Nant. Gerwyn was seventy-five then. He drove me into Aberystwyth to sign the unemployment register and then we went to the Housing Benefit Office to claim rent for me. "Whatever you do, don't say we're related," he told me. He knew how to do everything. He was born in Nyth Y Gigfran, when his father was the shepherd there, but unlike his father Gerwyn had travelled. He used to say: "The man who thinks the grass is greener somewhere else is never still." He'd say: "Emrys, I am a man of the world, and this is the best place in it." Then he'd look around and laugh. "Now, that doesn't say much for the world, does it?" Every now and again he'd rub his hands together: "Hell, go mad. Fetch a bucket of coal in. I'll pour us a tot."

He was always in his tweed jacket and flat cap with white hair sticking out everywhere, which a man of the world should have cut oftener, I used to say.

"This place isn't much, Emrys," he said to me. "But a house is a house, and there's a bit in the bank as well. You go and see Bryn Morgan the lawyer when the time comes. Just don't let them put me in a Home. And don't give my split-cane rod to nobody. It stays in this house. And my fly box is to be yours and nobody else's."

Llinos said she'd come to see the lawyer with me. Like Titch, she works in the Council Offices, in the Housing Department. She says she wants to have kids and then go back part time.

When we parted company after the reception, Glyn said: "Now you can come down from that godforsaken place. You're keeping Llinos on a string. Do you think she'll wait forever?"

But Mr. and Mrs. Jones can't run Pengarreg. They're too old. Since they gave up the cows they sell just three hundred lambs off five hundred acres. It's a pittance. They've struggled ever since the subsidies stopped. They'd be better off on benefit. If they were on benefit, and I took the farm on, I'd get the single farm payment that replaced the subsidies and we'd all be better off. Maybe I'm stupid working so hard for next to nothing, but Gerwyn never thought so. "You are good to them," he said. "I can see your heart with my glass eye, Emrys, and it is working all right."

"Course it is," I said. "I'm only twenty-seven."

He didn't have a glass eye, either. It's just how we used to joke.

I am happy in Nyth. Glyn's not happy, and Titch used to dream he could fly. "Where to?" I used to ask. "Anywhere," he'd say. "Over these fucking hills." Titch swears a lot. At the reception, he said: "Get yourself a fucking life, Ems."

"Everybody alive has got a life," I said. "Nobody is lying in a coffin all day, not even in the Council Tax Offices."

You can hardly forget you're alive mending fences and walls up here in the wind. Hell, we're desperate for new gates.

Titch said: "With her looks Llinos could have anyone. What are you offering her?"

Fortunately, Llinos doesn't think like that, but she asks me more and more often how I feel about her, and it's not enough anymore just to say I love her.

"Do you, though?" she said, when we came back here after the reception. "How much do you love me? What are you staring up in the air for like that?"

"Do you think swallows really sleep on the wing on their way from Africa? How can they?" I asked.

She gave a long sigh.

We used to go out with Titch and Glyn and their girlfriends on weekends, till they got married. Glyn gossips about who's pregnant and who's buying a house, as if it isn't bad enough having Llinos going on at me whenever a house comes up in one of the villages.

She's been spending a lot of time up here this last week since Gerwyn died.

"*Why* do you want to live up here?" she asked straight out the other night, sounding really disturbed. "Cause you do, don't you?"

"I'm used to it," I said.

"I don't know if I could get used to it," she said.

I looked at her, not sure what exactly she was saying.

"It's not so bad, Llinos."

"It's so damp," she said.

"There's a good fire," I said.

"Oh!" she said, turning her face away, as if there was nothing anyone could do with someone like me. "Oh!"

As she left she said: "Don't forget we're seeing the lawyer in the morning. I'll pick you up at nine."

"What about work?" I said.

"I'll ring in sick."

"But you're not."

"I probably will be, from sitting in the damp trying to have a conversation with you."

As she was leaving she pulled me to her. "Nobody lives like this anymore, Ems. Come down. Look how long it's been. I've been waiting years."

"I know, Llinos. But what would Mr. and Mrs. Jones do without me? I know what it's like when someone goes off all of a sudden, like my father did."

Llinos stared at me.

She said: "I'm so long-suffering I amaze myself." She was upset. "Honest to God," she said. "And this path out here! I'll break my neck one night."

"There's the moon. I'll walk with you."

"That's OK. I know the bloody way by now. Be ready in the morning."

In the morning the lawyer spoke in Welsh and read the will in English. He told us he was the executor and didn't foresee any problem with probate. Llinos had made herself look special and Mr. Bryn Morgan appreciated her, I could tell, her black hair around her shoulders and her made-up eyes. He had carefully combed grey hair and a dark suit with stripes. Llinos asked how long it would take, and told him the roof was leaking and there was no proper toilet and the whole place was damp. "Mr. Morgan, you've no idea," she said, and she recited a list of things as if she'd rehearsed it all. "It's not fit for human beings, Mr. Morgan," she said.

He said he'd hurry things.

"You could break your neck just walking in and out of the door," Llinos said. "There's not even a proper path. Please, don't let it take too long, Mr. Morgan. Please."

I was taken aback by this. You'd swear she was thinking of moving in. I'd lived there for fourteen years with it the way it was, and the roof wasn't leaking either. I'd bodged more stuff on it just a few weeks earlier.

Llinos drove us back and brewed some tea. She produced a packet of Jaffa cakes, which I love. "So," she said, sitting down after bringing me my tea. "Twenty-four thousand, four hundred and thirty pounds! Who'd have imagined? What will you do with it, Ems?"

"Well, I was thinking as we were coming back in the car," I said.

"What were you thinking?"

"I was thinking . . . if all those things you said to Mr Morgan got put right . . ." I stopped, knowing there should be better words.

"Yes?"

I racked my brains.

"Yes, Ems?"

In the end I just said: "If we get married, do you think you could live up here?"

She said: "All right, I'll get us a housing grant. The tree will have to go, though, and we'll have to work out where to put the oil tank for the central heating." All of a sudden she was one big smile. "We'll make it pretty, too, Ems. We'll get Glyn to bring a few loads of soil up here and see if we can't get some flowers and a few herbs to grow. *Something* must be willing to grow up here." Her voice softened. "We'll take some cuttings from the old tree and maybe get it to grow a bit further over. Though I don't suppose we'll be here forever. Oh, come here," she said, and threw her arms around me.

I had been thinking that land is cheap up here and that I could rent Pengarreg's land. I knew Mr. and Mrs. Jones would be glad to let me have it. I decided not to say anything yet to Llinos about buying Pengarreg's sheep . . . maybe buying some cows again, too. It might not be impossible to buy Pengarreg itself one day. Maybe Mr. and Mrs. Jones would even leave it to us. We could still keep Nyth. One of our kids might want it one day. Things could go back to being as they should be.

Since Llinos was so happy, I said: "You know, I think I'd like to have a large family."

AUTHOR BIOGRAPHIES

ANDONI ADURIZ is one of the most influential chefs of our times. He was born in San Sebastian in 1971, a city at the very heart of Basque gastronomy. On finishing his culinary studies, he went to Catalonia to work at elBulli, with Ferran Adrià. This experience opened a world of possibilities to him. Throughout his career, he has prioritized culinary evolution and an interdisciplinary approach. In 1998, Aduriz embarked alone upon his most risky and ultimately most satisfactory project: opening his restaurant Mugaritz, which has been recognized with 2 Michelin stars since 2006. Mugaritz closes for four months a year, a window which is devoted almost exclusively to developing new creations. The location offers the chef a canvas on which to unleash his creativity, as well as being a place surrounded by tradition and local products. In Mugaritz, Aduriz has managed to achieve a balance between avant-garde and traditional Basque cuisine. His refusal to conform has resulted in countless achievements: since 2006 Mugaritz has featured in the top ten list of *Restaurant Magazine*.

ALHIERD BACHAREVIC was born in Minsk in 1975. He studied Belarusian Language and Literature at Maksim Tank Belarusian State Pedagogical University in Minsk and worked as a teacher and journalist. His novel *The Magpie on the Gallows* was published in German translation by Leipziger Literaturverlag in 2010. In 2009 a short story collection *Talent do jakania sie* appeared in Polish translation. His writings have been translated into German, Polish, Czech, Ukrainian, Russian, Lithuanian, and other languages. His novel *Shabany. The story of a disappearance* was adapted to stage by a Belarusian theater in 2014. Bacharevic was a participant of the European Writers' Conference in Berlin in 2014, and has taken part in book fairs in Frankfurt, Leipzig, Warsaw, and Lviv. Bacharevic also translates poems, fairy tales, and short stories from German.

JUSTYNA BARGIELSKA, born in Warsaw in 1977, has published seven poetry collections, most recently *Nudelman* (Biuro Literackie 2014), and two works of fiction, *Obsoletki* (*Born Sleeping*) (Wydawnictwo Czarne, 2010) and *Małe lisy* (*Little Foxes*) (Wydawnictwo Czarne, 2013). She has twice won the Gdynia Literary Prize—in 2010 for her poetry collection *Dwa fiaty* (*Two Fiats*) and in 2011 for *Obsoletki*. She also won the Rainer Maria Rilke poetry competition in 2001. She lives in Warsaw and teaches poetry and prose writing to graduate students at the Jagiellonian University in Kraków.

CLAUS BECK-NIELSEN is a Danish author. In September 2001, Nielsen shed off his former identity and declared Claus Beck-Nielsen dead. In the ten years that followed he was the nameless subject of the company Das Beckwerk, carrying out a number of "interventions" in states of emergency around the world—in Iraq, Iran, Afghanistan, and Egypt. Since 2012, Nielsen has been part of The Nielsen Movement, producing performances, exhibitions, and political interventions— but first and foremost: prize-winning novels. Among Nielsen's novels are the trilogy and parallel world history *The Suicide Mission* (2005), *The Sovereign* (2008), and *Fall of the Great Satan* (2012). "The Author Himself" is excerpted from the autobiographical novel *My Encounters with the Great Authors of Our Nation* (2013), shortlisted in 2014 for Scandinavia's most prestigious literary accolade, The Nordic Council Literature Prize. Nielsen's work transcends not only national borders, but also boundaries of gender, the latest Nielsen novel being Madame Nielsen's *The Endless Summer*, to be published in the USA in 2016 by Open Letter Books.

BESSORA, born in Brussels from a Gabonese father and a Swiss mother, has lived in Europe, Africa, and the United States. After studying finance and anthropology, and working for international companies in Geneva, she wrote her first novel, *53 cm*. She was awarded the Fénéon Prize in 2001 for her novel *Ink Stains*. She received the Grand prix littéraire d'Afrique noire for her novel *Pick Me Pretty Sirs . . .* in 2007. Now dedicating herself to writing, she is the author of seven novels, some short stories, and she's experiencing writing in the digital age through her blog *Bessora, tendre peau de vache*. Her writings, satirical, ironic, and melancholic, focus on the representations of identity and taboos.

RUMENA BUŽAROVSKA was born in 1981 in Skopje, Macedonia. She is the author of three short story collections—*Scribbles* (2007), *Wisdom Tooth* (2010), and *My Husband* (2014)—and a study on humor in literature—*What's funny? Humor in Short Stories* (2012). She is a literary translator from English into Macedonian (Truman Capote, Lewis Carroll, J. M. Coetzee) and teaches American literature at the State University in Skopje.

ION BUZU was born in 1990 in the village of Ratuş, Criuleni region, Moldova. He graduated from the Moldovan Academy of Economic Studies in 2013, having studied part time so that he could devote the rest of his time to reading, writing, and wandering. He began but did not complete a Master's Degree at Chişinău University, on the subject of Romanian Literature in the European Context. In 2013, he made his literary debut with a collection of poems entitled *3ml de Konfidor*, published by Casa de Pariuri Literare, Bucharest. In 2014, along with two other poets and an artist, he founded *Lolita*, a Bessarabian literary magazine. Among other things, he has worked as a pollster, copywriter, market stall vendor, and software tester.

HARKAITZ CANO holds a degree in law from the University of the Basque Country. He works as radio, television, and comic scriptwriter and as a music lyricist, and has translated works by Hanif Kureishi, Paul Auster, and Allen Ginsberg into Basque. He has published poetry volumes—*Norbait dabil sute-eskaileran* (2001) and *Compro oro* (2011)—collections of short stories—*Telefono kaiolatua* (1997) and *Neguko zirkua* (2005, Spanish Critics Prize)—and the novels *Beluna jazz* (1996), *Pasaia blues* (1999), *Belarraren ahoa* (2006) *Blade of Light* (2010), and *Twist* (2011; Spanish Critics Prize, Euskadi Prize). Cano has taken part in a number of performance art projects that combine literature with music, cooking, and other arts. His books have been translated into nine languages, including English, German, and Russian.

EDGAR CANTERO, born in 1981, is a novelist, screenwriter, and cartoonist who lives in Barcelona. He is a contributor to the Spanish satirical magazine, *El Jueves*. His first novel in Catalan, *Sleeping with Winona Ryder* (2007), won the Premio Ciutat de Badalona. His Catalan fiction includes *Baileys 'n' Coke* (2008), *Days to be Deleted* (2008), and *Valvi* (2011). In 2014, he published his first novel in English, *The Supernatural Enhancements*.

ARTEM CHAPEYE was born in 1981 in Kolomia, Ukraine, and is active as a writer and journalist. His *Travels With Mamayota: In Search of Ukraine* (2011) and *The Red Zone* (2014) were both shortlisted for BBC's Book of the Year award. His latest work is a book of reporting about the conflict in Ukraine, *Three Letters: War* (2015), co-authored with Ekaterina Sergatskova. He has also translated books by Edward Said and Mahatma Gandhi into Ukrainian. *The Red Zone* is due to be published in English by Dalkey Archive Press.

ROB DOYLE was born in Dublin, and holds a first-class honors degree in Philosophy and an MPhil in Psychoanalysis from Trinity College Dublin. His novel, *Here Are the Young Men*, was published by Bloomsbury, and was shortlisted for the Irish Book Awards Newcomer of the Year prize. His second book, *This Is the Ritual*, will be published in January 2016 (Bloomsbury / Lilliput). Rob's fiction, essays, and criticism have appeared in *The Dublin Review*, *The Stinging Fly*, *The Irish Times*, *The Sunday Times*, *The Sunday Business Post*, *Gorse*, and elsewhere. Having spent several years in Asia, South America, the United States, Sicily, and London, he currently lives in Paris.

ILIJA ĐUROVIĆ was born in 1990 in Podgorica, Montenegro. After finishing music school, he went on to study literature. He has been writing short stories since 2005. His first book of prose, *They Do It so Beautifully in Those Great Romantic Novels*, was published by Yellow Turtle Press in Montenegro in 2014. Since 2013 he has been living in Berlin.

MICHAEL FEHR was born in Muri, near Bern, in 1982 and lives in Bern. Prior to studying at the Swiss Literary Institute and the College of the Arts in Bern and completing his MA in Contemporary Arts Practice, he played the drums for thirteen years, took percussion classes, and studied business and law (without completing the degree). In 2013, his first book *Kurz vor der Erlösung* ("The Verge of Release") was awarded the Bern Literary Prize by the Canton of Bern. Fehr was also shortlisted for the Franz Tumler Prize—a prize, in South Tyrol, for the best debut novel. In 2014, he represented Switzerland at the Days of German-Language Literature in Klagenfurt (Austria) and won two awards, including the Kelag Prize for second place in the main competition (Ingeborg Bachmann Prize). His second book, *Simeliberg*, will appear in Spring 2015. He maintains a website at www.michaelfehr.ch.

CHRISTIAN GAILLY (1943-2013) was a French writer known for his minimalist prose and his syncopated, rhythmic style. He had previously been a jazz saxophonist and a psychiatrist, and the two vocations strongly influenced his career as a writer, both thematically and stylistically. Beginning in 1987 he published fourteen novels, including *An Evening at the Club*, which won the prestigious Prix Inter in 2002, and *The Incident*, which was adapted for the cinema as *Wild Grass* by Alain Resnais in 2009. "The Wheel" comes from *The Wheel and Other Short Stories*, the final work published before his death.

NICO HELMINGER, born in 1953, studied German, Romance Languages, and Theater Studies in Luxembourg, Berlin, and Vienna. He worked as a teacher, then lived and worked as a writer in Paris before returning to Luxembourg. He has been awarded numerous prizes, including the most important cultural award in Luxembourg, the Prix Batty Weber, in 2008. He writes poetry, prose, drama, radio plays, and libretti in Luxembourgish and German. Most recently, he wrote the play *zu schwankender zeit und an schwankendem ort* ("in volatile times and in a volatile place," 2012), the novel *lëtzebuerger léiwen* ("Luxembourg Lions," 2013), the book of poetry *abrasch* (2013), and the novel *Autopsy* (2014).

MICHEL LAMBERT was born in the former Belgian Congo in 1947 and now lives in Belgium. Over the past quarter century, he has published four novels, eight short story collections, and a novella. He is the recipient of numerous awards, among them the foremost prize in Belgian francophone letters, the Prix Rossel; the 2006 short story prize of the Société des Gens de Lettres de France; and the 2006 triennial prize of the Belgian francophone community for *La Maison de David* ("The House of the Painter," 2003). In 1992 he cofounded the Prix Renaissance de la Nouvelle to honor preeminent writers of short fiction in French. His books and stories have been translated into some fifteen languages. His oeuvre was examined at length by Émilie Gäbele in *Michel Lambert: les âmes felées* (*Michel Lambert: Bewildered Souls*, 2013).

HUW LAWRENCE, born in Llanelli, Wales, was educated at Manchester University and briefly at Cornell University. Leaving a lectureship in Manchester, he worked as a quarry laborer in Blaenau Ffestiniog so that his children could grow up in Wales speaking Welsh. A teaching post took him to Aberystwyth, where he still lives. His story collection, *Always the Love of Someone*, was shortlisted for the Roland Mathias Prize in 2010. His stories have won several prizes, including a Bridport Prize and four Rhys Davies Prizes.

NIJAT MAMEDOV, born in 1982, is a poet, essayist, and translator. Author of the books *Map of Language* (2010), *A Meeting Place Throughout* (2013), and a multimedia hypertext, *A Walk* (accessible at www.proqulka.com). Mamedov was awarded the Russian Prize in the poetry category in 2013 and the prize of the Yeltsin Foundation for the best literary translation from Azerbaijani into Russian in 2007.

JOÃO DE MELO was born and raised in Achadinha, São Miguel, in the Azores, and served as a medic in the Angolan war. He is the author of eight novels and several books of short stories, poetry, and essays. He has won many international literary prizes, and his work has been translated into eight languages. His epic novel about the Azorean diaspora in the 1970s entitled *Gente Feliz com Lágrimas* ("Happy People in Tears") is forthcoming in English translation by Tagus Press.

ARMIN ÖHRI was born in 1978 and grew up in Ruggell, the northernmost village in Liechtenstein. He studied history, philosophy, and German linguistics and literature. Since 2009, he has published a variety of stories and novels in two independent publishing houses, including the well-respected German publisher Gmeiner. His works tend to be set against a historical backdrop and are based primarily on literary examples of the 19th century, such as entertaining feuilleton novels that fall into the crime genre. Öhri works in the education field at a business school in Switzerland. In 2014, his novel *Die dunkle Muse* won the European Union Prize for Literature.

VLADIMIR POLEGANOV was born in 1979 in Sofia, Bulgaria. He completed two Master's degrees in clinical psychology and creative writing at Sofia University, and is currently working on a PhD in Bulgarian literature. He is the author of one collection of short stories, *The Deconstruction of Thomas S*, published in 2013 by St. Kliment Ohridski University Press. His works have appeared in various literary magazines in Bulgaria, including *Stranitsa* (2014) and *Granta Bulgaria* (2014). In 2012, his short story "The Well" was awarded the prestigious Rashko Sugarev award for new writing. He is currently working on his first full-length novel.

MARIUS DANIEL POPESCU was born in Craiova, Romania in 1963. He left Romania for Switzerland in 1990. He wrote the novel *La Symphonie du loup* while earning a living as a bus driver in Lausanne. The novel was published by French publisher José Corti in 2007 and was awarded the Robert Walser Prize in 2008. It has since been translated and published in Spanish (Nocturna), German (Engeler Verlag), and Romanian (Humanitas). His following novel *Les Couleurs de l'hirondelle* was published, also by José Corti, in 2011. Since 2004 he has been editor of the French language poetry journal *Le Persil*. He has published two collections of poetry with the Swiss publisher Antipodes.

PAULINA PUKYTĖ is an artist, writer, and cultural commentator. She lives and works in London and Vilnius. She graduated from the Vilnius Academy of Art, and received a Master's degree from the

Royal College of Art in London. She writes for various cultural publications in Lithuania and in 2007 received the Lithuanian Ministry of Culture Award for her articles. She has published a collection of essays, *Netikras zuikis* ("Fake Rabbit," Apostrofa, 2008), a play, *Žuvies akys* ("Fish Eyes," Kitos Knygos, 2015), and two books of fiction— *Jų pročiai* ("Their Habits," Tyto Alba, 2005), and *Bedalis ir labdarys* ("A Loser And A Do-gooder," Apostrofa, 2013). Both *Netikras zuikis* and *Bedalis ir labdarys* were shortlisted for The Book Of The Year Award and the latter additionally for The Most Creative Book by A Lithuanian Author Award; it was also adapted to the stage.

VERONIKA SIMONITI's first short story collection, *Zasukane štorije* ("Twisted Stories," 2005), was nominated for the Best First Book of the Year and was one of the four nominees for the Best Short Story Collection of the previous two years (the Fabula Award) in 2006 and 2007. 2011 saw the publication of her second short story collection, *Hudičev jezik* ("The Devil's Tongue"), which includes the story "A House of Paper." Her stories have been critically acclaimed as "stylistically polished, atmospheric and lyrical short narratives, which playfully address a wide range of issues," including language. She is featured in an English-language anthology of short prose, *A Lazy Sunday Afternoon* (2007), as well as an anthology of Slovene women authors. Her stories have been published in German, Croatian, Serbian, Italian, Hungarian, and Czech. Her first novel, *Kameno seme* ("The Stone Seed," 2014), was nominated for the Best Slovene Novel of 2015.

ILMAR TASKA's novella *A Car Called Victory* ("Pobeda") won the Estonian short story prize in 2014. He is now writing his first novel based on this story. Taska was born to a family that had been deported from Estonia to Siberia. He graduated with a Master's degree from the Moscow Film Institute (VGIK). Taska has worked as a development executive for the Estonian film company Tallinnfilm with masters like Tarkovsky and Kromanov, and also cowrote and produced a movie for a Hollywood studio (*Back in the USSR*, 1992, starring Frank Whaley and Roman Polanski). In 1993 he established his own television company, which was the first private national network in Estonia. Taska is active in the fields of film, theater, art, and literature. He won his first literary award at the age of 16, and has worked primarily as a screenwriter. In 2011, Taska published the short story collection *Parem kui elu* ("Better than Life"). The critically acclaimed collection brings together Taska's short stories with his writings from literary magazines, and was translated into Swedish in 2014. Taska's short stories have also been translated into English, Bulgarian, and Latvian.

SRĐAN V. TEŠIN was born in 1971 in Mokrin (Banat, Vojvodina, Serbia). He lives in Kikinda, in the northern Serbian province of Vojvodina, and has written ten books. For the novel *Kuvarove kletve i druge gadosti* ("Cook's Curse and Other Nastiness") he won the Borislav Pekić Fund Scholarship for 2004. His collection of short stories *Ispod crte* ("Below the Line") was chosen as the book of the year by the Association of Writers of Vojvodina in 2010. His work has appeared in Serbian and foreign anthologies of contemporary Serbian literature, and has been translated into French, English, German, Polish, Czech, Macedonian, Albanian, Hungarian, and Slovenian. He is a member of the Serbian PEN Center.

KRISZTINA TÓTH is a Hungarian writer born in Budapest in 1967. Originally known for her poetry, Tóth has become a Central European master of the short story. Her novel *Akvárium* ("Aquarium," 2013) and her latest collection of short stories *Pillanatragasztó* ("Instantbond," 2014) were both shortlisted for the AEGON prize. *Vonalkód* ("Barcode," 2006) was also published in French by Éditions Gallimard, while *Akvárium* and the genre-defying *Pixel* (2011) were recently published in German by Nischen Verlag.

TSOTNE TSKHVEDIANI was born in 1993 in Kutaisi, Georgia. He entered the Tbilisi State University in 2011, where the main subject of his research were twentieth-century anarchist movements in the region of Caucasia. In 2012, Tsotne joined the eco-anarchist movement and took part in several strikes, which were an expression of solidarity for the people who live and work in industrial Georgian towns. He often visited these places and had personal interviews with the inhabitants. This is reflected in his short stories as well. The subject of Tsotne's works are varied: birdwatching and psychedelic music, politics and philosophy, and sometimes mythology too. *The Town and the Saints*, his first collection of short stories, was published in 2014 by Bakur Sulakauri Publishing and combines stories that tell the lives and problems of people living in abandoned and forgotten areas. The towns themselves are often the characters of the stories. His story "The Golden Town" was selected for the annual Georgian anthology *The 15 Best Short Stories of the Year*, and was also announced as the best short story of 2014 and received the BSP award.

JOSEF WINKLER (born in Kamering, Austria, in 1953) is one of the most important contemporary German-language authors. His work has been praised by figures as diverse as Günter Grass, W.G. Sebald, Elfriede Jelinek, and Alberto Manguel. The winner of numerous prizes, including the Grand Austrian State Prize in 2007 and the Büchner Prize in 2008, he is the current president of the Austrian Arts Senate. Winkler resides in Klagenfurt with his wife and two children.

MĀRA ZĀLĪTE was born in 1952 in Krasnoyarsk, Siberia, to a Latvian family deported to Siberia by the Soviet regime. A graduate of University of Latvia's Faculty of Philology, Zālīte has worked as poetry consultant for Latvia's Writers' Union, editor-in-chief of the Latvian literary magazine *Karogs*, director of the Young Writers' Studio and president of the Authors' Association. Zālīte has authored many volumes of poetry, numerous plays, lyrics for many Latvian choral and pop songs, several rock opera and musical librettos, and essays on Latvian culture and history. Zālīte's works have been translated into German, Russian, English, Estonian, Swedish, and other languages. Her first novel, *Five Fingers*, is an autobiographical portrayal of her family's return in 1956 from Siberia to Latvia and her subsequent life on her grandfather's farmstead, where she has to come to terms with the conflict between the life she sees around her and the fantasy image of Latvia that she grew up with in Siberia.

TRANSLATOR BIOGRAPHIES

MARTIN AITKEN has translated such Danish authors as Dorthe Nors, Helle Helle, Kim Leine—and Peter Høeg. His work appears in book form and in literary journals and magazines including most recently *Asymptote*, *The New Yorker* and *Harper's Magazine*. Forthcoming books include two novels by Josefine Klougart for Open Letter Books and Deep Vellum Press.

JESSE ANDERSON is a literary translator from Seattle. He has several forthcoming book-length translations, and his fiction and poetry have appeared in various literary journals and online.

PETER BACHEV holds a degree in International Relations and a Master's in Gender Studies from the London School of Economics (LSE). He is currently coordinating the sex and relationship education provision in secondary schools across London, and working as an editor with the press office of Eva Paunova MEP. "The Birds" is his first foray into translating fiction.

JASON BLAKE teaches in the English Department at the University of Ljubljana. He translates from Slovenian and German, primarily for Slovenia's annual Vilenica festival, which focuses on Central European authors. His most recent book-length literary translation is Marjan Rožanc's *Of Freedom and God* (with Jeremi Slak). In 2011 he published *Slovenia – Culture Smart!*, a guide to living in Slovenia.

ALISTAIR IAN BLYTH was born in Sunderland, England, and attended the universities of Cambridge and Durham. He ended up in Romania at the end of the last century and has remained there ever since. His translations from the Romanian include, most recently, the novel *The Bulgarian Truck* by Dumitru Tsepeneag.

NATHANIEL DAVIS is an editor at Dalkey Archive Press.

PAUL CURTIS DAW is a lawyer-turned-translator whose translation of Evelyne Trouillot's novel, *Memory at Bay*, is forthcoming from the University of Virginia Press. His translations of stories and other texts from France, Haiti, Belgium, Quebec, and Reunion have appeared frequently in *Words Without Borders* and have also been published in *Subtropics, Indiana Review, Cimarron Review, carte blanche,* and *KIN*.

WILL FIRTH was born in 1965 in Newcastle, Australia. He studied German and Slavic languages in Canberra, Zagreb, and Moscow. Since 1991 he has been living in Berlin, where he works as a freelance translator of literature and the humanities. He translates from Russian, Macedonian, and all variants of Serbo-Croatian. His website is www.willfirth.de

AMAIA GABANTXO is a writer and literary translator specialized in Basque literature. She currently teaches Basque language and literature and creative writing at the University of Chicago. She is the most prolific translator of Basque literature to date, as well as a pioneer in the field. She has published and performed on both sides of the Atlantic: in Ireland and Great Britain, the countries in which she carried out her university education, and in the US, where she lives since 2011. She moonlights as a flamenco singer.

MARGITA GAILITIS was born in Riga, Latvia, immigrating to Canada as a child with her family. Gailitis returned to Riga in 1998 to work as a translator of Latvian laws into English in support of Latvia's application for membership in the European Union, achieved in 2004. Today Gailitis focuses her energy on literary translation and poetry. She has translated some of Latvia's finest poetry, prose and dramaturgy and is a tireless advocate for Latvian literature worldwide, for which she was awarded in 2011 the prestigious Three Star Order by the President of Latvia. Gailitis's own award-winning poetry has been published in periodicals in Canada, the US and Europe.

OWEN GOOD is a young Northern Irish translator living in Budapest, where he teaches Translation Studies at Péter Pázmány Catholic

University. Good won first prize in *Asymptote*'s "Close Approximations" competition in 2014 with his translation of a selection of Krisztina Tóth's poetry. Good's work has also appeared in *Hungarian Literature Online* and *Krakow Post*, and in 2015 he was selected to compete in the European Literature Night Translation Pitch in London organised by the Czech Centre London, English PEN, and Free Word.

NADA GROŠELJ translates from English, Latin, and Swedish into Slovene, and from Slovene into English. Several of her translations into Slovene have won national translation awards (the Anton Sovre Award, the Best Young Translator Award, children's literature awards). Her translations of Slovene literature into English have been included in the Litterae Slovenicae and Vilenica series, in an English-language anthology of Slovene literature, and in the bilingual editions of three Slovene poets: France Prešeren and Tone Pavček (with co-translators), and Jože Snoj (as sole translator). Her latest translation, *Selected Poems* by Milan Jesih, was published by Dalkey Archive Press in 2015.

OLIVIA HEAL, writer and translator, has had short fiction published in a number of literary journals. She was shortlisted for The White Review Prize in 2013. Her translations include *Jealousy* by Marcianne Blévis (Other Press) and short works by Monique Wittig and Nicole Brossard. In 2014 she launched Dow House, a small press.

ALEXANDER HERTICH is an Associate Professor of French at Bradley University. His translation of René Belletto's *Dying*, which was a finalist for the French-American Foundation Annual Translation Prize, was published by Dalkey Archive Press in 2010. He has also translated Simone de Beauvoir, and his translation of Nicolas Bouyssi's "An Unexpected Return" was selected for *Best European Fiction 2015*. In addition to translation, he is an active literary scholar and has published in French and English on Patrick Modiano, Jean-Philippe Toussaint, Marie NDiaye, and Raymond Queneau as well as other modern French novelists.

MATTHEW HYDE is a translator of fiction and non-fiction from Russian and Estonian. After studying Russian and politics at London and Essex Universities, and gaining his Institute of Linguists Diploma in Translation with a distinction for literary translation, Matthew worked for 15 years for the British Government as a translator, research analyst, and diplomat, with postings in London, Moscow, and Tallinn (as Deputy Head of Mission). Following this last posting Matthew chose to remain in Tallinn with his Estonian partner and baby son, where he plays the double bass and translates.

MARIA JASTRZĘBSKA was born in Warsaw and came to England as a child. She is a poet, editor, and translator. Her most recent collection is *At The Library of Memories* (Waterloo Press, 2013). She co-translated *Elsewhere: Selected Poems* by Iztok Osojnik with Ana Jelnikar (Pighog Press, 2011). *Dementia Diaries*, her literary drama, toured nationally in 2011, and she was co-editor of *Queer in Brighton* (New Writing South, 2014). She lives in Brighton.

ROMAS KINKA works as a forensic linguist and a literary translator and finds that both disciplines complement one another. The best compliment he has received comes from the Lithuanian author Kristina Sabaliauskaitė: "It was a real pleasure to read Romas Kinka's translation . . . I felt as if I'd written it myself in English." His translation of her *Vilnius Wilno Vilna: Three Short Stories* will be published in 2015.

ELIZABETH LOWE is the founding director of the Center for Translation Studies at the University of Illinois at Urbana-Champaign. Her translation of João Paulo Cuenca's novel, *The Only Happy Ending for a Love Story Is an Accident* (Tagus Press, 2014) was on the short list for the 2015 International IMPAC literary award. Her latest translation is *Happy People in Tears* (Tagus Press, 2015), a novel by João de Melo about the Azorean diaspora during the Salazar dictatorship.

DONAL MCLAUGHLIN featured as an author and a translator in *Best European Fiction 2012*. In 2014, Dalkey Archive published both his new collection of stories (*beheading the virgin mary & other stories*) and his translation of Arno Camenisch (*The Alp*). He maintains a website at www.donalmclaughlin.wordpress.com

VERA RICH (1936-2009) was a British journalist, poet, and translator, and was one of the most active popularizers of Taras Shevchenko's poetry in the English-speaking world. During the 1980s she was Soviet Science Editor for *Nature*. In 1997 she was awarded the Ivan Franko Prize of the Union of Writers of Ukraine. In 2006, by decree of the President of Ukraine, she was awarded the Order of Princess Olha (Third Class). In 2007 the Union of Writers of Ukraine awarded her its "Pochesna vidznaka" medal ("Insignia of Honor"). Part of her ashes rest in a cemetery at Khaniv, near the Shevchenko tomb and memorial, where her gravestone commemorates her work for Ukraine.

ESMIRA SEROVA was born in Baku in 1983 and graduated from the Azerbaijan University of Languages. After trying her hand at writing for some time, she now translates modern Azerbaijani poetry and prose into English, while holding a permanent position as staff translator and interpreter at the Institute of Control Systems of the Azerbaijan National Academy of Sciences.

GEORGE SIHARULIDZE was born in Tbilisi, Georgia in 1990 to a family of artists. He moved to the United States in 1993, and now lives in Boston, Massachusetts. In 2014, he graduated from Boston University with an undergraduate degree in psychology, and has since been working on a series of translations of various short stories and film scripts.

ANICA TESIN was born in Serbia in 1948. She translated some of the works of Natalee Caple and Michael Crummey, Canadian writers, into Serbian, which were subsequently published by Serbian literary magazines. She has resided in Canada since 1987.

LAWRENCE VENUTI translates from Italian, French, and Catalan. He is, most recently, the author of *Translation Changes Everything: Theory and Practice* (2013) and the translator of Ernest Farrés's *Edward Hopper: Poems* (2009), which won the Robert Fagles Translation Prize.

ADRIAN NATHAN WEST is the author of *The Aesthetics of Degradation* and translator of numerous works of contemporary European poetry and fiction, including Josef Winkler's *When the Time Comes* and Pere Gimferrer's *Fortuny*. He lives between Spain and the United States with the film critic Beatriz Leal Riesco.

ACKNOWLEDGMENTS

DIREÇÃO-GERAL
DO LIVRO E DAS
BIBLIOTECAS

Elisabeth Kostova
FOUNDATION for
CREATIVE WRITING

Estonian
Literature
Centre

FÉDÉRATION
WALLONIE-BRUXELLES

MINISTRY OF CULTURE
AND MONUMENT PROTECTION
OF GEORGIA

GEORGIAN
NATIONAL
BOOK
CENTER

ILLINOIS
ARTS
COUNCIL
AGENCY

STYRELSEN
DANISH AGENCY FOR CULTURE

LATVIAN
LITERATURE
CENTRE

AMT FÜR KULTUR
FÜRSTENTUM LIECHTENSTEIN

culture.lu

Ministry of Culture
of the Republic of Macedonia

POLISH
CULTURAL
INSTITUTE
www.PolishCulture.org.uk

swiss arts council
prohelvetia

SLOVENIAN
BOOK
AGENCY

CYNGOR LLYFRAU CYMRU
WELSH BOOKS COUNCIL

PUBLICATION OF BEST EUROPEAN FICTION 2015 was made possible by generous support from the following cultural agencies and embassies:

DGLB — The General Directorate for Books and Libraries / Portugal

Elizabeth Kostova Fondation for Creative Writing

Estonian Literature Centre

Etxepare Basque Institute

Fédération Wallonie-Bruxelles

Georgian National Book Centre and the Ministry of Culture and Monument Protection of Georgia

Illinois Arts Council

Kulturstyrelsen — Danish Agency for Culture

Latvian Literature Centre

Lichtensteinische Landesverwaltung

Luxembourg Ministry of Culture

Macedonian Ministry of Culture

Polish Cultural Institute

Pro Helvetia, Swiss Arts Council

Slovenian Book Agency

Welsh Books Council

RIGHTS AND PERMISSIONS

"The Word Flew Away" ©2013 by Josef Winkler. Translation ©2014 by Adrian Nathan West.

"Streaming" ©2010 by Nijat Mamedov. Translation ©2010 by Esmira Serova.

"The Art of Being a Stutterer" ©2001 by Alhierd Bacharevic. Translation ©2009 by Vera Rich.

"Long Night" ©2008 by Michel Lambert. Translation ©2014 by Paul Curtis Daw.

"The Birds" ©2013 by Vladimir Poleganov. Translation ©2014 by Peter Bachev.

"The Author Himself" excerpt from *My Encounters with the Great Authors of Our Nation* ©2013 by Claus Beck-Nielsen & Nielsen & Gyldendal A/S. Translation ©2014 by Martin Aitken.

"Apartment for Rent" ©2011 by Ilmar Taska. Translation ©2014 by Matthew Hyde.

"The Wheel" ©2012 by Les Éditions de Minuit. Published by permission of Georges Borchardt, Inc., on behalf of Les Éditions de Minuit.

"The Golden Town" ©2014 by Bakur Sulakauri Publishing. Translation ©2015 by Bakur Sulakauri Publishing.

Excerpts from *Pixel* ©2011 by Krisztina Tóth & Magvető Publishing. Translation ©2014 by Owen Good.

"John-Paul Finnegan, Paltry Realist" ©2015 by Rob Doyle.

"The Major and the Candy" excerpt from *Five Fingers* ©2014 by Māra Zālīte. Translation ©2014 by Margita Gailitis.

"The Interrogation" ©2013 by Armin Öhri. Translation ©2015 by Nathaniel Davis.

Excerpts from *A Loser and a Do-Gooder* ©2013 by Paulina Pukytė. Translation ©2014 by Romas Kinka.

Excerpt from *Luxembourg Lions* ©2013 by Nico Helminger. Translation ©2014 by Jason Blake.

"Waves" ©2010 by Rumena Bužarovska. Translation ©2014 by Will Firth.

"Another Piss in Nisporeni" ©2010 by Ion Buzu. Translation ©2014 by Alistair Ian Blyth.

"The Five Widows" ©2015 by Ilija Đurović. Translation ©2014 by Will Firth.

Excerpts from *Born Sleeping* ©2010 Furgał & Wydawnictwo Czarne. Translation ©2014 by Maria Jastrzębska.

"Strange and Magnificent Powers" ©2015 by João de Melo & Publicações Dom Quixote. Translation ©2014 by Elizabeth Lowe.

From *La Symphonie du loup* ©2007 Marius Daniel Popescu. Translation ©2014 by Olivia Heal.

"Where Is Grandma, Where Do You Think She's Hiding?" ©2012 by Srđan V. Tešin. Translation ©2014 by Nadine Linton and Anica Tesin.

"A House of Paper" ©2011 by Veronika Simoniti. Translation ©2014 by Nada-Marija Grošelj.

Excerpts from *Mugaritz: B.S.O.* ©2012 by Harkaitz Cano & Andoni Aduriz. Translation ©2014 by Amaia Gabantxo.

"Aesop's Urinal" ©2010 by Edgar Cantero. Translation ©2014 by Lawrence Venuti.

"Voyage Under Narcosis" ©2015 by Bessora. Translation ©2015 by Jesse Anderson.

"The Apparent Fisherman and Real Drunkard" excerpt from *The Verge of Release* ©2013 by Michael Fehr. Translation ©2014 by Donal McLaughlin.

"Son, Please" ©2014 by Artem Chapeye. Translation ©2014 by Artem Chapeye.

"Restocking" ©2015 by Huw Lawrence.